BURDEN OF PROOF

CLUB RAPTURE: RISK AWARE BOOK TWO

KATE HAWTHORNE

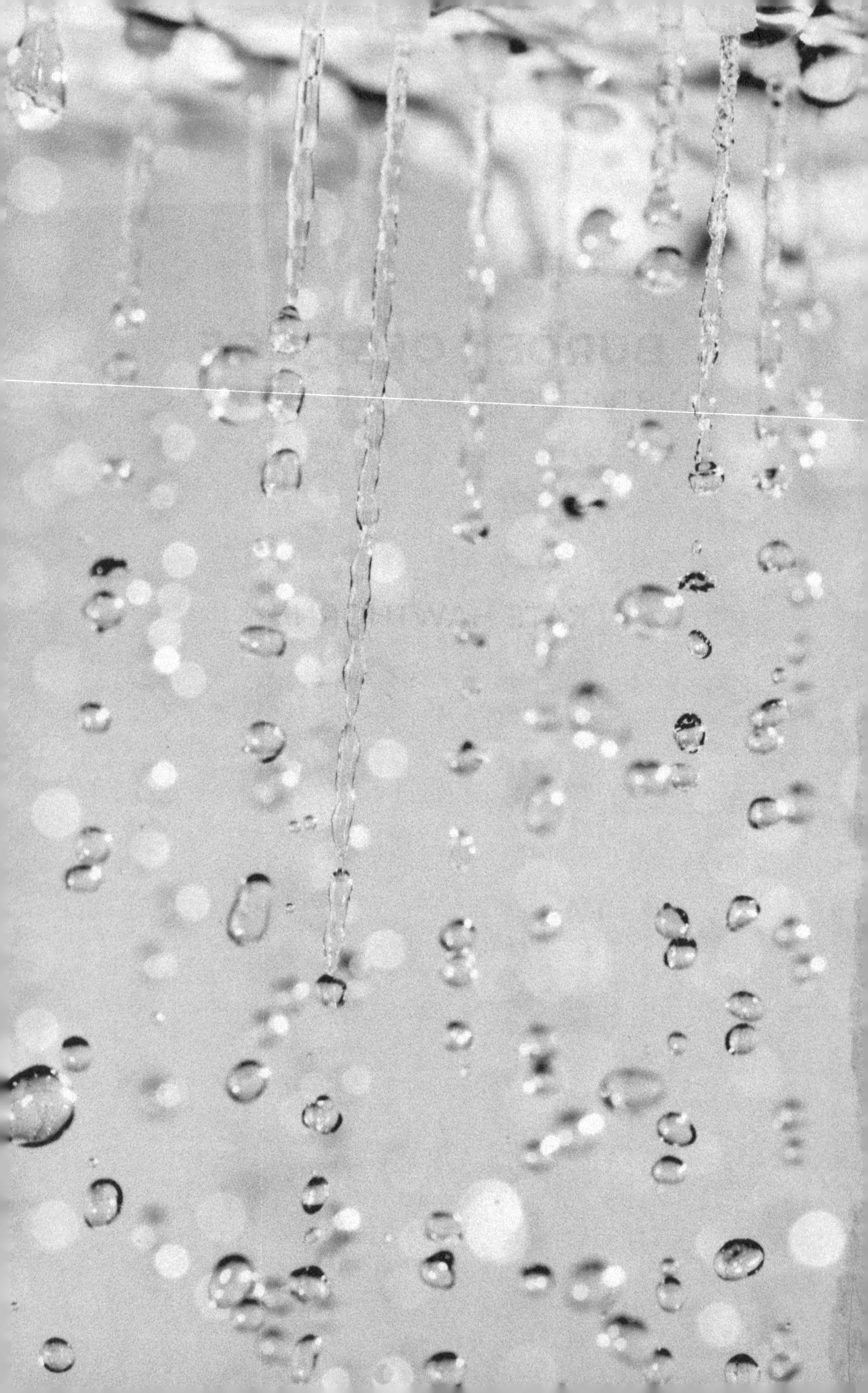

Burden of Proof

OF PROOF

CLUB RAPTURE: RISK AWARE BOOK TWO

KATE HAWTHORNE

Burden of Proof by Kate Hawthorne

Copyright © 2025, 2026
Kate Hawthorne

Edited by | Jordan Buchanan
Cover Design | Kate Hawthorne

CONTENT NOTE

Burden of Proof is a romance that includes on page sex outside of (and before) the main relationship, sex work, mild violence between secondary characters, poorly negotiated (but physically safe) power exchange scenes, and non-negligent death of a mega pet store-bought fish.

If this content is triggering to you, please proceed with care. If you have specific questions, please reach out to the author.

CHAPTER 1
LINCOLN

LINCOLN

The thing about fucking a twenty-five-year-old is…it's never a good idea. But I had made a lot of bad decisions in my life, though getting on all fours for a virgin might have taken the cake. I was only twenty-five myself, but *I* was far from a virgin, and I also made it a general rule to not sleep with anyone who was under thirty.

Especially virgins.

Smith Covington wasn't even technically a virgin. He'd just never been with a man before, and I liked being with men. He was easy enough on the eyes, and it had been awhile since I'd gotten anything other than a blow job, so I'd said what the hell. He also looked so pathetically sad when he'd been drinking and crying, and you might as well call me Lincoln Summers, patron saint of bad fucking ideas.

"Can we try the other way?" Smith asked, long and slender fingers rolling the condom off his cock. He tied it off and tossed it into the hotel trash can, and I stared up at the ceiling, my forearm covering my forehead and half my eyes.

"The other way?"

"Where you..." he trailed off, gesturing with a swirling motion of his finger, his chest covered in sweat.

"If you can't say it, you can't have it," I said, grabbing his wrist and pulling him down. He collapsed onto the bed beside me, our shoulders touching, toes touching.

"I want to bottom," he said. "I want to see which one I like more."

"What an eager beaver."

I ignored the way his pinky finger dragged across the top of my wrist, turning away from him and flinging my legs over the side of the bed. I would have thrown myself out the window if the damn thing opened, but the threat of a lifetime of undeserved therapist bills for Smith was enough to stop me from executing *that* bad idea. And if that hadn't been enough, my best friend being shacked up with Smith's oldest brother definitely would have been.

Falling into a shitty hotel bed with Smith hadn't been on my radar.

The night I met him, he was reeling from some bad news and nursing a bottle of wine like if he got to the bottom of it, the revelation of his new half-brother would somehow cease to be real. I'd sat beside him on the edge of a bed that wasn't his in a house that didn't belong to either of us and listened to him pour his heart and soul out to me over the last dregs of his wine. After he'd run through it all, I patted his forearm and tucked him back into bed, but his trembling voice stopped me before I could get out of the room.

"I think I might be bisexual."

I sighed and turned back to face him. "Everyone is bisexual, Smith."

"But I've never..."

He was too drunk, and I was too sober.

"And I have."

"Would you?" he asked, legs tangling around the sheets. "With me, I mean?"

"Maybe when you have some alcohol in your bloodstream and not the other way around."

After that, he'd left me alone for so long I thought he'd forgotten about me entirely.

But then he'd texted me with an address, a room number, a time, and one of those ridiculous little emoji faces that looked like a watery-eyed, kicked puppy. I'd gone back and forth for hours if I was going to go through with it or not. I knew Silas would probably not be thrilled with the prospect of me fucking his future brother-in-law, but I had no plans to make anything with Smith into something real. He was a sad man who wanted to fuck, and I was a sad man who wanted to fuck. Even though we were sad for very different reasons, the fucking part would be fine.

It would be *fine*.

Bracing my elbows on my knees, I stared down at the patterned hotel carpet and the tufts of dark hair on my toes.

"Do you think your brother is going to marry Silas?" I asked.

Behind me, the bed shifted.

"Marshall has never done anything by half."

I scrunched my nose, sniffling. "Silas has barely told me anything about him."

"Is there a question there?"

"Yeah," I grumbled.

"Marshall is a good person. A great man." The admiration in Smith's voice was enough to make me want to believe it.

"So, he'll be good to Silas?"

"The best."

I swallowed. Nodded.

"We can't do this again." I pushed away from the bed, grabbing my underwear off the floor and stumbling into them.

Smith had already gotten extremely up close and personal with every nook and cranny of my body. There was no need for me to be shy anymore, but still…

"Like, after tonight?"

Fuck.

How could one face hold so much hope?

"Like, after that." I gestured at him, sprawled out naked in the middle of a ruined hotel room bed. "If you want to bottom, find someone else to take that test drive."

"Do you not like to top?"

I grabbed my pants and stepped into them. Pulling up the skinny denim was a struggle considering my legs were shaking—Smith was not bad in bed—and I was covered in both of our sweat.

"I am happy to flip every day of the week if the opportunity presents itself," I said. "I just know that doing it with you would not end well for me. Silas is already going to kill me when I tell him."

Smith scrambled into a seated position, the sheets pooled in his lap, and his eyes comically wide. "You can't tell Silas."

"He's my best friend." I tugged my shirt over my head, pulling down the hem until I felt covered enough, which all things considered, was not likely to happen. "I tell him everything."

"If you tell him, he'll tell my brother."

"Probably," I agreed, "and also a valid reason that I'm making sure to keep *my* cock out of *your* body."

He covered his face with his hands, and I left him there on the bed to go take a piss. My stomach was still covered in drying cum, and I picked some of it off with the edge of my fingernail while I gave my dick a couple of shakes. Tucked back into my pants and as presentable as I would be without a shower, I padded back into the bedroom.

The youngest Covington brother had gotten dressed in

record time, and something about the fact he'd stepped into a pair of now wrinkled khakis was almost enough to make me take it all back and top him after all.

No, Lincoln.

Bad Lincoln.

I clapped my hands together in front of me, prayer position, with my lips grazing against the side of my steepled fingers.

Smith looked disheveled as all fuck, the outside of him doing a fairly decent job at unintentionally matching my insides.

"I like you, Smith," I told him honestly. "But I need you to trust that us finishing up here or doing that again is a horrible idea."

"I know," he agreed, though I imagined for different reasons.

He was worried about the social implications of sleeping with his older brother's younger boyfriend's best friend. I was worried about the recent revelations that I'd built my entire life around a part of my personality that was turning out to be a lie. Or if not a lie, at least a massive mistruth.

The unraveling of my personal understanding had started slowly. Coming of age in Hollywood was a very unique experience, and with parents who worked as much as mine did, I spent a lot of my formative years unsupervised. I'd started going to kink clubs as soon as I turned eighteen, and I'd quickly ended up with far more than just an eyeful.

Learning about and experimenting with power exchange relationships had been fundamental to my personal development, and while I wasn't as annoying about it as some people, I found a lot of comfort in my identification as a dominant. Meeting Silas, my perfect and sweet and submissive best friend who let me spank him when the mood was right, only solidified the things I knew to be true about myself.

The problem was I'd recently met a man named Ethan at Rapture. We'd hooked up, and somewhere in the middle of it, our roles reversed. I could tell he didn't find the change weird in the slightest, easily sliding into the more dominant one between the two of us. And for my part, I'd done the same but in reverse. The *problem* turned out to be that I very much liked the second half of my night with Ethan, but I hadn't been able to figure out what that meant for me.

Being a dominant made things simple. There were rules and expectations, and when I met a prospective partner, we both knew who was going to do what and how the night would go. Coming into a situation as a switch? That was…there was so much room for error there. So much gray area…confusion. It was enough of a shift in the dynamic that felt like a well-worn glove to me that I hated the idea of changing it up.

It was one thing to flip fuck. It was another entirely to go from dominant to submissive and back again with the same partner in the same scene.

Just the thought of it made my head hurt.

And the last thing I was going to do was bother my best friend about it because Silas was desperately and acutely in love with Marshall, and I'd be damned if a single thing I did or said would take that happiness away from him. It was bad enough he'd been so worried about me he didn't even want to move in with Marshall, but I'd nipped that one in the bud before it could cause any real damage.

I talked to Marshall about it instead. I asked him what his dominance meant to him, if it was something he could ever see himself giving up.

He told me he'd give up everything for Silas, then told me no matter what, I'd always have a place in his home. The guest room where Smith had propositioned me for the first time was now permanently mine if I wanted it, but my questions about dominance and submission remained unanswered. Or maybe I was being obtuse on purpose.

Patron saint of ignoring the obvious too.

Or something.

Smith finished getting his clothes in order, cracked his neck, then gave me a nervous smile. "Am I setting myself up for failure if I ask if we can stay friends?"

"Stay?"

"Become."

I folded my arms in front of my chest, suddenly cold. My first answer was a loud and resounding no, but then I remembered Silas had a boyfriend, and I no longer had a roommate, and my life was about to get a lot more boring. I could probably use a friend…or seven.

"Yeah," I said, grimacing. "I mean, no. You're not setting yourself up for failure, and yes, we can become friends."

"I don't want things to be weird," he said.

I cleared my throat, heat burning in the middle of my chest.

"They're not weird, but before you decide if you want to be my friend, I want to let you know that I'm a sex worker."

Smith blanched. "Do…do I owe you money? Did you expect…?"

I held up my hands, first telling him to stop and then beckoning him closer. Smith shuffled toward me the same way Silas always did when he felt sorry for himself, and I wrapped the tall, nervous man in my arms.

"Not that kind of sex work." I kissed the side of his face. "Just stuff on the internet."

"I don't care. It doesn't matter to me."

I thought about Riot—a quick fling from a couple months ago—about him not being out and him walking away from me on account of my work. The loss of him was still surprisingly sharp, and I hated the way it felt, like a barb lodged in my ribs. Instead of pulling away to rub at the ache, I held Smith closer.

"It's been a dealbreaker for people in the past."

"Not for me," he whispered.

"I'm also…affectionate," I mumbled.

"I've seen how you are with Silas," he said. "Even though I'd been drinking, I could tell that you two are used to touching."

"That's just how I am, not just with him. It's not a dealbreaker if you're not, though. It's…it's something I like."

"I'm sure I could get used to it," Smith said back, chin tucked toward his chest in an alarming display of bashfulness.

Which, thank God, another reminder of all the reasons I should take him up on his offer and definitely make sure we never even looked outside of the friendzone again.

I pushed him away enough to get a look at him. We were the same age, but something about him felt like we were decades apart. He was thoughtful like Marshall, but so off-puttingly innocent it was nearly impossible for me to find him attractive. Not that I was attracted to Marshall. I mean, objectively the man was nice to look at it, but not my type. He was too dominant.

Shit.

Was that really it?

Marshall on one end of the spectrum and Smith on the other, and I couldn't bring myself to muster up attraction for either of them.

"You're…you're something else," I said.

"That sounds bad."

"It sounds like the truth."

"You know…" He sighed, shrugging his shoulders and letting them fall. "I spent my whole adult life wanting to be just like Marshall, but the older I get, the more I think we're not the same."

"You're nothing like him. I mean, on the surface maybe, but not fundamentally."

He scrunched his nose.

"I don't mean it badly," I assured him. "I see it, but… you're both very different."

He sat down on the edge of the bed to lace up his sneakers, pausing far longer than necessary on the second one.

"You're not attracted to me, are you?" he asked.

I really fucking hoped I hadn't said any of that other stuff out loud.

"You're not my type, but you're not unattractive. You made me come, Smith. It's not like—"

He cut me off, cheeks burning red. "I didn't need an explanation. I just…thought it would be easier to be friends if we both agreed we didn't want to have sex again."

"You already over the idea of asking me to top you?"

He huffed out a laugh, shaking his head. "The more you talk, the more I want you to keep your clothes on."

"I think I should be offended."

He stood up, looking lanky and boyish and so fucking *kind*.

"But you're not," he said.

"No," I agreed, "I'm not."

After that, we ran through a quick check of the hotel room, gathering our things and making sure no wrappers had landed on the floor instead of the trash. With the exception of the bed, the room was in the same condition as when we'd arrived. Smith stopped me at the door, squaring his shoulders and sticking his right hand into the small space between us.

"Friends then?" he asked.

I couldn't decide if I wanted to kiss him—platonically—or run the other way screaming. I did neither, instead sliding my hand alongside his and squeezing.

"Friends."

CHAPTER 2
HUNTER

The hotel room was mid-range, but the bed was bolted to the wall and didn't squeak so I counted it as a win. The stack of crisp bills on the table beside my cell phone, another win, and the force of my orgasm as I shot long and hot stripes of cum across another man's chest, the biggest boon of all. He groaned, reaching up and smearing my load into his skin, and I carefully tucked my still-hard cock back into my pants before I'd even finished emptying onto him.

"Thank you," he whispered.

The app said his name was John, but I found that to be highly unlikely and also unoriginal.

"Thank you?"

John groaned and dragged the mess of my cum down his stomach. "Thank you, Sir."

I hummed, giving John one final look before grabbing my phone and the cash, pocketing them both. There was no kissing between us, no kindness, no goodbye. That wasn't what either of us were interested in, though if I were being honest, I wasn't interested in him at all. John wanted someone to degrade him, and I wanted someplace to come that wasn't my hand.

Finn was the one who'd suggested it, unintentionally of course. He'd probably be furious with me if he knew I was having sex with strangers for money, even angrier if he found out I hadn't told him about it. The whole thing had started on accident too. Finn had told me I was acting a little more high-strung than usual, and he'd stolen my phone and set me up on one of those hookup apps I'd never had the time for. I didn't even pay attention to what he put on my profile until I got the first message three days later.

Unintentionally or otherwise, my brother had painted me out to be a dominant man looking for a once-off. *High-powered attorney looking 4$ a quick, fun night. No strings and no obligations. I like to be in charge of everything in my life, the bedroom isn't an exception.*

After the fact, I realized the dollar sign must have been a typo, but it meant something to the first man who'd reached out. He said his name was Steve, and he looked like a Steve, and he offered me two hundred dollars to jerk off while he sat on his hands. I didn't need the money, but growing up in the Covington house had instilled many fundamental ideas in my brain. The first of which being never walk away from money, so…

And that was how I'd accidentally become an escort. A dominant escort.

My brothers were none the wiser, though Finn said to me the week after he set me up on the app, "You seem less stressed."

And I'd told him I was. We'd never talked about it again.

I walked out of the hotel without a second look back and headed for my car. As soon as I was in the driver's seat and the car was on, my phone lit up through the Bluetooth, an incoming call from my half-brother, Andrew.

"Hello?" I said, backing out of the parking spot to drive across town to Finn's house.

"Hey. It's Andrew."

"I know it's you. I have caller ID," I said, and he laughed nervously on the other end of the line, the sound filling my car. "What's up?"

"I was just calling to see how things had gone since dinner."

"Like usual."

"Have they said anything about me?"

I sighed, turning right and heading west.

My father was a piece of shit in every possible way, but he was also the most fertile—and promiscuous—man on the planet apparently. My four half-brothers and I were proof of that. Marshall was the oldest, four years older than me and Finn, fourteen years older than Smith. The four of us had been raised together—for the most part. Smith arrived as an angry teenager long after Marshall was out of the house, but his presence always loomed over the three of us. My oldest brother was the patriarch our family deserved, and it was only a matter of time until Willem Covington kicked the bucket and gave the title up.

Recently, we'd been made aware of a fifth brother, smack in between me and Smith in age. Andrew. His mother had done a commendable job of keeping Andrew away from all things Covington, but her will had included the truth of his lineage, so after she passed, he searched me out and the rest was quickly becoming history.

Andrew lived in San Diego, two hours away from us, and he'd very recently made the drive up to LA on a Friday for dinner and introductions. The meeting had gone well. Everyone seemed to like him, though Smith was the most hesitant when it came to opening up his arms. I didn't blame him either. Smith was barely twenty-five, and he'd only been in our lives for ten or eleven years. Any change to the status quo would have been sickening to me at his age too.

"No one has said anything good or bad," I told him.

"Smith is leery, but he's like a golden retriever trapped in the body of a black cat. He'll warm up to you."

"And Finn? Marshall?"

"Marshall is level-headed and sees the whole thing logistically. He's fine. Finn is——"

"Kind of an asshole," Andrew interrupted.

"My favorite brother," I corrected, though it might have been a lie. I liked all my brothers equally and for different reasons, but Finn and I were closest in age and closest in everything else too.

"Sorry."

"He can be a prick," I conceded, but it's just his humor. "They'll all warm up to you; I'm sure of it. We've just had a lot going on lately."

"Anything more exciting than a mystery brother appearing out of the ether?"

"Marshall has a boyfriend," I said.

"Is that…not normal?" he asked.

"He hasn't dated anyone since college as far as I know," I explained. "And his new boyfriend is young."

"How young?"

"Smith's age," I said, realizing Andrew probably hadn't committed my brothers' ages and birthdays to memory yet. "He's twenty-five."

Andrew let out a low whistle, and I chuckled.

It had been a two weeks since we'd all met Andrew, one week since we'd met Marshall's boyfriend, Silas, and I prayed we made it through the rest of the month with as little fanfare as possible.

"And Smith was okay with that but not me?"

I laughed. "Smith is…he'll be fine."

Whereas it had always been the four of us, it was also always me and Finn, Marshall and Smith. Whatever feelings Smith had about his idol dating someone fourteen years younger than him was between the two of them to work out and explicitly not my problem.

"Do your brothers know you and I have been talking?" he asked just as I flipped the blinker to turn onto Finn's street.

"They know we talked before you met them. I can't imagine they'd assume that would stop."

"So, no," he said.

"I'm close with my brothers, but I don't tell them everything." Andrew didn't know what to say to that, and I was thankful. "Speaking of, though, I just got to Finn's house, so I've got to go. Do you want to get together soon? If not everyone, maybe the two of us can grab lunch."

"Yeah. Yes. That would be nice."

"I'll talk to you soon."

"Bye."

"Bye, Andrew." I disconnected the call by turning off the car.

Dropping my head against the headrest, I let out a breath. The adrenaline from my hookup with John still raced through me, and I needed something to take the edge off. I just needed a minute to get myself together, but bright light washed over the porch and Finn's tall silhouette filled the open doorway. He gestured for me to come inside and didn't wait for me to follow before heading back in himself.

"You got this," I told myself, grabbing my things and following my brother into his house.

I kicked off my shoes at the door and dropped my phone and keys on the side table. He had an overgrown monstera that made it impossible to leverage any open space on the table, but he had made no moves to trim her back so I didn't say anything about it.

"Going to piss!" I shouted out to Finn, heading for his guest bathroom before finding wherever he'd gone off to on his own.

The fluorescent was damning, so I turned the light back off and locked the door, undoing my pants and pulling out my still sticky and half-hard cock. Using warm water from the sink and a washcloth I would make sure to bury at the bottom of his hamper, I cleaned myself up from the earlier rendezvous, then pissed because I wasn't a liar.

"It's fine," I said to my reflection in the mirror. My hair wasn't even out of place from work. The whole go with John had been so low impact I hadn't even broken a sweat. "You're fine."

"Everything coming out okay?" Finn shouted from somewhere in the house.

Even though he couldn't see it, I rolled my eyes, then dropped the washcloth on the top of his hamper on my way to find him because fuck him.

I found my brother in his office, which we'd recently painted some odd shade of pink that he assured me was meant to make the place feel calm and cool like a museum. It reminded me of the nipples of Annaleigh Watson, a girl I'd dated in college for a few months, but I didn't think Finn would appreciate the comparison.

"Do you really like this color?" I asked.

I couldn't imagine spending all my work from home time in a room the color of my ex-girlfriend's areolas.

"It's classy," he said.

Ignoring him, I went for the liquor Finn kept on his built-in bookshelves, pouring some bourbon for him and a vodka for myself. He wasn't behind his desk, instead on the cushioned window seat that overlooked his back yard. Finn was still dressed for work in navy slacks and a black button-up. He'd undone the top buttons and rolled up the sleeves, stretching a slender arm toward me when I got close. I passed him his drink and climbed onto the seat myself.

With our backs against opposite walls, and knees bent, we

didn't fit as well as we had when we were younger. The window seat in one of the guest rooms at our father's house had been our favorite place to escape to as children, then as pre-teens. At some point, we'd evacuated to the roof, seeking more privacy, but some of our most intense conversations had been with our feet aligned, his, mine, his, mine, and our faces tipped toward the ceiling.

"I never asked you," I started, raising my glass over our bent knees. He knocked his into mine, brow raised in question. "Did you buy this house just for the window seat?"

Finn snorted, but his cheeks flushed. "That's absurd."

"Of course," I agreed, having my answer.

Finn was an asshole sometimes, like Andrew had said, but it was a defense mechanism. I'd never met anyone who loved as hard and deep as Finn, but he was prickly about it. You had to break past the shell to get the gold, and he'd been locked up tight since his last breakup two years before.

"Tell me something interesting," he said, taking a swig of bourbon. "I've had a long day."

"Was the math being mean?"

"Don't make me hold you in contempt," he shot back.

"Literally not how that works, but good luck."

"Would you just tell me something?" he asked again, dropping his head against the wall behind him.

"The Psittacosaurus is a dinosaur with quills."

"The what now?"

"Psittacosaurus," I repeated.

"Has what?"

"Quills," I said.

"Like, for writing?"

"Like a porcupine." I took a drink and watched my brother's face as he tried to process what I'd just told him.

Eventually, Finn scrunched his nose and made a dismissive noise in the back of his throat. "I meant about you."

There weren't many interesting things about me. My name was Hunter Ethan Covington. I was thirty-five years old, my birthday was one month after Finn's, same year. I graduated summa cum laude from USC with my J.D., and I'd been working as an attorney ever since. Contract law was boring, but it was helpful for all of my brothers, and I wasn't miserable over the whole thing. Work was work for me, and I'd always managed to have a good work/life balance, even if my life was often the most boring part of my day.

Feeling bold, though, I took another swallow of my drink and gave Finn an answer I knew he wouldn't believe.

"I came straight over here from a hotel. Met a man named John earlier tonight and came all over his chest for fun."

That earned me a full body laugh and my brother pouring the rest of his drink down his throat. He slapped my knee and used my leg as leverage to get up from the window seat, clearly dismissing the truth as a lie, which was perfectly fine with me. Finn and I were close, the twins Marshall and Silas often called us, but that didn't mean he knew everything about me.

"That's a good one, Hunt." Finn helped me up from the far too small bench seat, and we both made eyes at my right hip when it cracked a little too loudly. "Let's go get something to eat."

CHAPTER 3
LINCOLN

Silas had moved in with Marshall.

I knew it was coming. I'd told him to do it. But moving from our overstuffed two-bedroom apartment to a studio that only held *my* things was a lot like relocating a twin size mattress into a castle.

Silas insisted I keep most of the furniture we'd bought together because Marshall already had a house full of furniture. The studio didn't require all of our furniture, though, so I'd unloaded a lot of it at the thrift store and made do with whatever was left.

The studio was spacious and angled in such a way I could tuck my bed into a corner and have some kind of privacy from the rest of the space. I'd turned the back of the loveseat toward the window so it faced the kitchen, a comfortable seat that doubled as a half-wall in the middle of the room. The kitchen was basically a counter against the wall, butting up to the door with a fridge and dishwasher, though the cabinet space was lacking so it ended up being the place I stored all my dishes.

I could have afforded something nicer, but the pay from my online work wasn't always consistent. There was a steady base that hadn't wavered, so I made sure the rent would be covered by that amount. Anything else, I could find a way to supplement. Worst case, I could get a different job. I could do both for sure, and a steady paycheck that offered health insurance wouldn't be the worst thing in the world.

I didn't want to think about that, even though the alternative turned out to be thinking about Ethan and the way it had felt so fucking good to be told what to do for once. Scrubbing a hand down my face, I flopped backward onto my bed and stared holes into the ceiling. It was a new experience to be so utterly alone, but not just alone…also lonely. Before, even if Silas and I hadn't been doing something together, I hadn't been alone. Hadn't been lonely. The silence of my new apartment was deafening, and I reminded myself pushing Silas out had been the right thing.

He deserved to be with Marshall, and I sure as shit wasn't going to be the one to stop that over something as childish as not wanting to live alone.

Maybe I would get a fish.

It wasn't a horrible idea, I convinced myself as I cleaned off a space on my dresser for a small fish tank. I had some extra cash from the month before, and Silas—who'd always made more money than me—had insisted I keep the whole security deposit on our old apartment. I checked my balance just to be certain, then headed to the big box pet store to peruse its wall of multi-colored betta fish.

I'd always felt bad for the betta fish, stuck in those tiny plastic tubs. How frustrating it must be for them to always be watched and poked at but never brought home. Ignoring the parallels, I picked out a fish that looked somewhere between alive and thriving and whatever the opposite of that would be.

Me, probably.

I bought him—or her—a much larger fish bowl, a treasure chest, some plastic coral, and some brightly colored gravel for the bottom. The girl working helped me pick out the right kind of food, assuring me betta fish were extremely low maintenance.

"How do I know if it's a boy or a girl?" I asked when she
was finished ringing me up.

"Why does it matter?"

"So I can name it," I said.

She gave me a silly look, scrunching her nose at me. "I
don't think names have anything to do with gender. Do you?"

I mean...

"Fair enough."

"You might want to wait, though," she said with a grimace,
bagging the decorations and the food.

"Why?"

"Sometimes these betta fish...they don't make it more than
a day or two. They get shocked from the move or from the
water temperature. Sometimes there's something wrong with
them, and we don't know."

I looked down at the fish I'd picked in its little plastic home.
It definitely didn't look robust, but I could tell there was some
fight in it.

"I think we'll be fine," I said.

"There's a seventy-two hour replacement policy." She
handed me my receipt. "If it does die, I mean."

I hated the idea of my fish dying, but I thanked the girl for
her help and explanation just the same.

I spent the whole drive home trying to think of a name for
the fish, but I wasn't any closer to a decision when I got home.
I carried everything up to the second floor, trying my best to
not jostle the fish any more than necessary. Groaning and
closing the door to the apartment behind me, I kicked off my
shoes and carried the fish and all its supplies to my dresser.

"Just a little bit longer," I told the fish, taking off the lid to
its takeout container of a home so it could get some air.

Did fish need air?

Fuck, I was going to be a horrible fish parent. Silas was out there falling in love, getting an awesome job, and starting his life, and I was in a shitty studio apartment, unsure of how to keep a four-dollar fish alive.

Twenty minutes later, I was confident the water in the bowl was the correct temperature as to not shock the betta, so I carefully scooped it into the tank and rocked backward to watch it acclimate to its new home. If a fish could look panicked, it did, but after about five minutes, the fans of its fins rippled in the water, and it began to swim in a wider circle around the bowl.

"Me too, buddy," I said. "Me too."

After cleaning up all the trash and finding a home for the fish food, I got a snack for myself, then propped myself onto the bed so I could watch it longer. I really hated thinking of the fish as an it, but I still had no idea what to name it.

I took a picture of the fish and sent a text to Smith.

> What's it look like to you?

SMITH

> A fish?

> I mean name-wise.

I could ask Silas, but it was Friday so he'd be over later anyway and I'd just ask him then.

> Betty?

> Betty the Betta??? BFFRL Smith.

> Bruce

> No wonder you're single

> Speaking of, have you found someone to pop that other cherry of yours yet?

You'd be the first person to know if I did.

Should I be honored?

I tossed my phone onto the bed and frowned at the fish tank.

"Is your name Betty?" I asked.

The fish ignored me.

"Bruce?"

Still ignored.

"You're gorgeous either way," I said, reaching again for my phone and muttering, "Beautiful names."

Typing the ask into my search bar, hundreds of baby name websites popped up with all the names you'd expect, but there was one that caught my eye.

"Cassandra?" I asked.

The fish stopped and floated to the side, facing me head on.

"Is your name Cassandra?"

The look said yes.

"Okay, Cassandra. Welcome home."

Cassandra looked at me for a couple more seconds then resumed their exploration of their new home. I dropped my phone back onto the bed and decided to follow their lead. There were plenty of boxes I hadn't unpacked yet, so I busied myself with pulling books out of boxes and stacking them against the wall. There was definitely no bookshelf to be found in my little studio, but I didn't hate the look of the haphazard and mismatched stacks beneath the window.

An hour later, I'd had enough of unpacking. With about two hours until Silas was due to arrive, I decided it was better to focus on money than on misery. I took a quick shower, styled my hair, then found the place in the studio that had the best light. It was—by design—my bed, tucked behind that corner with the setting sun coming in hot through the windows. I set up my tripod and my ring light, then realized that unless I wanted to film a hand job video, I had to find the box with all of my sex toys in it.

Fifteen minutes later, I found it in the bathroom. I lugged the whole thing to my dresser and used the bottom drawer to house all the toys. I grabbed lube and an average length dildo that had a thick knot near the base, set my phone to record, and climbed naked onto the bed.

On my knees, I made a show of fellating the pretend cock, stroking my own dick to hardness when the knot pressed against my teeth. Gagging, I tipped my head back and pulled the toy out of my mouth, making sure to let spit roll down my chin when I did. This was all I'd needed, maybe. Back in my element, back in my body.

I slammed the suction base of the toy against the wall, hoping it was strong enough to hold, then I made a show of using lube-slick fingers to prep myself for the larger penetration. It felt good to be filled. I hadn't been fucked since Smith, and I groaned happily as I pushed my asshole against the blunt tip of the dildo.

"Oh, fuck," I whimpered straight into the camera, stare rapt on the mirrored reflection of myself in the screen. Backing up until the flared knot kissed my rim, I sucked in a breath to steady myself, then I started to move.

I fucked myself on the toy, murmuring all kinds of generic things about how good it felt to be filled, about how the cock was so thick and my body so stretched. This was the type of video that always seemed to sell well. People didn't even care if the penetration could be seen. It was the eye contact and the noises that always earned me the most money, so I made sure to deliver on both.

It wasn't like I was really acting or anything. The toy felt really fucking good, and I knew if I could manage to get that knot into my ass, it would feel even better. The problem was, at the end of the day, it was still a toy and what I wanted the most was a real hot cock attached to a body with real strong hands. I didn't even care anymore about being dominant or not. I just wanted to be touched in a way that would lead to something that wasn't platonic.

I could call Ethan again, I thought, and I had to bite the inside of my cheek to stop myself from moaning his name and ruining the video. Instead, I licked the palm of my hand and reached between my legs to stroke myself. I'd set a manageable pace, but as soon as I touched my dick, the need to come turned into something unavoidable.

"I'm so close," I told the camera. "You're gonna make me come, oh, God…"

Two minutes later, I bore down against the knot, pushing hard against the wall. My rim stretched, it stretched, it fucking hurt, and then I came with a shout. Hot jets of cum shot all over my hand and the sheets, and I sank back another two inches, the swollen knot of the toy securely inside of my body.

Crying out, another burst of cum splattered against my stomach, my entire body alight with pleasure. I'd never had my hole stretched so far, the shocking pain of it enough to make sweat bead against my temples and the dips at the small of my back. I could feel the temperature difference in the room, and I paused long enough to remind myself I was filming. Forcing my eyes open, I stared hard into the camera when I reached back and dragged my fingertips across my stretched hole, the slick silicone toy.

"Holy shit," I whimpered, collapsing forward onto the bed.

Right into the wet spot.

I'd have to shower again, but I'd survive.

I caught my breath and waited for my heart rate to return to normal before extracting the knot from my body, which was a lot harder than I wanted it to be. The removal hurt, and I made a mental note to cut the clip before my discomfort showed. With a pained grunt, I moved off the bed and paused the recording, then took the toy into the bathroom to clean. After another shower, I dug out a black jock and my favorite pair of leather pants. I made sure to put socks on first, having learned that lesson a long time ago.

Half-dressed, I said, "Sorry you had to see that, Cassandra, but you should get used to it. That's my job."

I laughed to myself about apologizing to a fish for fucking myself in front of them, but when I saw Cassandra floating on her side instead of swimming around, the explanation died in my throat.

My phone chirped with an alert that someone was at the door, and I knew without looking it was Silas. I snatched my phone off the tripod and burst into tears. The response didn't feel appropriate to the loss, but it was the culmination of everything that had happened over the past couple of months and once I started to cry, there was absolutely no stopping it.

I heard Silas's footsteps coming down the hallway. This building really had no fucking insulation at all. Sniffling, I wiped snot off on the back of my hand and grabbed my phone, turning away from the door so Silas didn't see my face when he got to the door. He walked in without knocking, and with a deep breath, I forced myself to face him and smile.

"Hey, Silas," I said, smiling through the tears.

In the way he'd always had about him, Silas didn't ask what was wrong. He opened his arms to me, and I walked right into them, burying my face against his chest. He didn't smell like himself anymore. He smelled like Marshall, and that only made me cry harder.

Silas gently carded his fingers through my hair, his mouth pressed against the side of my head.

"Lincoln, what on earth is going on?" he asked.

"Cassandra died," I said, giving myself one last moment of weakness before extricating myself from Silas's arms.

"Who's Cassandra?"

I flung my arm in the direction of my dresser. "My fish."

"When did you get a fish?"

"Two hours ago," I said.

"Oh, Linc." He rubbed a gentle circle between my shoulder blades and urged me across the apartment back toward my dresser where Cassandra was still dead. "I'm sorry."

"The girl at the store told me they might die."

"Yeah, I think…I think they either live a really long time or the opposite," he said, sitting on the edge of my bed and frowning at my dead pet.

"Watch the sheets," I warned, which only earned me an eye roll.

I sat down beside Silas and rested my head on his shoulder. We both stared at Cassandra for a while, and then he petted his hand against the top of my thigh.

"Do you want me to…I don't know how to say this."

"Are you asking me if I want you to flush my fish?" I asked.

"I would do it for you if you did."

My tears had mostly dried up, and I managed a nod. Silas stood up, and I collapsed down onto the foot of the bed. I closed my eyes and listened to him move around my apartment, finding the other container in the trash and then coming back to scoop Cassandra out of the bowl. Then he walked away, the toilet flushed, and he was back, pulling me off the bed and into his arms. I wrapped myself around him, missing not just my best friend but the life that had been ours before he fell in love with someone else.

CHAPTER 4
HUNTER

HUNTER

Every Friday night, I got dinner with my brothers. Well, I got dinner with three of them. Andrew was in San Diego and lord knew how many other half-Covingtons were buried in the woodwork. I hoped they stayed there. Andrew had been hard enough on Smith, and even though Finn had put on his usual, sarcastic front, he wasn't pleased about it either.

I made it to Cunningham's the same time as Smith, catching up to him in the parking lot. He was leaning against the closed door of his car, brow furrowed at whatever he was looking at on his phone.

"Hey, baby brother," I greeted. "You good?"

He pursed his lips and shoved his phone into his pocket.

"My friend's new fish died," he said.

I grimaced, thinking about how much Finn had wanted a fish when we were kids and how emphatically his requests had been denied. Eventually, Finn had just stopped asking for what he wanted, and so had I.

"That sucks."

Smith shrugged, glancing up at me from the corner of his eye. "Have you talked to Andrew lately?"

Sometimes I forgot Smith was twenty-five. It was so easy to see him as the same long-limbed, angry, preteen he'd been when he came to live with us. It had been well over ten years, and sometimes it felt like it, but more often than not…it didn't. It was hard for me to believe he was in his twenties now, and Marshall nearly forty, while Finn and I were on the wrong side of mid-thirties.

How had my life gone by without me even noticing?

"Yeah, I talk to him a bit," I said, not wanting to be completely honest because I'd always put Smith's feelings above all else.

"Has he asked about us at all?"

"Yeah."

"Okay," he said, frown deepening.

Puffing out a breath, I looped my arm around his shoulder and pulled him away from his car. I had no idea what was going on in his brain, but I knew he wasn't going to tell me about it. Marshall was his confidant.

"Let's eat, alright?" I suggested, pulling him toward the restaurant.

"Yeah."

We walked into the restaurant and found Finn and Marshall already there, thankfully back in our normal booth and not at the five-person table we'd used for the last two weeks. Smith sank into the booth to Marshall's left, and I took my place at Finn's right. The two of them had drinks already, but the waiter was quick to arrive with a Manhattan for Finn and a vodka and soda for me.

"So glad you could join us," Finn drawled, clinking the edge of his glass against mine. "I was just talking to Marshall about his recent domestication."

"I'm not a raccoon."

"What's it like?" Finn asked next, scrunching up one side of his mouth. "Having someone to come home to at night?"

Something flashed across Marshall's face, and the look he answered Finn back with was scathing. But as soon as it was there, it was gone, and he said, "I enjoy Silas' company."

"Of course you do."

"You should try settling down, Finn," Marshall said. "Might do wonders for your personality."

Finn cocked his head at Marshall, another curious look passing between them. "I like myself just fine, thank you, Marsh. I sleep well at night."

Marshall hummed, and I could tell there was something happening between the two of them, though what was anyone's guess. The line of questioning brought me back to my earlier thoughts from the parking lot, though, and the absolute last thing I wanted to do was lose myself in a spiral in front of my brothers.

The way things had been going for me lately…it was all wrong.

I'd been on that app Finn set me up on for almost a year, and sex was fine. A lot of the time it was better than fine, but I wanted more. I'd watched Marshall fall in love with Silas. I'd seen firsthand the subtle ways my oldest brother had been changed, and I was man enough to admit I was jealous about it. I wanted that connection, that intimacy.

The only way I'd find it was to delete that app or at least take the stupid dollar sign out of my bio. But I'd taken all the money and dumped it into a high-yield savings account and the resulting balance wasn't a small one. I could make a good donation to a charity or something, and that felt like it balanced out the dubious way I'd earned it.

"Where are you at?" Finn asked, slamming his elbow into my ribs.

"Right here," I said, automatically.

"Physically," Marshall said, brow raised.

"We were literally just talking about you and Silas. I've been listening the whole time."

Smith made an amused sound in the back of his throat and, to my left, Finn groaned.

"Since then we've talked about Smith still debating taking his mom's maiden name and quitting his job."

"You want to what?" I said, eyes going wide.

Smith shrugged. "We talked about it in passing but nothing seriously."

"Are you thinking about it seriously now?" I asked.

Another shrug.

"The point is," Finn interrupted, finishing his drink, "we weren't talking about Marshall."

"I'm *right here*," I repeated.

"Thinking about?" Marshall prompted.

I slid my glass around the table, shifting the ice so it clinked and settled. "Nothing important," I lied, clearing my throat. "But I did want to see if the three of you were up for a little road trip soon."

"To San Diego?" Marshall asked.

I nodded.

Finn sank back against the corner of the booth, mouth tipped down into frown that made the family resemblance achingly clear. I steepled my fingers together and covered half my face, exhaling into my hands and staring at the leather gap between Marshall and Smith's shoulders.

"Excuse me," I muttered, climbing out of the booth and heading for the restroom.

I'd never wished for private bathrooms more than when Finn's shoulder stopped me from latching the stall door. He flung his body weight against it, and we both tumbled backward, and I narrowly avoided my entire forearm landing in the bowl.

"What the fuck?" I shoved him off of me, and then we both fell out of the stall and into the bathroom. Finn's hip landed against the sink, and he cursed under his breath, rubbing his hip with his eyes screwed shut.

"What is going on with you?" Finn asked, shaking off the pain long enough to point an accusatory finger at the middle of my chest.

"What do you mean?"

"You're not yourself."

I sighed. "Nothing is wrong that won't shake out."

I needed that to be the truth. I had to believe that, eventually, everything was going to settle, and I would feel normal again.

"Do you have an STI or something?" Finn asked next, cocking his head to the side.

"Why would I…what?"

"You told me you met some dude in a hotel room for sex," he said.

My mouth was immediately as dry as the Sahara Desert. I'd told him that, but I didn't think there was any way he'd believed it. He had to have thought I was lying the day I told him that, because if he for any second believed that to be true, he would have called me out on it immediately.

"Did you really believe that?" I asked.

"No, of course not." Finn shook his head at me like it was obvious. "But I don't know, Hunt. Maybe you picked something up, and you tried to plant the seed as a coverup or an excuse about why you're on a seven-day antibiotic track."

The corner of my mouth quirked up. "How do you know it's seven days?"

"Fuck you. What's wrong?"

"Nothing," I answered.

"I can't believe you're lying to me. Of all people."

Finn folded his arms in front of his chest and had the decency to look offended. When I rolled my eyes at him, he stuck out his lower lip and pouted.

"I'm not lying," I said. "At least, not in the way you think I am. I've just had a lot going on in my head lately, and I'm trying to sort it out."

"Talk through it with me."

"It's not a talking kind of thing," I said.

Finn frowned and let his arms fall to his sides. He propped himself up against the sink, and I leaned against the paper towel dispenser, head resting on the wall.

"Marshall and Silas have just made me a little lonely," I admitted.

"They are a little sickening, aren't they?"

I nodded. "But it's nice. I mean, it's nice for him."

"You want it to be nice for you?" he asked.

"It's been so long since I've been with anyone seriously, I don't even remember what it feels like," I said. "But I don't think I want to be alone forever."

"You should seriously use that app I set you up on. I'm sure you can find people there." He reached into his pocket and pulled out his phone, waving the black screen at me. "I find people all the time. Well. I…"

He trailed off, and I narrowed my eyes.

"You what?"

"There's lots of single people on it, Hunter," he said. "But I bet you didn't even open it up after I set it up for you."

"I've never gotten an alert since the first day," I told him, which was the truth, because the sound the app made was so glaringly obvious, I'd turned notifications off entirely. I only opened the app when I was bored and wanted to fuck. I didn't need it pinging off in my pocket at all hours of the day.

But none of that even mattered because I was going to delete the app. Dollar sign in the bio or not, I'd already seen what sort of people were there, and if that worked for Finn, more power to him, but I wanted more than a one-night stand. I wanted more for my brother too.

"You should give it a chance." Finn held out his hand, clapping his fingers against his palm like he wanted me to give him my phone.

Instead, I shoved him in the middle of his chest.

"I'm not giving you my phone." I exhaled a long breath, giving him the smile he was after. "I promise I'm fine. Just been working a lot and thinking about the future, and I'm a little too tired to be drinking vodka is all."

"Alright," he conceded after giving me a disapproving onceover. "I'll believe you for now."

"How magnanimous," I muttered, stepping into one of the bathroom stalls and slamming the door closed in his face. "Now if you don't mind."

Finn laughed, the joyous sound of it echoing off the walls before dying off with his exit. Only after he was gone did I take a second to balance myself and breathe. I waited until my hands weren't shaking to pull my phone out of my pocket, ready to clear all evidence of my use on the app into the trash in case Finn ever did get ahold of my phone.

There weren't any alerts. No messages.

"I'll delete the whole thing later," I told myself, deleting the old messages and shoving the phone back into my pocket. It was plausible deniability, but Finn hadn't tried to physically wrestle me since high school, so I was relatively confident I'd be safe for the rest of dinner.

I pissed—for good measure—washed my hands, then rejoined my brothers at our booth. Someone had ordered fresh drinks for everyone except me, and I didn't know if it was Finn trying to punish me for lying or him being thoughtful and not putting another drink in front of me when I told him I was too tired for it.

"So," Marshall said after I'd taken my seat, giving me one of his trademark calm smiles. "When did you want to go to San Diego?"

CHAPTER 5
LINCOLN

After my emotional meltdown over a fish I hadn't even owned for more than an hour, Silas kissed me on the mouth and convinced me to head out to Rapture. My best friend's never-ending affection for me made me want to cry again, but at least those felt more like happy tears. Silas had gotten so lucky when he ended up with Marshall Covington, an older, smarter, and achingly handsome man who also happened to be perfectly okay with the nature of Silas's relationship with me.

The two of us had always been physically affectionate with each other, often snuggled, sometimes kissing, occasionally scening, though never fucking. For as long as I'd known him, I'd only ever looked at Silas as a friend, but that didn't change the fact we liked to touch each other. Marshall had been great about the whole thing, not once shying away or encouraging Silas to be different with me after they committed to each other.

I admired the confidence and security that rolled off Marshall in waves and hoped that one day I could find a bit of it for myself. I'd cornered him in his living room a couple months ago, back when the doubts about my interest in dominance had first set in. The whole thing came so easily to him and lately, for me, it felt like a struggle. Not that I didn't enjoy being dominant, but watching the way Marshall was dominant made me wonder if I'd been faking it the whole time.

He'd told me there was no shame in submission, no harm in switching even. He told me the strongest man he knew was a submissive, and I knew he meant Silas. The confession only made me adore Marshall more, not for myself but for Silas. The two of them were so sickeningly perfect together I knew it was only a matter of time before Marshall stepped into the shoes I wore and slowly—unintentionally—pushed me out of frame.

But I'd let Silas finish getting me dressed, press my car keys into my hand, and tell me where to go. Submissive my ass, I thought, as I drove us to Club Rapture in Pasadena. The kinkiest club I'd ever been to, housed in the walls of an abandoned church, and Silas dragged me up the stairs and immediately onto the dance floor.

He obviously didn't have eyes for anyone else, knowing Marshall was at home waiting for him, and I didn't want to look for anyone to play with, considering the atrocious state of my mind since Silas moved out. Instead, we danced for hours until so much sweat poured down the small of my back I didn't know how I would ever get out of my leather pants.

At the end of the evening, he offered for me to stay at Marshall's for the night, but I said no, and after getting us both back to my apartment, we said goodnight. I lingered in the parking lot, tossing my phone from hand to hand, staring absently at nothing in particular. It wasn't that I didn't want to find someone to play with, it was just that I didn't want to find someone to play with at Rapture. Not like I was so important that I had a reputation to uphold, but all the regulars knew me as a dominant, and I didn't want to cruise for someone opposite that until I was certain the change was a real thing and not pretend.

Before I could talk myself out of it—patron saint of indecision and all that—I swiped open the One Night Stand app on my phone and scrolled through the profiles of people in the area. About fourteen people in, one of the faceless torsos stood out from the rest, and I paused, finger hovering over the scroll button. He was an escort, I realized, which...probably wouldn't be the worst way to try it out if I was serious about the whole thing. I could definitely afford to pay whatever his rates were, and that almost made him a professional. It wasn't the worst idea, but I also knew it was extremely unsafe to go into that kind of situation without an emergency contact of some kind. Maybe I could write down my location on a Post-it or something. If I went missing, Silas would find it eventually.

Groaning over the logistics, I sent a message.

Tonight?

The reply was almost immediate, like he'd been on his phone and waiting.

CEH13

You host?

I can, but my apartment is a closet.

I can. I have closets but don't live in one.

Snorting, I scrubbed a hand down my face. Great. The faceless torso had jokes.

What did you want to do?

Wanted to play. Maybe some...wanted to try being spanked.

I can spank you.

What else?

Kneeling.

Have you not?

Normally, I'm the one standing.

I see. So, something easy.

I don't know if I want EASY.

You do.

Are you seriously telling me what I need already?

;)

I think this is a bad idea.

Hey now. It's just fun, right?

You're professional. You get it.

So he'd checked my app profile, which had a link to my profile on the website I used to sell my own content. He'd actually…my phone gave a little buzz, and I realized I had a new subscriber with a very familiar looking username.

In reality, it was the best way to go. We were both sex workers, so there weren't going to be any feelings involved. I could find out what it meant to submit. He would get an easy payday, and that would be the end of it.

Loc?

He sent me his address and asked for thirty minutes to get ready, and also—discreetly—told me the rate for our little adventure. His apartment was twenty minutes from me, so the time wasn't an issue. Not wanting to talk myself out of it, I ran upstairs and fought my way out of my leather pants, showered the sweat of the night off of me—though some people liked it, it didn't feel appropriate for whatever trouble I was about to get into—got dressed again, and headed back down to my car.

Instead of a Post-it, I typed out a message to Silas and set it to send at six in the morning. That would give me plenty of time to cancel it if I survived and enough time for my body to still be warm if I didn't.

I swung through the bank on my way to CEH13's apartment, wishing I knew his name so I didn't have to think of him by his username, which was clearly initials of some type. Maybe his name was Chris or Cory or Calvin. I'd ask when I got there, not that it really mattered what his name was. He'd probably give me a fake one anyway, which was totally fine.

I spent the drive thinking about Ethan of all people, and the casual ways he'd been dominant without even trying. Sometimes it had been a firm look or a steady hand, but every time it had been enough to shift the scales *just* enough to throw me off-balance. Avoiding him the last time I saw him at Rapture had been hard, but I wasn't ready to admit to Silas that things just didn't feel right for me. I honestly wasn't sure if it was all about the submission or part that and part the fact I'd lost my best friend and my roommate in one blow. What I did know was I didn't want him to feel bad about falling in love, so I wasn't going to say anything to him one way or another until I figured it out.

A few minutes late, I parked in a guest spot at a very affluent-looking high-rise in Santa Monica, thankful that I'd made the decision to go inside and change out of my leathers. In addition to the address, the guy from the app had also given me the code to get into the front door, so I let myself in and rode up to the fourteenth floor. The hallways of the building were bright and sterile, which made the walk to the end of the floor feel a lot like a trip to the doctor's office to get my dick swabbed or something.

But when I reached the apartment, the front door was cracked open, the light streaming out of the unit a much softer glow than the bright fluorescents in the hallway. I knocked on the door anyway, it swung open, and I was met with not just the torso from the app, but the gorgeous face that went with it.

"Hey," I croaked, clearing my throat. "Are you…"

I still didn't know his name.

"Ethan," he said, and I groaned, clearly not hiding the way my face contorted because he laughed and said, "Is that bad?"

"I know an Ethan is all."

He stepped out of the way and ushered me into his apartment.

"Well, if it's any consolation, it's my middle name."

I chuckled, shoving my hair back from my face. "A small one. I'm Jay, also a middle name. Or, rather, middle initial."

Ethan's mouth quirked up into a smile. "Fair enough. Did you want a drink or anything?

"No, I don't think so."

"Straight to it then?" he asked, and I nodded.

"I don't want to talk myself out of this."

"I'm not a fan of being with people who don't really want to be with me," he said, aimlessly dragging his hand up and down the exposed length of his stomach. The man had to live in a gym to have abs and biceps like that.

"Oh, you don't have to worry about that. Trust and believe I very much want to get a taste of whatever you're selling. It's the rest of it that has me on edge," I told him.

"Do you not enjoy submission?" he asked.

"Never tried it."

Ethan arched a brow. "Not ever?"

"Kind of once on accident," I explained, "which is why I think I might want to try it again."

He smiled at me, and heat rushed through my veins like molten lava, melting me down into a pile of nothing.

"We can try it again," he murmured, reaching for me, crooking his fingers until I stepped close enough for him to touch.

I walked into his arms, groaning at how warm his body was, how sturdy, how tall. Ethan was gorgeous by anyone's standards, at least six foot tall, somewhere around two hundred pounds if you counted the muscle. He had brown hair that fell in soft waves around his face, almost reaching his shoulders but not quite, and penetrating eyes that looked like they couldn't decide if they wanted to be rum or whiskey.

He smoothed his hands down the outsides of my arms. His fingers were so fucking soft and delicate, long bones and slender digits, and fuck this man was gorgeous. If I looked as good as him, I'd ask to get paid too.

"I want to know your limits, Jay. Your wants…but first, can we get the logistics out of the way?"

His breath was hot against the shell of my ear, and I lost myself for a second until embarrassment flooded my cheeks.

"Right." I reached into my pocket and pulled out four hundred-dollar bills. He didn't check them and he didn't count, he simply smiled at me and slid them into the pocket of his obscenely low slung sweatpants.

"Let's go into the bedroom and talk, Jay. How does that sound?"

It sounded perfect, even as I tried to ignore the way it was another man giving me a command. My body responded with all the interest I hoped it wouldn't, but I nodded my approval and trailed after him down a short hallway and into a sprawling bedroom. The whole apartment was amazingly decorated, with a black leather couch, dark jewel tone pillows, and a noticeable amount of plants on shelves and hooks around the living room.

The bedroom was far more plain, and I knew without asking it had to be a guest room or a secondary. The bed was low to the floor with a minimal headboard but dark and comfortable-looking bedding. Throw pillows against the wall matched the ones in the living room, and to either side of the bed were matching nightstands with matching lamps. They were both on, the amber glow from the bulbs the only light in the room besides the sparkling brightness of the city that reflected in through the windows.

"I get the impression you'd prefer it dark," he murmured, sitting down on the edge of the bed. He patted the space beside him, and I sat down with an *oomph*.

"Dark is good."

He nodded. "Tell me your hard and fast limits, Jay."

My lashes fluttered, and I licked my lips, pulling them between my teeth and biting down hard enough that it hurt. I needed the spark of pain to ground me in the moment, in the quest of what I was after.

I realized, in hindsight maybe, that submission wasn't about pain. It was something I'd known all along, but when I ran through the checklist in my head of limits, I found I wasn't entirely sure if the impact parts of play were what I was truly after. I was certain I wouldn't hate it, and I didn't want to waste my money on something as simple as kneeling, but…

No.

It wasn't simple at all, was it?

"You with me?" Ethan asked, gently setting his hand on my thigh. "Is this okay? Did you want to change your mind?"

"I'm fine," I said quickly. "This is fine. The question was loaded. That's all."

"Loaded how?" he asked.

"Respectfully, I'm not trying to use my hour as a therapy session."

He huffed out a laugh, then drummed his fingers against the top of my leg. "Limits, then."

"Just spanking. I don't want any other impact play," I told him and he nodded along. "No blindfolds or gags, no real bondage—"

"What's real?"

"Not intense," I corrected.

"That's subjective," he said.

"Let's just go with no bondage," I said, and he nodded again, not looking miffed in the slightest that I was wishy-washy as a sponge covered in dish soap.

"That's fine and doable," Ethan said, giving my leg a squeeze before standing up. He turned to face me and, on instinct, I leaned back to stare up at him. With me on my ass, he towered over me, looking as casually dominant as ever.

I wondered briefly if this was how Silas felt with Marshall.

"That's not what you really want, though, is it?" He cocked his head to the side, and his hair finally brushed across his bare shoulder. "You really just want to submit, don't you?"

CHAPTER 6
HUNTER

Jay was so nervous that simply being around him also made me nervous. I'd planned for a last hurrah. A final hookup so I could go out in a blaze of glory, then delete the profile Finn had set up for me and move on with my life. But Jay had shown up, all awkward tension and glaring need, and I knew on sight the night was going to be anything besides expected.

"I don't know," he rasped, fingers splayed out over the tops of his thighs.

"I can't do much with that," I told him.

"I do want to submit," he said softly.

I tugged on the waistband of my sweats, pulling them low enough to expose the dark hair that curled up around the shaft of my cock.

"Are you okay with penetration?" I asked.

Jay swallowed hard and nodded.

"What if we don't do that? What if it's only hands or mouths?"

"That's…that's fine too."

I could practically hear him thinking, and it was a wonder to me that he hadn't come to submission sooner. Playing this part wasn't something I did in my not-for-profit sex life, not that I had one of those anymore, but it was clear as day that Jay was desperate to shut his mind off and give up control, even if only for an hour. He wasn't after any sort of physical impact, just the release that came from being told what to do for a while. Admittedly, that sort of thing wasn't entirely in my wheelhouse, as the men who were normally interested in my services cared more about the physical aspect of it, but I was confident I could play pretend for a little while.

"Will you feel shortchanged if you don't come at all?" I asked.

Jay looked down at his lap and frowned. "Not sure I could, even if I wanted to."

"*Do* you want to?"

He exhaled, cheeks puffing out. "You tell me."

I was halfway certain that wasn't how it was supposed to go, but I was more than halfway certain I could get both of us through the hour unscathed.

"Okay. For the next hour, you can call me Sir."

Jay swallowed and blinked, nodded almost imperceptibly.

"You can call me Sir," I said again.

"Yes, Sir." The words barely made it out of his mouth. He choked a little, coughed, then slammed his mouth shut.

"Does that make you feel wrong?"

Jay bit the inside of his cheek and answered with the slightest shake of his head.

There was so much terror inside of him. It clawed at his skin, trying to break through and put both of us out of his misery. I knew whatever I did with him wasn't going to be enough to fix whatever was going on with him, but maybe it could help get him on the right track.

"Strip then," I said next. "Take off all of your clothes and get on your knees."

He hesitated for the briefest moment, then did as I'd told

him. Once he was naked, he stood in front of me as proud as he could be, all things considered. If he wasn't so scared of himself, he'd be gorgeous. Average height and slim built with narrow hips and a slender waist. Jay had his navel and his nipples pierced, nothing more than small glints of silver in the darkness of my guest room that made my mouth water.

Did I actually *want* this man?

My gaze raked over him, sliding lower until I reached his cock, which based off his earlier comment was predictably limp. It was the nerves. It happened to the best of us. My cock, on the other hand, was far from soft, and I palmed my erection, groaning from the pressure of my own hand. Jay's stare flickered down to the motion, and his lips parted in a silent gasp.

Yeah.

Yes.

I definitely wanted this man.

"Get on your knees, Jay," I said, and he again hesitated. "Are you with me still?"

"What? Oh. Yes. It's…" He grimaced and sank down onto his knees. "It's the middle name. I—"

"Hush then," I said, closing the space between us so I could reach out and set my hand on top of his head.

He'd gone to his knees with little fanfare, but I was going to let him stay there long enough to get a feel for the submission he was after. We were obviously on the clock, but I was content to wait him out. Through the twitching and the shifting and the resettling of his weight until, finally, Jay sank into himself and went almost entirely still.

"There you are," I whispered, combing my fingers through his hair. I pulled him forward a couple of inches, his cheek resting against my thigh. "Stay here now. I've got you."

He went even more pliant, resting his weight against my leg and releasing a breath so long I found myself impressed with his lung capacity. I slid my hand through his hair around to the back of his head, and I held him there until my own leg started to tingle from the pressure of him against me.

"How's that?" I asked, and Jay answered me with a hum. "You don't want to get spanked, do you?"

"No, Sir," he whispered.

"I didn't think so." I shoved my sweats down to my ankles and stepped out of them, finally moving Jay's weight off my leg. He rocked back to support himself when I kicked my pants to the corner of the room, and I pressed the side of my finger against the underside of his chin.

Slowly, I tipped his head up, losing my own breath at the sight of him on his knees. Jay's cheeks were flushed, his lips parted, his pupils shot. It would have been easy to get lost in those identical dark pools of want, but this wasn't that kind of encounter. Jay was a man paying me to shoulder his burdens for an hour, not asking me to let my own feelings get the better of me and ruin us both.

"You look perfect on your knees," I stroked my thumb over the side of his chin. "I don't know how you could ever want to be anywhere else."

He blinked hard, eyes growing shiny and wet.

"Hey now," I coaxed, catching the first tear as it escaped the corner of his eye. "It's all right, beautiful. It's okay. You're okay."

Jay shifted his body as the tears began to fall in earnest, but he made no move to get up or pull away.

"Does it feel good down there on your knees?" I asked.

He nodded, tongue darting out to lick a stray tear from the corner of his mouth.

"You look good down there," I said, angling my hips so my cock was more directly in his face. "See how good you look."

He studied my erection with those blown eyes of his, chin quivering and tears still pouring down his face.

"Here," I said to him next, dragging my tip across his lips. He opened, and I plopped the head of my dick down onto the flat of his tongue. "You're being so brave, Jay, and I've got a reward for you if you can suck it out of me."

The message was clearly received. Jay closed his lips around my dick and sucked me like his life depended on it. He was loud and wet and messy, never using his hands even as he slid most of the way down my shaft. He gagged and choked on me, using the muscles of his throat to try and coax an orgasm out of me. His ministrations very nearly worked, but I'd jacked off before his arrival with the intent to last as long as possible for the hour we had together.

"Your mouth is…" I trailed off, words escaping me.

Tangling my fingers back into his hair, I tugged him off my cock, appreciating the way his lips were wet and swollen, still connected to my shaft with chains of spit. There was enough space between us I could look down and easily see his cock had thickened, pointing toward the wall behind me and spasming with every breath he took.

"Your mouth is decadent," I finally said, going down to the floor in front of him.

I pulled Jay's smaller body onto my lap and turned us so my back rested against the side of the bed. Using my feet, I hooked myself around his ankles and spread his legs apart, making sure my own cock was nestled neatly against his ass cheeks. Jay groaned after I got us settled, dropping his head against my shoulder and closing his eyes.

"Hands together behind the back of my neck," I said, and he looped his arms around my neck and held on. His palms were sweaty but steady.

I reached for the nightstand and jerked the drawer open, feeling blindly inside until I found the bottle of lube. Pumping a generous amount into my hand, I moved to grip him slowly, making sure he had more than enough time to tell me no if he wanted to. He said nothing, only moaning as my fingers tightened around him. His hips lifted away from my body, but my legs held him down, and he sank back into my lap with a whimper.

"Just relax," I whispered, stroking him from root to tip, ignoring how perfectly his body fit against mine. "Just submit."

He flexed his fingers against the back of my neck, sending a shiver down my spine. I fought down the swell of emotion his whimpers and sighs dredged up, focusing instead on stroking him with slow and measured twists of my wrist. I attended his cock lazily, not caring so much if he got off, only focused on keeping him pliant in my arms.

Ten minutes later, Jay's entire body seized and he cried out. I kept him pinned against me as he painted my knuckles with hot drips of cum, keeping the same pace and same tension in my hand. I dragged my fingers from root to tip, tip to root, root to tip, until Jay's orgasm quieted down, and he trembled like a leaf in my lap.

Kissing the side of his head, I let my other hand wander over the small swell of his hip and down lower toward his balls. They were high and tight, still churning from his orgasm, and I cradled them gently in my palm.

"Submit," I told him again, unhooking my ankles from his calves. Jay's legs fell more open, and he tightened his fingers against the back of my neck. He—unintentionally—tickled my hairline and I grunted, hips lifting off the floor and pressing my erection into the round globes of his ass.

A pained sound tumbled out of his mouth, and I didn't need to see Jay's face to know he was crying again. Maybe he'd never really stopped, but he'd also never stopped me, so I did not relent. I stroked Jay through another shuddering orgasm, and my own cock grew impossibly hard at the way he forced himself to stay spread for me while he came. His fingers had loosened their hold on each other, and instead his nails dug into my skin for purchase.

The third orgasm was more difficult to come by, Jay's body fighting him as hard as the clock fought me. Every stroke caused a violent reaction, but there was no way I was going to let him go without leaving it all on the table.

"Up," I said, reaching behind me and covering his hands with my own. Leveraging us both up onto our knees, I squeezed his hands far harder than I squeezed his cock. The change in position had been a guess that paid off. Almost as soon as Jay's knees hit the carpet, he came for a third—and final—time. Barely anything leaked out of his cock, but his face was soaked with tears and spit, his muscles trembling like I'd pulled him out of a freezing river.

"Oh, God." He cried, body bucking away from mine, but I held him steady until his breathing returned to almost normal and his teeth stopped chattering. Once he was only barely hyperventilating, I eased us back down onto the ground and let him rest against my bed.

Jay's entire body prickled with gooseflesh and sweat, his chest a dark and rich shade of red, nearly as dark as his over-worked cock. He dropped his head back against the mattress, eyes closed, and chest still heaving.

Our time had long ago run out, but I had no intention of sending him home yet.

Not that raw.

Not that exposed.

CHAPTER 7
LINCOLN

Naked and boneless would have been an understatement. Every nerve in my skin was over-sensitive, my bones…gelatin. The only reason my body remained upright was the steadiness of Ethan's body behind mine. Even when he reached down between us and stroked himself off, coming against the small of my back with almost no commotion.

After he spent, he eased me down onto my side. The bed was so close but also terribly far away, and I had no qualms with the floor. I could curl in on myself just as easily there as I could a bed. Getting up from the floor and leaving would be much easier than getting up from the bed, so the placement felt a lot like courtesy.

Ethan sat down beside me on the floor, gently stroking his fingers across my bare skin, down the length of my back until he reached my ass before tracing his way back up into my hair-line. I shivered, squeezing my eyes closed before rolling onto my stomach.

Before rolling away from *him*.

"How much time do I have left?" I murmured, scrubbing a hand down my face and forcing my eyes open. Ethan had a paneled ceiling, and not the paneled ceiling I grew up with. The fancy kind made out of beveled wood and intricate angle cuts.

"Don't worry," he answered. "Do you want a shower before you go?"

"That feels a little too…" I trailed off and frowned, rolling onto all fours, ready to push to my feet so I could find my clothes.

"I can't let you leave like this," he said, reaching out and grabbing my wrist. His hands were so warm, so steady. "So you can either lie here on the floor longer, or you can take a shower."

Whatever had just happened between us might have been a paid encounter, but he was following the rules of the game, and I appreciated that. I'd have to dig out some more cash to tip him or something. Were you supposed to tip escorts? I wasn't familiar with the protocol.

"If I get in the shower, I'll cry again," I admitted.

There was no harm in being honest, considering my eyes were probably swollen shut from the crying I'd already done, and there was no way in hell I was ever going to see this man again.

"There's no harm in it," he said, which only made me want to cry before I even got into the bathroom. "Do you want to talk about anything that just happened?"

"I don't think I can afford the therapy add-on."

Ethan chuckled and smiled, a dimple appearing in his right cheek. "Consider it a freebie then."

He stood first and held out his hand to me, which I took. Ethan helped me to my feet, and I was pleased to find standing wasn't as insurmountable as I'd feared. My knees were definitely worse for wear, the pile of the carpet worn deep into my skin on account of the kneeling.

Fuck.

I'd gotten onto my knees for another man. I'd submitted to another man.

And I'd done it seriously, not in the teasing back and forth kind of way the first Ethan had played at it.

And I'd liked it. I'd really fucking liked it.

"Come on," New Ethan said, leading me out of the bedroom and down the hall to the bathroom.

Even the guest bathroom had the same vibe as the rest of his apartment, dark jewel tones, golden light, and comfort. Fuck, his apartment was comfortable.

"How do you like the water?" he asked.

"Hot," I said, clearing my throat. "Sir."

He paused, halfway to the taps.

"You don't have to call me Sir anymore."

"What if I'm trying to get used to the feel of it?" I asked.

Ethan turned on the water, waved his hand under the spray to check the temperature, then moved out of the way so I could climb in.

"Do you plan on calling someone else Sir?" he asked quietly.

I pulled the curtain closed halfway, and Ethan sat down on the closed lid of the toilet, his sticky cock now soft against the top of his thigh. He rested his elbows against the back of the toilet tank, leaning toward the wall so he could still see me in the shower.

"I don't know," I said, grabbing what looked like a clean washcloth off a small rack by the soap. "Can I use this?"

"It's clean."

Off the bat, he hadn't struck me as the kind of man who had clean towels at all times in a guest bathroom, but if he hosted often, it made sense for him to be prepared. I wasn't sure how that made me feel, so I did what I did best and ignored the feeling. Instead, I squirted some body wash onto the cloth and lathered it in my hands.

"I've made some assumptions tonight based on your cagey answers that you prefer to be dominant in the bedroom," he said.

I washed my armpits, then reached back to clean the place on my back where he'd painted my skin with hot stripes of his own cum.

"And out of it."

Ethan made a thoughtful—if disbelieving—noise.

"That's why I wanted to try this," I told him. "I hooked up with a guy a few weeks ago, and he…I don't know. He was playful about it, but the whole time we hooked up it felt like the tables kept turning."

"And you didn't like that?"

"I did like it," I said. "That's the problem."

I lowered the soapy cloth to my cock and balls, washing them gingerly as to not accidentally turn myself on again. Not that I could come again if I wanted to. Ethan had wrung three orgasms out of me, and the last one was barely anything but air. If I came again, it would be nothing more than thoughts and prayers between me and God.

Ethan frowned at me, his hair falling over his face when he cocked his head to the side.

"Why does that stress you out so much? Can't it just be fun?"

I thought about Silas and Marshall. I wondered if Silas found the things they did fun or if he found them necessary. Ethan posed a fair point, though. I'd been single for so long, was it really that important to me? I'd clearly lived just fine for all the weeks at a time I went without it. Why did I make such a big deal of it when I did finally get it?

"I don't know," I answered, rinsing out the washcloth and returning it to the hook. "Maybe."

I turned and tipped my head back under the water, slicking my hair away from my face and letting the spray wash over me.

The soap raced down my body, and I did a turn under the water to make sure I was fully clean.

"I had fun tonight," Ethan offered.

I swallowed hard, impressed I'd made it through the shower without crying again while knowing if he'd left me alone, I would have. Fucking subtle-ass, aftercaring motherfucker.

"I had fun too."

I turned off the water and shoved the curtain all the way open. Ethan stood up from the toilet and faced me, catching my stare and holding it. He didn't look away when he reached toward the wall and pulled a towel off the bar, and he didn't look away when he held it between us. He looked at me like he saw me, like he had something else he wanted to say, but he knew I wouldn't want to hear it.

I snatched the towel out of his hand and made quick work of drying off before shoving it back into his hands.

"I should go," I said, stepping out of the tub and brushing past him. I needed to get back to the bedroom to find my clothes, needed to get dressed, needed to get the hell out of there.

"I'm not in a rush," he said from the bedroom doorway, towel still in hand.

"I've overstayed. I'm sure of it."

Ethan didn't say anything to that.

My clothes were scattered near the foot of the bed, and I dressed as quickly as my shaking hands would allow. The jeans rubbed against my legs like sandpaper, the shirt stuck to my still damp skin like glue. I fought my way into my socks and shoes, then checked my pockets for my wallet, phone, and keys.

"Are you good to drive, Jay?" he asked, and I almost didn't understand who he was talking to until I remembered we were both lying to each other about our names.

"I'm fine. Thank you for the night. For your services. Whatever."

He chuckled under his breath and tucked the towel under his arm. He was still fucking naked, and he was so fucking comfortable about it, following me around his house with his limp cock hanging out. In the living room, I grabbed whatever extra cash I had in my wallet. It couldn't have been more than fifty dollars, but I tossed it down onto his coffee table just the same.

"You paid me already," he said.

"A tip."

"Don't need one."

"Well, I'm not taking it back. Donate it to a fish sanctuary or something."

Ethan snorted, and I turned in time to see him roll his eyes at me. "Is there such a thing?"

"They have sanctuaries for every other kind of animal. I don't know why they wouldn't."

"I'll be sure to find out and donate accordingly," he said.

I scrunched my nose, wanting to fall down onto my knees in front of him and kiss his feet. Ethan hadn't given me a single answer, just a dozen more questions I definitely didn't have the answers to. It was worse than before I'd arrived, and I'd have to go home and be alone with it.

"I think I hate the way you make me feel."

He studied me carefully, biting his tongue between the tip of his teeth. "I don't think you hate it all. That's the problem."

"Well." I clapped my hands together in front of me, the tears I'd expected in the shower finally threatening to spill. "Thanks for that."

Without another word and only a hundred other thoughts, I spun on my heel and let myself out of Ethan's apartment. I slammed the door closed behind me which I knew wasn't entirely necessary but made me feel better anyway, and I all but ran to the elevator. It took forever to arrive, and I knew Ethan wouldn't come after me, but whatever part of my body didn't know that wouldn't quiet down.

I sniffled, swiping the back of my hand under my nose, and the elevator finally arrived. I rode it downstairs, tears leaking from the corners of my eyes while I did everything I could to ignore the sight of myself in the mirrored doors. After they slid open and let me out, I ran to my car and collapsed into the driver's seat. The doors were closed, and it was late. I grabbed the steering wheel and screamed at the top of my lungs. I screamed until it hurt to scream, and then I took a deep breath and another and another.

The clock on my dash ticked over to the top of the hour, and I grabbed my phone before I forgot to delete the message I'd scheduled to send to Silas in the event of an untimely demise. Ethan had killed me, just not physically. It was the awareness of this new side of me that hurt more than any rugburn on my knees or any ache in my balls.

Had I always known that I wanted both?

Was it greedy of me to want both?

I'd grown up seeing bisexuals scorned for being indecisive, for not wanting to pick a side. Would people view me the same way for being vers *and* wanting to switch?

"Fucking fuckballs," I said to no one in particular.

It was so late it was early, but there was no way in hell I could go home to my empty apartment and my drained fish-bowl, so I did the only thing I knew to do.

I called my best friend.

He answered with a lingering laugh on the third ring. "Hello?"

"Did I wake you up?" I asked.

"No. We were up," he said. "Are you okay?"

I pinched my lips together between my teeth and shook my

head, even though he couldn't see me. And even though he couldn't see me, Silas knew.

"Do you want to come over? You can stay here tonight. We can talk in the morning? Have some bacon?"

I screwed my eyes closed and nodded.

There was a silence, and then Silas' worried voice, "Are you okay to drive?"

"No." I cleared my throat. "No, I'm not okay. Yes, I want to come over. Yes, I can drive."

"Are you sure? Marshall and I can come get you."

"I can drive," I said.

"I'll unlock the door," Silas promised. "Get here safely, Lincoln. Whatever's wrong, we'll figure it out and fix it in the morning. Okay? Just like we always have. Right?"

I didn't believe him, but I didn't know what else to say.

"Yeah, Silas. Just like always."

CHAPTER 8
HUNTER

Saturday morning, I felt like shit.

Finn wasn't answering his phone, and it was too early for Smith to be awake, so I did the only thing that made sense. I drove myself to Marshall's house.

"You look like you got hit by a train," he said instead of hello, stepping out of the doorway to let me in.

I scrubbed a hand down my face, my unshaven jawline abrading my palm.

"I know it's early on a weekend. I don't mean to interrupt anything, it's just Finn wasn—"

My oldest brother cut me off with the press of his fingers against my lips. I snapped my mouth closed and narrowed my eyes at him.

"You don't have to make it sound like I'm the last resort," he said, inclining his head toward the kitchen. "You're always welcome here."

I toed off my shoes in his entryway and padded after him. The house was mostly dark, save for a light on in the kitchen and the sunlight streaming in through the window. I climbed onto one of the barstools at the counter and propped my chin in both of my hands.

"Where's your better half?" I asked.

Marshall pressed some buttons on the coffee pot and the smell of liquid heaven quickly filled the room. I inhaled deeply, groaning when my stomach growled.

"He was up late with his best friend," Marshall explained, placing a mug of coffee in front of me. "Are you hungry?"

"You heard that, then?"

He huffed out a breathy laugh. "Do you want me to make you some breakfast?"

"I can cook." I slid back off the stool, coffee in hand, and eased around the island until I was in the kitchen beside him. "The least I can do for pulling you out of bed this early."

"I was already up."

Marshall yawned, stretching his arms high above his head and arching his back. He was still in pajamas, and I wasn't sure I believed he'd already been up when I gave him a two-minute text warning of my arrival.

"Sure, Marsh."

I elbowed him out of the kitchen and turned my attention to his fridge, finding a carton of eggs, half a package of bacon, and an apple. Taking it all out of the fridge, I shot him a dubious look. "I see domestication has hardly domesticated you."

"I like you better when you talk less."

I gave him the finger, then made myself at home in his kitchen, scrambling eggs and slicing the apple into eighths while I waited for the pan to get warm enough to fry up the bacon. I'd just laid the first strips down when Silas staggered out of the bedroom, eyes half closed and hair sticking up in every direction. He had on an old hoodie and the outline of a pillow in sharp angles across his cheek. He went straight to Marshall, walking into his arms and letting my brother kiss him on the head.

"Good morning, Hunter," Silas muttered, accepting his kisses before taking a seat on the stool to Marshall's right.

"Good morning, Silas. Coffee?" I offered since I was in the kitchen.

Since I was in *his* house.

"Yes, thank you." He sniffed the air, smiling. "And bacon once you've gotten enough."

I poured Silas some coffee and set the mug in front of him.

"Eggs and apple too?" I asked.

"Please. Thank you."

Silas yawned and leaned against Marshall's arm while I finished frying up breakfast. The two of them spoke in hushed tones, which was lovely for them but less great for me, considering the reason I'd come over in the first place was because the last place I wanted to be was alone with my thoughts. They were so deep in it, much like they had been from the start, so there was no way of avoiding thoughts of Jay and the time we'd spent together the night before.

He'd been so nervous and earnest on his arrival, so broken and defeated by his departure. I shouldn't have let him leave, but there was no way I could have let him stay. I could—I should…maybe—text him to check on him later in the morning. To at least make sure he got home okay, even though there was no reason for me to do that.

I wasn't anything more than an experiment to him. A transaction where he paid and I delivered goods. If he'd wanted someone to follow up on his mental state, he wouldn't have hired an escort.

Fuck, I needed to delete that app.

I dished up some eggs, bacon, and fruit for my brother and his boyfriend, then reached into my pocket for my phone. I was going to delete that ridiculous app once and for all, and maybe someday in the future if I felt brave enough, I'd tell Finn all about how his fat fingers caused me to accidentally become a sex worker. I swiped a greasy finger across my phone screen, finding two notifications on the app. Ignoring them, I pressed my finger down until the One Night Stand app began to wiggle, ready to delete it. Whatever notifications the app had for me could go unread. I needed to be done with that part of my life once and for all.

"Smells so good," an almost familiar voice said from the hallway, and my head snapped up at the sound of it. I had the spatula in one hand and my phone in the other, dropping them both when Jay shuffled into the kitchen wearing nothing more than a pair of way too big pajama pants. They hung low enough there couldn't have been more than an inch of skin between the waistband and his cock, and I would know since I'd gotten up close and personal with the latter only hours before.

Jay had both hands over his face, rubbing sleep out of his eyes, but when my phone landed against the tile, he dropped his arms to his sides and squinted the room into focus. He saw me first, his nose clearly chasing after the bacon I'd finished cooking, and his eyes went wide as the two plates I'd just loaded up with food. I tore my stare away from him, bending down to pick up my phone. The corner of the screen had cracked, but other than that, the damage looked minimal. The hookup app still danced on my screen, and I turned the whole thing off and shoved it back into my pocket.

"I thought you'd sleep longer," Silas said from behind me.

Jay blinked hard, tearing his stare away from me and looking directly at Silas.

"Good morning, Lincoln," Marshall greeted, unbothered and unaware. "I don't think you've met my brother, Hunter. Hunt, this is Silas's best friend, Lincoln."

Jay—no—Lincoln and I faced each other head on, bodies tense and jaws locked.

"Good to see you," I said softly.

"What are…" He stopped himself, snapping his mouth closed before taking a step closer.

"I'm making breakfast," I said. "Did you want some coffee?"

"I can get my own," he muttered, stepping around me to get to the coffee pot. I turned back to the stove, and we were shoulder to shoulder, staring at the wall.

"Ethan," he said under his breath.

"Middle name."

Lincoln made a derisive noise in the back of his throat. "Hunter Ethan Covington."

"Lincoln Jay…?"

"Lincoln Jesse Summers."

He poured a cup of coffee for himself, adding two spoonfuls of sugar and swirling the granules around. This was clearly not his first time spending the night because he knew his way around Marshall's kitchen as well as I did.

"Does Silas…"

"No," he said quickly, raising the mug to his mouth. "Does Marshall?"

"No."

"Good."

Lincoln turned away from me and went for the empty barstool beside Silas. I watched every movement until he settled into the seat, only tearing my attention away after Marshall cleared his throat. Maybe not so unaware after all. I risked a quick glance at my brother, who looked like he was ready to slap my hand out of the cookie jar, and I held them up in surrender before plating breakfast for Lincoln and myself. There was no way I was going to take the barstool at his edge of the island, so I put one of the plates in front of him and opted to eat mine standing on the kitchen side of the counter.

Silas made an overtly sexual sound when he bit into the bacon, which earned him a sharp pinch to his ribs. Jesus, my brother was so head over heels for that man. I dared another look at Lincoln, who watched Silas and Marshall with an expression I could only describe as disgusted yearning.

He was jealous.

And he hated it.

The four of us ate breakfast in a silence that made me want to slice my skin and peel it off my bones. Lincoln looked equally uncomfortable, but Silas and Marshall were in their own little honeymoon world. After everyone ate, I took the plates and stacked them in the sink.

"I'll wash them," Lincoln offered. "Since you cooked."

"You don't have to," I said.

"I don't mind." He jumped off the barstool and joined me in the kitchen. "Breakfast was great, by the way. Thank you."

"Did the best I could with the tools I had," I mumbled.

Marshall loosed a curious laugh at me, then stood up himself. Another stretch and another yawn. "I'm going to hop in the shower and get the day started."

"I'll join you," Silas said eagerly, scampering after him.

There was no way the two of them were going to get out of that shower without fucking, which left Lincoln and me alone in the kitchen. For his part, Lincoln had meant what he said about washing the dishes. His eyes were narrowed as he scrubbed bacon grease off the frying pan, not even stopping when I approached him and turned off the water.

"Lincoln."

"Don't," he warned, turning the water back on.

I shoved the tap down again. "You might be the boss of other people, but you're not the boss of me."

"I'm clearly not the boss of anyone."

"Submitting once doesn't make you less dominant," I said, confused why I even had to explain that.

"Easy for you to say. You're *clearly* a fucking Dom."

"I'm *clearly* an escort who can role play anything for an hour."

He turned the water back on, and this time I let him.

Lincoln went back to scrubbing his troubles away, and when he finished the pan, I took it from him to dry. He watched me swirl the dish towel around the handle and the bottom, then he reached for one of the plates and sponged it off before thrusting it into my unprepared hands. I fumbled it, like I'd done earlier with my phone, but managed to save the plate.

"Seems unfair for you to take whatever is going on in your head out on Marshall's dinnerware."

"Don't," he warned, passing me another plate with more care than the first.

We finished the dishes without exchanging another word, sighing in equal measure when we realized Marshall and Silas were still in the shower and probably would be for a while.

"Can we talk about last night?" I asked, scratching the back of my neck. I was scared to move, scared to say the wrong thing. Lincoln was skittish and scared, and I didn't want to out him to his best friend, but he needed to talk to *someone*.

"I can't afford that," he bit out.

"You probably won't believe this, but you are my last client, so..."

He scrunched his nose, glancing up at me from the corner of his eye. He was so small, so delicate, but also so strong.

"You're right. I don't believe it," he said.

"Doesn't matter anyway. I'm not asking in that capacity."

Lincoln turned and rested his ass against the counter, those borrowed pajama pants still indecently low on his hips. He crossed his arms in front of his chest and stared at the stove.

"What do you want to talk about?" he asked.

"I want to make sure you're doing okay. I think...I mean I

don't know a lot about this, but I don't think I should have let you leave."

"I couldn't afford to stay," he snapped.

Frustrated, I stepped in front of him, grabbed his arms, and gave him a little shake. He was still frowning but glared up at me with an exhausted kind of venom filling his eyes.

"Would you stop with the money shit?"

Lincoln's nostrils flared, and he sucked in a sharp breath. "I don't know what any of it means anymore," he finally said.

I licked my lips, rubbing them together and trying to think of the right thing to say. I wasn't good with words like Finn, and I wasn't good at understanding the things people needed like Marshall.

"I've never known what any of it means," I admitted to him softly. Down the hall, the water turned off, and I flexed my fingers around his arms, not ready to let him go. "But if it's a secret you're keeping and I'm the only one who knows, maybe we can figure it out together."

Lincoln studied me thoughtfully, a knot appearing between his eyebrows.

"It's more complicated than that," he said.

Marshall's and Silas' voices grew louder from down the hall, and reluctantly I let go of Lincoln and took a step back.

"I donated it to Angeles Fish and Wildlife Rescue," I said quickly.

His eyes went wide, his lips shaped into an O that had me thinking all sorts of things that had no place anywhere near that moment. "What?"

"The fifty-three dollars."

"What's fifty-three dollars?" Silas asked, bounding into the kitchen like an overgrown puppy. He threw an arm over Lincoln's shoulder and kissed him on the cheek, achingly close to his mouth which had settled back into its usual unhappy line.

"Nothing." Lincoln hiked up the oversized pajama pants, turning to face Silas and kissing him messily against the slope of his neck. It was clearly a distraction from the conversation Silas had walked in on, but seeing Lincoln's mouth move against Silas's neck in the exact ways I wanted his mouth to move against me…

It was horribly intimate, but Marshall seemed absolutely unbothered, smiling fondly at the two of them instead of looking like he wanted to put Lincoln through a wall.

"Are you okay with this?" I mouthed, gesturing at the two younger men in the kitchen.

Marshall squinted, rolled his eyes, nodded, and mouthed back, "Harmless. Platonic."

If Marshall didn't have an issue with the over-affectionate nature of his boyfriend's relationship with Lincoln, what could Lincoln have meant when he said it was more complicated than that?

What else was he hiding?

But more importantly, why did I care?

CHAPTER 9
LINCOLN

managed to avoid Hunter for the rest of the day on Saturday, making an escape from Marshall's house just before lunch. My only saving grace was that he couldn't directly try and corner me in front of his brother because then we'd both have a lot of explaining to do, and neither of us wanted to get into that.

Sunday, he messaged me seven times, and I left him on read.

Monday, three more messages, all before lunch. Two more after dinner.

Tuesday, two at lunch, one just before eleven at night.

All of the messages said some variation of the same thing.

Please can we talk about Friday night.

I know we're strangers, but I'm worried about you.

Why won't you answer me?

There was no tangible reason for him to want to talk about Friday or to worry about my mental state afterward. He might be my best friend's boyfriend's brother, but he wasn't anything more to me than an escort I paid to dominate me for an hour. I'd paid and he'd done his part, and he'd even donated the extra cash to a fucking fish rescue.

Like… why?

What?

Wednesday morning, I woke up to one single text message that simply read *Lincoln.*

I groaned, rolling onto my stomach and burying my face into the pillow. It was time for me to get my head out of my ass about lots of things, but Hunter Covington was not on the list. Not only was he not submissive—my type—he was also not dominant—my vice. He could clearly play the role well in the bedroom, and that was great, but at the end of the day, I did want a partner who *lived* it.

I wanted what Silas had with Marshall. Or what Marshall had with Silas.

Or something.

Patron saint of who-fucking-knows.

Eventually, I forced myself out of bed and into the shower. I needed to film some content, which I normally did in batches. I'd spend a few days making as many videos as my body would allow, and then I'd post until I ran out. The last one I'd posted was the one with the dildo against the wall, so I needed to not just make some more, but I needed to get creative about it.

Hunter's house would have been great for filming. He had moody lighting and lots of square footage. Being confined to the walls of my studio was limiting, and I didn't want things to get boring. Maybe I'd splurge for a hotel over the weekend and see what trouble I could get into with a wall-size mirror and a glass-walled shower.

In the meantime, I prepped myself in the shower, styled my hair, had some coffee, then sat down on the edge of the bed to go through ideas. I had a running checklist on my phone of content suggestions, and I often doubled up, especially if there were things that ended up with a lot of views. My income always seemed to go up whenever I focused on sounds over visual so, to start, I propped myself up against the wall with a bottle of lube and silicone cock sleeve.

With one more swallow of coffee, I set up the tripod and the ring light at the edge of my bed, then arranged myself against the wall with my feet flat on the mattress and my legs bent at the knee. The frame cut my face off, which was fine, because it gave an impressive view of my piercings and my package. If I lifted off the bed, my asshole was barely visible, and that was the kind of tease that earned me tips and comments.

I'd probably end up filming a follow-up in a couple of weeks, the same pose with a toy inside of me. It was the thing people generally asked for. If I played with my ass, they wanted me to involve my cock. If I played with my cock, they wanted me stuffed from the back. If I fucked one of those silicone assholes, they wanted me spit-roasted by toys.

Greedy, but I didn't mind.

I started recording and leaned against the wall, trailing one hand up my chest and the other down my stomach. I'd put more than enough lube on my hand, so when I wrapped my fingers around my half-hard cock, it was already slippery and loud. Groaning, I pinched my nipple and began to stroke myself.

My last orgasm had been Friday night with Hunter. I hadn't even touched myself since then except to wash in the shower. A hand around my dick triggered a Pavlovian response, and I could practically feel his feet hooked around my calves, pinning me like a butterfly while he worked my shaft.

Dropping my head against the wall, I moaned loudly, twisting my wrist the way he twisted his. The sensation was overwhelming, and I had to slow down to make sure the video wasn't a two-minute deal. I released my cock and sighed as it slapped hard and loud against my stomach, then I cupped my balls and tugged at the barbells in my nipples until they hurt to touch.

My body was on fire, unable to stop thinking about how it had felt to be on my knees with Hunter behind me. His chest warm and sweaty against my back, his breath hot on my ear, his hand…

His fucking hand.

I came with a pained cry, arching away from the wall as cum shot onto my chest and slid down my stomach. Fuck, it felt good. It felt horrible. It felt just as confusing as it had Friday night when it happened. With another dramatic grunt of pleasure, I jacked my cock until my balls were empty, then I ended the recording and collapsed onto my bed.

This was absolutely unacceptable.

There was no way I could spend the rest of my life jerking off thinking about the way Hunter jerked me off. There was no feasible scenario where I would survive that. I'd simply have to get him out of my system and hope for the best.

Or something.

Sliding down to the foot of my bed, I yanked open the top drawer in my dresser and grabbed a clean pair of underwear. Cum-covered cock be damned, I pulled them on then went into the kitchen to wash my hands. I got some water and an apple, and brought it all back to my bed. The rest of the job was boring, loading the video onto my laptop, importing the file and fixing the lighting, adjusting the sound, editing and piecing together clips to make it longer and better. Great use of that certificate I'd gotten after high school in video editing, right?

Just shy of noon, I got an another text, this one in my actual messaging app from a Covington I actually liked.

SMITH

Do you have plans later?

Not a single one.

Will you come shopping with me?

It's Wednesday.

Need to eat.

You want me to come shop for groceries with you?

Will make you dinner too.

I hadn't even started eating my apple, and my stomach groaned its approval of Smith's plan.

Alright.

Is this weird?

Yes.
Very.

No.

Okay, good. Just kind of lonely.

Heard.

Come to my apt and I'll drive?

6?

See you then.

I dropped my phone onto the bed and bit into the apple, then I watched the final video to make sure it didn't suck.

It didn't.

But it was hard to pretend I didn't imagine Hunter's hand around my dick instead of that sleeve.

"Patron saint of being a fucking dumbass," I muttered under my breath, uploading the video and slamming the lid on my laptop closed.

Normally, *normally*, I needed at least half an hour to recover. Hunter had reduced that to minutes on Friday, but Hunter wasn't here, as I reminded myself. Even as his messages sat read and ignored in the app we'd connected on. He could be here, if I wanted. If I answered him. But being with Hunter, answering him…it was like opening a can filled with those exploding coiled snakes. Once the top was off, there was no way to get everything back in, and just because I'd searched him out when I'd wanted to maybe poke at the lid, I wasn't ready to unscrew the cap entirely.

I finished the apple and tossed the core into the trash, heading back to my box of tricks to find something to play with for the next video. I was half off the bed, digging through my toys when my phone chirped with an alert from my subscription app. Someone had already commented on the video, and I hoped it was a request for more so I would know what to film next.

Swiping through my profile to my videos, I clicked the comment and when I saw the username, my heart immediately skittered to a stop.

CEH13

Closer to the camera next time, Jay.

It was clearly an order, and once my heart kicked back into a survivable rhythm, my blood burned a hundred times hotter than before.

I'd completely forgotten that he'd subscribed and knowing it was the middle of a workday and he'd immediately stopped whatever he was doing to watch my video sent a thrill up my spine.

Against my better judgment, I flipped back to the hookup app and his ignored messages.

Lincoln.

I tapped my finger against the screen, somehow knowing if I did reply, there was no going back.

What do you want with me?

I closed my eyes and hung my head over the edge of the bed, my search for a toy abandoned. My phone vibrated an incoming message, and I dropped my hand down in front of my face to see what Hunter had to say.

I don't know.

What do you want with me?

I don't know.

What a fucking pair.

I meant closer to your face, by the way. I didn't get to see on Friday. I want to see.

"Nope," I said out loud, throwing my phone out of reach. "Absolutely the fuck not."

I abandoned my quest for content, muted all my notifications, then fucked off down to the beach until it was time to meet Smith at his apartment for our shopping excursion. He lived in an apartment downtown, a stylish loft with exposed ducts and concrete everywhere. I thought the whole thing was horribly bland, but I supposed there were people into that kind of thing. It actually reminded me of something Marshall would like, if Marshall was in his twenties not his forties. How

Hunter's taste was so far off from the two of them, I'd never know.

I lingered near the door while Smith changed into something more comfortable, then I followed him down to his car and let him drive us the few blocks to the grocery store. The ride was quiet until we parked, and he turned the car off and grabbed the steering wheel, making no move to get out of the car.

"What's wrong?" I asked, grateful for a distraction.

He swallowed hard, and I reached over, grabbing one of his hands off the wheel and pulling him toward the center console. He fought me at first, but eventually I got him into my arms and kissed the top of his head. It was the same thing I would have done to Silas, the same thing I told Smith to expect. Instead of pushing away, he melted into me a little and sighed.

"No one was affectionate like this when I was growing up. I don't know how to…"

"Receive it," I said.

He nodded, and I smiled into his hair. "Just like this."

Smith let me hold him for almost five minutes, which did as much for him, I think, as it did for me. My arm fell asleep, but I wasn't going to pull away until he did. Finally, Smith groaned and extricated himself from my arms, rubbing at his eyes and doing his best to cover the blush on his cheeks.

"You're just like that all the time?" he asked.

I shrugged. "It's nice, right?"

"Yeah." He cleared his throat and made quick work of getting out of the car.

It was fine.

I was committed to being friends with the youngest Covington brother, which meant waiting him out until he became comfortable with the only kind of friend I knew how to be. Unfortunately, the three orgasms his older brother had given me and the ignored order in my pocket hung between us like an invisible axe blade.

There was no good way to tell Smith I'd hooked up with Hunter, and maybe even no reason to tell him if I wasn't going to do it again. Maybe the best course of action was to wait until I figured that part out and then tell him. Silas would know what to say, but that would also involve telling Silas that I'd hooked up with not one, but two of his boyfriend's brothers.

"What's wrong *with you*?" Smith asked when we reached the front of the store.

I gave him a smile and yanked a shopping cart out of the carousel.

"Nothing is wrong with me," I said. "Beyond an absolute crisis of character and a dead fish."

Smith's eyes went wide. "Betty died?"

"Cassandra," I corrected.

Smith scrunched his nose and followed me into the store. Once we were through the sliding double doors, I stopped and let him take the lead. He had a list written on paper, because of course he did. He was more Marshall's brother than Hunter was, that was for sure.

"Tell me about Cassandra." Smith stopped at the produce, bagging up some lettuce, onions, and celery.

"She died," I answered with a shrug. "I think she must have been shocked from the transfer. I don't know. Maybe the water was the wrong temperature, or I moved her too fast, or I gave her bad—"

Smith gestured angrily at me with a carrot. "It's not your fault the five-dollar fish died on arrival."

I swatted the carrot out of my face, and he shoved it into a bag.

"That's what Silas said."

"Silas is right."

I snorted and rolled the cart along behind him as he

collected his produce before making a left toward the butcher counter at the back of the store. Propping my elbows on the handlebar of the cart, I rested my chin in my hands while Smith consulted his list and then asked for two ribeye steaks and four chicken breasts.

"Why are you lonely?" I asked, which earned me a sharp glare.

He collected his meat and dropped it into the cart, hooking his fingers around the edge and pulling me toward the chips and crackers aisle. I trailed behind him, frowning at the back of his head until he stopped and grabbed a bag of tortilla chips from the shelf.

"You know, when my mom basically sold me out for a seven figure payday, I was angry."

"Wait, wait." I pushed the cart into his hip. "When she what?"

He let out a sardonic laugh. "Do you not know the Covington lore?"

"I don't know anything about payouts."

"Our father cares about nothing more than the Covington name," Smith explained. "Every time a child pops up, he offers a huge like, I don't know, child support payout or something, and then he ends up with full custody."

"Normally it's the other way around?"

"Yeah. Well, we found a new brother recently," he said.

They'd found out about the new brother the night I'd met Smith for the first time.

"I remember."

"*His* mom didn't take the money. Raised him without ever letting him know shit about our father. Only put it into the will so he could do whatever he wanted with the information after she died."

Smith reached for a box of Cheez-Its next, then a package of cookies, and another package of cookies, and a third.

"Sweet tooth?" I asked.

He scoffed.

"I've always looked at Marshall as being more of a father figure than our actual father, but I really don't want anything to do with the Covington name."

"That's fair."

We headed into the soup and spice aisle, and Smith collected some boxes of chicken stock and vegetable stock, some bottles of pasta sauce and some dehydrated onions.

"I thought for a while about taking my mother's name, but she's the one who got tired of raising me and sold me out, so…"

I knocked into him with the cart again, this time on accident.

"She what now?" I asked, eyes wide.

"I was almost a teenager. She…she'd had the offer for a while but had told Willem no, until one day she just said yes."

I didn't know what to say. I didn't think there was anything *to* say.

"And that's what happened with all of you?"

"In varying degrees," he said, frowning down at the contents of the cart before turning his attention back to his list. "Just need hummus and cheese, and we're good."

I grimaced, uncomfortable with how easily he was about to move on from admitting all of their mothers had basically sold them into boarding school for some zeroes in their bank account.

My parents had been shit, but at least they kept me. Even when I'd wished they hadn't.

Smith set off for the last two items on his list, and I followed behind, waiting for him to say something else. When he didn't, I couldn't stop myself from saying, "You know you didn't deserve that, right?"

"Yeah," he said automatically. "But without it, I wouldn't

have Marshall and Finn and Hunter, so it was worth it in the long run."

He sounded like he wanted to believe it, and I wanted to believe it too.

For him.

"It just…sometimes I just…" He rubbed his sternum, and the ache was so acute, I felt it myself.

"Yeah," I agreed, not needing him to finish. "I hear you."

CHAPTER 10
HUNTER

don't know what the fuck I'd been thinking leaving that comment on Lincoln's most recent video, but watching him jerk off for the camera had made me so hard I'd almost come in my pants. I was late to a meeting with one of the partners because I had to stop in the bathroom on my way to his office to rub one out, but I figured the only thing worse than being late would have been showing up on time with a raging erection.

After our brief exchange, Lincoln went back to ignoring me, and I went back to work with the implications that I was one handshake away from making partner myself. My mind raced at the possibility and the opportunity. Something I'd spent years working for was almost in reach, and the only thing I could think about was Lincoln and the way he cried on his knees and the way he moaned when he came all over my fingers.

How had one man thrown my life into a tailspin in barely more than an hour?

Maybe it was selfish, and maybe it was wrong. He hadn't indicated any intention to talk to me ever again, let alone try to see me again. But I hated only having access to him in that stupid hookup app, so before I logged out at the end of the day, I texted him my phone number. Just like the rest of my messages, he read it and didn't reply.

At least, not until Friday, seconds after I pulled into the parking lot at Cunningham's to meet my brothers for dinner. I caught my phone as the messages started to pour in, the final one coming in as soon as I reached the door.

UNKNOWN

I know you're busy.

Probably texting you right now on purpose because I know you won't reply.

I'm so jealous of your brother and Silas.

I've been ignoring you because it's like Marshall swooped in and stole my best friend and then set the bar so fucking high. And the last thing I want right now is a pity fuck. The last thing I need is a guy I paid for an hour of sex to chase me around trying to get me to talk to him about shit he doesn't really care about. Alright?

We're gonna be stuck together because I don't think they're ever going to break up, and I'm never going to leave Silas, and I don't want to have to look at you every time I see you and think about THIS when I could think about last Friday instead.

Not that I'm thinking about last Friday. You clearly are, coming into my JOB BASICALLY and trying to ask for more than what I paid you for. What is your angle, Hunter?

I'm so confused, and my fish died so just ignore me.

He was crazy if he thought I would really not respond to any of that, but before I could get a message from my brain to my fingers, Smith was at my left with an arm around my shoulder.

"Fancy seeing you here," he said.

I scoffed and pulled open the door. "You're in a better mood."

"Than when?"

"I don't know. The past few weeks," I said. "Since Andrew."

"Well, no matter how much I tried, I couldn't wish him away."

He laughed like he was teasing, but I wasn't sure he was. We moved into a single file line to get from the front of the restaurant to our booth in the back. Marshall and Finn were already there, deep in conversation about something. They both looked up when we took our seats beside them, Marshall raising his hand to flag down a waiter.

"You look distracted," Finn said on sight.

I bit the inside of my cheek and weighed my options, cell phone still clutched in hand.

"Winters wants to make me a partner," I said, setting my phone on the table facedown.

The waiter arrived with drinks for me and Smith, and I took a sip of mine, avoiding the penetrating stare of my oldest brother.

"You sound like you hate that," he said.

"It's just…I've waited a long time for it. And now that it's here…"

"You'll say yes," Finn said to my left, nudging me in the ribs.

"Of course I'll say yes—"

My brothers interrupted the rest of my statement, raising their glasses and cheering. With a groan, I clinked the edge of mine against theirs and took another drink, waiting for them to settle down so I could finish my thought. "Of course I'll say yes, but it feels anticlimactic is all."

Marshall cocked his head to the side. "Why?"

"Because if I get it—"

"When," Finn interrupted, and I looked at him, my mouth pulled into a tight line. My half-brother, my *twin*, my biggest advocate in all things for as long as we'd been in each other's lives. He'd never given up on me, never stopped fighting for me. Even on the days I felt like I didn't deserve it, Finn had fought.

"When I get it," I corrected myself, and his mouth twitched into a smile. "It's just like...what's next?"

"You don't enjoy the victory," Smith said.

I shook my head.

"Maybe you're due for a vacation," Marshall suggested, and I shot him a scathing look across the table.

"When have I ever taken a vacation?"

"Exactly."

"*You* take a vacation," I shot back.

He rolled his eyes at me like I was a teenager again. "Stop trying to act like Finn."

"Fuck off, Marsh," Finn said, giving his drink a shake to jostle the ice before having a swallow.

"A vacation sounds nice," Smith said, the hint of longing clear in his voice.

I didn't want to take a vacation, but I loved that all my brothers thought I was high-strung enough to need one.

"I'll think about it," I said, sliding out of the booth and pocketing my phone. "I've got to piss, but we are also due for a trip to San Diego."

"Family matters don't a vacation make," Finn sing-songed, stare flickering from my phone to my face and back again.

"Don't come after me or I'll piss on your shoes."

"Joke's on you," Finn muttered, finishing off his drink. "I'm into that shit."

I made my way to the bathroom, taking the time to make sure my brother didn't follow me before locking myself in a stall and reading back through the messages Lincoln had sent me.

Instead of texting him, I called. He answered on what had to be the last ring.

"Yeah?" Lincoln sounded so tired, so weary.

"What was your fish's name?" I asked.

A pause.

"Cassandra."

"Was she pretty?"

"They were," he said.

"They." I cleared my throat. "Did you have them long?"

"No."

"Is that why I donated fifty-three dollars to a fish rescue?" I asked.

"Yeah."

"Okay," I said. "Good."

A pause.

"Did you really call to talk about my fish?" he asked.

"Not only your fish," I admitted.

"I thought you were at dinner with your brothers."

I rubbed absentmindedly at my throat, constricted even though I'd taken my tie off as soon as I got out of the office.

"I am. I'm in the bathroom."

Lincoln made a noise that sounded a little like he was choking on his own spit.

"I'm meeting Silas for dinner in five minutes," he said. "I'm sitting in my car in front of the restaurant."

"I don't want to keep you, I just—"

"Why did you call?" he interrupted.

"It's not pity," I told him, the words feeling strong and true as they formed against the roof of my mouth. "My questions or any of it. It's not pity."

"What is it, then?"

"Interest," I said, because it felt like the truth.

"No wonder you were giving up escorting if you catch feelings for every John you fuck," he said, laughing bitterly.

"I never caught feeling for any of them," I said, hushed. "I started the work on accident, and I kept it up because I was lonely and bored."

"And now?"

"You're far from boring," I told him.

Lincoln made a noise I couldn't make sense of, then said, "I've got to go."

"Can I see you later?"

"Why?" he rasped.

"Do you want the truth?"

"Always."

I leaned against the closed door of the stall, pressing as much of my overheated neck against the cool metal as I could manage.

"Partly because I want to talk and partly because I do really want to see your face when you come."

On the other end of the call, Lincoln sucked in a sharp breath.

"I haven't been able to stop thinking about that video since you posted it. Haven't stopped thinking about you since last Friday."

He groaned. "What do you do for work, Hunter?"

"I'm a lawyer."

"So, of course you know the right things to…fuck…" Lincoln stopped talking, and there was indistinct noise in the background of the call. "Just listening to a voicemail, Si. I haven't forgot about you."

And then the call disconnected.

"Fuck."

I shoved my phone back into my pocket and unlocked the door. Taking a look at myself in the mirror, there was no denying the flush in my cheeks and the dilation of my pupils. I turned the cold water on and splashed some on my face, pressing my damp and cool hands against the back of my neck before drying them off. When I felt like I could think again, I headed back to the booth.

"Long piss," Finn said when I slid back into my seat beside him.

"You know how it goes."

He hummed agreeably, scratching the side of his lip.

"So, when do we want to go to San Diego?" He looked pointedly at Smith. "Do we all even want to go?"

"Silas is worried about how his best friend is adjusting to life on his own," Marshall said, "so I'd like to stay close for them both while they sort that out."

"Both?" I asked.

"The two of them are close," he said. "And if you must know, I'm rather fond of Lincoln."

Finn smirked. "Trying to start a harem or something?"

"It's platonic," Marshall said.

I tried to fight my frown, thinking about how close Silas and Lincoln had been Saturday morning at Marshall's house. How they'd come so close to kissing and right in front of us both.

"That's just how he is," Smith offered with a casual shrug.

"How would you know?"

"We're friends," he said. "Or becoming friends. I don't know. It's...he was at Marshall's the night we found out about Andrew, and I went over there after dinner. We talked a bit."

Marshall scrunched his nose, glancing down at our youngest brother. "Did you?"

"After you were asleep, we talked a bit, yeah. We talk. We hung out earlier this week."

I worried the inside of my cheek, earlier bite mark still tender, as I waited for any indication from Smith that Lincoln had outed our hookup to him. But Smith looked as innocent and earnest as he always did, so if Lincoln had talked about me, Smith wasn't going to say a word.

"He's a little lost without Silas attached to his hip," Smith said, "but I think he'll be fine."

"I'd still rather wait awhile," Marshall said. "Maybe in a couple of months."

It had been a bit since I'd spoken to Andrew, and he wasn't against seeing us, but I wouldn't have classified him as chomping at the bit either. A couple months between visits wasn't going to be a hardship on any of our social or familial calendars.

"I'll let him know next time I talk to him," I said.

Shortly after that, the waiter arrived with food because Finn had apparently ordered me a steak while I was in the bathroom. It wouldn't have been my first choice considering how tangled my stomach was over the whole thing with Lincoln, but I managed to force down enough of the it so as to not raise suspicion.

The conversation over the rest of the meal was casual and normal. Finn teasing Marshall about Silas's age, Smith making heart eyes at Marshall like he hung the fucking moon, Marshall telling Finn he was an annoying human while also making worried eyes every time Smith got quiet for two long. The three of them never ignored me but were happy to let me live on the outskirts of the conversation.

I appreciated it more tonight than normal since it let my thoughts wander back to Lincoln, back to last weekend and the conversation earlier. I still wanted to see him, but he hadn't given me an answer one way or another, which left my hands tied. Seeing him was going to be like cracking open Pandora's box, though, because Marshall knew him and Smith knew him, and there was no way to keep anything a secret for long with that many Covington men involved.

We all moved too fast, for better or worse.

We finally made it through dinner, Marshall begging off first so he could be home for Silas, and Finn following soon after. I walked Smith back to his car, told him goodnight, then tossed my keys into the air and headed for mine. I double-tapped the key fob and slipped into the driver's seat.

It took a minute for my phone to connect to the Bluetooth, but then the computer-generated voice I'd downloaded for my nav that sounded a lot like Henry Cavill said, "Text message from unknown. If you were serious, I'll come over after I'm done with Silas. If you weren't serious, just don't open the door or whatever. See you soon. Or not."

CHAPTER 11
LINCOLN

Not only was the door to his apartment unlocked when I finally talked myself out of the elevator at Hunter's building, it was also hanging open. That didn't stop me from hesitating in the doorway, shuffling my feet and rapping my knuckles against the wood just the same. The door swung wider, and Hunter came into view, no shoes, no shirt, and a drink in his hand.

He didn't say anything and neither did I.

We stared at each other for a breath, then I stepped inside and closed the door behind me. He made no move to come closer, and I imagined I looked as skittish as I felt.

"Do you want a drink?" he asked.

"What have you got?"

"I'm a vodka guy, but Finn drinks bourbon, and Marshall and Smith drink wine, so…"

"What if I drink rum?" I asked, lip twitching.

Hunter swallowed hard. "I've got rum."

"Vodka soda's fine," I said.

He studied me for another breath, and I tried my hardest to not let my eyes wander down to his bare chest. It wasn't the first time I'd seen him without a shirt on, but that didn't make the sight of him any less glorious. Hunter had the body of a model. There was no arguing about that.

I held strong until he turned to go to the kitchen, and I finally let my stare drift down the exposed length of his back. The broad swell of his shoulder muscles and the narrow dip of his waist right down to the perfect little divots over his ass. I crossed an arm in front of my chest and scratched my neck, following after him.

I hadn't spent much time in the main part of his apartment the night we hooked up, but while he busied himself in the kitchen, I was able to take a look at his things for the first time. It was still as broody as I remembered, dark green walls and a ceiling to match, vibrant velvet pillows on a black couch, and a scattering of plants and books on every dark wood surface I could see. There was a laptop open on his coffee table, a stack of what I assumed to be court notes scrawled illegibly on yellow legal pads.

"You can sit," he said over his shoulder, and I tried to make myself comfortable on his couch. I shifted some of the pillows around to make room, finally tucking one onto my lap and using it for emotional support.

Hunter came back to me and passed a crystal glass into my hand. He sat down and angled his legs toward mine, but not close enough to touch.

"I don't know where to start," he said at the same time as I said, "I kind of hoped we could just cut to the fucking."

It took a second for what I said to register with him, and his cheeks flushed. He smiled down into his drink.

"Sounds like we're definitely not on the same page," he said.

"You asked me to film my face while I came so you could see it," I reminded him. "I'm not sure what page that is in your book, but in mine…"

"You came over the first time because you wanted to

submit. Whatever that meant to you. And you did. And I would love to have closed the door on you and never thought about you after that, but that's not what happened." Hunter took a sip of his drink, the ice clinking against the edge loud enough to sound like a gunshot.

I hadn't even tried mine.

"What about me kept you up at night?" I asked.

"Besides how attractive you are?" He arched a brow and cocked his head to the side, and I nodded for him to go on. "The way you cried from your chest like your bones were cracking open in my arms."

Well.

I raised the glass to my mouth and took a swallow of what was mostly vodka with a splash of soda. Hunter watched my mouth, his nostrils flaring when I licked the wetness off my lips.

"Why, though? I hope you don't think you can fix me."

"That's no one's job except yours," he said, setting his glass down on a cork coaster on the table that I hadn't seen, tucked between the notes and the books. "Did you get what you wanted from it? From our time together I mean? Did it answer your questions?"

I snorted and rolled my eyes. "I only have more now," I admitted.

"Do you want to talk about them?"

I worried the inside of my lip until it bled, biting hard enough—on accident—to grimace.

"What?" he asked.

"I bit myself," I muttered.

Hunter leaned in closer, moving fast like a predator. My breath caught in my throat as he curled his hand over the top of my shoulder.

"Are you bleeding?"

"Yes."

With his free hand, he tapped the underside of my glass, lifting it toward my mouth. His eyes were dark when the glass connected with my lip, and darker still when he tipped a swig of the cocktail into my mouth. I don't know how I managed to swallow. I could barely remember how to breathe with his hand on me and his drink on my tongue.

"It'll sterilize it," he murmured, pulling back reflexively.

The tension between us snapped like a taut wire, and he reached to take the drink out of my hands the same moment I moved to give it to him. He set it on the table and then was back, his fingers sliding around my neck and coming together in my hairline, thumbs tracing lines along the underside of my jaw.

"Do you want to talk about them?" he repeated his earlier question, and I could barely think, let alone speak.

"No," I said.

His thumbs pressed harder against my jawbone. "Do you need to?"

I pulled my lips between my teeth, making sure to not draw more blood. "Probably."

Hunter groaned, but it sounded like a sigh, and then he let me go. But at some point, he'd moved closer, our legs finally touching and the proximity to him made me feel like I could breathe, even though I also felt like I was choking. I was so tired of everything existing inside of me at the same time. The dominance, the submission, the top, the bottom, the want, the rejection. It was unfair and it was too much, and there was no way I was going to cry in front of this man again. Or so I thought until he reached up and quickly swiped away wetness from beneath my lashes.

"I miss my best friend," I said.

"It sounds like you still have him."

"It's not the same."

Hunter nodded, saying nothing.

"I'm friends with your brother," I blurted, scrunching my nose. Something flashed across his face, but he stayed silent. "Smith, I mean."

"He mentioned that at dinner."

If Hunter knew Smith and I had fucked, he gave no indicator of it, and I didn't know which was worse. If I was going to have to be the one to tell him, or if it was going to be Smith. Quickly, I weighed the options, thinking about Smith's earnestness and eagerness and knew it had to be me.

"My older brother is fond of you as well," Hunter said.

"Just wait until I meet the fourth one, and I'll win them all over." I laughed and took a deep breath, knowing there was no time like the present to bare all my truths. "I've had sex with Smith."

Hunter sucked in a breath, the flickering change in his expression hardly noticeable. He was a lawyer after all, I reminded myself. Of course he would have an impeccable poker face.

"Have you now?" he asked quietly.

"Just once. It..." I scrubbed a hand down my face. "If you wanted to talk about a pity fuck—not that I pity your brother, he just..."

"He was a virgin," Hunter guessed.

"He'd never been with a man."

The gears turned, almost imperceptible twitches around the corners of his eyes. I rubbed my sweating palms on the pillow, wishing it was a blanket I could crawl into and use to hide from Hunter's impassive stare.

"Have you and Silas had sex?" he asked me, which was the absolute last thing I expected.

The idea was preposterous.

"No." It was impossible to hide the distaste from my face. "I'm not attracted to him."

"You were kissing each other at Marshall's. I saw it with my own eyes."

Hunter leaned away from me, resting his back against the arm of the couch and propping one leg up on the cushions. Bent at the knee, he rested his forearm there, and the positioning was so detached I wanted to cry again.

"As friends," I said.

"Do you kiss Smith as friends?"

"I never kissed Smith…" I trailed off, trying to read his face before continuing.

"What about Marshall?" Hunter asked next.

"I've never kissed him."

"Do you want to?"

"I don't kiss Silas with any intent," I said. "There's no attraction there. We are friends, and we are affectionate. We are physical, but platonically. I haven't kissed Smith, and I'll never kiss Marshall."

"You've never kissed me," he rasped.

I tipped my head back and stared up at his color-washed ceiling.

"No," I said softly. "I haven't."

For a while, neither of us said anything, and it was too much for me to sit through any longer. I shoved the pillow onto the couch between us and leveraged myself onto my feet, but Hunter moved fast, grabbing my wrist and pulling me back down.

"I was just gonna go," I explained.

"Is that what you really want?"

I shook my head.

"Then don't."

I situated myself back on the couch, and Hunter returned the pillow to my lap.

"I'll be right back," he muttered, standing up and turning away from me so fast the movement almost gave *me* whiplash.

He walked out of the living room and disappeared down a hall, whether to throw himself out a window or what, I wasn't entirely sure.

I didn't know what I'd expected coming over, but it definitely hadn't been anything this deep. I mean, I'd expected things to get deep, but not conversationally.

Exhaling a long breath, I leaned over and grabbed my glass from the table and finished it in one swallow. Hunter was gone for well over five minutes, plenty of time for me to stand up and get halfway to the door, turn around, sit back down, and repeat it a second time before giving up and sitting on my hands. My stomach was in knots, violent churning waves of a dozen feelings I didn't have a name for.

I was being an idiot.

I'd set out to find someone to dominate me to see if I liked it as much as I thought I did. What I ended up finding instead was a person I actually liked. For whatever misguided reason, Hunter cared about me, and I was so caught up in my own shit I was going to lose out on that entirely. And at the end of the day, wasn't that what I wanted in the first place?

I was jealous of Silas and Marshall, their closeness, their exchange, and somehow I'd stumbled onto a Covington brother of my own offering me the very same things. There might be more complicated layers about the dominance and submission, but it could all be taught. It could all be learned, right? It wasn't even like I knew what I really wanted from Hunter in that regard anyway. Because I found the thoughts of kneeling and having him kneel equally appealing for very different reasons.

Hunter finally came back to the living room, and I glanced over the back of the couch in time to watch him flex his hands into fists before shaking them both out and closing the space between the hallway and the couch. He sat down next to me, eyeing my empty glass before clearing his throat and looking me in the eye.

"I'm back," he announced, and there was no way of stopping the laugh that bubbled up in the back of my throat and burst out of me at full volume. I doubled forward, covering my mouth with both hands and laughing so hard my ribs hurt. Tears streaked down my cheeks, but this time not from sadness or confusion, but absolute astonishment over my situation.

"Sorry." I sat up, wiped the tears from my cheeks and swallowed back another bubble of laughter. "Sorry, I'm good."

"Was that particularly funny?" Hunter asked, the corner of his mouth twitching.

"I'm back," I repeated, trying my best to affect the matter-of-fact tone he'd used, which was enough for his mouth to finally spread into a full-on smile.

Fuck, he was even prettier than before.

"I haven't been being fair to you," I said, giving my face one last wipe. I dried my hands on his pillow, which he watched but made no comment on. "I'm just. It's very messy in my head right now, and you're trying to be nice about it, and I'm not helping the situation."

Hunter studied me, that poker face of his back in place, making it impossible to decipher the small changes in his features. I tangled my hands together nervously, wringing them until he reached out and put his hand over mine and sent me into stillness.

I closed my eyes and let out a trembling breath. I relaxed.

"I don't know much about the things you like," he said quietly, stroking his thumb across my knuckles. "I know how to play a role, but it's not supposed to be a role. At least, I don't think it is."

"What…" I cleared my throat and blinked open my eyes, staring down at his longer fingers and the way they wrapped over my hands. "What do you mean?"

"It's a responsibility. Being a dominant."

"Sounds like you know plenty," I murmured.

"It's a big responsibility, and it's okay to…not want to be responsible all the time," he said.

"Only some of the time?" I asked, hating the way my voice cracked.

"Only some of the time."

The way Hunter looked at me was somehow the best and the worst thing that had ever happened to me. Even if he didn't have words to say what he saw, I definitely got the impression he saw *me*. Like, he saw me in the ways Silas saw me, and that was…

A lot.

"Do you want to be with me?" he asked, squeezing my hand.

I forced my fingers to unclench, turned my palms up toward him, and he threaded our fingers together.

"I don't know you."

"You know a bit," he said. "I think."

I knew as much about him as he knew about me, which wasn't a lot but it was still something.

"Do you want to be with me?" he asked again.

"Do you want to be with me?"

Hunter frowned, shook his head. "Don't do that. Don't… don't be scared of being honest just because it's unknown territory."

That was a punch to the chest, enough to cave my sternum in and stop my heart. I took my free hand and rubbed a circle over the invisible wound, realizing that he'd been holding my hand so long I had already gotten used to the way his fingers felt twined with mine. He shook me loose, but only to cover the hand on my chest with his. The barest amount of pressure, and his other hand slid around my back and just like that, he pressed me back into my body, back into place.

"Yes," I admitted to him. "I do."

CHAPTER 12
HUNTER

It would be far too easy to fall in love with Lincoln, I realized. With one hand on his back and the other on his chest, his lungs expanding with every breath between my grip and his watery eyes blinking up at me with a desperation I could almost taste.

"What do you need right now?" I asked, sliding my hands up to his face so I could wipe the dampness from his cheeks. "I don't know you well enough to know yet."

Lincoln snorted, scrunching his nose. "And you say you don't know how to do this."

"I don't."

"When you pretend, don't you feel it here?"

He pressed his hand against the middle of my chest, and I didn't have any option besides to tell him the truth.

"When I'm with you, I do."

"What does it feel like?"

I licked my lips, trying to make sense of the way I felt the first night with Lincoln when I'd put him on his knees. He wasn't the first hookup, the first paying customer, the first man I'd dominated, and yet everything about him had been different. I had been different.

"Feels like the only thing I want to do is put you on your knees and keep you there. I don't even care about fucking you. I mean, I want that, but…"

"You could put me on my knees," he murmured.

I glanced at the empty glass on the table, the weary redness of his eyes.

"You've been drinking," I reminded him.

"I'm not drunk," he said, rolling his eyes. "I'm just tired."

"Then let me take you to bed."

He groaned, but when I pulled him to his feet, he didn't argue. When I walked him to the bedroom, turning lights off along the way, he made no protest. And when we reached my bedroom, he made an amused sound in the back of his throat.

"I knew the other room was a guest room," he said. "There's no way you fuck strangers in your own bed."

"I don't fuck strangers in my apartment," I corrected, plucking at the hem of his shirt before tugging it over his head and tossing it onto the floor.

Lincoln turned and tilted his head back, tears dry but cheeks still splotchy. "What do you mean?" he asked.

"I don't bring men home."

"Paying?"

"Ever." I turned him back around and slid my arms around his waist, undoing the fly of his jeans and shoving them down to the floor. He stepped out of them and went for his underwear, but I stopped him. Both of our hands grazed over the warm bulge between his legs, and he pressed back against the thick erection between mine.

"Why me?" he asked quietly.

I didn't have a real answer, so I settled with, "Why not you?"

The only light in my bedroom was the green glass banker's lamp on my nightstand. It barely illuminated the book and the water glass in front of it, and I wondered what Lincoln's impression of my otherwise dark bedroom was. The furniture was a combination of mid-century and Victorian, lots of wood and texture, a four-postered bed with an ornate headboard and matching nightstands on either side.

"I'm on PReP," Lincoln said, and I buried my smile into the crook of his neck.

"So am I."

He inhaled sharply, breath clicking, and I gave him a gentle push toward the bed. I wanted him, my body wanted him, but there was no way I was going to fuck him. We both reached the bed, and he looked from one nightstand to the other, correctly judging which side I preferred and climbing into the other one.

"I have clear test results," he said.

I tugged the blankets until he lifted himself off the comforter and slipped his feet between the sheets.

"So do I," I said.

Lincoln gave a little wiggle into the mattress and blinked so slowly I thought he'd fallen asleep. I sat down on the edge of the bed, one leg raised up and the other one hanging off the side. Reaching over, I brushed his hair back from his face, and he practically purred into my hand.

"I'm vers," he murmured, the words disappearing into a yawn.

I couldn't answer him in the affirmative to that because while I'd definitely enjoyed both placements before, it had been too many years to count since I'd bottomed.

"What about you?" he asked, when I didn't reply.

"It's complicated," I said.

"It always is."

He rolled onto his side with a heavy sigh and gathered the blankets in his fists. He looked so small in my bed, almost weak, and I hated it as much as he would have if he could see himself.

"Roll over," I said, finally committing to getting in bed myself.

Lincoln groaned and turned to face the side of the bed, and I pulled him into the middle, bringing our bodies flush. He pushed back against my erection, hips swirling. "I hope we can uncomplicate it."

"Go to sleep."

"Yes, Daddy," he teased, but the words caught in his throat, and my breath caught in mine, and neither of us moved.

When it was impossible to hold my breath any longer, I let myself kiss the back of his head. "Get some rest, Lincoln. We'll figure this out in the morning."

I wasn't sure if he heard me because his answer was a quiet snore, and I was jealous that sleep had taken him so easily. The *Yes, Daddy* had me up for at least another hour, my brain trying desperately to understand the intent and the implications. He hadn't even meant it seriously, but he'd asked how it felt in my chest and hearing him call me that definitely made me feel some kind of way.

The whole kink thing wasn't new to me. Beyond the roles I'd played for money, I'd watched more than my fair share of porn. Some of it was more fucked up than others, but I knew about dominance and submission, knew how to spank and where. I'd experimented with bondage and nipple clamps, and my favorite way to play involved drawing out and denying orgasms to the brink of tears. There was a heady kind of arousal in that sort of power, and it made me hungry for more.

Finally, sometime before sunrise, sleep took me alongside Lincoln, who hadn't moved an inch since he'd passed out. His body still molded to mine, his fingers still tangled in the sheets. He was…God, he was gorgeous, and he was trusting and hurting and scared, and I wanted him.

Just after eight, Lincoln stretched and yawned, his toes

reaching down toward the tops of my feet before he curled back into a ball against my front.

"Do you know about free use?" he asked sleepily.

"Good morning," I said, "and no."

"It means you can take without asking."

I still had my sweatpants on, but it was easy to imagine the way my dick would slide between his ass cheeks and notch against his hole. "Is that something you like?" I asked, eyes still closed.

"In theory. I've never had a partner who was into it, considering they've all been submissive."

"We can try it."

My dick was sticky with an entire night of leaking precum, but I wasn't going to fuck Lincoln the way he wanted…the way we both wanted…until we'd set some ground rules. I'd seen that in porn too, normally at the end when they'd replay the little videos they took at the beginning, talking through all the things I'd already watched them do.

"Now?" Lincoln asked.

"After we talk about it. After we have an agreement."

He grunted and rolled to face me, staring at my throat instead of my face. He busied himself tracing swirls and lines from one side of my chest to the other, his mouth pulled down into a frown.

"Just like your brother," he muttered.

My blood ran cold.

"I can live with the fact you've slept with my brother, but I would sincerely appreciate if you didn't bring it up in my bed." Maybe it was the wrong thing to do, but I pulled away from Lincoln, sitting on the edge of the bed with my feet on the floor and my back to him. Even though he could certainly hear the jealousy in my voice, I didn't need him to see it in my face.

"I meant Marshall."

I stood, bracketing my hands on my hips and staring up at the ceiling. "You told me you and he never—"

"We didn't," Lincoln interrupted.

I turned back toward the bed, fingers digging into my waist and my eyes narrowed down at him looking like a mussed-up angel in my sheets. Lincoln's legs were tangled in the comforter, but he tried to sit up, slide toward me, his hand outstretched.

"I have no designs on your older brother," he said, "or the younger one, or any ones you don't know about yet."

"Don't even joke about that."

He flashed me a smile that quickly fell away. "I did mean Marshall but only based off the things Silas has told me."

Sighing, I scrubbed a hand down my face, not wanting to regret what I was about to ask, but also needing to get the question out there. "What do you mean?"

Lincoln managed to get himself out of bed, blankets discarded behind him. He stood toe to toe with me, and we both ignored the morning wood jutting out from between our legs. A night spent in each other's arms had clearly the same effect on us both.

"Do you…God, I don't want to be the one to tell you this."

"Talk," I demanded.

Heat flooded Lincoln's cheeks, and he said, "Marshall is a Dom."

I would have sworn the floor dropped out from under me with those four simple words. The room fell away and the only thing that remained was me and Lincoln there, still half asleep and all the way horny. That, and the knowledge my brother was apparently into BDSM.

"Did you not know?" Lincoln let out a quiet laugh. "It's kind of obvious."

Well, now that he said it, of course it was obvious. Marshall had always been the natural caretaker of the four of us. He was commanding without being controlling, confident without being cocky. And none of us had ever talked about our sex lives together, beyond some good old-fashioned teasing and ribbing, but the pieces of that puzzle still slotted into place.

"I didn't know," I said.

"Don't tell him I told you."

"He doesn't even know you and I know each other." I groaned, scratching at the side of my face. "Does Smith know that you and I…?"

Lincoln shook his head, rubbing absently at the back of his neck.

"This needs coffee," I said, shaking my head and gesturing toward the door.

Lincoln huffed out a laugh, but he shuffled out of my bedroom in nothing more than his underwear, already making himself at home in my space. I would have been lying to say I didn't like the look of him mostly naked on my couch, so I swallowed down the thought. I made us both coffee, and we drank half of it before addressing any of the elephants in the room. Finally, Lincoln cleared his throat and faced me head on.

"I am friends with your youngest brother," he said. "He knows the things I like, so if he knows that you and I are together, he's going to know you like those things too. Same with your older brother. Silas and Marshall both know. So if you're not okay with this…"

"It's—" I stopped myself, tapping the tip of my nose until the urge to speak had gone away.

"Cute trick," he murmured.

I let out a breath that made both of my cheeks puff up and deflate, one then the other and back again. "It's fine."

Lincoln sipped his coffee and arched a brow at me.

"They can't out me without outing themselves," I explained. "And even then, they'd have to prove it."

Whatever the right thing to say was, it wasn't the thing I

actually said. It was so unfamiliar for me to feel as unsteady in conversation as I did with Lincoln. I was used to going back and forth with sharp-tongued lawyers, but one unsteady twenty-five-year-old was enough to throw me off my game entirely?

What were the odds.

"What did I say?" I asked. "I didn't mean to say the wrong thing."

Lincoln pulled his lips between his teeth and bit down, clearly fighting a smile as he shook his head at me before looking down at his lap.

"It's not anything to prove or defend. It's just...it's who I am. Who I want to be." He let out a long breath, then leaned over and set the coffee down on the table in the midst of the chaos I'd brought home from work. "Maybe wanting you isn't enough. Maybe—"

"I just meant what I do in the bedroom isn't their business."

I reached out and grabbed Lincoln's wrist. He was two inches off the couch, and my fingers wrapping around his wrist brought him back down. Relief rolled over me, but I didn't let go of him. I handed him back his coffee and waited for my heart to slow back to a normal response rate, not so close to fight or flight.

"Free use means that whenever you want to take me, you can," Lincoln said softly, and my heart was right back at emergency room levels.

"We're back to that then? And that's something you want?"

He nodded, slowly at first, and then faster.

"There has to be limits, though, right?" I asked.

"Not with that. I mean." He shrugged. "Nothing that will get me arrested or put on a list."

God.

Fuck.

I couldn't believe this was real.

"Where are there limits, then? What are the things you want?"

Lincoln took a deep breath, held it, then sucked some more in on the top. It raised his shoulders, puffed out his chest, and he cocked his head to the side to study me thoughtfully. "You have all the right words, you know," he said.

"In most cases, I can handle words better than everything else."

"Then use them."

"Elaborate, Lincoln." I scooted closer and cupped his cheek in my palm. He had the softest scruff I'd ever touched. When he leaned into my hand, it tickled.

"If..." He paused. Cleared his throat, and I slid my hand from his cheek to the side of his neck. "If I'm submitting and I do good, you can tell me."

I ignored the way my dick pulsed in my sweats. "What if you don't do good?"

"You can tell me that too," he whispered.

"Lincoln."

"You can humiliate me," he blurted, rolling his eyes back and staring up at the ceiling. "I've always kind of wondered. And if you're submitting, I want you to talk then too. Do you even want to submit? Do you even know what it means?"

"It's more than just getting on your knees, I know that."

He made a sound in the back of his throat I couldn't quite decipher, and I waited to see if he had something else to say, but he remained quiet.

"Last night in bed when you called me Daddy——"

"I was teasing."

"But you liked it," I told him. "*I* liked it."

He dropped his chin back toward his chest and looked me right in the eyes, much more himself than he had been before, which made me feel much more me too. So, I kept talking. "To me, it meant that you recognized I was looking out for you. That I was capable of taking care of you. Guiding you."

My cock agreed with all of those statements, and the timing couldn't have been worse.

"I don't want a Daddy," he said. "Not all the time, like I…I don't want it to be all the time the way it is with your brother."

Grunting, I scrubbed a hand down my face. It was too early to know this much about my brother's bedroom habits.

"You just want to play at it sometimes," I wagered. "When you've had a long day."

"Maybe."

"I can work with that."

"And when would…I'm more familiar with this. I know when I want to submit and when I want to lead. How will you know? How will we make it balanced?"

Lincoln was talking faster and faster, and I didn't know how to make him stop short of kissing him or tightening my hand around his throat.

So, I did the latter.

"The only serious part of this needs to be that we are on the same page," I told him. "The rest we can figure out as we go, right?"

He swallowed hard, Adam's apple pressing against my palm. I couldn't ignore the burning hot arousal between my legs any longer, and I reached down to adjust myself with my left hand. Lincoln's eyes tracked the movement, and he let his whole body lean forward into the collar I'd made around his throat.

"Right," he whispered. "Yes."

"Yes?"

Lincoln groaned, so rumbling and low that it vibrated straight to my balls.

"Yes, Sir."

CHAPTER 13
LINCOLN

Nothing had ever felt as perfect to me as Hunter's fingers around my throat. So many times I'd handled my own partners the same way, and it was always a rush of exhilaration and arousal that coursed through me. The feeling of being on the receiving end of my favorite kind of necklace was something else entirely.

When I called Hunter *Sir*, his nostrils flared and his pupils grew impossibly wider. It was almost like watching a science experiment unfold in real time. He flexed his hand around my throat, and in the same movement, he stood up and pushed me down toward the floor. Sinking to my knees in front of him felt as right as the rest of it, though I was curious if I'd like it when we turned the tables.

"Look what you've done to me," he whispered, releasing my throat and carding his fingers through my mess of sleep-tangled hair. His dick was thick and hard in front of my face, warm and musky even though the material of his sweatpants. "All night I've had this because of you."

He tugged down the waistband of his sweats and tucked it behind his cock and balls, pushing both into my face in an unavoidable way. I licked my lips and let my ass sink down onto my heels. Hunter gave his dick a slow, overhanded stroke, his fingers tightening in my hair when his palm reached the slippery tip.

"Sorry," I murmured, though I was anything but.

"I'm sure you can figure out a way to make it up to me," he said, using his hand to guide my mouth toward his dick.

I could definitely figure that out, so it was easy to open my mouth and flatten my tongue, to take him as deep as he could reach until I choked around his length. My throat spasmed and Hunter groaned, sliding deeper until every inch of him was in my mouth. Neither of us moved, except I blinked hard, huffing a breath out of my nose so I didn't make a show about choking over how thick he was.

"Go on," he said softly, releasing my hair. "Make it up to me."

I slid my hands up the front of Hunter's thighs and dug in, then swallowed hard around him and started to suck. He moved like he wanted to touch me and guide me but was more interested in seeing how I handled him on my own. I sucked up and down his length, staring up at the underside of his chin while he stared up at the ceiling. Pulling off of him, I used the back of my hand to wipe spit off my mouth.

"Look at me," I begged, and when he did, I sealed my lips around him again.

Hunter's whole body swayed as I took him into my throat, and I groaned when my nose pressed against the curly hairs at the base of his shaft. I set a slow and tight pace, sucking half of his shaft with hollowed cheeks and all of the spit I could manage. He kept his stare on me the whole time, the heat of his gaze almost enough to make me combust.

I sucked him harder, ignoring the insistent ache between my own legs in favor of the rod between his. He was close. I was sure of it, but he was a greedy man and he needed more. Without asking—trusting he would stop me if I overstepped—I tugged his sweatpants down to his knees. Hunter moaned, a little gasp, and I eased my mouth off of him in favor of my left hand. I slipped the first two fingers on my right hand into my mouth, making sure he understood my intent, then I slid them back between the globes of his ass.

"Sir," I teased, voice nothing more than a raspy whisper.

"I'll come," he warned, his hand back in my hair, fingers trembling against my scalp.

"I hope so."

Spit was nowhere near enough, but the tip of my finger breached his hole, and he became a man of his word. Jets of hot and salty cum shot out against my cheek and my lips before I even had time to get him back into my mouth. The look on his face was pure arousal mixed with shocked embarrassment, and I laughed as I took him back into my mouth in time to catch the last bursts of cum on the back of my tongue.

I sucked Hunter until his asshole clenched around my finger hard enough to feel like the bone would shatter, then I let him go entirely. He stood there on trembling legs, mouth agape and chest heaving. His cock was still dangerously hard, and so was mine. Shoving my underwear down, I made a tight fist around my cock and stroked, leaning back and jerking myself off right in front of him.

If he wanted me to stop, he could tell me.

He didn't say a word, nothing good and nothing bad, but when the first spurt of cum shot out of my cock, Hunter's chin quivered. I had to look away from him, the pleasure of my own hand too much for me to stay present, though, and as the last remnants of cum leaked out of my cock, a hand on my chest pushed me down hard onto my back.

I hit the floor with a thud, and then Hunter was between

my legs, yanking my underwear the rest of the way off and stroking his cock right against my exposed asshole. He braced himself with his other hand beside my head, and I spread my legs wide to make room for the width of his body.

"Do it," I begged.

I'd wanted this man inside me since the first night we met, and he was only centimeters away from making that happen. He jerked himself off, knuckles slapping against my ass cheeks with every stroke, and I spread my legs even wider, reaching down to hold myself open for him. Finally getting the hint, he pressed the sticky head of his cock against my pucker, but instead of pushing inside, he shot his load right against it. Hot wetness spilled against my hole and ran down onto his floor, and above me Hunter groaned and shuddered through a surprisingly forceful second orgasm.

After he finished, he collapsed, landing on top of me before rolling off onto the floor in the small space left between me and his couch. He flung an arm over his face and struggled to catch his breath, and the only thing I could do was lie there beside him covered in both our cum.

"Is that why it's complicated?" I finally asked.

He scrubbed a hand down his face and pushed up into a seated position, his back resting against the couch.

"What?"

"Last night, when I asked if you were vers, you said it was complicated. Is it complicated because you come at the drop of a hat when someone touches your asshole?"

Hunter grimaced, bending one leg at the knee and propping his forearm up to cover his face.

"Mostly," he said. "And partly because the nature of my work."

"Being a lawyer?"

His cheeks flushed, but the corner of his mouth twitched into the hint of a smile. "You know what I meant."

"I do." I laughed, but it was mostly a tired exhalation of breath. "Does it embarrass you?"

He didn't answer.

"I think it's hot," I told him. "You can basically come on command. You could make a killing if you wanted to get into making videos."

"It's fine that you do, but I don't think that's for me," he said, the pink on his cheeks spreading down to his throat.

"It's not for everyone," I agreed. "Just like power exchange."

"This was…this was hardly that," he said, scratching absentmindedly at his hairline.

"I got on my knees for you, and you fucked my face, Hunter. I called you Sir…more than once. How is that not a power exchange?"

He shot me a scathing look and realization dawned on me. "Oh."

"Oh?"

"You weren't lying when you said it was role play before. All you've got is vibes and what you've seen in bad movies, isn't it?"

"Well, when you put it like that."

Hunter pushed onto his feet, but I managed to catch him by the ankle before he could get too far. Grabbing him twisted me onto my stomach, which smeared cum across the gorgeous wood planks of his floor, the friction against my shaft enough to make me wince. He noticed the change, stopping before he dragged me any farther across the floor. Shifting back onto my knees, we both looked down at the streaks of cum I'd left on the wood.

"Do you want to see how it works?" I asked him. "How it could be?"

"What do you mean?"

His pants were still around his ankles.

"Get on your knees, Hunter," I said carefully, voice low.

As he sank down to the floor, I rose to my feet. The shift in control was almost electric, arcing between us as we traded places.

"God," I murmured, flexing my hands at my sides. "You look good down there."

He laughed nervously. "I don't know what to do with my hands."

"You can put them on your thighs, palms up, or you can thread your fingers together behind your head."

"Which do you prefer?" he asked softly.

"Behind your head."

Slowly, he raised his arms and tangled his fingers together at the back of his head. The position caused his biceps to flex and his shoulders to swell. He looked so fucking delicious down there, pupils still shot and lips half parted.

"How does that feel?" I asked.

"Not sure."

I hummed, taking a step backward. "I made a mess on your floor, Hunter."

He blinked down at the white puddles on his floor, then up at me.

God, he had a perfect mouth. He looked so fucking pretty on his knees.

"You did," he rasped.

"You should clean it up."

He exhaled and it sounded a little bit like a groan and then slowly, so fucking slowly, he untangled his hands from behind his head, flattened them against his own floor and lowered himself down until his chest pressed against the planks.

"Go on," I coaxed, and then with his back arched and his ass in the air, Hunter stuck out his tongue and licked my cum off his floor.

I was hard again, cock in hand, watching him swirl his tongue around and lap up my cum like he was a cat and I'd offered him a bowl of fucking milk. When he'd licked up the last drop, he rocked back onto his heels and gazed up at me, his entire expression hazy.

"Hands," I chided, and he was quick to put them together again at the back of his head. "You did a good job there."

Hunter growled, licking his lips.

"Good job, Sir," I said again, softer, closing the space between us and covering his hands with mine. I pressed his face against my cock, shivering at the way his warm breath breezed over my bare skin. "But you missed a spot."

Hunter opened his mouth and licked the underside of my shaft, around the flared tip of my crown, and across my slit. He covered my cock with saliva and then smeared it across his face, making absolutely indecent noises the whole time. On his knees, Hunter sucked my cock like he was feral for it, and it took all my willpower not to shove him onto his back and handle him with much less care than he'd done for me only minutes before.

"Good boy," I said, grunting when he took the whole length of my shaft into his mouth. "Fuck, just like that."

He gave me one final suck before pulling off, chest heaving with every breath. I forced myself to let go of him and put enough space between us that I could find some air to breathe myself. The floor between us shined with his spit, his lips swollen from how hard he'd sucked my cock. How was it possible for him to look so achingly perfect on his knees while also the same way when I was on mine?

"I like it when you call me that," he said, tilting his head back to look at me.

"Good boy?" I asked.

He nodded, swallowing. "And Sir. And Daddy."

That felt a lot more complicated than Hunter's answer as to whether he was vers, but there was no way around the truth of it.

I pulled my lips between my teeth and bit down hard, hoping I wasn't about to make the biggest mistake of my life.

"Yeah," I agreed. "Me too."

CHAPTER 14
HUNTER

Monday brought two new cases onto my desk, which was a blessing because work was the only thing stopping me from backsliding into thoughts of Lincoln. Being on my knees in front of him and him calling me Sir as he stood over me with his cock in front of my mouth had been one of the biggest mind-fucks of my life, and while the whole thing felt wrong, it was also somehow desperately right.

At lunch, I received two text messages at the same time. One from Lincoln and the other from Marshall.

MARSHALL

Lunch?

LINCOLN

Plans tonight?

I texted my brother the affirmative and Lincoln the negative, then closed the case file I'd been studying to wait for answers from both of them.

MARSHALL

I'm out front.

That didn't bode well. It wasn't like Marshall to loiter.

I called Lincoln, and he answered on the first ring.

"I was just texting you back," he said. I could hear the smile in his voice, and it was enough to have me relaxing against the back of my chair, pretending my older brother wasn't on the sidewalk waiting for me. "Did you want to come over? Or I can come over to yours?"

As curious as I was about Lincoln's living situation, the twinge in his voice was unavoidable.

"You can come to mine," I told him. "Do you want to spend the night?"

"Yeah," he said, a little breathless.

"I get home around six on a good night. Meet me then?"

"Yeah. Yes."

I paused, glancing out the window. "What are you doing with the rest of your day?"

"Filming some content," he said.

Swallowing, I worried my bottom lip between my teeth. Lincoln and I had already talked about this. I knew making adult content was how he paid the bills, and I'd meant it when I told him I didn't have a problem with it, but knowing he was going to be at home getting off while I was stuck at work did have me feeling some kind of way about the whole thing.

"Is that a problem for you?" he asked, ever defiant.

"No," I assured him. "It does make me jealous, though."

"Why?"

"Because every time you come I want to see it," I told him.

On the other end of the line, Lincoln sucked in a sharp breath. "You asked for a close up before. Should I film that today?"

The yes was on the tip of my tongue, but heat pooled deep and dangerous in my belly before I could get the word out.

"Would you let me film it?" I asked instead. "Later tonight?"

Lincoln hummed, so low it almost vibrated the phone. "For me to upload or for you to keep?"

"Why not both?"

"Fuck," he cursed and cursed again under his breath. "That shouldn't be so hot."

"Is that a yes?"

"Yes."

"Something for me to look forward to then," I said, the original intent of my call lost to me until my ear pinged with an incoming text message that I simply knew was from my brother. "As delightful as this revelation is, I was calling to ask if you'd told Silas about us yet…or Smith."

"I haven't talked to your brother, but Silas…"

"Did you tell him?"

"Not explicitly," Lincoln murmured. "He knows me well, though, and he's good at putting the pieces of my secrets together."

"Marshall knows, I think," I confirmed for us both. "He just messaged me about getting lunch, and he's already downstairs waiting for me."

I turned off my monitor and stood up, checking my pockets for my wallet and keys before heading to the elevator.

"Shit. I'm sorry. I wasn't thinking…" He trailed off before adding, "Silas used to keep my secrets."

"I don't want to be a secret," I said, maybe with more force than I meant because the receptionist's head snapped up and her eyes went wide. I gave her a conciliatory wave before stabbing my finger into the elevator button and repeating, softer, "I don't want to be a secret."

"I don't want you to be," he whispered back.

"But I'd like to be the one to tell Smith. Do you think…do you think that would cause issue with your friendship with him?"

The elevator doors slid open, and I stepped inside, turning

to rest my ass on the back handrail. The doors closed, and I gave my reflection a quick onceover, wondering what exactly Lincoln saw in a man like me.

"If it does, he's not a friend worth having."

"All of my brothers are friends worth having," I corrected.

"Then it won't cause an issue."

"I'm in the elevator," I said, "so if I lose you, I'll see you at six."

"I can't wai—"

The annoying trill of the disconnect notification rang sharply in my ear, and with a frown, I shoved my phone into my pocket. Seconds later, I reached the ground floor. The doors slid open into the busy reception lobby, and it was easy for me to pick Marshall's imposing silhouette out on the street. He paced the length of the building, a tense frown on his face.

Poor bastard. I needed to quickly put him out of his misery.

I closed the space between us with long and sure strides, pushing open the glass door and joining him on the curb as he turned for another length of sidewalk.

"Sorry for the wait," I apologized.

"It's fine," he grumbled, pale eyes searching my face.

"I'm sleeping with Silas' best friend." I loosened the knot on my tie and smiled up at my protective—and apparently dominant—older brother. "Just thought you should know."

"I do know," he said.

"Has your mind been racing with curiosity over the things I do in the bedroom now?" I inclined my head toward the corner, toward the deli Finn and I frequented. "Because I know quite a bit more about your bedroom habits than I ever wanted to, if we're being honest."

Marshall let out a breath, falling into step beside me. "We're always honest."

"That's why I'm telling you now."

"How long has it been going on for?" he asked.

"It's new."

We reached the deli and quickly made our way to two vacant seats at the counter. The place was packed, all the booths and tables taken, the volume almost impossible to have a conversation over, which would only work out in my favor if things got too hairy with Marshall.

"Does this mean that you…" he trailed off.

"I don't think we need to go into details, Marsh."

"Right."

I handed him a menu, picking at the cuticle on my thumb while he perused the sandwich offerings.

I ordered the same thing every time, so did Finn, so I couldn't even remember the last time I looked to see what other options they had available. I'd always imagined myself to be the kind of man who liked what he liked, but then Lincoln had shown up and neatly tossed that idea into the trash. Or maybe he'd only shined a light on it. I got the same thing because I knew I liked it, but that didn't mean there weren't other things out there that I would also like.

A frazzled-looking waitress came by, notepad in hand. "The usual?" she asked me.

I shook my head and jerked my thumb toward Marshall. "I'll have whatever he's having."

From the corner of my eye, I could see Marshall's raised brow. The waitress looked at him, and he ordered a hot turkey and swiss with bacon, then slipped the menu back into place behind the napkin dispenser.

"You need to be gentle with him," Marshall said slowly, like the words were as curious to him as they were to me. It was the way I imagined he'd warn someone away from Smith, but the protectiveness toward Lincoln was unexpected.

"I know," I said.

Maybe—hopefully—I knew better than Marshall did.

"He's…there's been a lot of upheaval for him. He's not steady."

"He's steady with me."

Marshall dragged his tongue across the front of his teeth and let out a long breath that took at least three inches off the height of his shoulders. "He's adjusting to—"

I raised my hand and frowned at my older brother. "I'm gonna stop you right there."

"Hunter."

"I'm sure he appreciates your brotherly concern, but I think it's safe to say that he and I have had conversations the two of you have probably not shared together."

Marshall turned toward me, and I wanted to ask him when he'd gotten so old, when he'd gone so gray around the temples. Sometimes, in my head, we were still young. Finn and I teenagers, Marshall almost twenty, all of us still a few years off from Smith's arrival.

Growing up under the watchful eye of Willem Covington had been a trial for the whole lot of us, but we'd come out mostly unscathed, if not extremely protective of each other's interests. Our brotherhood was different from most. We all understood that, even if we never spoke about it, and seeing Marshall spread that out to someone who wasn't even partially related to us by blood sent a shock of emotion through me that I didn't have the words to explain. Lincoln needed to have people looking out for him, we all did, but where was that same care and grace for Andrew, our actual brother?

"I'm fond of Lincoln," Marshall answered. "He's Silas' best friend, and as long as Silas wants to be with me, Lincoln will have a place as well."

"Are you talking to me as my brother right now or a concerned surrogate father?" I asked.

A different server dropped off our sandwiches, and at the

sight of the melty swiss cheese bubbling out from beneath the toasted bread, my stomach growled.

"Can't it be both?" he asked.

"Did you have a talk with Lincoln too? About being gentle with your dearest brother?"

"I didn't think I needed to," he said.

I frowned, picking up half of the sandwich and taking a bite so I didn't have to answer him. It was a good sandwich. Different from my usual corned beef in just about every way possible, but tasty still in its own right. I chewed and swallowed, took another bite, and repeated the process.

"You're right," Marshall said, setting down his half-eaten sandwich. "You're my brother, of course I need to."

I bit the corner of my tongue and stared down at my lap, swiping my greasy fingers across the flimsy white napkin and hoping it would be enough to stop my hands from staining my slacks.

"I don't need coddling," I told him. "That's not what I meant."

"It's not coddling, and you know it."

I thought about the revelation that my brother lived and breathed dominance in his private life, that even though there'd been instances in our youth when he'd conceded things to me or Finn or Smith, even though there'd been times he had to cave in or that he faltered, Marshall was as he'd always been. Calm and collected, and very much in charge of his life and the people in it. After all, he was the first person I'd called when I found out about Andrew's existence. He was the one I'd gone to for guidance. He was apparently also the one Lincoln had sought out during his own confusion and struggles. Marshall was the patriarch of all our lives, whether we liked the mess that made or not.

"I like him," I told my brother. "Sincerely, I do. Even

though there's things…God, I don't want to go into this with you."

He chuckled and picked up his sandwich again, raising it halfway to his mouth. "You don't have to, believe me."

"I just…I have good intentions with him, with the whole thing."

Marshall finished the bite he was chewing, then polished off the rest of the half before turning his attention to the pickle spear on the side of my plate. He made quick work of it, then reached for mine, which I gave him freely.

"I know you do," Marshall said, licking pickle juice from his fingers. "I can't think of a better man for him than you."

I snorted, rolling my eyes. "I'm confident that's not true."

Beside me, Marshall went still, and without much thought, so did I.

"If he can do better than you, then you shouldn't be with him," he said. "And if you don't think he's the best choice for you…"

My breath hitched in my throat, and I balled my napkin up in my hand, tossing it onto the counter. "It's new, Marsh."

"You're a smart man, Hunter. Smarter than most."

"I appreciate the vote of confi—"

"I want the best for you," he said, cutting me off. "I want the best for Finn and for Smith and for Silas *and* for Lincoln too."

"You're a bleeding heart," I muttered, flagging the waitress down for a box.

"If that's what you want to call it."

We boxed up our leftovers and Marshall walked me back to the office. He didn't say anything else about Lincoln, but when we parted, he hugged me extra hard, kissed the side of my head before pulling back to look at me. Like…really look at me.

"For what it's worth, Hunter, I did mean what I said.

You've grown up to be a good man, and you'll be a good partner. But if you don't think the same…"

I sighed, scrubbing a hand down my face. "It feels arrogant to assume I'm the best he can do."

"It shouldn't feel arrogant." The corner of his mouth twitched up and he shrugged before taking a step past me, then another. "It should feel like a goal."

CHAPTER 15
LINCOLN

Avoiding Smith made me feel like shit. He'd been texting incessantly about getting me set up with another fish, and I'd been leaving his messages unread because I didn't think I could see him and not tell him about Hunter, and Hunter had explicitly said he wanted to be the one to tell his youngest brother about us first. I made a mental note about telling Hunter at some point in the night that I needed him to come clean and instead turned my attention to Silas.

I waited until I was on the way to Hunter's apartment to call Silas, also knowing there was a gap in the night between when Silas got off work and when Marshall got home. They were both workaholics, but one was far worse than the other. The phone rang through to voicemail, and I frowned out the windshield. Thankfully, almost as soon as the call disconnected, my phone rang and a picture of me and Silas lit up the screen.

"Hey," I answered, rubbing my palms on the steering wheel.

"Sorry I missed you," he said. "I was in the shower."

"That's fine."

"What's up?" my best friend in the world asked, and

suddenly I felt like shit for telling him this over the phone and not in person.

"Nothing," I lied. "Just driving around and thinking about you."

Silas let out a low laugh. "Just cruising the city?"

"You know. I like my apartment, but it gets boring when it's just me," I said.

It was a lie wrapped in truth.

"Have you got another fish yet?"

I made a dismissive sound in the back of my throat. "Are you and Smith in cahoots?"

"Me and Smith?"

I could hear Silas' eyebrows raise into his hairline, and I grimaced. "He's been on me about a Cassandra replacement too."

"I didn't know the two of you were that close."

We were closer, but I *definitely* wasn't going to tell Silas that over the phone.

"We're friends," I summarized, pulling my car into the parking garage at Hunter's apartment building. "Going into a parking garage, might lose you."

"That's convenient," Silas mumbled. "Do you want to go out Friday night? Maybe hit up Rapture?"

"Maybe, yeah."

The call disconnected before he could question me, and I'd never felt more relieved. Here I'd spent the last half of the day looking forward to going over to Hunter's apartment and losing myself in him, but the more time passed, the more shit there was for us to talk about. I had been so wrapped up in overthinking all of it, I hadn't even filmed any of the content I'd woken up ready to record.

What the fuck was I doing?

I was an absolute mess of a human, and I shouldn't take Hunter down with me. Just because he'd been blind enough to fall for me didn't mean I needed to *let* him. I was on the cusp of devising a way to break up with him when somebody knocked on my window, scaring me enough that I jumped out of my seat and screamed. I snapped my head toward the left and found Hunter there, hand still lifted and eyebrows raised.

I screwed my eyes closed and cursed under my breath, turning off the engine. Hunter pulled up on the door handle and the rush of cool garage air was almost enough to snap me out of my spiral.

"Good timing," he said, adjusting a leather strap over his shoulder. "I was running late."

I let out a weak laugh, scrubbing a hand down my face.

"You okay?" he asked.

I unlatched my seatbelt and moved to get out of the car, instead my feet landed on the concrete and my elbows landed on my knees. Cradling my head in my hands, I took some deep breaths that did little to steady me. I needed…

I needed…

Hunter dropped into a squat in front of me, his fingers raking through my hair over and over again until I leaned forward and pressed my forehead against his shoulder.

This was what I needed.

"What's wrong?" he asked quietly, breath hot against my ear.

"Nothing."

Because in that very moment, it was true. Nothing was wrong when I was with Hunter. It was all the hours I wasn't with him when everything felt unmanageable. Admitting that out loud felt grossly codependent, so I swallowed the thought back into the pit of my stomach.

"This doesn't seem like nothing."

"I didn't film today," I said.

It was a start.

"That's okay," he said, fingers still sliding through strands of my hair before ghosting down the back of my neck. "Let's talk, Lincoln. But upstairs, okay? More comfortable."

He stood up and helped me out of the car, pulled my keys out of my hand to lock the door, then walked me to the elevator. We stood close, shoulders touching, but he didn't ask me anything else. I took the short ride to study our reflections in the closed doors of the elevator car. Hunter in his slacks and shirt and tie, me in my jeans and crop top, my messy hair and my piercings. There'd never been two people more different, but the elevator doors opened as soon as I thought it, and the mirror images of us were gone.

Still in silence, Hunter walked me to the front door of his apartment and unlocked the door. We both stepped over the threshold and as soon as the door closed behind us, Hunter was on his knees at my feet. With a low hum, he rubbed his cheek against the outside of my thigh and started to pluck at the laces of my shoes.

He did look good on his knees.

"What do you need?" he murmured, hands skating up the backs of my thighs once he finished with my shoes.

There wasn't a single thing I needed more than what I had. Hunter on his knees in front of me, his mouth inches from my cock. This was the only thing I'd ever wanted, and it all made sense when we were together.

"Just you," I answered. "I need to be able to tell people about you, though. I feel like—"

He cut me off, tipping his head back. Even in the low light of his hallway, I could see the way his pupils had dilated into big, black pools that nearly obscured his irises.

"I told Marshall today. He already knew, but…"

I swallowed hard, understanding there didn't need to be any further explanation. He knew in the way Silas knew, even if I'd tried to pretend Silas didn't know.

"When are you going to tell Smith?" I asked.

"Friday," he said.

"I can't avoid him for a week," I said, taking Hunter's face into my hands.

"Tomorrow," he corrected, and I wanted to cry for how quickly and simply this man understood me.

"Okay."

Hunter smiled, nuzzling his cheek into my palm.

"What else do you need?"

I swallowed hard, ignoring the way my throat clicked when I opened my mouth to speak. "I need everything to be as easy without you as it is with you."

He hummed, kissing the heel of my hand. "When are you without me?"

"Earlier today."

Hunter frowned, almost a parody.

"Are we together, Lincoln?" he asked, jaw working back and forth. "Should I call you Sir when I'm down here?"

"Definitely not."

"Are we together?" he asked again. "Just us?"

I bit down on the inside of my cheek but managed to answer him with a tight nod.

"That doesn't feel like we're ever without each other then."

I wanted to be angry because the comment felt so dismissive of the way it actually did feel to be without him, but it was impossible to muster the necessary rage to do so when I stared down at Hunter's wide and earnest eyes.

"That's fair," I agreed.

"It'll be easier once it's in the open," he promised, fingers flexing against his legs. "And it'll be in the open tomorrow."

"Will Smith be mad I haven't told him?"

"I'll take the blame," he said so quickly, so simply.

"I don't—"

"It's my fault," Hunter interrupted me again. "I asked to be the one."

Pulling my lips together between my teeth, I slid both of my hands into his hair, working my fingers through the still-styled strands. His hair product stuck to my fingers, but I carefully worked my way toward the back of his head, even as he grunted and groaned through it all. Every happy sigh that left Hunter's mouth also unwound the tension in my own shoulders, and I could have stood in the entryway there for the rest of the night and died a happy man.

"Is it okay to ask you for something?" he finally asked, voice so quiet I almost missed him over the rapid beating of my own heart.

"Always."

I wanted to call him Sir. It felt right to call him Sir.

"Would you spank *me*?"

Of all the things I'd expected him to say, that was nowhere on the list, and I took a quick step backward. Hunter's entire body swayed forward, but he didn't fall. Instead, he rebalanced himself on his knees and threaded his fingers together behind his head like I'd shown him.

"Say that again," I croaked.

"Would you spank me?"

"Are you asking because you want to be spanked or because you think I want to spank you?"

He swayed a little, like he was drunk.

"Can't it be both?"

"Yes."

"Would it make you hard to spank me?" he asked.

I forced out another nod.

"I want you to spank me," he said then, telling instead of asking, and heat flared like a volcanic explosion between my legs. "And then I want to film you jerking off for your website."

"Jesus."

The corner of Hunter's lip twitched. "I have to admit, I do like Sir better."

The air left my lungs in one, long, whooshing exhale, and I flexed my hands at my sides, feeling so certain of what to do and also so confused by it at the same time. Hunter stayed on his knees in front of me, still dressed for work, tie still knotted around his neck and feet still crammed into shiny black dress shoes that I very desperately wanted to grind my balls all over.

"Crawl then, Sir," I murmured, taking another step back and another. "Crawl to your bedroom and let me watch you go."

Hunter's cheeks burned a violent shade of red, his chest heaving as he fell forward onto his hands and knees. I followed him through the apartment, down the long hallway to his bedroom, appreciating the way his ass filled out his slacks. It was an indecent thing, a man dressed like him, with as much money and class as him, crawling with his ass in the air begging for a spanking from a man who barely had his life together. It was all right…we could pretend.

Together, we reached his bedroom, and Hunter rocked back onto his heels again, immediately clasping his fingers together at the back of his head without being told. I closed the space between us and covered his fingers with my hand, tilting his head back until his throat strained.

"You look so fucking hot like this," I told him, licking my lips.

His chin quivered, lips parted. "I feel so fucking hot like this," he whispered back.

"I know we said spanking then filming, but I think I want to do it the other way around."

Hunter groaned, and I pulled my cell phone out of my pocket. I swiped through to my camera app and adjusted the settings to accommodate the low light in Hunter's bedroom, then I held the device out for him to take.

"You film it," I told him, plucking open the button on my jeans.

They were skinny and torn, and there was no sexy way to get out of them, so I was glad Hunter didn't start recording until I'd stripped down to my crop top and my black briefs.

"Do you still want to see my face?" I asked, trying to see him from around the phone. "I'll edit your voice out, don't worry."

"I want to see everything."

The toe of his shoes squeaked on the floor, and I thought about exactly what position I wanted to put him in to spank him. I imagined how hot his cock would burn against my leg as I did it.

Hunter stared hard at the screen of my phone, and I knocked the damn thing out of the way enough so I could get to his throat. He made a very desperate noise as I undid the knot of his tie, and an even more agonized one when he realized what I was about to do with it.

I wound the length of his tie around my hand, curling my covered fingers around the quickly growing length of my cock. I liked to use lube, but silk would have to do in this case. Taking a step back, still stroking myself, I crawled up onto the bed. I knew my body well enough to know what Hunter was recording. The backs of my thighs, the pucker of my asshole when my ass cheeks spread apart, the low hang of my balls, and the dark blue of the tie that wrapped around my shaft.

"I want to see your face," he murmured, shifting on the floor.

I threw him a look over my shoulder and then stroked my dick until my entire body trembled.

"What else do you want?"

"I want to fuck you," he rasped.

"What else?" I asked, flattening myself against his sheets before turning onto my back, arching my hips off the bed and spreading my legs.

For a while, Hunter didn't answer. He also didn't move.

Still filming.

I kept stroking my cock, dragging my other hand up the swell of my chest to toy with my nipple piercings. The friction between my legs was agony, and I'd never wanted anyone more than I wanted him. I wanted to come, I wanted to spank Hunter, and then I wanted him to fuck me until he burst. After that, I wanted to close my eyes and pretend we never had to leave his apartment, never had to leave his bed.

"Everything," he finally answered. "I want everything."

CHAPTER 16
HUNTER

Lincoln came all over my tie, his breathy whimper sounding a lot like the first syllable of my name, and I prayed he didn't edit that out when he pieced the clips together. I waited until after his cock stopped pulsing before ending the recording, then I set the phone down on the floor beside my leg and laced my fingers together at the base of my skull.

My body vibrated with the need to get inside of this man, but there was something to definitely be said about the anticipation that came from being on my knees. On the bed, Lincoln groaned again, then sat up, stripping out of his shirt awkwardly with one hand. My cum-covered tie still wrapped loosely around his other fist.

"How do you feel about gags?" he asked, sitting upright and bracing his bare feet against the floor.

I was so overdressed, but I'd never felt more exposed.

"Yes, please," I whispered.

"Pull down your pants," Lincoln said, chin raised. "Just down to your knees and then come get on my lap."

"I'm too big, I'll—"

"Come get on my lap," he said again, licking his lips. "Sir."

It was impossible to tell him no when hearing that three-letter word made me desperate to only tell him yes.

I pulled open my belt and tugged down my fly. I shoved my pants and my underwear down to my thighs, then fanned myself out over the top of his lap. It was awkward until he adjusted my position so my erection was tucked between his thighs, and I groaned for how tight his muscles held me.

"Open," he murmured next, pulling my head up with a tight grip on my hair.

I swallowed and parted my lips, grunting when he used sticky fingers to shove the balled-up—and probably ruined—tie into my mouth. The salty taste of his cum immediately filled my mouth, and I groaned, the sound turning into a moan when he dropped my face back onto the sheets.

"I'm not holding you down," he said, stroking his fingers over the small of my back. "If you hate this, just get up and I'll stop."

There was no way to tell him that I knew, without a shadow of a doubt, I'd never hate this. I nodded, my lashes fluttering when he dug his fingertips into my ass cheek. One hand pressed between my shoulder blades, more affirming than restricting, and then Lincoln's hand landed against my ass with a deafening crack.

My body tensed, and he went still, and then without any prompting from my brain, my hips thrust downward, pushing my cock toward the sheets. Lincoln let out a quiet laugh, drawing swirls over the place he'd just spanked me.

"Sir likes it," he said softly, then he spanked me again.

It was easy to get lost in the steady and expected cadence of Lincoln's hand against my ass. The calming strokes of his fingers up and down the length of my spine. Even the tight squeeze of his thighs around my cock as he continued to strike my ass. He moved his attention lower, alternating between firm slaps against my already tender ass and the extremely sensitive backs of my thighs. Every nerve in my body lit up like a live wire, the only thing stopping me from getting lost in it entirely was the embarrassing amount of spit rolling down my chin.

Lincoln wouldn't have been embarrassed if it were him. I didn't think he would be, at least, but he had a lot more experience with this kind of thing than I did. My know-how was limited to an hour here and there spent reenacting porn I'd seen on the internet. Suddenly, being over his lap felt more like role play than anything I'd done with any men before him. Kneeling had been okay, kneeling had been *more* than okay, but this…

Rocking my shoulder, I moved enough to dislodge his hand from between my shoulders.

"Enough?" he asked quietly.

I climbed off his lap, the balled-up and soaking tie still in my mouth.

Lincoln flung himself backward on the bed and spread his legs, almost the same pose as when he'd been jerking off earlier except now he cradled his balls in his hand, lifting his sac and cock up to show me his asshole. My mouth went dry, and with a surprising flash of reluctance, I yanked the tie out of my mouth.

"Want to fuck you," I said, tongue sticking to the roof of my mouth.

"You better."

It was easy to cover Lincoln's body with mine. Easier still to slick my fingers with lube and shove them between his legs. His body was hot and tight, but he made room for me like I was made to be inside of him. Maybe I liked the spanking more than I thought because, on top of Lincoln, I moved like a man possessed. My fingers thrust and scissored him open, and I only used my hand until the fine lines around the corners of his mouth went slack.

"Take me bare," he said on a gasp, the tip of my dick already notched against his slippery asshole.

He didn't need to tell me twice.

He barely needed to tell me once.

I thrust into Lincoln with enough force it slid us both up toward the headboard, and I had to force myself to go still inside of him so I didn't come on the spot. With my head hanging low and the curled ends of his hair tickling my nose, I fought my way through a tremble that threatened to knock all of my joints out of place.

"Oh," Lincoln exhaled, his hands coming around my waist with an exceedingly noticeable sort of delicacy, especially considering the fact those hands had most definitely left purple bruises on my ass.

"Hmn?" I pushed forward, making sure every inch I could fit had sunk inside of him. Needing more of a pause, I pressed my mouth against the side of his neck, kissing and sucking and baring my teeth against the thin skin behind his ear.

"Oh," he said again, fingernails sharp blades against my waist.

I was still dressed. I realized too late, my slacks down around my knees and my dress shirt still buttoned and hanging too low for my liking. I wanted more of Lincoln. I wanted all of him, but there was no way in hell I was going to take my cock out of him until we'd both finished at least once more each.

"Take off my shirt."

I shoved into him again, only so I could rock back enough to toe off my shoes and shake one leg out of my pants, and then the other. I got my underwear down to one ankle, and then Lincoln had finished with my shirt and it was enough. It was enough.

"If you don't move, I might die."

"I might die if I move," I whispered, still fighting to catch my breath.

"Okay," he said quietly, hands finally settling in the dip of my waist. "Alright."

Lincoln gave me space to breathe, not just in bed, but out of it as well. It was easy for me to kneel in front of him and easier still for me to put him onto his knees. There was no thought involved, only muscle memory, which was absurd considering we barely knew each other. But somehow, my body knew his, like for a thousand parallel lives this was a dance we'd learned and rehearsed and perfected.

"Hunter, I…" Lincoln blinked hard, voice trailing off into nothing louder than his next breath.

"Sir," he said next, swallowing hard, and then I kissed his throat, tilted his head back to make room for myself, and he whimpered, "Daddy."

There was something electric about the word, sending gooseflesh down the back of my neck at the sound of it. I kissed my way up the underside of his chin and slanted our mouths together, kissing this man that I had somehow fallen in love with overnight. He dug his nails into my waist and parted his lips for me, moaning when my tongue twisted with his, and the only thing I could hear was *Daddy*.

Daddy.

"I'm here. I've got you," I promised him, and then I started to move.

Lincoln came apart beneath me, his entire body shuddering with pleasure as I pulled my cock almost all the way out of him. Thrusting back in, I set a pace that didn't make my brain want to explode, and just like everything else…

It was enough.

It was *enough*.

Reaching down, I hiked Lincoln's legs up and buried myself deeper into him, pumping down hard on top of him, pushing him into the mattress. I groaned when Lincoln took his dick into his hand and stroked himself, all of his muscles going taut, especially the ones that gripped my cock on every thrust.

Lincoln cursed under his breath and tried to cover his face with his free hand, but I grabbed it away from him and pinned it to the mattress. His cheeks were flushed red and his lashes were clumped together, his stare focused on me even when he blinked long and hard.

"What the...How the..." Lincoln screwed his eyes shut, arched his back, and then came all over my chest. The heat of his pleasure and the tight friction of his knuckles against my stomach while he kept stroking himself off was more than enough to push me the rest of the way over my own edge. Trying to not come inside of him had been a struggle from the start and letting go of that control had pleasure rolling through me like a tidal wave. Burying my face into the crook of his neck, I thrust into Lincoln until my balls were wrung out and empty, the final exhale of my orgasm leaving me with a shudder.

"Hey." His voice was hoarse against my ear, his lips damp. "Kiss me, please."

I'd never make him ask twice for that, leveraging my way back up to bring our mouths together. Gentle at first, then with more feeling, until I was thrusting against him again, groaning with arousal when Lincoln fought against me and flipped me onto my back. On top of me, he arranged himself neatly between my legs, breaking the kiss to sit upright and play with his nipples.

"You've seen me come twice today," he told me, fitting his body between my spread thighs...finally getting my underwear the whole way off. "I've only seen you come once."

"I'll come for you again if that's what you want."

"I know," he murmured, sliding two fingers into his mouth.

I gasped, watching him fellate his two longest fingers and then press then down between my legs. My hole was so sensitive. It would have been even if my entire body wasn't absolutely primed for pleasure, but Lincon's slick and swirling fingers didn't do me any favors.

"Did you like when I called you Daddy?" he asked, plucking one nipple and twisting it to the point that watching it made my own nipples ache.

"I like when you call me anything," I admitted.

"Sometimes Daddy feels right," he said, sliding his hand down lower and stroking his cock. His damp fingers still toyed with my asshole, and it was a wonder I hadn't already shot my load all over us both. "Sir feels better."

"What about Hunter?" I asked.

A second later, Lincoln twisted his finger and slid it all the way up to the knuckle. I bit down on the inside of my cheek, bucking us both up off the bed.

"Hunter is nice," he teased, sliding his finger out before pressing it back in. "Outside of the bedroom."

I huffed out a desperate little laugh at just how astute that observation truly was.

Lincoln made a soft mewling sound, reaching behind his back and dragging his fingers across his ass.

"You're leaking out of me."

"I should have asked if it was okay to come inside of you."

"We've already had these conversations." He grunted, and it didn't take a stretch of the imagination to know he'd shoved his fingers up his own ass. "I want you to take me whenever you want me."

I had to close my eyes because the sight of Lincoln on top of me, his chest flushed and his cock swollen was almost too much for me to bear, all things between us considered. Reaching forward, I dragged my fingertips up his stomach toward his chest, and without prompting, he scooted a little closer so I could reach him.

"You like these to hurt, don't you?" I murmured, flicking one of his nipples.

In response, he groaned and pulled his fingers out of his ass.

"I do." He showed me his fingers, sticky with lube and cum, and then he reached down again between my legs and shoved my own spend right into my asshole.

"Oh fuck."

"Stop fighting it, Daddy," Lincoln coaxed.

I didn't even need to look at his face to see the playful smile that split his lips, but I did anyway.

"Lincoln," I murmured his name because, in that moment, it was the only thing I knew.

"Be a good boy and come for me, Daddy."

His mouth spread into a smile so bright it could have eclipsed the sun, and I had no choice after that, except to give him exactly what he wanted.

CHAPTER 17
LINCOLN

t was the smell of coffee and a dull ache between my legs that woke me up the next morning. Stretching my arms over my head and pointing my toes toward the end of the bed, Hunter's sheets tangled around my thighs like the very best kind of bondage. With a groan, I rolled onto my side, finding the other pillow empty and a light on somewhere else in the house that cast an amber glow down the hallway.

Climbing out of bed, I stumbled blindly toward the light—which was from the kitchen—wiping sleep out of my eyes the whole way.

"You look well and properly fucked," Hunter said, and wearing nothing more than my underwear, I smiled at him sleepily.

"That might be an understatement."

"Did I wake you up?" he asked, pouring coffee into a sleek, black tumbler and twisting closed the lid.

I shook my head.

It was the absence of his body beside mine that had eventually woken me up, but I didn't think we'd been involved with each other long enough for me to tell him that. I was never not craving the closeness and warmth of him.

"I was going to leave you a note," he went on, bustling around and arranging things in neat piles on the counter. His coffee, his wallet, his keys, his cell phone. He was mostly dressed, tie undone around his neck and his feet still bare, but he had on his standard slacks and a button-up combo.

"Dear John," I teased, but he cut me off with a roll of his eyes.

Hunter shoved a sheet of yellow legal paper across the island toward me. I was still half-asleep and everything was blurry, but his handwriting was crisp and legible, short and sure strokes of the pen making up every letter.

Lincoln,

I had to go to work and you looked too good to wake up. I like the sight of you in my bed, so stay there as long as you want. Film a little, if you feel so inclined. The door locks automatically when it closes, so don't worry about a key. Last night was amazing. You are amazing.

xx, H

I folded the note in on itself, determined to shove it into my pocket once I found my pants.

"Two kisses?" I asked.

"As many as you want now that you're up."

He walked around the counter and fitted himself between my naked thighs. There was no thought involved with taking the ends of his tie into my hands and knotting it into place at the base of his throat, which was a blessing, because I had to spend all of my brain power on remembering how to breathe with him so fucking close to me.

After I adjusted the knot, I smoothed my hand down the silk, finding his green tie to be as soft as his blue one. Before my fingers could drop off the end, he covered my hand with his and raised it to his mouth, kissing my knuckles, my palm, the inside of my wrist. A wave of goosebumps rolled up my arms, and I closed my eyes so I could better appreciate the feel of his mouth.

Patron saint of head over heels in love with a man I barely even knew.

"I'm going to have lunch with Smith today," he said, my fingertips pressed against his lips. "I'll let him know we're… well, shit."

Hunter's normally gorgeous mouth turned down into a frown, and I pulled my hand out of his grip in order to stroke my thumb across his cheek. His face was still damp, smooth… he'd shaved. I imagined him leaning over the sink, a towel loose around his waist and shaving cream streaked down his throat and toward his ear.

"What?"

"I'll let him know that we're…what's the word, Lincoln?"

"Involved," I murmured.

"Is that all?"

I appreciated him putting the ball in my court, but it wasn't a decision for me to make. Normally deciding your involvement with another person was a collaborative kind of thing, but he said it had been awhile since he'd been in a serious relationship so maybe he'd forgotten how it worked.

"What do you want it to be?" I asked.

"I'm a Covington, sweetheart," he said, angling his face into my hand and kissing my palm again. "We're greedy men by nature."

"Be greedy then."

He closed the space between us and slanted our mouths together, making quick work of slipping his tongue past my sleep-chapped lips and into my mouth. I flung my arms around his neck, happy to let him steer the kiss, relishing the way the taste of his coffee and his toothpaste quickly overpowered the sticky remnants of sleep that lingered in my mouth. It didn't take long for my cock to wake up as much of the rest of me, and it was only a reluctant groan from Hunter's mouth as he broke the kiss that put enough space between us that we could breathe.

"Boyfriend," he whispered, the word dusting across my lips like a kiss on its own.

"As long as you call me sweetheart again," I said softly, my whole body swaying after his.

"I'll call you anything you like."

"I'll call you Sir," I promised, because it felt right to do so. "I'll call you my best boy." Hunter smiled against my mouth. "I'll call you Daddy."

"I'll be all of those things for you."

He took my face into his hands and kissed me hard. Rough enough that I saw stars around the corners of my vision before I closed my eyes and melted into him again.

"I'll tell Smith you're my boyfriend," he said again.

"You just like saying it."

The corner of his mouth quirked up, and he looked so fucking young. "I'll tell him I'm your boyfriend. That sounds better."

Something unexplainable and terrifying knotted itself together in the middle of my chest, and I was glad Hunter had ended the kiss because if his tongue was still in my mouth, I might choke.

"What else?" I asked.

"I'll make sure he knows that you've been honest about your relationship with him. That it doesn't bother me. That it won't bother me."

"And tell him he can talk to me about it," I said. "I don't want things to be weird. I…your brother is a good friend, and I don't want to lose that."

"You won't." Hunter kissed my forehead, then took two steps back, smoothing his hand down the front of his tie. "I have to go to work, but I was serious about you staying."

"About filming."

"Do whatever you want," he said. "There's coffee if you want it. Use my shower, rub yourself all over my sheets, come on my pillows—"

I cut him off before he could say anything else, "You're being ridiculous."

"I want you here as much as you want to be here," he said, face going so very serious.

My tongue stuck to the roof of my mouth, but I slid off the stool anyway and cradled his face in my hands. I loved how he was taller than me, broader. I loved the way he bent and buckled for me when I needed it the most.

"Kneel for me before you go," I said quietly, stroking my fingers over his carefully styled hair. I didn't need to ask twice, barely even once, before he was on his way down to the floor, hands coming up to join at the base of his skull. "I love the sight of you down there."

"I like being here," he whispered.

"Rub your face against my cock," I told him. "Give me something to jack off about after you leave me here."

Hunter growled, doing what I'd asked and then doing more. He mouthed the shape of my growing erection through the thin material of my underwear, bobbing his head and using his tongue as if there wasn't a barrier between us. Heat wrapped around my spine, and I thrust my hips forward, desperate for him in a borderline obsessive way.

"Go to work, Sir," I managed to force out the words, sliding my hand between my cock and his mouth. "Before I put you onto your hands and knees and find out just how quickly you can really come."

He cursed under his breath, but righted himself to his feet, making a show of adjusting the bulge between his legs before swallowing hard and grabbing his things off the counter. It was routine as I watched him slide some things into his pocket and others into his bag. He gave me one last lingering look before heading for the door and stopped with his hand on the knob, throwing a quick look at me over his shoulder.

"I do want to try that," he said, chin tucked toward his chest. "With you."

How the man could disarm me with his dominance and his submission was a mystery that belonged in the history books because I'd surely never make sense of it.

"There's lots I want to try with you," I assured him.

He lingered long enough for me to watch the red flush flare up his cheeks, and then the door opened and closed, and I was alone in Hunter's apartment. Of course, I planned to snoop around. It was the easiest way to get to know him, but there was definitely a more pressing matter to attend to.

Since I'd just filmed a video, or rather, he'd filmed me on his bed the night before, I opted for a change of scenery, taking my phone into his primary bathroom. The setup was less than ideal, especially since I didn't have my tripod or my ring light, but I would do the best I could. Even if the video wasn't fit for the public, it would be good enough for Hunter.

I worked through a couple placement options, trying the angle on the bathroom counter, but it was too far away from the shower on account of Hunter's massive bathroom. The next best was in the shower with me, so I sent up a prayer of thanks over having a waterproof phone, then propped it up on his unused built-in soap dish. It wouldn't get a full body shot, but it would get my face, which was what he'd wanted in the first place.

Yeah, this was going to be a video just for Hunter.

Turning on the hot water, I pressed record and stepped under the spray. I was still hard from Hunter being on his knees, and I told him so, pressing my shoulders against the back wall of the shower and curling my fingers around my cock.

"You just left for work, and I'm so fucking hard for you,

Daddy." I moaned, trying to not overthink the endearment, the honorific. "Fuck. Fuck. I can still feel you inside of me."

It wasn't a lie.

I dropped my head back and closed my eyes, getting into the rhythm of stroking my cock and playing with my nipples. My own hand felt good, but nowhere near as perfect as Hunter's mouth or his fist. Even the way he tweaked my piercings was better, and I thought how rude a stranger knew my body better than I did.

When I closed my eyes, I could see him. Could see the way he screwed his eyes closed before he came, the way his mouth quivered a little when he held back his own pleasure. Like the most addicting aphrodisiac. I didn't need to close my eyes, though, and that wasn't what he'd wanted. He wanted to see my face, wanted to see *me* come. Prying my eyes open, I looked directly into the camera and gave a long and slow overhand stroke down the length of my shaft.

"I want to tie you to your bed and tease your asshole until you come," I told my phone, a shiver tearing up my spine at the memory of how sensitive Hunter was. How violently his body reacted to me. "And then tease you until you can't come anymore. Until you're just gasping and begging."

I wanted him to do the same to me. To reduce me to nothing more than a guttural need for him and the pleasure he wanted me to have.

"And then I want you to wake me up in the middle of the night…I need it. Need you to just take me." A whimper fell out of my mouth, almost lost beneath the sound of the shower. I tightened my hand, stroked myself quicker. "Want you to…"

I wanted Hunter to do vile things with my body.

Wanted him to shove a dildo in my ass and DP me, stretching me out until I came for him. Wanted him to roll me onto my stomach in the middle of the night and shove his dick into me, fuck me until he came, and then go back to sleep. And between all of that, before and during and after, I wanted him on his knees for me, my cock in his mouth and my hands in his hair.

"Tell me where to come. Tell me where I can come," I pleaded, the orgasm so close that even if I was supposed to wait for permission, I wouldn't have been able to hold off one second longer. "I'll come on your face, Daddy. Sir, oh *fuuuuuuck...*"

I came with the memory of Hunter's slack jaw and hooded eyes on the backs of my eyelids. Imagined pulling my cock out of his mouth, slick with spit and tears, shooting my load across his swollen lips and his freshly shaven cheeks. Hunter's name tumbled out of my mouth as loud as a thunderclap, and when the first shot of cum burst out of my cock, my knees trembled and gave out entirely.

My ass hit the floor of the shower hard enough to hurt, but the cum still geysered out of my dick like I had an endless supply of it for this one, earthquaking orgasm. Two more strokes and it hurt to touch myself, but the orgasm was still tight and aggressive in the base of my spine, so I fought through it until I had to cover my eyes and cry out for how bad —how good—it felt.

Finally, my balls were empty, and my arms fell uselessly at my sides. The warm water rained down against my chest, my face, my stomach, rinsing me clean while I caught my breath. Groaning, I forced myself onto my hands and knees, then up onto my feet. The camera still recorded, and I made sure to give Hunter a good look at my dilated pupils and my flushed cheeks before swiping my finger over the record button the end the video.

"I think I'm in love with you," I muttered.

And fuck if that wasn't the worst news I'd had since Cassandra died.

CHAPTER 18
HUNTER

As soon as I sat down across from Smith at lunch, he knew something was up. It was written clear as day in the lines around his mouth that he had no business having on account of how young he was. He eyed me warily, and I adjusted the knot on my tie to give me some breathing room.

"Is there another one?" he asked, mouth pulling down into a frown.

"What?"

"Another brother."

I scoffed, leaning back in my seat and hoping it portrayed an air of casualness. I didn't want to set off any alarm bells with the conversation, and I definitely didn't want him to think whatever I had to talk to him about was serious. Telling him about Lincoln should be an easy thing. If they were really just friends, then it shouldn't matter at all that I was involved with him. At least, that's what I'd been telling myself all morning.

"Statistically, I'm sure we have another brother," I admitted to him, "but I don't know about him yet."

He barely looked relieved. "Is someone dying?"

"What? No." I scrubbed a hand down my face. "Why would you ask that?"

"Why did you invite me to lunch?" he countered.

I shot a scathing look at him across the table. "Because I'm your brother."

"Yeah," he agreed. "You're the quiet brother. Marshall is the controlling one, and Finn is the talker. So why are you the one talking?"

I paused, reflecting on his observation about the group of us. He was clearly right on the mark about Marshall, though there was a much better word to use than controlling, even if I surely wasn't going to be the one to introduce my baby brother to...

No.

Wait.

Lincoln had told me Smith knew about *him*, which meant Smith...

I shuddered, not wanting to know about any of my brothers' sex lives, least of all the youngest one. He was barely of age in the first place.

"You're not wrong that I keep to myself more than the rest of us," I conceded. "But if that's the truth of all of us, which brother are you?"

Smith scrunched his nose and shrugged. "What did you want to talk about, Hunter? If it's not a new brother or someone dying."

"We have a mutual friend," I said, not sure how else to start.

Smith arched a brow at me, and he looked so much like Marshall, even though they shared hardly any facial features between them. "Okay."

Sitting across from my brother in a loud Thai restaurant in the middle of a Tuesday, on the brink of telling him about Lincoln, suddenly felt silly. Smith wouldn't care at all. Marshall had spent so many years trying to coddle him and shelter him from the realities of the world, and that was the last thing Smith needed…or wanted, probably. I didn't think any of us had ever bothered to ask.

"In hindsight, I thought this would be more of a problem," I muttered, which at least earned me a smirk. "I'm seeing Lincoln."

Smith exhaled, tilting his head to the side. "Seeing him like…*seeing* him, seeing him?"

"Yeah."

My brother licked his lips, pulling them together between his teeth and working them back and forth until they were both a darker shade of pink than usual. "How'd that happen?" he asked.

"It's a very long story."

"And you know…" Smith groaned, staring down at the napkin in his lap.

"I know."

"You don't care?" he asked next, the unspoken part clear between us.

You don't care that I fucked him first?

"Do *you* care?" I countered. "That I am now, I mean?"

"Lincoln and I are friends," he said simply.

"And Lincoln and I are more than friends." I paused, clearing my throat. "I wanted to be the one to tell you."

Smith regarded me cautiously, and it was then that I really saw him for the first time. A man on the cusp of the rest of his life, constantly being throttled by three older brothers who loved him beyond measure but didn't always know how to show it. Growing up after being abandoned by all of our mothers and shoved into a house owned by a man who could have cared less about being our father had fostered a fucked-up sense of camaraderie between us. Mostly, it was for the better, but sometimes…

I wanted to ask Smith again how he saw himself in the mix of us.

What brother was he?

"He deserves someone like you," Smith finally said, snapping me back to the crowded noise of the restaurant.

"I…I'm rather fond of him," I confessed.

"He needs someone to be gentle with him, even if he won't admit that out loud."

It was such a thoughtful—and true—assessment. I wondered if Lincoln knew Smith had pinned him so fast, seen straight through to the heart of him.

"I know," I agreed.

"Don't hurt him," Smith said.

I huffed out a laugh, rolling my eyes and asking him the same thing I asked of Marshall. "Are you going to tell him the same about me?"

He stared at me, hard and unmoving. "Of course."

"Of course you will," I agreed, and then everything between us felt normal again. We ordered drinks, ordered food, and made small talk.

Smith asked if Silas knew about Lincoln and me, and I shared that he did, in no certain terms. Marshall knew, so of course Silas knew, but I didn't think Lincoln and Silas had talked about the whole thing. Smith agreed with me, changing the topic of conversation next to our newly found brother, Andrew.

"Do you talk to him often?" Smith asked.

"Not often. A couple weeks ago was the last time."

"Does he…does he want to talk to any of us or just you?"

"I don't know," I answered honestly. "He's still very private when it comes to us, like he doesn't want to let us in all the way. I think he's adjusting to the idea of having brothers."

"What even does that mean?" Smith shook his head, picking at the noodles he'd been working through for the past ten minutes before dropping his fork unceremoniously on the edge of the plate.

"The four of us grew up together."

"I didn't grow up with you."

"Over a decade, Smith," I reminded him. "It's nearly half your life."

"I had friends," he said quietly. "Before Mom…"

"Smith."

"I can't believe I ever thought of taking her name over Covington," he muttered, rubbing his fingertips across his cheeks. He looked so young and so old at the same time, and I had to admit I was out of my depth. This was Marshall's territory for sure. I had no clue how to talk Smith through this in a productive way.

"I'm sure she took care of you as best she could."

"She sold me out," he snapped.

It might have been the first time my brother had ever raised his voice at me, and I reeled back accordingly. My back hit the seat, and Smith sucked in a sharp breath, shaking his head and holding up his hands.

"I'm sorry," he said. "I didn't mean…"

"You don't have to apologize for having feelings."

It was then, I realized, I didn't know my brother at all. I knew him in the ways that he mirrored Marshall and me and Finn, and I understood him in the way I understood the others. In a way that resonated down to my marrow because we shared the same blood, and we would always be who we were, but each of us had half of someone else. In my case, someone I'd never really known, but Smith…

He had lived a whole life before coming into ours.

"It's complicated, isn't it?" I finally said.

He made a dismissive sound in the back of his throat but nodded his agreement just the same.

"I didn't mean to open up this can of worms," I told him, which earned me a laugh and a watery smile.

"This is more Marshall's speed, isn't it?"

Even though I didn't have the right words, I was ready to force myself to answer anyway. Saved, or not, by the ping of a meeting reminder chirping out of my cell phone that sat face down on the table. I flipped it over, frowning at the last-minute calendar invite from Caleb Winters, one of the equity partners at the firm. There was also a message from Lincoln, but I definitely wasn't about to open that in front of my brother.

I huffed out an exhale and shoved my plate into the middle of the table. "I know this is horrible timing, Smith, but—"

"You've got to get back to work."

"Yeah." I pulled my wallet out of my pocket to pay. "I hate to…but are you…"

"I'm good, Hunter," he said. "I promise."

"We can talk more on Friday?"

"You talk less when Finn is around," he said. "I'm good, though. I promise. And you know, Hunter…not like any of you have asked, but I do have friends."

Smith gave me a smile that felt a lot like scorn, then he stood up and fussed with his shirt.

"Thanks for lunch," he said, jerking his chin toward the wallet I still held in my hand.

"Anytime, Smith."

I watched him walk away, waiting until he was out of the restaurant to drop cash onto the table. I had fifteen minutes to get back to the office, and my heart was lodged in my throat for all of them. Last minute meetings were never good, but I was relatively certain I wasn't about to get fired. We'd just talked about me being made partner. Had I messed up a case or done something wrong that would jeopardize that? Lunch meetings weren't uncommon, but last-minute ones certainly were less usual.

By the time I made it back to the office, I didn't feel any better about the situation, but time was short. I made it to my desk with seconds to spare, barely enough time to throw a mint into my mouth before heading for the other side of the floor where Caleb's office took up the whole corner.

I knocked on the metal frame of his door, sticking my head around the corner to find him behind his desk with two of the other partners—Walsh and Shaw—sitting opposite him. My tongue stuck to the roof of my mouth like I'd used Velcro on it.

"Covington," he greeted, gesturing toward the other open seat across from his desk. "Thanks for coming on such short notice."

The comment was asinine. Like I had any choice.

"Of course," I said, sinking into the expensive leather.

"This will be quick," Caleb said. "We just wanted to congratulate you."

My teeth chattered together once, and then I clamped my jaw together hard so they didn't do it again. "Congratulate me?" I echoed.

"We've talked it over," Walsh said simply. "You've been here for your whole career, Covington, and you've done good work by us."

"You've been on an upward trajectory since day one," Winters said, nodding agreement with Walsh. "And you've taken the rest of us with you."

"We're thinking non-equity, Covington."

I nodded, grateful for the offer and even more so that I wasn't being asked to come up with a six figure buy-in for the honor.

"I'm…I don't know what to say."

"Hopefully yes," Winters said with a low laugh.

"Yes," I said quickly, nodding along in case the word didn't make it out of my mouth loudly enough. "Obviously, yes."

"We'll finish drafting up the papers then and get them to

you before the end of the day." Caleb stood up and shook my hand, then Walsh shook my hand, and that was that.

The thing I'd waited my whole career for was finally mine, and it had been fifteen-some-odd years of work for a two-minute conversation. The reality didn't feel real, and I made it back to my desk with sweaty palms and trembling fingers. I had known this was coming. Caleb had told me as much, but hearing the actual words, knowing the new contract was on its way to my inbox…

Lincoln was the first person I wanted to tell.

Fishing my phone out of my pocket, I opened my messaging app to text him, finding the one he'd sent me over lunch still unread. It was a video, and the freeze frame thumbnail looked like he'd taken it in my shower. Groaning, I jumped up from my desk, closed my office door, and locked it before sitting back down and digging out my headphones.

I pressed play and Lincoln's face filled my screen, his hair wet and slicked back, his chest dripping.

"You just left for work and I'm so fucking hard for you, Daddy," he said, voice not much more than a long and drawn-out moan. "Fuck. Fuck. I can still feel you inside of me."

Arousal churned low and hot in my belly, my cock immediately jerking to full mast at not just the sight of him, but the sound of him. I watched rapt as Lincoln stroked himself off in my shower, twisting and tweaking the barbells in his nipples while he dirty-talked me the whole time.

I want to tie you to your bed and tease your asshole until you come, and then tease you until you can't come anymore. Until you're just gasping and begging.

And then I want you to wake me up in the middle of the night…I need it. Need you to just take me. Want you to…

Tell me where to come. Tell me where I can come. I'll come on your face, Daddy. Sir, oh fuuuuuuck…

Lincoln was a vision, flushed and coming apart against the

back wall of my shower, and I was seconds away from coming in my fucking pants at my desk, dick untouched. I wanted to do all of the things he'd asked for. I wanted to give him everything. Even as I watched him pull himself together long enough to get back to his phone, my mind raced with fantasies of flip fucking him until we were both a sticky and sated mess.

I needed a detour to the bathroom, but right as I pulled the headphones out of my ears, I heard Lincoln's voice. The video cut off abruptly, and I sat back down in my chair, restarting it from the beginning and dragging the cursor back through to the very end. The camera was focused on his chest, water droplets racing down over his nipples as he picked his phone up from wherever he'd propped it up to film.

"I think I'm in love you," Lincoln whispered, and then the video cut to black.

The words were so quiet I almost missed them. They were clearly an accident, not meant for me, but I'd heard them just the same. At the sound of his voice, my balls churned and heat exploded at the base of my spine, shooting hard and fast like a gunshot.

I think I'm in love with you, he'd said.

And in reply?

I'd shot my load into my pants.

CHAPTER 19
LINCOLN

At five on the dot, Smith called me. I stared at his name on the caller ID until the very last second, swiping to accept the call because avoiding it would have been worse.

"Hello?"

"Hey."

I leaned my hip against my dresser, holding the phone to my ear. After spending a lazy morning at Hunter's, I'd spent the rest of the day at home, cleaning up and unpacking things I'd been ignoring since moving into the smaller studio apartment. I hated being there, and I hated being alone, but it was something I was going to have to get used to. I'd texted with Silas on and off throughout the day, and it was messages from him that confirmed Hunter had told Smith about us.

SILAS

I knew it.

Marshall just called.

Okay?

Smith had lunch with Hunter today.

I am shocked, Lincoln.

I thought for sure you and Smith were hooking up.

When did you even meet Hunter?

It's complicated.

But I thought you'd already figured it out.

"What are you up to?" I asked Smith.

"Just got off work." His frayed nerves were almost louder than his voice. "I wanted to see if you wanted to go pick up a second Cassandra."

"I'm not sure the point of it."

"So you're not alone," he said softly, trailing off before making a thoughtful sound.

"Hmn?"

"Nothing," he said. "Just realizing what brother I am."

I forced out a laugh, wondering if it was loud enough to make it around the elephant in the room. "The cryptic one?"

"Do you want to meet me somewhere or do you want me to pick you up?"

"If you want to pick me up, that's fine," I said.

"Alright. See you soon."

We hung up, and I tossed my phone on the bed, wringing my hands together, desperate to know for how long we were going to ignore the fact I was in a relationship with one of his brothers. The answer was apparently thirty-four minutes, because as soon as I sank down into the plush leather passenger seat of Smith's Range Rover, he turned to me with as much steel in his eyes as I imagined he could muster.

"So, you and Hunter?" he asked.

"Me and Hunter," I said. "I…we didn't want to keep it from you. He wanted to be the one to tell you is all."

"He's like Marshall sometimes."

"Are you mad?"

"If I was mad, do you think I'd be chauffeuring you to the pet store to get a new fish?"

Smith put the car into drive and pulled away from the curb. Some EDM bumped through the speakers, too low to hear the melody but loud enough to feel the bass of it. I swallowed hard, wiping my palms on the tops of my jeans.

"I just don't want it to be weird."

"If I didn't think the way you're affectionate with my other brother's boyfriend was weird, I don't think you actually dating another would be." Smith threw me a sidelong glance as we cruised through a green light. "I never had any delusions that you and I were anything besides what we were. It would be weird for you to *not* date my brother. I mean, if you were interested in him."

I arched a brow.

"Because that would mean we'd lied to each other about what we are," he explained, shrugging up one shoulder. "I just want to make sure you're serious about him."

Palm trees flew by, and I was very close to telling Smith exactly just how serious I was about his brother, but being in love after a week or two was probably the biggest red flag to ever red flag.

"Your brother is a good man," I said. "I'll do right by him. At least, as right as I can."

That seemed to be satisfactory, judging by the quiet way Smith's jaw clicked after I finished speaking. I stared out the window as Smith drove us out of my part of town and into his. The strip malls were nicer, taller, whiter. The neon signs were crisp and clean fonts, a sharp contrast from the bright mismatched colors of my neighborhood. Eventually, we pulled up in front of a nondescript looking pet store, and Smith cut the engine.

"Do you think I'll have a better chance of keeping a bougie fish alive?" I teased, unbuckling my belt.

"It's your best shot," he agreed, reaching over the console and sliding his hand around the back of my neck. His fingers were warm and long, and he hauled me toward the center console, pressing our foreheads together and letting out a long breath.

My first reaction was to tense up, worried that Smith was going to kiss me, which…would have been fine. It wouldn't have meant anything, even if that might have been a blurrier line than some of my other ones. He didn't kiss me, though. He didn't hug me either. He only held me there, our noses brushing together and our breath mingling in the very small space between our mouths.

"Hey," I whispered, reaching up and covering his hand with mine.

"Hey."

And still, no movement. I lifted my other hand toward his face, my thumb grazing over his cheek while my fingers stretched around the side of his neck. Smith let out a little moan, leaning into my hand while still keeping our foreheads in close contact together.

"Just another minute," he murmured.

I exhaled, shoulders relaxing.

"I get it," he finally said, giving my neck a squeeze before extricating himself from the car. I chuckled, following him out and onto the sidewalk in front of the store.

"Get what?"

"The affection thing."

Stepping up beside him, I hooked my arm through the crook of his elbow, pulling him toward the door.

"It's nice to know you're not alone sometimes," I said.

He nodded, holding open the door to the pet store for me.

We walked inside and were met with more white, more

uniform displays, more minimalism. It looked like the antithesis of a pet store to me. No kibble on the ground, no bright and squeaky pet toys lining racks along the wall.

"This place is very beige," I said.

"Mostly."

Smith walked us to the back of the store where the beige finally gave way to a massive wall of colored fish. Some in large aquariums and some in small take-home containers. They were all stacked in the wall like a rainbow mosaic.

"Oh," I breathed out.

Smith laughed, untangling our arms so I could browse the wall freely.

There were fish in the wall I'd never even heard of and probably could never afford, but mixed in with all of those were the occasional goldfish and the brightly colored bettas. I walked the wall three times, scanning from top to bottom, middle to bottom, top to middle. This was my second chance at having a fish, and it was probably also my last chance. If Cassandra Jr. didn't make it, I was sure there would be no third attempt. I needed to pick a fish who would survive the transfer, but I didn't want to ignore the sad little swimmers either.

"Hey."

Smith crooked his fingers, calling me over toward the other end of the wall. He stood in front of a massive aquarium, but immediately I saw the fish he was pointing out for me. It was a betta, like Cassandra, but their container was twice as big, their tail twice as frilled. They were a dark reddish orange, and I imagined if a Phoenix were a real animal, it would look a lot like that.

"Good call," I agreed.

"I'll go find some help."

Smith ventured off to find someone who knew how to Jenga the fish out of the wall without collapsing everything, and I took a step closer until I had to tip my chin up to look at the fish. They were perfect.

"You find something you like?" a female employee asked, Smith flanking her on the approach.

I nodded and pointed toward the fiery betta. "This one."

"A good choice."

"They'll make it," Smith said to me, brow knitting together when the employee threw him a curious look. "His last fish died."

"On arrival," I muttered.

The employee looked shocked, adjusting her keys on her arm. "From here?"

"No. From a store by my house."

She gave me a quick onceover, obviously assessing the differences between me and Smith, correctly judging what part of town I came from.

"Most places neglect their fish," she said, busying herself with shifting the fish's container out of the mosaic. Once the fish was free, I realized there were a series of intricate and thin shelves jutting out from the wall to hold the containers. The foundation was sturdy, even if it didn't look that way.

"And you don't?" I asked.

"No," she said simply. "We don't. Do you need a bowl or food?"

"I still have it," I rasped.

She nodded, carrying my second chance at fish fatherhood toward the register area. Smith and I followed after her, and I paid her twice as much as I'd paid for Cassandra, accepted her upsell of some treatment for the water, and then Smith and I were on our way. I held the fish on my lap the whole drive back to my apartment, lifting the container off my lap when Smith took a turn too hard. I didn't want the fish jostled or scared.

I wanted them to have their best chance at a life with me.

"Can I come up?" he asked after we parked.

"I've been unpacking all day; my apartment is a mess."

"I don't mind."

"It's small," I said.

"Okay."

"I don't even have a couch right now."

"I can stand," Smith said.

I realized there was no getting out of it now. Smith Covington was my friend.

"Okay," I conceded.

We rode the elevator up to my apartment, and if Smith found my studio lacking in any way, he didn't say a single thing about it. He walked right to my bed and sat down on the edge of it, leaning back and holding himself up with his arms behind him.

"It's not that small," he remarked.

"It's the size of your brother's bedroom."

"They're all extravagant."

I set the fish down on my dresser beside the empty bowl.

"And you're not?" I laughed at him, taking the bowl to the kitchenette. Silas had cleaned the whole thing out for me after Cassandra died, and he'd tucked all the rocks and coral and decorations into individual zipper baggies.

Smith shifted his positioning on my bed so he could talk at me while I reassembled the fish home by my sink.

"I'm not."

"You drive a Range Rover," I reminded him.

Smith shrugged, and I couldn't help but roll my eyes at him.

"I didn't grow up with money," he said. "My mom didn't take the deal, you know. It took me a long time to get used to the extravagance."

"But you managed."

He chewed at the inside of his cheek, and I dumped the rainbow rocks into the bottom of the fish bowl.

"I didn't have a choice," he said.

"You got a college education out of it."

"I got a lot out of it." Smith's mouth pulled into an adorable little frown that made him look a lot like a kicked puppy. He was going to be a handful for someone someday, that was for sure. He wasn't quite a brat, but the way that man needed a fucking Daddy was a study for the textbooks.

"Worth it in the end?" I asked, shoving a plastic stalk of leaves into the rocks, then another.

"Sometimes I'm not sure."

"I think it's easy to be jaded on silver spoons when you're surrounded by them."

He didn't have anything to say to that, and I worried it might have been a little harsh. I filled the bowl with water and carried it back to the dresser, sitting down beside Smith on the bed before dealing with the fish transfer.

"You look like you need a hug," I said, pulling him into my arms before he could argue with me.

Smith came easily, allowing me to pull his much taller and lankier frame halfway onto my lap without so much as a single protest. He weighed more than I remembered, and I grunted through rearranging our bodies on the bed so I could prop myself—and him—against the wall. He wrapped his arms around my waist, cheek pressed against my chest, and I sighed, kissing the top of his hair.

"What's going on with you?" I asked. "I've been very focused on me and my fish, and I'm also used to Silas telling me everything without prompting. You seem like the type to need prompting."

Smith's shoulders jiggled with a laugh, and I held him tighter.

"I'm just questioning *everything*." He squeezed me, then unfolded himself from my arms and collapsed onto his back beside me.

"Everything could mean a lot of things."

"When I was younger, I really wanted to be just like Marshall. I even went into design because of him. I drink wine because of him."

I didn't say a word.

"I love my brother. I love all of them, but they're all so…" he trailed off, frowning himself into that puppy look again.

"Controlling," I offered. The word I'd wanted to use was dominant, but…

"That's a nice way to put it."

"They love you," I said. "I don't know Marshall well, but it's clear how much he cares about you and your feelings. He would do anything for you."

"I know."

"And Hunter," I added, because I did know that Covington brother better than the rest, and Hunter's devotion was unmatched. "I'm sure Finn too."

"Sometimes, it feels like I can't make decisions for myself. Like there's this Covington mold, and I can't get out of it."

I thought about what I knew of Smith, and of Marshall, and of Hunter, and for the life of me, I couldn't understand why anyone would want to get out of that mold. All the Covington men I knew were thoughtful, devoted, and loyal beyond measure. But I also appreciated that I viewed all of them and their lives from the outside. Smith was the one who'd lived it. He would know better than anyone else the burdens and responsibilities.

"Your brothers are smothering," I tried, and he nodded, flinging an arm over his eyes. "You can't figure things out for yourself because they're always offering their ideas for you before you even get the chance."

"How did you know?" he asked with a watery laugh.

"I know their type," I said, noncommittally.

Smith groaned, rolling onto his stomach and folding his arms together beneath his head to form a makeshift pillow.

"Your fish is staring at that bowl like it's heaven," he said, the words garbled around his arm. "You should let them into it."

I wasn't sure if he was talking about himself really or the fish. Wasn't sure if he was talking about *me* or the fish.

"You're right," I agreed anyway, sliding away from him and scooting toward my dresser.

Careful as could be, I transferred Cassandra Jr.—which definitely felt like the wrong name—from their plastic takeout container into the forever bowl. As soon as they landed in the water, their tail frilled up and they swam in a circle before settling into a calm and quiet float in the middle of the bowl.

"How're they doing?" Smith asked, crawling across my bed and propping his chin on my shoulder.

We both watched the fish hover in the water, and even though I didn't know how to explain it, they just looked a lot happier in their new environment.

"Sometimes change is good," I murmured.

Smith licked his lips, the movement gouging his chin down into the soft meat of my shoulder.

"Sometimes," he agreed, then a long pause before asking, "What are you going to call this one? They're not a Cassandra."

"I know." I tilted my head to the side to rest against his. "Phoenix feels right, but also too on the nose."

"I'd say Finn, but that's my brother's name."

"Feeny?" I tried. "Short for Phoenix, and we'll just never tell anyone that?"

Smith nodded his head beside mine. "Feeny is a good name."

We watched Feeny swim around the bowl, feeling out the

space before making a big loop around the stalk of leaves. Yeah, the fish was definitely happy to be home, and I hoped that eventually I would be too.

CHAPTER 20
HUNTER

I hadn't heard a peep from Lincoln since he'd sent me that video before lunch. I didn't know if he realized he'd sent me the hottest jerk-off video on the planet with an accidental love confession at the end or not, and I also hadn't decided if I was meant to ignore it until he told me in person, or if I should say something about it the next time we talked. The video was enough to throw me off-balance for the rest of the day, the partnership offer was going to have me off-kilter for the rest of the week.

Getting out of work, my phone was still quiet.

Getting home, still quiet.

Just before six, Smith texted me a photo of a red and orange betta fish, so I took that to mean he was with Lincoln, and I didn't know how that made me feel. Instead of trying to figure it out, I called Finn. It went to voicemail, but I was in the middle of leaving one when he called me back, and I answered that call on the first ring.

"Busy?" I asked.

"A bit, but…" He let that go unfinished. "What's up?"

"Needed to talk to someone is all," I said.

"Are you looking for advice because I'm the last person—"

"I'd call Marshall if I wanted advice," I interrupted, which earned me a sharp laugh.

"I should be offended, I think," Finn muttered. Somewhere behind him, a door slammed closed. "But I don't have grounds for it today."

"Everything good with you?"

"Peachy," he answered, sarcasm dripping off every syllable. "Do you want me to come over?"

"Already too tired of your pretty pink office to have me over?" I teased.

"I'll see you eventually."

The eyeroll was loud enough for me to hear, even over the beep of the call being disconnected. Scrubbing a hand down my face, I dropped my head back to stare up at the ceiling. I still held my phone, and it would have been so easy to call Lincoln, to ask what he and Smith were up to, to ask the name of his new fish, to make him tell me again that he loved me.

Love was such a foreign concept for me, at least romantically. It had been years since I'd even entertained the idea, and not for lack of wanting, just lack of trying. All of my brothers had been single for so long, wrapped up with careers and legacies, there hadn't been much time for anything serious to develop. I'd been perfectly content taking orgasms from the random men who paid for them, but now that I had Lincoln, everything I'd enjoyed before him felt lacking to me.

I imagined it had been the same way with Marshall and Silas at first. What an odd experience to not even realize how empty your life was until someone came along and filled a hole you'd never even been aware of. That was how I felt about Lincoln, and maybe it was fast, maybe it was wrong… He was so confused about who he was separate of Silas and who he was apart from being dominant. I worried he was using me—even unintentionally—to work through the mess in his own brain, and that once he figured out which way was up, he wouldn't want me anymore.

He said he was in love with you, my brain helpfully reminded me, but my heart still fought against it, terrified somehow of the notion. Any other man would have been scared of the comfort I found from being on my knees in front of Silas, but that was truly where I felt the most at home. I had no problem having him kneel for me when it suited him either, even though I was starting to think he really only craved it because he was chasing after the feeling of being cared for, which I could do even if we were standing eye to eye.

I would prove it to him.

To myself.

A loud and annoying knock on my door announced Finn's arrival, and when I opened it to let him in, my brother stood on my front mat, looking less put together than I could remember ever seeing him. His normally styled hair was loose around his face like it had started coiffed and come apart after having too many hands run through it. There were bags under his eyes and scruff on his jaw that looked like it had been there longer than the day. He was still dressed for work, slacks and a button-up, but he'd managed to get the cuffs undone, though not rolled.

"You look horrible," I greeted, and he narrowed his eyes at me, pushing past me into my apartment.

He was quick to make himself at home on my couch, kicking off his Oxfords before propping his feet up on the edge of my table and letting his head fall against the back of the couch.

"I look like I need a drink," he said.

"I guess you're in the right place or something," I cracked, even though I could tell he wasn't up for it.

I closed and locked the door, then headed into the kitchen

to get him some whiskey. I poured myself a vodka and soda, then joined him on the couch, mirroring his pose.

"Are you sure you're not the one who should have called Marshall?" I knocked my elbow into the outside of his arm, and he took it as a signal to lift his glass and take a drink.

"Marshall would not be impressed with my most recent life choices." Finn sucked his tongue across the front of his teeth… just like Marshall.

"I'm sure it can't be as bad as masquerading as an escort on a hookup app and accidentally getting into a relationship with a client."

My brother made a dismissive sound in the back of his throat. "That would be a story."

"I know," I agreed.

"But no, it's worse."

I stared down the length of our legs, straight down to our sock-covered toes. Finn and I were so much alike and so different at the same time. And still, nobody knew me better than him. Tension knotted together in my shoulders, guilt over letting him think all my jokes about hooking up with men for money were just that…jokes. I'd convinced myself it was okay to have secrets sometimes, especially if they weren't hurting anybody, but when it came to Finn, I felt the worst about it.

"How is it worse?" I asked instead of coming clean.

"You're going to laugh."

"Probably."

Finn took a healthy drink of his whiskey and sighed. This was so often the way of things with us, one of us needing something and the other needing something different at the same time. I'd called Finn because I didn't want to be alone with my brain about Lincoln and his admission, but Finn had clearly needed me to work through something with him as well. It was a give and take, a balance…

A brotherhood.

"I've been seeing someone," he finally admitted. "A couple someones."

"Dating, then?"

"Yes, but also…" My brother grimaced, downing the rest of his drink before smacking his lips together. "I was dating a married couple."

Another unanticipated confession.

"Okay," I said, because there wasn't anything else. "Are you not now?"

"No."

"Is this recent?"

He shook the ice around his glass and frowned. "Very."

"For how long?" I asked.

"A few months."

"When did it end?"

Sighing, Finn pushed himself up off the couch. He stretched and walked into my kitchen to mix himself another drink, then returned to the space beside me. He set his glass on the arm of the couch and finally finished rolling up his sleeves, then took a normal person-sized sip of whiskey.

"Today." He sniffed a little, rubbed his nose with the knuckle on his thumb.

"Did you want to talk about it? Do you want to tell me their names?"

"Not really," he mumbled. "Neil and Annette."

"How did you meet them?" I asked.

Finn exhaled dramatically and angled his face toward mine. "Why did you call me? What did *you* want?"

There was no accusation in the tone, only the simple recognition that I'd needed something from my closest brother when I'd made the decision to dial his number and not Smith's or Marshall's. It was also a clear deflection that when he said he didn't want to talk about Neil and Annette, he'd meant it.

"I've gotten involved with Silas' best friend."

Finn snorted and rolled his eyes at me. "Involved."

"We're seeing each other," I corrected.

"I always expected Marshall to go for someone younger, but never pinned that taste onto you."

I took a drink of vodka and then kicked Finn in the ankle. Hard.

He grimaced and used his other foot to rub away the ache.

"He's not even ten years younger than me, and I don't even notice the difference most of the time."

"Most of the time."

"Ever."

Finn puffed out his cheeks. "Go on."

"I'm not asking for advice," I reminded him, and it was doubly true now considering Finn was obviously working through some messy and complicated sort of heartbreak. "He said he was in love with me, but I wasn't supposed to hear it. It was on the back end of a video he sent me earlier today."

"A video," Finn mused.

"Oh." I lifted my glass, ignoring the amusement in his voice. "I also made partner today."

"Nice try to change the subject."

"No, really." I leaned forward and set my drink down on the coffee table, pressing my knees into the outside of Finn's thigh. "I made partner."

His expression went from weary to elated in less than two seconds, and then I was in my brother's arms, his face buried into the crook of my neck.

"I'm so fucking excited for you," he said into my skin.

I clapped him on the back, and he tightened his arms around me, which felt so fucking good. Finn held me for longer than he had in years, but by the time the hug ended, the pressure of it had shifted. He was the one holding on to me, and my hand against the back of his head kept him steady and still against my chest. He breathed heavy and hard, and I knew him well enough to know he was fighting back tears.

I also knew they had nothing to do with my new partnership.

"I'm so proud of you," he said, trying to pull away even though I stopped him. "You've worked so hard for this."

I nodded, smoothing my hand down the back of his neck.

We stayed in that embrace for another few minutes, finally untangling our arms from the other at the same time. Finn's eyes were red, but mostly dry, and he ran his hand over the front of his shirt and smiled at me.

"You're the first person I've told."

"You'll bloat my ego, Hunt, be careful." He smoothed his hair back, but there was no keeping the stray strands in place. "Is this news for dinner on Friday then?"

"Yeah, probably."

"Is Silas' little bestie also news for Friday?"

Jesus, Finn was a master at keeping the conversation right where he wanted it to be and not a smidge offtrack.

"Marshall already knows and so does Smith."

Finn frowned. "That counters all the work you just did on my ego."

I chuckled, shaking my head. "Smith and Lincoln have become friends, and I wanted to make sure he was okay with the idea of us dating. And Marshall obviously knows because of Silas."

"Sounds like excuses."

I shrugged and held my hands up helplessly.

"And he's in love with you?" Finn asked.

I nodded.

"Why is that so bad?" he rasped, voice cracking.

I cocked my head to the side and arched a brow at his break.

Finn cleared his throat and shook his head, and I loved him enough to not press the issue further.

"I…" I didn't have a good answer. "It's just new."

"That's not a real reason."

"I know," I whispered.

He pulled his lips together between his teeth, working them until they were both dark pink and indented from the pressure.

"Do you think there's like…some metric about this? That you're not allowed to have feelings until x amount of time has passed?"

"It sounds ridiculous when you say it like that."

"It sounds ridiculous when you say it your way," he countered.

I sagged against the couch, against my brother, my closest confidant for all of the life that I could remember.

"I'm sorry things didn't work out with Neil and Annette," I told him gently.

His arm tensed, but he lifted it and took a drink of his whiskey.

"I'm not," he said.

"Finn."

"Are you in love with…I don't even…what did you say his name was? Lincoln?"

"Lincoln," I confirmed.

"Are you in love with Lincoln too?"

This was the real reason I'd called Finn. I needed someone else to ask the question, to put me on the spot and force me to sit down and really think about it until I was able to get to an answer. If I shoved away all the ideas of what society felt an appropriate time for those feelings to develop, if I ignored the —very small—age gap between us, if I only paid attention to the two things that mattered the most…me and him…

"Yes," I confessed to my brother. "I am."

CHAPTER 21
LINCOLN

Smith left just after nine, and as soon as the door to my apartment was closed, I had my phone out to text Hunter.

> Hey

> Smith just left. It went well.

> We got me a new fish.

> Smith sent me a picture

> What name did you settle on this time?

> Feeny.

> Cute.

> What are you up to?

> I didn't do it to get a response, but I sort of thought I would hear from you after I sent that video earlier today.

The idea had been brewing in my head all day long, eating away at me a little more every hour that went by without a response from Hunter. I knew he worked, and I knew his work was often busy, but the fact I'd sent him that video, which was one of the most revealing things I'd ever done, and he'd ignored it did not sit well with me. By the time Smith called it a night, I was barely able to hide the way the silence had me crawling out of my skin.

> I liked it A LOT, Lincoln.

> Do you want to come over?

I frowned down at the lower half of my body, clothed in threadbare plaid pajama pants. My piercings glinted under the shitty light of my studio fluorescents and nothing sounded better than being in the warm comfort of Hunter's apartment, but the last thing I wanted to do was put on shoes and a shirt and drive across down. In answer to his question, I sent him a picture of my bare chest, my low-slung pajamas, the tangled sheets beneath my legs. His next text came quickly.

> Do you want ME to come over?

> My place is small and cramped.

> If you don't want me to come over, that's okay, Lincoln.

> I'm not feeling very myself.

> And you don't want help with that?

> Let me get you a ride. Come over here and spend the night with me.

> I want to watch this video with you next to me.

Heat burned my cheeks.

> That sounds horrible.

Is that a limit?

My breath caught in my throat, a violent knot of emotion.

No, Sir.

Then send me your address, and I'll arrange a ride. You don't need to change out of your pajamas if you don't want to.

Okay.

I sent him my address and rolled over onto my stomach, burying my face into a pillow and screaming. I had no idea if I was excited about this or terrified, if I was only uncomfortable from the unintentional pity party I'd had with Smith earlier, or lonely from the fact my time with Silas had been reduced to one a night a week. There'd been so much change in such a short time, and to say I felt lost was an understatement.

Patron saint of broken compasses and bad directions, even though I knew the way to Hunter's by heart.

I pulled on a t-shirt and some sneakers, then shoved a change of clothes and my toothbrush into an overnight bag. I got everything together with two minutes to spare, and then there was a black town car on the street and a kind-looking driver who confirmed my name before opening the back door for me.

Was this how Julia Roberts felt in *Pretty Woman*?

The ride to Hunter's house went quickly, and as usual, his door was cracked open when I got there. He was still dressed for work, at least halfway, wearing not much more than dark gray slacks and a black leather belt. He had a mostly drunk glass of whiskey in his hand and a tilt to his head that spelled trouble for me. As soon as I closed the door behind me, he jerked his chin upward.

"Are you good?" he asked.

I nodded.

"Go into the bedroom and get naked," he said. "Get on your knees."

Heat tore up the length of my spine, and I only stumbled twice trying to get out of my sneakers in the entryway. Getting naked would be easy, considering I didn't have any underwear on beneath the pajama pants to begin with. Hunter stayed still as I passed him, and I went into his bedroom alone, stripping out of my pajamas and going onto my knees in front of his bed.

Even though we'd been playing with this switch kind of dynamic, this was the first time Hunter had truly taken control without prompting, and the arousal was already a tangible and growing thing inside of me. Threading my fingers together at the base of my skull, I exposed myself fully and waited for Hunter.

When he made it to the bedroom, he had a fresh drink, same glass but a lot more clear, like he'd topped whatever he'd been finishing off with water. He took a sip of it before resting his ass against his dresser, facing me head on. I don't know what I expected of him, and the nerves of trying to anticipate had me feeling all sorts of awkward. It seemed he could sense it, or worse, that he was okay with my discomfort. He waited me out until I'd exhausted myself of worrying, until my weight sank heavier down onto my heels.

Finally, he reached into his pocket and pulled out his cellphone, swiping through the screen until the sound of a shower filled the room. His mouth twitched in the corner, and he held his phone out for me.

"Hold this so I can see it," he murmured.

I took the device and held it in front of my chest, screen out. Honestly, it was a relief he wasn't going to make me watch it, but I was a little miffed he wanted to watch it when he had the real thing right in front of him. My body didn't seem to care much, my dick jerking toward arousal at the sound of my own noises filtering out of the phone.

Hunter set down his drink, then with one hand, took off his belt and pulled down his fly. His cock was already hard, and he stroked himself with a rough, overhand pull from root to tip. I watched him quietly, ignoring my own erection while he stroked his, allowing my eyes to roam over his body while he focused his attention on the phone in my hand. It was a fucked-up kind of game, this little box between us, but I appreciated the tease of it, even as precum leaked from the slit of my cock.

About halfway through the video, his attention shifted from the phone to my face, his pupils blown into wide black pools. I desperately wanted to watch his hand move up his shaft, but it was impossible to look away from his chin quivering with pleasure right in front of me. I listened to myself finish, and Hunter was close himself but not quite there. He stroked himself faster, the sound of the shower the only thing left in the room, and then...

"I think I'm in love with you."

It was my voice not his, almost overshadowed by the strangled cry that tore out of Hunter's throat as he came all over his hand. I tightened my grip on the phone, all of the heat immediately draining out of my face. My palms went clammy and my jaw slack, but Hunter held my stare as he stroked himself through the rest of his orgasm. With cum smeared across his fingers and his stomach, he dropped his weight fully against the dresser, and the video on his phone started to play again from the beginning.

I was such an idiot.

Still on my knees, still holding the phone, I closed my eyes and dropped my chin against my chest. My cock was still annoyingly hard, not put off in the least by what had just happened, by what I'd just confessed. After what felt like a lifetime of silence, Hunter took another sip from his glass, fingers leaving cum streaks across the crystal.

"Did you mean to send me that?" he asked.

"I think it's obvious that I didn't," I muttered, my own moans still drifting from the speakers as the video restarted.

I need it. I need you to take me.

"Did you mean it?"

I hoped my face didn't give me away. I hoped he wasn't going to make me answer.

"What were you thinking when you were saying those things? Not the last part…the rest," he asked instead. "What were you fantasizing about?"

I blinked hard, frowning at Hunter's still half hard and cum-covered cock and the way it rested against his thigh.

"It's…" I was more embarrassed and exposed than I'd ever been in my life, and that was saying a lot.

"It's all right," he said, tone going soft. He crooked a finger and beckoned me closer. I knee-walked from my place in front of the bed to right in front of him, close enough I could have pressed my mouth against his cock if I wanted.

"I…"

What were words?

"Lincoln." Hunter took the phone out of my hand and set it down beside his drink, still playing, then he very gently carded his fingers through my hair until I took a breath and closed the space between us, resting my cheek on his thigh, my mouth inches from his cock. "Tell Daddy what you were thinking about."

My eyes rolled back, and I groaned, wrapping my arms around his legs and using his body to keep myself from melting into the floor. I'd never been into the Daddy thing before, not on either side of it, but something about casually using it with Hunter had me so fucking hot for it.

"I was thinking about you DP-ing me," I admitted.

"Fucking me with your cock and a dildo at the same time. I was thinking about your waking me up and using me to get off then rolling over and going back to sleep."

His fingers tightened in my hair briefly, then he was back to the same gentle glide from top to back and top to back. "What else?"

I chewed at the inside of my cheek and shook my head. There was no way I would tell him the rest.

No way I *could*.

He made an unhappy sound, moving me toward his cock and feeding it into my mouth, one inch at a time. He wasn't fully erect, so it was easy to fit the whole of him against my tongue, and when I sealed my lips around his base, Hunter groaned low and long.

"When I fantasize about you, I think of all sorts of things," he murmured, pumping his hips and burying my nose into the trimmed hair around the root of his shaft. My eyes watered as his cock swelled against my tongue, but I blinked the tears away instead of fighting it. "I do think about using you whenever I want. Sometimes, I imagine having you come to my office and sucking me off under my desk. I made partner today. It would have been a great way to celebrate."

The unanticipated announcement was enough to make me choke, but Hunter's hand on the back of my head tightened, and he kept me in place between his legs when I tried to pull away.

"I like you like this," he said, and it was enough to make me go still. "You can't argue with a mouthful of cock. You can't overthink."

I grunted, and he thrust himself deeper into my mouth.

"Let me tell you what I think about it, yes?"

I hummed my agreement around his cock and relaxed against him, even as spit bubbled out of the corners of my mouth.

"I think you're tired, Lincoln. I think you're tired of always trying, but you don't know how to stop, don't feel safe to stop."

Even if I wanted to argue, I couldn't have. Hunter was almost fully hard, and it took all my focus to not accidentally clamp my teeth into his cock when I tried to breathe around his thickness.

"But you feel safe here. Don't you?" He angled my head a little so I was forced to look up at him, and the look of pure and utter sincerity on his face was enough to push those earlier tears right over the edge of my lash line.

Hunter stroked his thumbs over my cheeks, catching them as they fell. The corner of his mouth tipped into a sad kind of smile and he nodded his agreement. His confirmation.

"You feel safe with Daddy, don't you?"

I answered him with a garbled nod and a hard suck.

His smile turned into a grimace, and he thrust deeply once, twice into my throat, fingers digging hard into my skull in the most pleasurable way possible.

"You feel safe like this, and you feel safe when I'm the one on my knees too, isn't that right?"

I blinked hard and nodded again.

"That feels a lot like love, doesn't it?" Hunter groaned, pumping his hips again. He was fucking my throat with the shortest and most gentle thrusts, and he'd eased his way so far into my throat I couldn't ever imagine having him anywhere but there again. It wasn't overwhelming; it wasn't consuming.

It was perfect.

"So." He pulled out and I cried, chasing after him but being held back by his punishing grip. "Did you mean it?"

"I meant it," I swore, staring up at him to make sure he knew it. "I meant it. I'm so fucking in love with you, and I don't think I've ever—"

I couldn't even finish the confession. Hunter had clearly heard what he wanted to hear because his cock was back in my mouth and the first spray of cum shot hot and wet against the roof of my mouth. Another on my tongue, the rest of his orgasm spilling down my throat.

Fuck.

Fuck.

Fuck, I loved how sensitive he was. How easy it was to get him off.

Moaning, I hollowed my cheeks and sucked the cum out of him, no longer embarrassed over the confession I'd never meant to give. Hunter liked that I was in love with him, but more than that, I was *safe here* to be in love with him. And it was so unlike any feeling I'd ever had before. The sense of protection and homecoming when I was with this man was so different from the way I felt for Silas, for Smith.

My friends.

Hunter was so much more than that. He was everything.

With a shudder that rippled through his entire body, Hunter pulled his cock out of my mouth and cradled my face in his hands, holding me so I couldn't look away from him even if I'd wanted to.

"Tell me."

"I love you. I'm in love with you."

My chin trembled, the tremor getting worse when Hunter traced his cum-stained fingers across my swollen lips, hooking them over my teeth.

"I love you too," he whispered, and then he was on his knees and his mouth was on mine, his fingers still in the way of our tongues, but I didn't mind. He pulled my mouth open to make room for his teeth against mine, his lips, his tongue. I swirled mine around his fingers, chasing the taste of him and sighing happily when he finally took them away so he could kiss me deeper.

He kissed me so fucking hard I forgot my name, and then I was on my back, Hunter on top of me. Our mouths still fused together, Hunter took my own aching dick into his hand, rutting against me while he stroked me off. It didn't take long for me to come after that. Before Hunter, I would have called my duration embarrassingly short, but after a recurring first row seat to how perfect he looked when *he* came in seconds, that worry was long gone. Hunter swallowed down my cries when I came, only breaking away to pepper kisses against my jaw when it was too hard for me to breathe.

He kept his hand fisted around my cock long past the end of my orgasm, and his face buried into the crook of my neck. With one last groan, Hunter thrust over the top of me and shuddered before collapsing onto his back beside me on the floor. We both struggled to breathe, but when his fingers sought out mine and he raised our hands to his mouth for a kiss, catching my breath had never been easier.

CHAPTER 22
HUNTER

After getting us both off, I scooped Lincoln off the floor and set him on my bed. I rarely found myself aware of the difference in our sizes, but when he nestled himself against my chest it was impossible to miss. Lincoln had been so strong for so long, especially when it came to the front he put on around Silas, and I wondered—but was afraid to ask —if the only time he was able to stop pretending was when he was with me.

"Under the blankets," I said softly, tugging down the sheets and lifting them up over his legs. Lincoln sat up against the headboard and blinked slowly, reaching out to slide his fingers through my hair.

"You're the best Daddy," he murmured. "The best submissive."

I made an affirmative sound in the back of my throat and pulled his hand out of my hair, bringing it down to my mouth to kiss his knuckles. Being both to a man like Lincoln was a terrifying prospect, but I'd never felt more up to the challenge. Playing both sides of this coin came naturally where he was concerned, and we both found ourselves moving easily from one to the other and sometimes back again. But in that moment, I was the one calling the shots, and Lincoln needed some quiet care and attention.

"I'm going to get you something to eat and drink, and then we're going to bed," I said.

Reluctantly, I left him there in my bed, but only long enough to get some cheese, crackers, and a bottle of water from the kitchen. By the time I made it back to the bedroom, he had slid halfway down the wall and was fast asleep. I did debate the merits of waking him up, but decided sleep was acceptable, all things considered. We'd both had long days with confessions to our friends and to each other. Rest was most likely the best course of action, and even though I had to work the next day, I loved the idea of Lincoln staying over and lazing around my apartment until he was ready to leave.

After all, that was how we'd admitted our feelings to each other.

Lord fucking knew what would come next.

Popping a cube of cheese into my mouth, I stripped out of my soiled pants, turned off all the lights, and tucked into bed beside him. Lincoln groaned and rolled over into my arms, sighing happily before letting out a quiet snore against my chest. Sleep came quickly for me, and I followed right after Lincoln into my dreams.

I woke hours, minutes…sometime later, the blankets tangled around my thighs and sweat pooled between my pecs. Beside me, Lincoln was on his stomach, face buried in the pillow and the sheets shoved off him and onto me. Blinking slowly, I waited for my eyes to adjust to the darkness of the room, waited until the moonlight was enough for me to make out the pale and round swells of his ass.

I want you to wake me up in the middle of the night and take me.

Lincoln's interest in free use had been an elephant between us from the first time he'd brought it up. I knew going into a relationship with him there were things he understood about himself that I wasn't privy to, and I also knew he had far more experience in the world of kink than I did. I didn't hate that imbalance between us because kneeling for Lincoln came as naturally as putting him onto his knees instead. I was under no illusion that things between us were typical—or even right—but they worked for us and that was the only thing that mattered.

I'd just made partner at work, and Lincoln Summers was in love with me.

I couldn't ask for much more than that.

It was with that happiness that I found myself reaching over to the nightstand for the lube, and with that sense of fulfillment that I slicked my fingers and my cock, stroking myself until I was hard and leaking. I wanted Lincoln, of course I did, but something about the premise of using him just for my pleasure felt wrong. Of course I wanted to get off when we were intimate, but I wanted him to enjoy it as well.

Would he really enjoy me climbing on top of him in the middle of the night and fucking him? I knew from my time on the app that there were plenty of things people were into that didn't necessarily do it for me…and that was fine, but I loved Lincoln. The last thing I wanted to do was hurt him or make him feel unsafe with me. He called me Daddy when it suited him, but it was important to me he found that comfort and protection when we were together.

Honorific or not.

My dick hurt for how hard I was. He wants this, I reminded myself, and if the state of my cock was any indicator, so did I. Before I could talk myself out of it, I mounted Lincoln's sleeping form and pinned his hands together over his head. He was a deep sleeper, making a grunt at the movement but not much else. With my other hand, I lined my cock up with his hole, wondering if free use meant no prep.

I'd have to ask him in the morning what he wanted, but I

didn't feel right about going in cock first without being certain. I shifted my weight over the top of him and eased one of my fingers into him. He roused, eyebrows lifting, but his eyes didn't make it to looking awake. I pumped one finger in and out of him, relishing how tight his body fought against me when I pushed a second in. It was the middle finger that woke him up, and that had me switching my fingers for my cock.

Lincoln whimpered, and I pushed his wrists down firmly against the pillow, thrusting slow until the entire length of my cock had entered him. A shiver rippled up my spine at the sleepiness of the whole thing, an unexpected sort of pleasure and arousal wrapping around both of us when I began to move.

"Hmph." He rolled his face into the sheets, dipping a steep arch into his back to take me deeper. "You feel so good. Oh, fuck."

He was the one who felt good. Pliant and warm and tight in all the right places. I didn't need to reach around the front of him and grasp his cock to know he was also hard. Any other time or place, I would have, but he'd been specific with his ask. He wanted me to take him and not worry about his pleasure, only my own. Considering I was also still half-asleep, that didn't take a lot of work. My body was the only part of me awake, and Lincoln's whimpers and moans only spurred me on.

"Gonna come inside of you," I whispered, dropping my face down beside his, kissing the shell of his ear. His fingers scrabbled against the sheets, and I sank fully into him with a groan.

"Fuck. Fill me up."

I grunted, the orgasm already too close to stop.

"Ask nicely," I demanded.

A violent tremor wracked through Lincoln's entire body,

every muscle beneath and around me contracting and tensing at the order.

"Please come inside of me, Daddy," he whimpered.

Our hips stuttered and jerked, and that was the end for me. Cum poured out of my cock, and I had no idea what it looked like since I was buried balls deep inside of him, but it absolutely felt like a geyser. My body was on fire, and all I wanted to do was roll us onto our sides and fall asleep inside of him, but that wasn't what Lincoln had wanted. But…it was what *I* wanted, and if we were in a relationship…

"Quiet down," I warned, hooking an arm around his chest and turning us both onto our sides. I wrapped a leg around his thigh and pulled him flush against me, driving myself deeper into him. My cock still throbbed and pulsed through the end of my orgasm and I shivered, squeezing Lincoln tight.

"I'm so full," he rasped.

"Just how I want you," I told him. "Now go to sleep."

He loosed another whimper, and one final dribble of cum pulsed out of my cock. I closed my eyes and within seconds was asleep.

———

The incessant trill of my alarm was never welcome, but the next morning it was louder and more insistent than it had ever been before. Lincoln made an unhappy sound, and I reached behind me to search out my phone on the nightstand to quiet the noise. My bed was so, so warm, Lincoln's body so perfect, I knew I'd fall asleep and not wake up until lunch, so I allowed myself one snooze before gently extricating myself from the sheets and my boyfriend's perfect body.

As soon as I was on my feet, Lincoln rolled onto his stomach with a grumble, stretching his arm toward my side of the bed. His front was clearly his favored sleeping position, and

I didn't dislike it either. Being able to feast my eyes on the smooth globes of his ass while I got dressed for work wasn't something I would ever complain about. I would complain, though, about the streaks of dried cum on the backs of his thighs, a reminder that at some point my dick had slipped out of his tight hold and sometime thereafter my cum had followed.

I was so focused on his ass, I didn't notice his eyes open, didn't see the way his mouth twitched into a sleepy grin.

"You did so good last night," he murmured, praise I should have been laying on him.

I finished tightening my belt, then sat down on the edge of the bed beside him to put on my socks.

"I didn't know if you wanted to be prepped or not," I said, dusting my fingertips down his crack, teasing one against his hole.

"What you did was perfect," he said. "But I didn't expect the snuggles."

"It felt important to keep my cum inside of you."

Lincoln thrust his hips down against the mattress. "Use a plug next time. If you want."

"Was the method I used not satisfactory?"

He smiled and hummed. "I only meant if you wanted it to stay in longer. The way you did it was far beyond satisfactory, Sir."

Brushing Lincoln's hair back from his face, I bent down and dropped a gentle kiss against his forehead.

"I love when you call me that," I told him. "When you call me any of those names, to be honest."

"I love when you act like one." Lincoln's lashes fluttered, and I kissed his eyelids.

"Does the…" I paused, groaning at myself for trying to broach the subject. It was too early to talk about the mechanics of our dynamic.

He rolled onto his back and stretched, reaching toward the headboard with both hands. "Tell me."

"It doesn't matter," I assured him, untucking my socks from each other so I could put them on and finish getting ready for work. "What other people think or do isn't important. The only thing that counts is what we think and do."

With a tired grunt from behind me, Lincoln flung himself out of bed. He wrapped around me like a cat, taking the socks out of my hands before settling on his knees at my feet.

"We are whatever suits us," he whispered, rucking up one sock before using his chin to gesture at me to lift my foot for him. "As we've always been."

It was a simple—yet profound—observation, one that had any further comment dying in the back of my throat. Lincoln put my other sock on and adjusted them both around my calves before smoothing my slacks back into place. He rocked back on his heels and let his hands rest on his thighs, palms up.

He was a sight, on his knees with a hard cock and eyes still half-closed. His hair a tangled mess on top of his head, skin flushed from sleep and pierced nipples hard as rocks.

"I particularly like calling you Sir when you're on your knees for me," he murmured, letting me manipulate the angle of his head with every stroke of my hand through his hair.

"Do you now?"

He nodded, closing his eyes with a smile.

My heart slammed against my sternum, and I surged forward and down, taking Lincoln's face into my hands and crashing our mouths together. He startled, but quickly fell into the kiss, curling his hands around my forearms and holding on while my tongue dipped deeper into his mouth. I kissed him until I couldn't breathe and then longer still until I could breathe again.

"I love you," I promised, sealing it with a hard press of lips against the corner of his mouth. "Are you staying here today?"

He smiled sleepily. "I don't even know what day it is."

"Wednesday."

"For a while. My laptop is at home, and I've got to catch up on editing or I won't have enough money to pay rent this month. And I have to check on Feeny."

"Feeny?"

"My new fish," he said.

"Right."

I had paid for a subscription to his videos, and if he was always around, I'd never get a chance to watch them. The real thing was of course better, but there was something to be said about the way he played for the camera that really got me going. Even the video he'd made for me in the shower was something special from the way he acted when we were face to face. On camera he was less restrained, and that was saying something.

But I wanted to tell Lincoln not to worry about rent, that I could easily afford my apartment, and I wanted him and all of his things inside of it. That we could make a spot for Feeny in whatever room made him happiest, but we'd already confessed we were in love and that was on the cusp of being too much, too soon. Lincoln was the kind of man who valued his independence, even if he hated it, and I didn't want to take that away from him.

"Okay," I said instead, trusting there would be a time and a place, and neither of them were here and now.

"Friday nights are my nights with Silas, by the way," he said. Our mouths were still so close, his fingers still so strong around my forearms. "Since you're with your brothers."

"Every Friday?"

He nodded. "Sometimes we go to Rapture. Does that bother you?"

I pulled back enough to see his face, to stroke my thumbs across the stubble on his cheeks.

"Are you doing something there that would bother me?"

He swallowed hard. "Sometimes Silas and I kiss, but it's not…not the way I kiss you."

I knew this about him already. I knew the way he chased affection in any and all forms. It wasn't for me to question or doubt his intentions. That wasn't what love was about, and it was surely not the love I was going to show him.

"I know," I reminded him. "Nothing about you bothers me."

Except the fact you're not here all the time.

He smiled up at me, eyes narrowing into slits until he looked like a cat. I kissed the tip of his nose, then gave his face a squeeze.

"We have three days until Friday, and I need to get to work."

"Would it be bad if I asked you to call in sick?"

I bit the inside of my cheek, forcing myself away from the minx at my feet. "It would be very bad for me to call in sick the day after I was made partner, yes."

Lincoln was up like a flash, grabbing me by the biceps and pulling me to a stop.

"I almost forgot all about that. I can't believe you snuck it in last night, but now that I remember, this calls for a celebration!"

I huffed out a laugh, nodding my agreement. "Tonight?" I asked.

"Tomorrow," he said, chuckling when I frowned. "Don't be greedy. I need time to get it ready."

"This sounds like you already have a plan."

"Of course I do," he said, grinning and taking a step away from me. He was giving me the space I needed to go to work, which was patently unfair because the last thing I ever wanted to do was leave him. But Lincoln understood I needed to go, and that was the way he loved me.

Respectfully and wholly.

CHAPTER 23
LINCOLN

I did go home eventually and film some content. After editing the new videos and my backlog, it was barely three in the afternoon, which meant everyone I wanted to spend time with was still busy at work. Hunter would be wrapped up the entire day, and even though I very much wanted to spend every night with him, I didn't want to come off as being clingy or possessive. I'd stay home at least until the weekend, even if it killed me. But he was at work and so were Smith and Silas, which left me to my own devices for the rest of the afternoon.

I started off by spending an irrational amount of time staring at Feeny to make sure he wasn't going to die on me like Cassandra had done. He seemed happy, at least as happy as a fish could, even though I did briefly feel bad about stealing him away from his fish friends just to bring him to my tiny apartment and leave him there all alone for hours on end.

"It wasn't like he could talk to the other fish," I assured myself, which only made me feel moderately better.

Flopping onto my bed, I covered my eyes with my forearm, trying my very best to not think about how small my apartment was or how much I missed sharing my space with Silas. Was I so desperate all the time for human contact that I couldn't even manage a handful of hours alone in my apartment? Was there something wrong with me? The way my body craved connection…

No.

Nope.

The patron saint of pity parties was not going to fall down that rabbit hole again. Instead, I forced myself out of bed and into the shower where I very stoically ignored my cock. I freshened up in all the important ways, dug out some clean clothes, and got dressed. I did stop to admire myself in the mirror, doing my best to see myself the way Hunter did.

Sliding my hands over my hips and then my stomach, I took in the flat planes of my muscles and the silver balls in my nipple piercings. Higher, I dragged my hand up to my throat and tilted my head back, imagining it was Hunter's fingers curling around my neck instead of my own. Closing my eyes, I tried to imagine my hand wrapped around his throat, but I came up short.

It hadn't been so terribly long ago that I had been very confident in my role as a dominant, and what had started as a little bit of curious exploration had, in fact, turned my entire life on its head. It wasn't like being with Hunter made me less dominant, but it did give me space to be more submissive, and I very much enjoyed the balance of that. Putting him down onto his knees and calling him Daddy made me painfully hard, but knowing he was at work and I wouldn't see him for days was enough incentive to change my train of thought to something else entirely.

I pulled my cell phone out of my pocket and sent him a text.

> I don't want you to come until we're together again.

Three dots appeared on the screen, disappeared, and reappeared.

HUNTER

Are you asking?

Heat burned low in my belly as I typed out my reply.

I'm telling.

Then I'm telling you the same.

Fine.

Fine??

Did you want to try again?

Jesus Christ, this man was going to be the death of me.

Yes, Daddy.

I didn't need to be in the same room as him to picture the pleasure washing over his face. Hunter fucking *loved* when I called him Daddy. It was an honorific I never expected to use with another person, but there were times with him when it felt like the only appropriate thing to call him. I liked that he never asked for it, that he was never disappointed when I did or didn't use it. It meant so much that he accepted all the jagged parts of me, finding ways to make them fit into his life without a single complaint.

Sliding my phone back into my pocket, I tore myself away from the mirror and texted someone else. They were quick to respond, and five minutes later I had an address keyed into my GPS and I was on my way downtown.

I met Marshall Covington at a small coffee shop in the lobby level of his office. He didn't let me pay for my iced latte, because why would he, and he didn't ask if I wanted to sit or if I wanted to walk. Marshall found a small table on the sidewalk and waited for me to join him. He was like his brother in that way, a quiet kind of unassuming dominance that overtook them both without feeling forced or unwelcome.

"Is everything all right, Lincoln?"

The question was absurd, all things considered, and I answered Marshall with a weak shrug.

"Has Hunter done something to hurt you?"

A laugh bubbled up out of me, and I chased it back down with a swig of iced coffee, shaking my head until my throat was clear enough for words.

"No, he hasn't," I said, then added. "He won't."

That answer seemed to be the right one, and Marshall looked pleased to hear it, leaning back in his seat and crossing one ankle over the top of his other knee.

"Did you need to spend more time with Silas?" he asked next, and that one felt much more like a loaded question because no, I was not adjusting well to their relationship and how it affected *my* relationship.

"I don't think I would ever say no that," I mumbled. "But I respect that he wants to spend time with you, so I won't ask about it."

"I'll tell him," Marshall said simply.

I scratched my upper lip and frowned. "That's not why I texted you."

A smile pulled at the corners of his mouth, and I almost hated how smug it made him look. He didn't prompt me to continue, but the amusement in his face said it without him even needing to use the words.

"I'm just feeling very lost," I finally told him, and all the earlier tease from his upturned mouth disappeared. Marshall leaned forward, setting his coffee on the table and bracing his elbows against his thighs.

"The same as before?" he asked.

I swallowed hard. Nodded.

I'd already confided my confusions to Marshall my wavering commitment to dominance and how that would impact me as a person. I knew it sounded silly, but for a very long time I had clung to that identify like a security blanket, and losing it and Silas at the same time sometimes felt impossible to recover from.

"I don't think I want to know what you and my brother do in the bedroom, but is he giving you space to explore that?"

"Yeah. Yes." My cheeks burned with embarrassment. "I think where I'm at now is…"

He waited, not pressing me at all.

"I love him," I admitted, a truth my best friend wasn't even privy to yet. I threw a sideways glance up at Marshall, who didn't look surprised in the least. In fact, he looked relieved. "When I'm with him everything is great, but when I'm not…"

"It feels more out of your control if you're not there to oversee it constantly."

"Yeah." I nodded. "Exactly."

"Oversight isn't love, Lincoln." He pushed my coffee toward me, and I obediently took a drink. "It's control. You don't want to control Hunter, do you?"

"No. I mean…well…no."

I very much wanted to control Hunter in all the ways I also wanted him to control me, but I was aware that wasn't what Marshall meant with the ask.

"I know this is rich coming from me, considering I moved Silas in as soon as the opportunity presented itself, but that kind of thing will only strangle the fire out of a relationship. It won't foster growth."

I made a dismissive sound in the back of my throat. "I know that, and that's not what I want. I just don't know what

I'm supposed to do with myself during the times we are apart. Until those voices quiet down."

"What do the voices say?" he asked.

"That he's too good for me."

Marshall raised a brow and cocked his head to the side. "Maybe the other way around too."

"I love that you think that, but your brother has his shit together. He just made partner and—"

Marshall sat up straight, eyes wide. "He what?"

I cursed under my breath. "I think he's going to tell everyone on Friday. Please don't ruin it."

He settled back into his seat, crossing his arms in front of his chest. "I'm happy for him. He deserves that, and I won't ruin it for either of you."

Scratching the back of my head, I sighed, trying to remember my train of thought so I could get back into it. "So, he's got his shit together, and I really do not."

"How so?" Marshall pressed. "You have an apartment, a job, a pet."

I smiled at the thought of Feeny swirling his way around his bowl on my dresser.

"I'm a sex worker."

"Does Hunter care?"

"No."

"Then how does that matter?" he asked.

"It just...."

"Does it matter to you?"

I bit the inside of my cheek, shrugging again even though we both knew the answer was yes. "I don't want him to be ashamed or embarrassed about me."

"Has he ever led you to believe that he is either of those things?"

"No," I grumbled.

"So, it's your own hangups then."

"Marshall—"

He cut off my protest with a raised hand that brokered no argument, so I bit my lips between my teeth and stopped arguing.

"Do not manufacture problems that don't exist." He looked down at his watch and frowned. "I'm sorry, Lincoln. I have a call upstairs that I've got to take."

"Yeah." I forced a smile and stood up, grabbing my coffee. "I didn't want to keep you. Thanks for the coffee."

I tried to step away, but Marshall reached out, stopping before closing the space between us and curling his fingers around my wrist to prevent me from leaving. I looked up at him, feeling more lost than when I'd called him in the first place.

"The call will keep," he said. "I'm not leaving until you feel better about whatever is going on up here."

Marshall did let go of my wrist to tap his fingertips against my temple.

"I just want to be enough," I whispered.

"Lincoln, let me tell you a couple of things that I know to be true, okay?"

I nodded again. Clearly it was the only response I was capable of.

"I've known Hunter for almost all of his life. He's the quietest of my brothers, but he is also the most loyal. He is fiercely dedicated to the things and the people that matter to him, and if you've spent any time at all with him, then you know that to be true. I've never met anyone who loves as hard and true as he does, and I've never met anyone who loves so infrequently."

Marshall paused, letting the intended effect wash over me. I'd heard him right the first time, but he stayed silent, and I took the end of his confession in a second time.

"My brother is sparing with his affection, Lincoln. And it's because of that he is generous. You hear me?"

"Yeah. Yes."

"If he loves you, you are worth it," he said.

I blinked back a very unwelcome rush of tears, tilting my head back to stop them from sliding down my face.

"And Silas," he went on, clearly unmoved by my thwarted display of emotion. "Silas loves everyone, and I love that about him, but he doesn't love anyone the way he loves you."

I scoffed.

"Not even me," he said, and I rolled my eyes at that, finally letting one or two of the tears escape. "You can roll your eyes all you want at that, but you know it's true. Silas cares for you in ways he'll never care for me, and I love that for him. I love it for *you*."

"Alright," I mumbled, wiping my lash line.

"And if these two men, whom I hold in the highest regard, think you're deserving of that, who are you to tell them otherwise? Who are you to tell someone I myself have grown rather fond of, that he shouldn't trust the love that is so graciously and freely given to him?"

"Marshall, shut up."

"The only person you need to prove you're deserving of this to is yourself, Lincoln. No one else, least of all them."

"Good talk, big guy." I slapped my hand against the center of his chest, giving him a watery smile before taking a step back.

He waited and studied me, giving me a onceover that must have answered whatever question he had about my ability to make it through the rest of the day without having an emotional meltdown in the middle of the sidewalk.

"I love you, Lincoln," he said, ruffling my hair and kissing the top of my head.

"I love you too," I muttered, sliding my arms around

Marshall's waist and pressing my cheek against his sternum. He was so tall and so broad, and while I wasn't attracted to him, I was very aware of the safety that came from being near him.

I cleared my throat and took a step back, still feeling the same kind of protection. Nodding, I smiled up at him as sincerely as my tears would allow.

"Thank you," I told him.

"I didn't do anything, Lincoln." He took a step toward the building, glaring down once more at his watch. "But I am going to tell Silas to have dinner with you tonight, so you might as well be prepared for company."

I nodded, taking a slurp of my coffee. "Yes, Marshall."

The corner of his mouth quirked up, and he laughed softly, then shook his head and went back to work.

CHAPTER 24
HUNTER

Lincoln had been scarce the rest of the week. We talked every day, and he'd sent me a handful of pictures, including some of him and his new fish, but I hadn't actually seen him in person since Wednesday morning when I left for work. Our conversation that afternoon about not getting off until we were back together hadn't helped matters much, so to say I was on edge would have been an understatement.

When I rolled up to Cunningham's for dinner with my brothers on Friday night, I was beyond irritable, but Marshall's amused smile was almost enough to temper me back down to something passable as social.

"I've been looking forward to this all week," he said, leaning back against the booth and sipping at his wine.

"Is that so?" Finn asked. He looked tired, and I realized it had been too long since I'd spent time with him one on one. It was too easy to get swept up in the magic that was Lincoln, but I needed to be better about not forgetting the other people in my life. I also had two missed calls from Andrew on my phone, and I swore to myself I'd call him back over the weekend.

Marshall answered with a noncommittal sound, and I

didn't know how…but without a doubt, he somehow heard about me making partner.

"How have things been?" I asked Finn, knocking my elbow into his.

"Peachy." He popped his lips on the P and raised his brows mockingly, and I knew he was obviously anything but.

"Anything you want to talk about?" Marshall asked.

"No, but thanks, Dad."

"Be nice," I warned.

"I was too nice," Finn snapped. He paused and cleared his throat. "Can you let me up. I've got to piss."

Against my better judgment, I moved to let Finn out of the booth, and no sooner had my ass hit the leather seat did Marshall and Smith send me matching—and equally judgmental—looks.

"What?"

"Go after him," Smith said.

"He's just going to take a piss," I said.

Marshall pursed his lips and shook his head at me, disappointment clear.

"Oh, my God." I climbed out of the booth and gave them both the finger. "Fuck you and your meddling."

I made it two steps away from the table before deciding to backtrack, picking up my and Finn's drinks. "I made partner by the way," I said to them both, turning on my heel and chasing after Finn.

He was easy to find. Hadn't even bothered to go into the bathroom. Instead, I found him pacing the hallway, hands bracketed around his waist as he walked.

"Hey," I said, holding out his drink.

For what it was worth, he didn't even startle, taking the glass out of my hand and pressing his shoulders against the wall.

"What's wrong?" I asked.

He shook his head.

"Is this about Neil and Annette?" I asked, aligning myself to his side so our shoulders touched. He tightened his grip on the glass and stared up at the roof.

"Sometimes I wish I'd never gotten involved with them."

"Why?"

"Because none of it was worth this." Finn poured the rest of his drink down his throat, then clinked his empty glass against mine. "I really do need to piss."

And with that, he disappeared into the bathroom.

I knew better than to follow him, understanding his moods better than most. Finn would talk when he wanted to talk, and not a second before. We were quite a bit alike in that way, and I tried to think about how I would feel after having Lincoln and losing him. The thought of it alone was enough to have my chest tightening to a point where it was hard to breathe. I rubbed at my sternum and pulled my cell phone out of my pocket, scrolling through my messages until I got to Lincoln's name.

Have fun tonight if you go out.

In response, he sent me a picture of him and Silas on Marshall's couch, limbs tangled together and a remote control in Silas' hand. It definitely looked like the two of them were gearing up for a wild night in.

Can I see you this weekend?

I hope so.

My dick is about to explode.

Mine twitched at the thought.

Do you want to go to Rapture tomorrow?

Can we talk about it later?

Definitely.

Enjoy your snuggle.

Enjoy your brothers.

I slid my phone back into my pocket, thinking about Lincoln's invitation. The only things I knew about Rapture were the things Lincoln had told me. I'm sure Marshall could shed some light on the goings on, but I'd meant it when I said I didn't want to know that much about how any of my brothers fucked.

It was a weird thing to think about putting my bedroom preferences on display in public, but it wasn't like Lincoln's bedroom activities were top secret. He had a healthy following on his video account and was clearly a lot more comfortable with being out about his special interests than I was.

Sighing, I scrubbed a hand down my face. I just wanted things to be as easy outside of the house as they were inside of it. It seemed unfair I couldn't wrap me and Lincoln into a cocoon and stay there until I was ready to be somewhere new.

The bathroom door pushed open and Finn emerged, looking marginally better than when he'd gone in.

"You're still here?"

"Of course I am."

He swallowed hard and nodded. "I'm good, Hunt. I promise."

"You'd tell me if you weren't?"

"Yeah."

He didn't sound believable, but I needed to take him at his word. "Dinner, then?"

"Another drink." Finn hooked his arm through the crook

of mine and walked me back out to the dining room with a pit stop at the bar so he could get another Manhattan.

When we arrived back at the table, Marshall had already done the honors, and Finn looked positively giddy at the promise of two fresh drinks waiting for him.

"Did you know Hunter made partner?" he said, raising one of the glasses for a toast. It was just like him to deflect, and since Smith and Marshall didn't know about Finn's couple, I decided not to call him out on it.

"He mentioned it," Smith said, clinking his glass against mine.

"When did this happen?" Marshall asked.

"Earlier in the week. I was waiting to tell everyone tonight."

"*I* found out earlier in the week," Finn said, and I rolled my eyes at him. Every drink and every jab, he turned more into his usual self, but I couldn't shake the feeling it was a mask and not reality.

"Congratulations, Hunter," Marshall said, adding his glass to the mix. "I know you've worked really hard for this."

I nodded, tucking my chin toward my chest.

He wasn't wrong. I had worked very hard for a very long time to land this accomplishment. Even though I'd known it was coming for a while, the reality of it was still a little hazy. I was half-drunk on being in love with Lincoln and the change in rank at the firm was like a cherry on top. Delicious, but somehow absolutely unimportant when the rest of the dessert was considered.

And to me, Lincoln was the rest of the dessert.

"Partner at the office and a boyfriend at home," Finn said, cocking his head to the side. "I'm glad to see you finally coming into your own a little."

Across the table, Smith made a sound I couldn't quite make sense of, and Marshall threw him a worried look.

"It's definitely all very surreal," I conceded with a shrug. Finn was the one who enjoyed being the center of attention, not me. "But I'm fortunate. And I'm glad I get to share it with the three of you."

"We should have a proper celebration," Marshall suggested. "Invite Andrew up maybe, Lincoln and Silas."

"I never imagined you'd willingly invite Andrew anywhere," Finn teased.

Smith let out an unimpressed breath, taking a drink of his wine and swishing it around his mouth before he swallowed. It was as much of a reply as Finn was going to get.

"We're going to have something next weekend," I told all three of them. "Work sponsored."

"Free drinks," Finn said.

"It's Saturday, I think. I'll let you know."

I saw the email come in earlier in the afternoon, but I'd been too distracted by my never-ending interest in Lincoln to pay too much attention to it. Was it really too soon to ask him to move in?

"Silas has been settling in with Cory," Marshall offered, launching into a conversation about some innovative design techniques Silas was trying to get into a proposal he was working on with his new boss. A lot of the terms were lost on me, as always, but Smith nodded along, and Finn pretended to care.

We made it through dinner relatively unscathed, and Marshall was the first to call it a night. The four of us said our goodbyes in the parking lot, and I tried to not be jealous Marshall was going home to *my* boyfriend, and I was going home alone.

"Why don't the two of you come over?" I asked, though it was less of a question and more of a statement.

With one brother on either side of me, they both nodded their agreement. We didn't bother saying goodbye because we were reunited twenty minutes later. Finn kicked off his shoes in my entryway and Smith followed suit, the two of them collapsing into the middle of my couch and making themselves at home. I went into the bedroom to change into something more comfortable than wool slacks, then detoured to the kitchen for drinks before joining them in the living room.

With a jokingly violent shake of my hips, I made room on the couch between the two of them, shoving a bottle of wine into Finn's hands and two glasses into Smith's. I had the third in mine, and Finn didn't need any instruction to know what to do. He poured all three of us a healthy dose of wine, reaching behind him to set the bottle down on the sideboard.

"What do you want to watch?" I asked, giving him his wine and taking mine from Smith.

"I honestly don't care," Finn said. "I would be perfectly happy to sit here and listen to you talk about Lincoln for the rest of the night. Remind me that love isn't miserable."

"Are you in love, Finn?" Smith asked, dropping his head against my shoulder.

"No."

He said it so quickly, I did wonder if it was a lie.

"Are you?" Smith asked softer, the question directed at me.

"Yes."

"That's good. He needs that."

"How do…" Finn sat up, angling his body to size me and Smith up. With narrowed eyes, he took a drink of his wine, brow knit together like he was solving a crime. "I've had a few drinks before this one, but this feels very incestuous."

"I assure you it's not."

Finn scratched the back of his neck and slowly sank into his spot on the couch, taking a drink of wine and smacking his lips together.

"If you say so."

"I do," I told him at the same time as Smith said, "We do!"

"They're friends," I said.

"Same as Lincoln and Silas?"

"Exactly," I said.

Beside me, Smith muttered, "Not quite."

"Not you too. Don't downplay how fond he is of you."

"I know he is," Smith said. "He's a good man. You're both good men."

"So are you," Finn and I said at the same time.

Smith frowned but shrugged his shoulders. "For a really long time I was jealous of the two of you. You've always been so close."

At the observation, Finn moved closer to me, but not in any way that Smith would notice. Just a subtle shift of his weight, a gesture we'd perfected over the years.

"Are you still hung up on being a Covington?" Finn asked, reaching over me to clink his glass into Smith's.

"Hung up on a lot of things, I think," he admitted.

"Do you still want to quit your job?"

"Sometimes."

Finn snorted. "I think we all want to quit our jobs sometimes. As long as you don't want to quit life."

"I don't," Smith said quickly.

We both looked at Finn, and I asked him, "Do you?"

He licked his lips and smiled down into his wine. "No," he said quietly. "Not that."

We sat together in silence for a few more minutes, and then Finn grabbed the remote from the arm of the couch and turned on the TV, scrolling through my streaming apps until he found one he liked. After he had it cued up, he tossed the remote into Smith's lap.

"Would you find something to watch?" he asked, taking my wine out of my hand. Finn leaned forward and set both our glasses on the coffee table and pulled me to my feet. "And would you let me borrow some fucking clothes? These slacks are driving me up the wall."

"Hey," Smith whined, clicking through the true crime documentaries and not really paying attention to either of us. "I don't want to wear work clothes all night."

"Your work clothes are jeans," Finn accused. "You can wait your turn."

Laughing, I shoved Finn toward the bedroom, promising Smith after he found us something to watch he could change into a pair of sweats. I followed Finn down the hallway, not caring in the slightest when he made himself at home on my bed while I dug a pair of sweats and a shirt out from the dresser for him.

"Can I spend the night?" he asked softly, taking the clothes out of my hand but not getting up from the bed.

The uncertainty in his voice stopped me in my tracks, and I ruffled my hand through his hair, smoothing it back before kissing the top of his head.

"Of course you can," I promised him. "You never even have to ask."

CHAPTER 25
LINCOLN

The music was loud, thumping up through the floor and vibrating my legs. I had my hands in the air, swaying with Silas pressed against my back and another gorgeous man inches away from my front. He'd tried to get closer, but I pushed him off. There was no real harm in letting him watch since he'd never get to touch. It wasn't like my ass wasn't already all over the internet anyway.

Silas slid his arm around my waist and splayed his fingers out across my stomach, singing along to the remix of the song we'd been dancing to, lips moving into a kiss against my ear when the DJ remixed the beat into a new song that wasn't familiar to either of us.

"I need some air," he panted, hooking his finger through the belt loop of my shorts and hauling me backward toward the patio door.

It had been months…probably longer, since we'd come to Rapture just to dance, and I was having the best time and never wanted to let it go that long again. We'd started the night on the couch, and I'd had nothing but plans to stay there, but as the night wore on we both got a little bit antsy. There were no words exchanged when we decided to go, and I knew I'd missed Silas, but I hadn't realized just how much until we were back in the swing of something that used to be very common for us.

Outside, the music was barely more than a drumbeat, still ringing loud in my ears. We headed toward the corner of the patio, and I pressed Silas against the wall, slanting our mouths together and licking past his teeth. He groaned against me, spreading his legs to make room for me between them, laughing when I broke the kiss to trail my mouth up his jaw to his ear.

"I'm having the best time with you."

"Same." Panting, I turned so my back pressed against the fence, our shoulders touching as we both caught our breaths and people watched. "What do you think they talk about at their little dinners?"

He chuckled. "You mean Marshall and the rest of them?"

"I mean Hunter and the rest of them." I laughed and rested my head against the fence. "But yes."

"Boring shit, I imagine. But sometimes not. Like, they've talked about me before, and their other brother Andrew. I'm sure they talk about their love lives."

I bit the tip of my tongue between my teeth, wishing the pain would be enough to settle my breathing back to normal.

"I'm sure they have weeks of content with me," I said.

Silas knocked his shoulder against mine. "Why do you say that?"

"Because of us." I gestured weakly between the two of us, the fact we'd been plastered against each other all night, kissing half the time and touching the rest. "Because I've slept with Smith, because I'm a sex worker, because I'm in love with Hunter."

My best friend's eyes went wide, and he arched a brow at me. His reaction was clearly in response to the last part of my confession, not the rest of it. I'd, of course, left out the story of how Hunter and I had met, because him being a sex worker was something I was certain he'd want to take to his grave. Not because he had issue with it for me, just…it wasn't something he wanted to talk about with anyone else.

"In love?"

I nodded, and Silas's mouth settled into a soft smile. "I like that for you."

"I like it too."

"I don't know any of them to be cruel men, Linc. No one is judging you at their table." Silas paused, and I could feel his stare on me. "Are you judging yourself?"

Patron saint of being called the fuck out.

"Yes and no," I answered. "He just made partner at his firm, you know. And it feels like a choice for him to be dating a man who lives in a studio apartment and puts his asshole on the internet to pay rent."

Silas scoffed, rolling his eyes at me. "It is a choice, and he's made it."

I don't know what I wanted Silas to say, but I'm not sure that was it. Not like I wanted him to argue with me about whether I deserved a man like Hunter Covington or not. I couldn't bear it if he thought not, if anyone did, but that didn't make the differences between us any easier to manage.

"I don't think like this when we're together," I muttered.

"Something to work on then," he suggested.

I was about to argue the point when a group of three men I'd seen on more than one occasion stepped onto the patio from the club. I'd seen them around for years, knew them to be friends of the owners, but didn't know their names. They were very clearly in a throuple, one of them wearing an actual collar, holding the hand of the other while the third looked between the two of them approvingly. The one who was clearly the dominant of the three scanned the patio, his attention fixing on Silas. He gave a little shove toward his partners, and then all three of them were heading toward us.

"Do you know them?" I asked.

Silas shook his head.

"Silas?" the taller of the three men asked.

The dominant.

"They know you," I muttered under my breath.

"Yeah," my best friend answered. "That's me."

"I'm Justin." He extended his hand, and Silas gave him a quick shake. "This is Micah and Keith. We're friends of Marshall's, and I don't think he's ever properly introduced us."

Micah was the one with the collar, Keith the hand holder.

"Oh." Silas smiled, ever the friend to all. "Nice to meet you. This is my best friend, Lincoln."

"We've seen both of you around," Justin said, scrunching his nose. "I didn't mean that as ominously as it sounded."

"Yes, you did," Keith said, raising Micah's hand and kissing his knuckles. "Will you get us some drinks?"

"I can't carry five," Micah grumbled.

"Callum will help," Justin promised.

"Yes, Sir." Micah's stare darted to me and Silas. "Are you drinking?"

"Water for me," I said. "But I can come with you, help you carry everything. Si, did you want something?"

"Vodka soda."

"It's nice meeting the two of you," I said to Justin and Keith, brushing past them and gesturing for Micah to join me. "And you."

"It's fine," Keith said under his breath, and Justin nodded his agreement. Only after his two partners approved my help did Micah relax and follow me. The closer we got to the door, the louder the music became, and after the quiet of the patio, it was impossible to not wince stepping back into the busy club.

Micah and I made our way to the bar where the bartender

greeted him warmly, like old friends. I stood there awkwardly while Micah rattled off all five of our drink orders, then turned to me with his elbow propped on the bar.

"You didn't need to help," he said.

"I know."

"Thanks."

"You're welcome." I dragged my tongue across the inside of my lower lip, really looking at Micah for the first time. He was older than me, probably closer to Hunter or Marshall's age, but it was obvious he took care of himself. He was good-looking by anyone's standards and surprisingly soft-spoken when he talked. "So, you're with both of them?"

There was no real easy way to broach the subject, so I went with the direct approach. If he'd come out with one partner not two, I would have asked the same thing. It just would have sounded a lot less judgmental.

"Yeah," Micah said simply, nodding. "Justin and I are legally married, but we've been with Keith for over five years now."

I let out a whistle, eyebrows inching toward my hairline.

"That's impressive." I thought about being with anyone that long, let alone two anyones. "And…fuck…is it rude to ask about…"

I let my words hang there, gesturing toward his collar.

Micah smiled and pressed his fingers against the leather. "Not rude, no. Justin has always been my Dom, and Keith is… he's a bit of a switch."

"If you don't mind me asking, how does that work?"

I was definitely thinking about me and Hunter when I asked the question, my brain racked with the circular nature of our own power exchange relationship.

"It works well." His mouth quirked into a smile. "Especially when Keith and I both do what we're told."

"Keith is dominant with you?"

"When Justin allows him to be." Micah tilted his head to the side, studying me carefully. "Why do you ask?"

Embarrassment flooded my cheeks, and I looked up, cheeks puffing out on a very melodramatic exhale. "I just…"

What was the point in lying about it?

"I thought I was a dominant, but I've recently learned that maybe I'm not."

"It's okay to be both," he said, nodding. "Keith is at home either way."

"Sounds like I should have gone with him to get drinks instead of you."

Micah huffed out an amused laugh, and the bartender, whom I assumed to be Callum, set all five of our drinks on the bar. Micah thanked him, and I thanked him, and then I grabbed Silas's drink and my water, and we headed back out to the patio.

Justin, Keith, and Silas were engaged in some kind of interesting conversation that came with some very dramatic hand gestures, and Silas had his phone in his hand, laughing. When we made it back to them, Silas took the vodka from my hand, leaning in and resting his head against my shoulder.

"I let Marshall know I'd met his friends. They're done with dinner if you wanted to go chase down Hunter."

I very much wanted to go chase down Hunter, but I'd missed my best friend, and I was not interested in cutting my night short.

"In a bit," I told him, and Silas exhaled happily, settling in against my side. I slid my arm around his waist to hold him up and knew by the weight of his body against mine that in a bit would definitely be sooner rather than later.

"Micah was telling me you've been together for five years?" I said, directing the question at Keith.

He was just as attractive as Micah, maybe more. Tall and slender with dark curly hair that was close-cropped against his head and eyes dark as the sky above us. He wore no collar, just a ring on his left ring finger that matched the bands belonging to Justin and Micah.

"Feels like months," Keith said at the same time Micah said, "Feels like forever."

Justin chuckled, gazing fondly at both of his men. I admired his casual dominance, the way protecting and owning both of his partners seemingly came so easy to him. There was no posturing or pretending about who he was or who they were, and I wanted that. Swallowing a mouthful of cold water, I tried to think about all the times Hunter and I had been together. None of it felt like pretending.

When he was on his knees, it was right, and when I was on mine, it was right. And maybe I'd never entertained the idea of being a switch before, but seeing how easy it should be was enough incentive to try. Even though Hunter and I had been flipping and changing, the back of my mind had always felt like it would have to settle on one or the other. Keith was a reminder that wasn't the case.

"How did…God, never mind." I scrubbed a hand down my face, and Silas linked his arm around my waist.

"None of that," Justin chided. It was playful, but sure.

"It was presumptuous."

Keith chuckled and pushed out his lower lip. "There's no such thing."

"How did you realize you were a switch?" I blurted.

Silas's fingers dug into my waist, and he breathed in sharply against my ear.

Keith tucked his chin against his chest, and at the same time, Justin tilted his up. It was the most subtle shift in power I'd ever seen, poignant enough to suck the breath right out of my lungs.

"It was situational," he said, licking his lips. Something dark flashed across his face, and even though there was no way

Justin could have seen his expression, he reached out and rubbed his hand in small circles against the middle of Keith's back. "It…Justin… he just, brings it out in me. So does Micah."

"There was no point in trying to pretend we were anything else," Justin said. "This is who we're all meant to be."

Keith breathed in deep and let it out, the three of them standing together as cohesive a unit as I'd ever seen any couple be on their own.

"I love that," I rasped, wondering the whole time if I would ever be that comfortable in my own skin.

Wondering if Hunter would be there until I was.

CHAPTER 26
HUNTER

Smith and Finn fell asleep on my couch, one after the other, and I carefully untangled myself from their limbs so I could go sleep in my own bed. I hadn't heard from Lincoln since dinner, but I wasn't surprised to be woken up just before three in the morning by a phone call.

"Hello?" I answered sleepily, rolling onto my side and rubbing my eyes.

"Sorry for calling so late," Lincoln said.

"Never apologize for that."

"Are you home?"

"Yeah. Yes. In bed."

There was a small pause. "Will you come let me in?"

I bolted upright, suddenly wide awake. "Are you here?"

"In my car in a parking spot, but yes," he said.

"I'll unlock the door, but be quiet. Finn and Smith are asleep on the couch."

Lincoln made a tired, but amused sound in my ear. "I'll be up in five."

He made it in four, locking the door behind him and tiptoeing through the apartment and right into my bedroom.

Lincoln closed my bedroom door and pressed his shoulders against the wood, and I sat on the edge of my bed, mouth dry.

"Did you end up going out after all? To Rapture with Silas?" I asked.

He nodded, and we both looked down at the loose tank top he had on, the huge scoops that showed all of his ribs and the tease of his nipples, the tight black shorts, the leather boots.

"Did you have fun?"

"Met some friends of Marshall's," he answered, chewing at the inside of his cheek.

"Were they nice?"

"Yeah." He nodded, sucking in a deep breath.

Tension rolled off of him in waves, but I couldn't figure out what was making him so uncomfortable. When we'd texted at dinner, I didn't get the impression anything was amiss, but the man standing in front of me now was more uncomfortable than I'd ever seen him, seconds away from itching like he wanted to peel himself out of his skin.

"Are you all right?" I asked.

"Just confused."

I scratched an itch beneath my right eye, not letting my stare waver. "Did you want to talk about it?"

He shrugged.

"Take off your boots, Lincoln." I scratched the same spot a second time, letting out a breath. "Take off everything."

His chin quivered, but he didn't argue.

Lincoln undid the laces on his boots, then stepped out of them and peeled out of his socks. The tank was next, then his shorts and an indecently tight pair of briefs that I almost told him to keep on. The sight of him was breathtaking. My need to come after three days aside, Lincoln was perfect…even if he didn't see it when he looked in the mirror.

"Come here." I beckoned him with a crook of my finger, and as soon as he pushed off the door and headed for me, I scooted back until my head was against the pillows. Lifting the covers back, I made room for him on the side of the bed that had already become his, then waited patiently while the sheets fanned out on top of us.

There was space between us, more than I would have liked, but clearly what Lincoln needed, so I forced myself to sit with it.

Five minutes, ten, and finally he said, "I miss Silas."

"I know."

"I don't like that I miss him because it makes me feel like I'm nothing without him." Lincoln swallowed hard, throat clicking. "I don't like missing you."

"I don't mind missing you," I whispered. "It reminds me of how much I love you."

His weary eyes went wide, and I finally closed the gap between us, reaching out and tracing my fingers over the rise of his cheekbone. I shook my head, letting him know he didn't have to say it back. He didn't need to say anything back.

"I..." Lincoln pressed his tongue against the roof of his mouth, sucked in a sharp breath. "I feel like I don't know who I am anymore. I thought I was one way when I had Silas, but now I don't have him—"

"Yes, you do."

"Not in the same way," he said quickly. "And that's fine. But I don't have him the same way, and it's making me question all the other things about myself."

I thought about my brother then. About how forlorn Smith was over the same things and how much it hurt me to see him struggle with finding his own footing separate of us and of our last name.

"I think that's just something that happens in life sometimes," I told him, even though I wasn't sure it was the right thing to say. "But I know that doesn't make it easier to go through."

Lincoln didn't say anything.

"I felt the same way before I met you," I whispered, leaning in a couple of inches but not too far, not too close. "Finn was the one who put me on that app, who wanted me to be different than I was."

"A man who fucks for money," Lincoln teased, smiling sadly.

"No lies detected."

He leaned into my hand and I curled my fingers into his hair.

"Are you different?" he asked.

"Very, and it's because of you, but I don't think that's a bad thing. I'm grateful for the things you've shown me about myself. For what I've learned being with you."

"Tell me." He breathed the words more than spoke them.

"I learned how good it feels to be on my knees for you," I said, because it was the truth. "How amazing it feels to trust you enough to give that to you. But I've also learned how amazing I feel when you kneel for me."

"I like it too," he said. "I like the things I call you and the way it makes me feel to use those words no matter who is kneeling."

I slid my fingers a little further into his hair, and Lincoln scooted closer, bringing our chests flush. It brought my mouth toward his forehead, and I kissed his still sweaty skin. The only thing between us were my pajama pants, which I wouldn't have worn if I'd known he was going to come over, but didn't think to take off before he'd arrived.

"I also like when it's not either of those things, when it's none of those words," I told him, skating my fingers down his back, relishing the way he shivered in my arms. "I like just being with *you*, all of *that* aside."

He was quiet for a moment, then he tipped his head back

enough I could see his face. His eyes were watery, but he wasn't crying, and I shifted enough to take his face into my hands and bring our mouths together. He let out a soft cry when I slipped my tongue into his mouth, and I kissed him slow and deep until the noise turned into something more like a needy kind of whimper.

There was probably a conversation that needed to be had about Lincoln's insecurities around himself, but we talked just fine with our bodies. It was late, and we were both tired, and it was easier for us both this way.

And that was okay.

"You really love me?" he asked, breathing hard when I broke the kiss to make my way up the curve of his jaw with my hungry lips.

"I love you," I told him again, drowning in the rightness of my confession. "I love your little fish and your indecision."

He made a very unimpressed sound, and I brought my mouth back to his until the only sounds he made were gibberish. I reached behind me, not willing to separate our mouths again, slapping my hand around the nightstand until I found a discarded bottle of lube. I made a mess of my hand and the sheets trying to get my hand wet with it, but when I reached down between our bodies and speared two of my fingers into Lincoln's body, his gasping moan was worth a thousand laundry bills.

"I love your sharp edges," I said next, hooking his leg over my thigh so I could get closer and deeper. "I love your softness."

Lincoln shook his head, and I shoved down my pajama pants, replacing my fingers with my cock. Sinking into him felt a whole lot like coming home, and he shivered and trembled in my arms, gasping harder after every inch. Once I was fully inside of him, I pumped my hips, thrusting deeper. He made the most perfect sound I'd ever heard in my life, and I rolled him onto his back, adjusting his knee into the crook of my arm and pumping into him once more.

He threw his head back and moaned, and I buried my face against his neck and kissed him hard. I wanted to fuck him hard, rut into him with abandon and let out three days' worth of pent-up frustration, but I was nowhere near ready to walk away from how his body trembled beneath mine, so I went slow and easy with him. Long and measured thrusts that punched the air out of his lungs until Lincoln was a sweaty mess, his cock hard and leaking between our stomachs.

"I love who you are right this second," I promised, arousal burning hot at the base of my spine. "And I'll love who you are tomorrow, and when you learn to love yourself, Lincoln…I'll love you then too."

He cried out, definitely loud enough to wake my brothers —and the neighbors—a searing splash of cum shooting against my chest as he came untouched. I curled my hand over the top of his head and thrust into him, stare locked on the wash of pleasure on his face as he came, and that was all it took for me. My hips slapped against the backs of his thighs, and the first shot of cum burst out of my cock like a firehose on full blast.

Burying my face into the sheets beside his, my entire body ached with the force of my orgasm, spilling into Lincoln's body until my cum dripped down his sac. My orgasm was long finished before my cock softened, and I rolled us onto our sides so I didn't have to pull out of him again.

Lincoln's cheeks were flushed and streaked with tears, and I kissed both of them, not wanting him to say another word. I understood how hard it was to not know yourself, to not trust yourself. It had been a very long time since I'd had those feelings for myself, but I remembered how unmoored I'd felt…all the days I'd spent questioning myself and my life.

I was grateful I'd come through it.

Grateful now that my brother had a friend like Lincoln, and they could see each other through it together.

"This is probably horrible timing, but my firm is hosting a party to celebrate me becoming partner. Would you come with me?"

"Yeah. Okay. Of course."

"Not right now."

Lincoln snorted, nodding his agreement. "That's a relief because I don't think I can meet your colleagues with your cum dripping out of my ass."

I laughed harder, easing my softening dick out of him with a wince. "You are definitely going to meet them with my cum dripping out of your ass. Just not this second."

Lincoln rolled onto his back and covered his eyes with his forearm, breathing hard.

"I feel so silly for coming over here like this," he muttered, hiding his face from me. "It felt so dramatic and horrible when I wasn't with you, but as soon as I you were here…"

He didn't need to finish the thought because I agreed with it fully.

Everything was easier when Lincoln was around, and I was relatively confident that had to do with the being in love with him thing, but I wasn't going to bring it up if he wasn't ready to talk about his feelings on his own. He'd already given me so much, I didn't need three words out of his mouth that his body told me every day anyway.

"I'm glad you came home and found what you needed."

He hummed, making a loose fist around his cock and giving a slow, overhanded stroke downward toward his thigh. His shoulders shook, and he turned onto his side, pressing a chapped kiss against my sternum.

"So am I, Daddy." An amused exhale, a smile against my heart. "So am I."

CHAPTER 27
LINCOLN

Saturday morning arrived with a loud bang and a slew of curse words meant to be quiet but still said far too loudly for anyone to sleep through. Rolling onto my stomach, I buried my face into the pillow, reaching out to feel for Hunter on his side of the bed and finding it empty. Another crash of sound from somewhere in the house, and my eyes flew open.

Smith and Finn were here.

They'd both been asleep on the couch when I arrived the night before, and I hadn't paid them much mind. Hunter had walked me right into the bedroom and done his best to make sure I forgot everything I'd been worried about on the drive over. It worked for the most part, but it worked better still when I was with him.

My own feelings of inadequacy were something I would have to get over if I wanted things with Hunter to work out in the long term, and considering we'd already admitted our very serious feelings to each other, I very much wanted things to work out in the long term.

"Oh," Hunter's voice from the door startled me out of my thoughts, and I shifted onto my side so I could see him. He was half-naked, wearing nothing more than a pair of pajama pants and a smile. Hunter had a mug of coffee in one hand, and he shoved his messy brown hair out of his face with the other. He looked nothing like the put-together lawyer I knew him to be, nothing like the confusingly submissive dominant partner he was exploring.

"Oh?"

Unlike Hunter, I was all the way naked, but thankfully he scooped up a pair of pajama pants from his dresser and tossed them to me before sitting down on the edge of the bed.

"You're awake," he said.

"Hard to not be."

He grimaced, taking a sip of coffee. "Did we wake you?"

"You didn't wake me up. I just woke up." I shoved the pajamas under the blankets and fought my legs into the right holes, shimmying the waistband into place. Hunter tore the blankets away less than a second too late. He frowned over the rim of his coffee mug, plucking at the elastic to get a peek for himself anyway. "I assume both of your brothers are still here?"

"Smith is trying to leave, but Finn seems like he's going to hang on for a while. He's going through some shit in his personal life, and I don't think it's ideal for him to be alone."

"I can get out of your hair," I offered quickly, flinging my legs over the side of the bed. "I don't want to interfere."

Hunter grabbed my wrist, pulling me back down to the bed. "You're not interfering."

I swallowed hard, catching my breath. "I believe you."

I didn't.

"Would you come meet him?" Hunter asked.

"Can I steal a shirt first?" I glanced down at my chest, my piercings glittering against my skin. "I don't really need your brother knowing about all this."

The corner of Hunter's mouth twitched, but he nodded

and gestured dismissively toward the dresser. "I don't care if he knows, but if you'd feel better with a shirt on, then help yourself."

"Would…" I trailed off, the question preposterous on the back of my tongue.

Hunter stood and took a step toward the door, glancing over his shoulder with one eyebrow lifted. He was clearly waiting for me to speak, but the words were a mess.

"Yes?" he prompted.

"Would you pick one for me?"

Hunter worked his jaw, sucking in a loud lungful of air. "If I had my way, you wouldn't put one on," he said softly, going to the dresser and pulling out one of his plain white undershirts. "But if you want one, you can use this one."

He passed me the shirt and bent down, kissing the top of my head, whispering into my hair, "Daddy loves when you show off, sweetheart."

And before I could say a single thing in reply, he was gone. The bedroom door closed behind him, the smell of coffee and sweat lingering in the air like a quickly thinning fog. There wasn't anything special about the shirt he'd picked for me. It was white and it was his, the material soft and thick. It smelled like his laundry soap, it smelled like him, and I wanted to put it on because I wanted to be surrounded by him in all ways and at all times.

Daddy loves when you show off, sweetheart he'd said to me.

This was Hunter Covington, a man who had more success this week than I'd ever have in my whole life. A man who didn't care what I did for work or that I kissed my best friends or that I'd had sex with his brother. Hunter was a man who accepted me for exactly the person I was, even if I didn't like myself all the time. He had stumbled into kink on accident and taken to it so readily, all to support me in chasing after my own understanding of myself. He would get on his knees for me without thinking, indulge my fucked-up fantasies, and God knew what else he'd do for me. There was no way I deserved him, but if Hunter didn't want me to wear a shirt…

"Fuck it," I cursed under my breath, throwing the shirt onto the pillows and heading out after him into the living room before I could talk myself out of it.

I found the three of them in the kitchen, Smith leaning against the fridge with his arms crossed over his chest, looking so much like Marshall I had to laugh about it. Hunter faced the stove, the sound of sizzling bacon filling the space. And then there was Finn, sitting on the kitchen counter and swinging his legs back and forth like a teenager. If there was something going on with him personally, his face definitely didn't show it.

He was the first to turn when I walked in, dark eyes inquisitive and hair a mess. His inscrutable stare raked over me, clocking each barbell and every missing piece of clothing before returning to my face.

"He is risen," Finn said.

At the sound of his brother's voice, Hunter turned around, a pleased and slightly turned-on smile taking over his face when he realized I'd gone shirtless after all. I hope he knew it was something I'd done with the sole purpose of making him happy. It was bad enough I'd fucked 66% of the Covington brothers in the room and 40% of them overall. I found myself hoping for a handful of new ones to pop out of the woodwork so I could knock my bang rate down to something more socially acceptable.

"You're up," he said to me, soft and pleased. I joined them in the kitchen, standing against Hunter's side and resting my head against his shoulder in greeting. He left another kiss in my hair, spatula-ed some bacon onto a folded stack of paper towels, then turned off the burner.

"I'm Finn," Finn said before Hunter could even get the words out. "Nice to meet you."

"Lincoln," I said with a nod.

"And you know Smith," Hunter said, not a single hint of jealousy or malice in his tone.

Smith hadn't left his perch against the fridge, but his expression was the wariest in the room. Part of me wanted to close the space between us and touch him until he wasn't sad anymore, but the other part of me didn't want to make things weird for Hunter.

No.

Hunter knew who I was. He knew how I treated my friends.

We'd already agreed we weren't going to hide our relationship from them, and there was no reason for me to hide my friendship with Smith from him—or anyone else.

"Of course I know Smith," I said, walking right toward him and sliding my arms around his waist. I kissed him on the cheek and waited until he slipped his arms around me and returned the hug, shoulders relaxing. "He took me to pick up Feeny."

"Feeny?" Finn asked, expression still unreadable.

I gave Smith a squeeze, noting it was a struggle to get out of his arms and return to Hunter, who took me in without so much as a pause.

"My fish," I explained. "I got him after Silas moved in with Marshall."

"You should get a fish," Hunter said to Finn, who answered that with two middle fingers raised. "So you have company."

"Do you talk to your fish, Lincoln?" Finn asked. "Does he keep you company?"

"I do talk to him," I said. "And he doesn't argue with my choice of takeout for dinner, and he doesn't leave dirty socks all over the floor, so that's a win."

"And he's beautiful," Smith said, finally pushing away from the fridge. He went to the counter and poured me some coffee, then disappeared into the living room.

I drank some of my coffee and smiled up at Hunter. "Is it just bacon you've got?"

"And toast," he said. "If Finn would put it in the toaster like I asked him to."

"I am a guest in your home," he protested, feigning offense.

"If you're a hungry guest, you'll put the bread in the toaster." Hunter looked from Finn toward the living room, then said to me. "Do you want to go sit down?"

"Are you asking me to check on him?"

He pursed his lips, head bobbling side to side indicating he was very much asking me to check on Smith without wanting to admit it.

"Bacon and toast sounds perfect," I said, lifting onto my toes to brush a quick kiss against his mouth before passing by Finn for the living room.

Hunter's apartment was relatively open concept, so it wasn't like there was any real separation between the spaces, but it was also big enough that two conversations could happen in the two separate spaces without being overheard. As soon as I reached the couch, the hushed whispers started from the kitchen, and I laughed at them as I took a seat beside Smith.

"They're the closest of all of us," he said, stretching his legs out and propping them up on the coffee table. He had on Hunter's clothes, a little too large around the shoulders and the waist for him.

"Why?"

"They're the same age." Smith shrugged one shoulder. "Marshall says they're twins."

"And you?"

"The baby," he answered. "You know all this."

"I do," I agreed, sliding closer so our thighs touched. "What brought the two of you back here last night?"

"Just needed some brotherly bonding, I think."

"Are you bonded?"

Smith scoffed. "I feel better than I did when I got here, if that's enough of an answer."

"I feel better than when I got here too."

He glanced at me, stare penetrating. "Is there anything you need to talk about?"

There were probably a dozen things I needed to talk about, but none I wanted to talk about in that very moment and probably none that I should talk about with Smith. I needed Silas for this, or maybe even Keith. Keith would probably be a better choice, a very uninvested third party who was also a switch.

Fuck.

Was I a switch?

Scrubbing a hand down my face, I dropped my temple onto Smith's shoulder with a sigh.

"If this is better, I'd hate to see the before," he muttered.

"That part of me is exclusively reserved for your brother," I teased.

"Ew!" Finn hollered from the kitchen, jumping off the counter. He had coffee in one hand and a plate of golden toast in the other. "Too early for sex talk."

"I wasn't—"

Finn dropped the plate of toast on my lap and sank down into the couch to my left, squishing in between my body and the arm of the couch. It pushed Smith toward the other end, but Hunter was there with bacon, and the four of us were shoulder to shoulder like an overfilled sandwich of our own.

"He won't believe you," Hunter said. "Even if it wasn't a sex thing."

"It's always a sex thing," Finn said, stretching out his legs and propping his feet on the coffee table. He was also in Hunter's pajamas it looked like, if the short length of the pants was anything to go by. Finn was easily the tallest of the three Covingtons currently in my company, muscular in his own right, but not aggressively in the way Hunter was.

"Of course it is," Hunter agreed, reaching over Smith's lap to pick up a piece of toast. I caught his stare, and he smiled at me, and I'd never seen him happier. "Now make yourself a meat sandwich and shut up."

CHAPTER 28
HUNTER

On Monday afternoon during my lunch break, I called Andrew. He answered right before it went to voicemail, which was very much like him. I was still trying to put him into the right Covington boxes, trying to figure out which of our traits he possessed, even though not being raised with us. Sometimes, he was predictable, and other times, not so much.

"Hey," he said, his voice echoing. "You're on speaker."

"Am I in mixed company?"

"No. Just me, this Epsom bath, and these sore muscles."

"Everything all right?" I asked. "Shouldn't you be at work?"

"I just worked out a little too hard on Saturday, and I'm paying the price. Took the day off." He laughed, and it was all Smith, rare but precious. "What's up?"

"I know we'd talked a couple weeks ago about me and my brothers—" I grimaced. "Your brothers…coming down to San Diego, which clearly hasn't worked out."

"I don't think they like me," he interrupted.

"It's not that. Marshall just moved his boyfriend in, and they're very head over heels about each other. He said maybe in a month or so. But I wanted to see if you could maybe come up again? I hate to ask—"

"Yeah," Andrew said before I could finish. "It's not a long drive."

Even if he hadn't meant for there to be accusation in the words, I heard it anyway. San Diego was not so far from Los Angeles that it should ever be an ordeal for us to get together. I realized then I'd been approaching a relationship with my newest brother all wrong. I'd wanted to set out a unified front as to not alienate Finn, Smith, or Marshall, but in doing so, I'd definitely done the same to Andrew. He didn't seem like the type to ever admit it—very Finn of him—but that didn't take away the fact it might have happened.

"I got promoted last week at work," I explained. "Made partner. Finally."

Andrew hummed thoughtfully, water swishing in the background. "That sounds like congratulations are in order."

"Yeah. Thanks. Uhm, the other partners are hosting a little party for me this coming Saturday. My…our brothers will be there, and my boyfriend too. Lincoln."

"Did you tell me you had a boyfriend?" he asked.

"It's very new," I said, clearing my throat. "But I would like you to get to know him. If you…if you want to come up early on Saturday, maybe the three of us could get lunch or something."

A pause, and then, "I'd like that."

Relief rolled through me, and I sank back against the well-worn leather of my desk chair. I hadn't realized how nervous I'd been about inviting him until I actually did it, and now that the hard part was out of the way, we could have a normal conversation, which we did.

We talked about mundane things, the weather and traffic, and we complained about work. He lamented the dating scene in San Diego, which I found impossible to believe could be slim, and then he told me about his mom. About what it was like for him growing up. In return, I offered him my own stories of what it was like to grow up under the punishing expectations of Willem Covington, and then it was time for him to get out of his bath.

"I think I've been too hard on the four of you," he said softly. "Maybe."

"In what way?"

"I'm jealous sometimes, I think…that the four of you have each other. But it was borne of necessity, wasn't it?"

I opened my mouth to reply, but not a single sound came out.

"Sorry, that was…" Andrew laughed nervously. "I hate to end the call on that note."

"It's fine," I told him quickly. "I just…it's fine."

"I'll see you Saturday then? And your boyfriend?"

"I can't wait," I said, and it was the truth.

We said our goodbyes, and after the call disconnected, I leaned back in my chair and scrubbed a hand down my face. I truly needed there to come a day when I didn't feel like I was the intermediary between Andrew and my brothers. Andrew was also my brother, but I couldn't manage the relationships between him and the other three on my own. That was for them to build.

I started a new group text. Adding Marshall, Finn, Smith, and Andrew to the same chain.

> Figured now is as good a time as any for all of us to be able to get in touch with each other.

The read receipts filled the screen one after another. Andrew's being first, then Smith, then Marshall, and lastly Finn. Instead of responding in the thread, he messaged me privately.

FINN

WTF

He's our brother too.

On a technicality.

He's as related to you as I am.

He's a stranger.

Does this have to do with N&A or are you really just this cranky? Because I promise you, there's more out there than just him.

My phone rang, my brother's face filling the screen with his name across the top.

"What?" I answered, already annoyed.

"What do you mean there's more than him?" Finn asked.

"Statistically," I said. "It's probable."

"Have you heard anything specific?" he pressed.

"No, Finn."

My brother made a very unhappy noise on the other end of the phone.

"What are you doing right now?" I asked.

"Trying to find a spoon to dig my eyes out with so I can stop looking at this spreadsheet," he said. "Why, what are you doing?"

"Telling myself I need to take a lunch but not actually getting up from my desk."

He laughed at me. "Glutton."

"I didn't make partner by taking lunch breaks."

"Did you want to get lunch?" he asked.

"Definitely."

"I'll text you a place," Finn said, then he hung up.

A handful of seconds later, he sent me the address of a Thai place in Venice, so I powered down my laptop and headed to the parking garage. In the elevator, I ended up with Winters, who asked if I was looking forward to the little celebration they'd put together for the coming weekend. I was, so I told him as much, and I told him my brothers and my boyfriend would all be coming. This seemed to please him, and we said our goodbyes before heading to our respective cars.

Before I backed out of the parking spot, I texted Lincoln to let him know I missed him. He was quick to respond, sending me a selfie of him and Feeny. A shot of disappointment rolled through me knowing he was at his apartment and not mine, but I also knew he was exceedingly mindful of where he spent his time. I would've had him film all of his content from the comfort of my place, and unpack his clothes in my closet, and his sex toys under my bed, but I didn't want to scare him off.

Even after we'd confessed our young and possibly premature feelings to each other, Lincoln was skittish. He was careful to not take up too much room in my life, to always clean up after himself, leave no trace behind. If I was being honest, I hated that. When he went back to his apartment, it was as if he didn't really exist, and I hated that more than anything else. I wanted him to leave underwear on my floor or a toothbrush on the edge of my sink.

I texted him back.

Will you come over later?

I was there all weekend.

You don't have to. But I'd like you to.

If you're sure.

I have some work that I'll need to take home, so bring your laptop if you want. You can edit while I finish up. I'll order dinner. You can stay the night.

Okay.

I could hear the hesitation, even through the phone.

Bring an extra toothbrush too. To leave.

I don't mind traveling it.

I mind.

A long pause, so long I pulled out of the parking spot and headed to the street. I'd just swiped my parking card to get out of the lot when he replied to me.

Is that an order?

Heat flared out from the base of my spine, and I tried to shove it back down considering I was at a green light in the city and on the way to meet one of my brothers for lunch. Of all the things Lincoln and I had talked about as we set the ground rules for the things we did in the bedroom, taking those things out of the bedroom had never been on either of our radars. I had the impression that was the way Marshall chose to live his life, and kudos to him for that, but it wasn't something I'd imagined for myself. But I'd never imagined someone like Lincoln for myself either. Never imagined this kind of relationship, but here we both were.

I left the message on read until I pulled into the parking lot of the Thai place Finn wanted to meet up at. His car was already there but empty, so I imagined he'd already gone in to get us a table.

Do you want it to be?

Does it need to be?

> I don't know.

> If it needs to be, it is. If you want it to be, it is.

> If you don't, it's a suggestion. It's my preference.

He didn't say anything else to that, so I shoved my phone into my pocket and went to find Finn. It was easy enough, considering how tall he was, tucked into a very small table in the corner, his legs stretched out into the walkway and a bottle of beer held loosely in his fist.

"One of those days?" I asked, sinking down into the chair opposite his.

"It feels like it's never-ending," he admitted.

"Do you want to talk about it?" I asked.

Finn shook his head, blinking hard. "Would you tell me something interesting?"

My heart twisted in my chest at my absolute inability to help my brother in any ways that really mattered. "Not dinosaur related?"

He frowned at my joke, and it was answer enough.

"Alright. Let me think a minute."

I'd known Finn for almost my whole life, and he was many things, but miserable was rarely one of them. He'd always been the most happy-go-lucky of the bunch of us, ready to crack a joke or give someone a hard time when they needed to be put back in line. And Finn did a very good job of hiding his current unhappiness when Smith and Marshall were around, but when it was the two of us, he dropped that mask entirely. I was grateful, I realized, to give him that. Wondering how much I would have to give in order for Lincoln to feel the same way with me.

Maybe someday.

Across from me, Finn's frown deepened, and he picked at

the corner of the beer label with his thumb. I knew there was only one thing for me to tell him that would shock him out of his mood.

"Alright," I said, clapping my hands together. "I've got it."

He scoffed. "I don't think I've ever seen you this animated."

"This interesting fact deserves some extra pizzazz." To demonstrate, I waggled my fingers at him, and he chased his amusement at me back with a swig of his beer.

"I should have called Marshall," he said.

"Wrong." I flagged down the waiter and ordered a beer for myself and another for my brother. "Do you remember when you set up that account for me on that hookup app?"

"The one you never bothered to use?" Finn arched a brow at me. "I remember."

"I have used it," I informed him.

He narrowed his eyes, but his mouth twitched up from a frown and into a straight line. "You little liar."

"I never lied. I told you I'd never gotten an alert on it, which is true because I never turned them on."

"That sounds like the opposite of using it," he said.

I pulled my phone out of my pocket again and set it on the table, stopping short of pulling up the app to show him, but letting him know I would if I had to.

"I have used it, but not for the way you expect," I told him. The waiter brought our drinks, and I took more than a healthy swallow of mine. "If I tell you this, you have to promise not to tell."

"Oh." Finn finally smiled, leaning in and resting his chin in his hands. "This is *definitely* interesting."

"You have to promise," I repeated, raising my pinky in the air. "Lincoln is the only person who knows."

"I bet he does." Finn was positively giddy, bursting at the seams.

"Alright," I said.

I had to be certain of this. If I confessed this to Finn, there was no going back from it. And even though I was relatively confident he wouldn't tell Marshall or Smith, there was no way of being positive.

"Out with it, brother," he demanded, hooking his pinky around mine and kissing his thumb.

I pressed my lips against my thumb to seal the promise, then as quietly as I could manage while still getting the words out, I told Finn the story of how Lincoln and I met.

CHAPTER 29
LINCOLN

"It's just his preference," I told myself, standing in front of the brand new toothbrushes in the drug store. "It's just a toothbrush."

What was the harm in leaving a toothbrush at Hunter's apartment? It would make staying over a little more convenient, and it was also something I wouldn't mind throwing away or losing when things inevitably went south between us. But also…would things go bad between us? He'd basically ordered me to bring a toothbrush over, what would stop him from ordering me to stay if I wanted to go? And not like wanting to go in a *this situation is toxic* kind of way, but in a *self-preservation* kind of way.

Pinching the bridge of my nose with one hand, I dug my cell phone out of my front pocket with the other and did the only thing that had ever made sense in my life. I called my best friend. And even though he was at work, he answered on the second ring.

"Hey!" Silas's voice carried genuine happiness.

"Hi." Mine did not.

"What's up? Are you okay?"

"Uhm, yes and no," I admitted. "I'm trying to pick out a toothbrush to keep at Hunter's, and it's harder than I thought."

"To…pick a…toothbrush?"

"The other part," I said.

"Oh. *Oh*." Silas hummed thoughtfully. "To leave at Hunter's."

"Ding. Ding."

Unable to look at the toiletries for a minute longer, I walked over to the pharmacy and flung myself down in one of the uncomfortable plastic chairs in their waiting area, phone still pressed against my face.

"It's serious with him then?" Silas asked.

"He loves me."

"Aww. I love that, Linc. You deserve that."

The lie twisted violently around my ribs, and I screwed my eyes closed. "Do I, though?"

"Why wouldn't you?"

"Why *would* I?" I shot back. "There's…I don't know, Silas. There's a lot that's been going on. A lot happening with me and him that you don't even know about. So you can't really say that."

There was a biting silence, and I replayed what I'd just said to my best friend, hating every scathing word of it.

"Does Smith know?" Silas asked calmly. "Should you call him?"

"Jealous much?"

He sighed, sounding like Marshall in my ear. "I just want to make sure you have the support you need."

The idea was honestly laughable, considering the support I needed had moved out of our apartment and into his boyfriend's bougie house. The support I needed had essentially forced me into a studio apartment so he could live his best life, and I'd encouraged it every step of the way. Patron saint of self-sacrifice or something much fucking worse.

"I shouldn't have called," I said, disconnecting before Silas could argue with me.

There was a part of me that knew I was acting irrationally, but there was also no way it was something I could get a hold of. With my phone still in hand, I texted Marshall.

> Can I have Keith's phone number?

> Justin's Keith?

> Please.

He sent it over almost immediately, and I pretended the gears weren't turning in his head about why I wanted to talk to his switch friend in the polyam relationship. I'd already talked to Marshall about what it meant to be dominant, so he had to suspect there was some wavering happening. I only hoped he'd not talk to Silas about it, which I also knew was impractical. He and Silas talked about everything because that was healthy and normal and because Silas was a submissive and Marshall was a dominant, and Marshall told him to and Silas obeyed.

That all felt very straightforward and simple.

I fired off a text to Keith, reminding him of who I was and asking if we could get some coffee. He answered within a couple of minutes, letting me now he was out with a like-minded friend, but I was more than welcome to join them as they were already on their way for coffee.

I figured there was no harm in it because I could not care less if a stranger wanted to judge how messy I was, so I bought the cheapest toothbrush on the rack, then keyed in the address Keith sent me and headed toward it. The traffic was impossible, but forty minutes later, I finally found parking and Keith.

He was at a small outside table on the sidewalk, his curly black hair falling across his forehead. His friend was...

gorgeous in every possible way, maybe a little taller than average with long black hair that looked like silk in the sunlight.

"Lincoln!" Keith waved me down, and I stumbled toward the table, giving him and his friend an embarrassingly awkward wave.

"Hey. Hi. Thanks for meeting me."

"Any friend of Marshall's is a friend of mine," he said, gesturing across the table. "Have you met Verity?"

Verity.

I shook my head.

"Verity and their best friend Landon are the ones who own Rapture," Keith explained. "Well, Gregory and Aaron have a bit in it now too."

"I don't…"

"Gregory is Landon's partner, and Aaron is mine," Verity explained, pushing a plastic cup of iced coffee from the center of the table toward the empty seat. "We made a guess on your drink."

"Caramel," Keith said.

"I don't hate it." I sank down into the seat and took a swallow of the drink they'd picked out for me. It was really good, not too sweet and not too bitter. "Thank you."

"So, not that I hate it, but what brings you around?" Keith asked. "I have my suspicions, but I don't want to assume."

"You know what they say about people who assume," Verity teased, flipping their hair behind their ear. "It makes you an asshole."

A laugh formed in the back of my throat, and I swallowed it down, but not before the noise made it out of my mouth. As a silence fell over the table, I realized they were both still waiting for me to answer. My cheeks heated, and I found myself suddenly embarrassed over the call in the first place. They were both strangers, closer to Marshall's age than mine, and there was no way either of them would even care about me, let alone my problems.

"It feels silly now," I muttered, pinching the straw between my fingernails.

"Maybe, but that doesn't mean it's unimportant." The two of them shared a knowing look, and I frowned at the condensation rings on the table.

"Well, while we try to figure that out, Keith, have I ever told you about how my relationship with Aaron started?" Verity asked.

"No," Keith said, clearly lying. "I don't think you have."

"I met him at Rapture, and he was the most persistent little thing—" Verity said, only to be cut off by a short laugh from Keith.

"He's hardly little."

"Oh, I know."

I looked up in time to see Verity suggestively waggle an eyebrow before smirking at me and continuing their story.

"He wouldn't leave me alone for months. I finally gave in and went out with him. Mostly to put him out of his misery."

"I'm sure that was it," Keith drawled, swirling ice around his cup and rolling his eyes. He obviously more than knew Verity and Aaron's history. I imagined he'd been there for it.

"I was very certain when I met Aaron that I was a switch. He was not, and I truly didn't see how we could be compatible there…all things considered."

If my ears perked up, I hoped neither of them noticed, but I imagined they both did.

"When all ended up said and done between us, I think I still am. At least in the heart of me, but I also think it feels very good to submit whenever it suits me…which is more often than not."

I licked my lips, pretending I didn't see them staring at me.

"I get that," Keith said, going on like I wasn't there. "When

Justin and Micah brought me into their relationship, I wasn't sure how it was going to work. They were already very established in their roles, and Justin is…he's an amazing Dom."

"He is," Verity agreed. "Comes by it very naturally."

I thought about Hunter, and how easy it was for him to command me, even from his knees. And then I thought about myself and how it was so often a struggle to maintain my own handle on that control.

"I thought I was submissive, and I am, but it made sense for me to switch between the two of them," Keith said, even though I had the suspicion Verity was intimately aware of how things were between Keith, Justin, and Micah. "I'm dominant to Micah because that's what he needs. It's what he brings out in me. And I'm submissive to Justin because that part of me is safe to breathe when he's around."

Verity hummed their approval.

"Justin gives me a safe space to be both at the same time," he said, and I scratched absently at the back of my neck. "It's a real special bond."

After that, neither of them said anything, but both of them watched me quietly, waiting.

"I, uhm…" Fuck, this was difficult. "I'm a Dom."

Neither of them laughed, and I didn't realize how much I needed that recognition.

"Or I thought I was. I…recently, maybe. I've been…things with my boyfriend…"

Verity took pity on me, reaching across the table and patting my forearm until I looked at them. Their expression was soft and earnest, finely arched brows raised over the kindest eyes.

"Aaron brings out parts of me I didn't know before I met him," they explained. "Is that what it's like for you?"

"Yes, no. Kind of. I suspected before Hunter that I might enjoy it."

Verity nodded, giving my arm a squeeze before settling back into their seat. They wore a silk shirt with cranes on it, the flowing fabric never looking still, even when they were. It was…hard to look at them being so stoic when my brain felt like it was actively trying to claw itself out of my skull.

"It doesn't need to be a serious thing," Keith said, and we both looked at him next. "I mean, it's obviously *serious*, but it's supposed to also be fun. You're supposed to enjoy it, right? It's meant to be a benefit not a burden."

"If it was a burden to serve Aaron, I would never." Verity laughed and chased the sound down with some of their coffee. "And he'd be happy with that, I think."

"Things with Justin and Micah would be different if I wasn't a switch," Keith agreed. "But I'm certain we'd still love each other. And things between us have changed so much since we first got together."

"Five years now?" Verity asked.

"Six, I think." Keith shrugged and smiled. "I'm honestly very bad at keeping track, but Micah could probably tell you down to the hour."

"He's a bleeding heart."

"Hopeless romantic," Keith agreed, nodding. "The moral of the story is, there's always room for growth and under-standing in these kinds of relationships. Maybe more than in relationships that don't play with power exchange. It's…it's meant to be fluid and evolving."

"Like you wouldn't have the same limits your whole life, would you?" Verity asked, tapping my arm with one of their slender and manicured fingers. "Even as a dominant?"

"No," I rasped. "They'd change."

"So why is it okay for your limits to change, but not your likes?" They chuckled. "And isn't that kind of the same thing."

I groaned, dropping my elbows onto the table and catching my face with my hands. Verity was so fucking right. I'd locked myself into a box, built partly out of self-preservation and also a little bit out of fear. Dominance had been a safe place for me when I needed it to be, but Hunter showed up and made a new kind of safety, a safety that allowed me to explore things from the other side.

If I'd ended up with anyone else for that very first hookup, it was very possible I'd still be thinking I was only a Dom. And maybe I was, but it was easy to not be that way with Hunter. It felt right to let myself have both.

"I can still be a dominant man," I said, mostly to myself, "who is submissive to one person."

"Yes!" They both said at the same time, Keith louder than Verity, but Verity clapped their hands and stomped their feet onto the sidewalk, their joy contagious.

"I'm embarrassed about this" I mumbled into my lands, loud enough for them to both hear. "You don't even know me, and I just dumped this whole sob story—"

"What sob story?" Verity asked, curling their fingers around my wrist and giving my arm a shake until I looked up at them. They smiled at me so sincerely, it made me want to cry. "We're just three friends getting coffee, talking about how scary it is to be seen by someone for the first time."

"But also wonderful," Keith said. "Empowering."

Verity hummed their agreement.

"Our stories are all very different," he said. "But submission gives me more control than dominance ever could."

"Hey now," Verity chided, tutting their tongue against the roof of their mouth. "It's balanced and you know it."

"I like to call him Sir when he's on his knees for me," I blurted, sending their casual conversation straight to silence.

A moment passed, then another, and Verity finally said, "Damn, Lincoln. That's…really sexy."

I laughed then, covering my face again with my hands and blinking back tears I didn't want to cry in front of these two strangers who'd dug my brain out of a miserable black spiral in less than half an hour.

"Does Micah call you Sir when you're on your knees for Justin?" Verity asked Keith, who pouted and shook his head.

"No, but he's going to tonight."

The two of them burst into laughter, and it was impossible to not join in. I always felt good and secure when I was with Hunter. It was the away times that had been the problem, but at that coffee shop with Keith and Verity laughing about something I'd always imagined to be so very serious, for the first time in a long time, I felt okay on my own too.

CHAPTER 30
HUNTER

When I got home from work, Lincoln was sitting in the hallway, legs bent and his forearms resting on his elbows. He had his head against the door, and when I stepped out of the elevator, he glanced up but made no move to stand.

He had a new toothbrush dangling between his fingers, and the surge of unbridled pleasure that washed over me would have been embarrassing to admit out loud, so I didn't. Besides, the look of absolute dejectedness that colored Lincoln's face was enough for me to swallow the small victory anyway, at least temporarily.

"What's wrong?" I asked, holding out my hand and helping him to his feet. The plastic of the toothbrush packaging crinkled beneath his grip.

"Can we talk?"

"Of course," I said, unlocking and opening the door. "Always."

Lincoln followed me inside and toed off his sneakers, looking a little bit like a wounded deer. He had on striped socks and skinny jeans with holes in the knees, a t-shirt with the arms cut out so his ribs—and the occasional nipple piercing—were on display.

He was breathtaking.

"I brought a toothbrush," he said, holding it up.

"I saw. It…makes me very happy that you listened."

Lincoln groaned, covering his mouth with his hand and shaking his head. I gave him a minute to gather himself.

"Where should I put it?" he asked, the words muffled behind his fingers.

"The bathroom," I told him. "Next to mine."

He nodded like it was an order.

I stayed standing in the hallway while Lincoln marched himself down the hallway and into my primary bathroom. He fought through the plastic wrapper—if the noises filtering down the hallway were any indication—then shuffled his way back to me, shoving his hair out of his face.

"What did you want to talk about?" I asked.

"I don't want you to let me fuck this up," he said, blinking hard before looking up at me with watery eyes.

"What do you mean?"

"I don't want you to let me fuck this up," he repeated. "I am going to sabotage this somehow, and you're a really good man, Hunter. You're a good man for me, and I don't want to ruin it. But I know I will."

"I disagree."

"You'll see."

I shook my head, reaching for him. I hooked a finger through the cut-out hole in his shirt and pulled him close. He went right into my arms, pressing his forehead against my chest and sliding his arms around my waist. Lincoln felt impossibly small like this, and every protective instinct I had swelled to life right there in the space between us.

"I love you," I reminded him, kissing his hair. "I will not let you fuck this up."

"What if I ask for too much?" he muttered into my shirt. "What if I don't give enough in return."

Sighing, I slid my hands down his back, let them graze across the top of his ass before falling away.

"Get on your knees, Lincoln."

He complied with a practiced and comfortable grace.

"Hands behind your back."

He twined his fingers together at the small of his back, arms straight and his chest puffed out. Beneath his shirt, I could see his nipples were hard, so I shoved the shirt out of the way to reach one of his piercings. Tweaking the barbell between my fingers, I smiled when he grunted in pain but didn't pull away.

It took one hand to get my belt undone, to pull down my fly, to drag my half-hard cock out from behind the confines of my briefs. I fed my length into his waiting mouth, pushing until his nose was buried against my skin. Lincoln gagged around me a little, the muscles of his throat flexing against the tip of my cock.

"What could you give me that's better than this?" I asked him honestly, threading my fingers into his hair and tilting my own head back.

Lincoln's mouth was wet and hot and tight, and his tongue against the underside of my shaft was heaven on earth. The longer I was in his mouth, the harder I got, the more he choked around me, the more he refused to give up.

"You let me wake you up to fuck in the middle of the night," I reminded him. "You send me videos that make me hard all fucking day."

His lashes fluttered and he moaned, swallowing around me. Precum pulsed out of my slit and painted the back of his tongue.

Lincoln whimpered.

In our time together, I'd learned a handful of things about

Lincoln Summers. The most pressing being he didn't feel important and he didn't feel seen. That was why I'd obliged him so quickly with the free use after the night he mentioned it. I needed him to know I saw him for who he was. That I loved him for who he was. And if he thought there was any chance in hell I was going to let his insecurities ruin this for me, he had another think coming.

"Tomorrow when I'm at work, I want you to film something for me. Can you do that?"

He nodded, spit streaming down his chin.

My cock throbbed.

"I want you to DP yourself, sweetheart."

Lincoln's eyes rolled back, and he gagged again around my cock, which I was certain had never been harder in my life.

"If you can't do it yourself with two toys, I want you to use the biggest one that fits. Can you do that for me?"

He nodded again, entire body trembling.

"And I want you to talk to the camera while you do it. I want you to talk to me. I want to know exactly how it feels to be split in two for the man you love."

I tightened my grip in Lincoln's hair and fucked my cock further into his throat, thrusting deep and then shallow before pulling out of his mouth entirely. He sputtered and gasped for breath when I pulled free, streams of spit connecting his lips to my dick.

"I need to be inside of you. Can we stay like this or…"

"Like this," he whispered. "Like this please, Daddy."

How Lincoln could unman me with a single word, I'd never know. Part of me didn't want to understand the power he had over me. I just wanted to relish it while it lasted because I could do my best to stop him from sabotaging us, but both of us knew how to make this stop entirely.

I tugged at the knot on my tie, loosening it enough I could get the top button of my shirt undone, then I undid the bottom few buttons. Just enough I could pull the tails of the shirt out of the way. I was still fully dressed, but I'd never been more ready to fuck.

"Go to the spare bedroom, Lincoln. Take off all your clothes."

His shoulder cracked when he unlaced his fingers from their place at his lower back, but that was the only sound he made before rising to his feet and making his way down the hall. I followed after him, stroking my spit-slicked cock, stopping in the doorway and watching him strip out of his clothes.

Once naked, Lincoln turned and faced me, his cock as red as his cheeks. He looked so fucking unmoored. I closed the space between us and sank to my knees in front of him, kissing his navel and dragging my mouth across to his hip. Lincoln's cock pressed urgently against my chin, but I ignored it.

"I would never let you ruin this," I promised him again, leaving a kiss against the V that funneled my attention right to his dick.

With a gentle shove, I pushed Lincoln onto the bed and crawled up between his thighs. He spread his legs to make room for me, grunting as I used my body weight to shove him sideways across the bed.

"There's a lot we can do together." I leaned away to get to the nightstand, feeling around for the lube. "We can do it in this room, or we can do it on our room."

He whimpered, tilting his head back and baring his throat in the most gorgeous display of submission. I wanted to capture it forever. Save it to jerk off to.

"Lincoln, can I record you?"

"What?" The question was barely more than a breath.

"The way you look right now…" I licked my lips. "I want you to see it."

"Yeah. Yes."

The lighting was probably horrible, and the angle was

going to be far from perfect, but I didn't care about any of that. It was the feeling I wanted to preserve. Shoving all the pillows off the bed, I propped my phone against the headboard and pressed record. I didn't even know if we were in frame, and I didn't want to waste time checking. It was angled at his face, and I hoped that would catch it all.

I turned my attention next to lubing my cock and my hand, wasting no more time before reaching down and getting two fingers into Lincoln's tight hole. There was that gorgeous arch of his neck again, a breathy whimper that went straight to my balls.

"Who am I, Lincoln?" I asked, starting the slow work of stretching him to take my cock.

"Daddy."

"Who else?"

"Sir," he rasped. I fought a third finger into him, using my hips to knock his legs wider apart on either side of me. Lincoln fisted the sheets and arched off the bed, crying out when I pushed all three fingers in up to the last knuckle.

"What do you want?" I asked him next.

"Your cock."

There was no work in giving him that. It was easy to replace my fingers with my shaft, and I sank into him fully with one short snap of my hips. I leveraged myself over the top of him, his legs bent back against my chest, his body nearly folded in half. I took Lincoln's face into my hands, brushing away spit and tears, kissing all the places my fingers had cleaned.

"Who am I now?" I asked softly.

His breath was my breath. His approval, my life.

"Good boy," he panted, his entire body seizing with pleasure. "Oh, God."

He'd managed to get through the trinity that had become my existence, so I rewarded him with a long, hard thrust.

"I'm so proud of you for bringing that toothbrush over," I

whispered against his mouth, fingers still dancing across his face. "You did what you were told, and now can you feel how happy you've made me?"

Lincoln's muscles clamped down around me, and he squeezed his eyes shut, answering me with a silent nod.

"When I'm at work tomorrow, I want you to go back to your apartment, and I want you to bring some spare clothes next. Can you do that, sweetheart?"

I fucked into him with a slow and leisurely pace, rewarding him with a deep and sharp thrust when he answered me.

"Yes, Sir."

"How do you decide?" I asked, rubbing my nose against his. "Daddy or Sir?"

"Daddy always," he murmured, lifting his head just enough from the bed to search out my mouth. "Sir sometimes."

I chuckled, snapping my hips against the back of his thighs.

"Sir always," he corrected. "Sir, can I come?"

I wrapped one of my hands around the top of his head, using his body to fuck myself deeper and harder into him. I held Lincoln's body beneath mine, getting harder every second from the sounds he made, from the smell of his sweat. I wanted to tell him not to come, wanted to ask him to put me onto my back and come inside of me, but I also knew that wasn't what either of us needed it that moment, least of all Lincoln. He needed submission, to be taken apart and held in pieces, and reassembled after time had softened his edges a little bit more.

"You may not," I answered.

Lincoln let out a sputtering sob, and I slanted our mouths together to swallow the rest of it down for myself. I was so greedy for this achingly messy man, and if he truly thought I'd ever let him ruin the way I felt about him, the pleasure he brought into my life, he didn't know me at all.

I grabbed him roughly around the waist and rolled us both over at the same time until l was on my back and he was on my lap. My phone fell on its side, and I grabbed it, arranging it close to my face to get it more like a POV.

"Can you make me come?" I bracketed my hands loosely around Lincoln's slim waist, coaxing him to find his own pace on top of me.

"Yes, Daddy," he whispered, grinding down hard against my thighs.

I slid my hands over his ribs and his stomach, tweaking his piercings and groaning in arousal at the way he threw his head back when he felt good. I loved the sight of him unrestrained and in the throes of his own pleasure. And he was right. It took no time at all for Lincoln to work me up into a frenzy. With his fingers steepled against my chest, my orgasm tightened into an impossibly thick knot at the base of my spine.

"I can feel you," he panted, words barely audible over the loud slap of our skin. "Please let me have it. Please fill me up with your load."

I was seconds away from my release, and I grabbed Lincoln by the throat, not tight, but hard enough to get his attention.

"Do you deserve it?" I rasped.

He went still, but he was so tight and hot, there was no stopping me from continuing down the road I found myself on. Lincoln's eyes went wide, and my cock thickened and pulsed, spilling spurt after spurt of cum up his ass. It was work to keep myself steady, to keep my eyes open, to watch him.

"Do you deserve this?" I asked, pulling him down and biting his lip between my teeth.

Lincoln whimpered and trembled, and I shoved my free hand between us, stroking his cock until he came in a rush across my knuckles. He screamed his orgasm into my mouth, onto our stomachs, and I held him rough and strong through the whole of it. Something inside of me shifted, the balance of submission and dominance clicking into place in a new way for me. The circle of it all, the infinite need for satisfaction, pride, and control. It lived on both sides, and it always would.

"Answer your Daddy," I said against his lip, licking a hot stripe against the place I'd bitten him. "Answer your Sir."

"I deserve it," he whimpered, collapsing against me.

I wrapped my arms around him and pressed him tight against my chest. Mouth hot and wet against his ear when I said, "Yes. You do. That's why I trust you with it. That's why it's yours."

CHAPTER 31
LINCOLN

The more time I spent at Hunter's, the less I liked my own apartment. I'd tried really hard to hype myself up about it after Silas moved in with Marshall, but I hadn't spent enough time there for it to even start to feel like home. Hunter's apartment, though, with its soft bed and its dark colors...that felt like home. He would have had me over at his place every night of the week if I'd agreed to it, but I still didn't trust things enough to bite that bullet.

Even though I'd been staying over most nights, I still came back to my place during the day. I filmed content, I fed Feeny, and I stared at the wall wondering if my stubbornness was going to be the death of me or not. It was a nice routine that Hunter didn't know about, and I'd made it through the week without cracking. It was Friday, and he had dinner plans with his brothers after work, and I had plans with Silas to do a whole lot of nothing. For real this time, not like last week when we'd caved and gone out to Rapture after all.

It was going to be a low impact night, considering Saturday morning I was going to meet the fifth Covington brother for the first time, and then Saturday night all of us were going to the party at Hunter's office celebrating his new partnership. It was a lot to do in a short amount of time, and I hoped I'd be too busy to even stop and think about the comparisons people were sure to draw when they saw the two of us together. His brothers had accepted me because I was friends with Silas, but it was easy enough to wonder what their reactions would have been if we'd just met on the One Night Stand app with no background relations.

After getting all of that out of my mind, I filmed a wank scene, edited it, and sent it to Hunter before scheduling it on the website. It was a bit of fun between us. Me sending dirty videos to him while he was playing the role of buttoned-up-and-definitely-not-kinky partner at one of LA's most up-and-coming law firms, and me pretending we were a fair match.

Fifteen minutes after the video left my outbox, Hunter texted me a shaky and grainy video of himself in the bathroom at work. His pants were undone, his shirt rucked up enough for me to see the bottom of his stomach. His breathing was hard, punctuated with the occasional soft grunt, and then far too soon, Hunter came all over his knuckles and the recording cut away.

I definitely hadn't planned on filming two videos, but as hard as watching Hunter had me, I could easily go for two. Before starting, I called him. The phone rang twice before he answered with a breathy laugh. He must still be coming down.

"Hi," he answered.

I grinned, covering my face with my hand even though he couldn't see me.

"Hi. Did you like that?"

"Very much," he said, still breathing hard. "Obviously."

"I liked watching you like it," I told him. "I might make another one today."

"More power to you, but if you expect the same response from me, I might die over it."

"Oh, come on, Daddy," I teased. "You've got the refractory period of a teenager, and you know it."

There was a short pause on the other end of the line, and for a breath, I worried I'd done or said something wrong. Those old fears began to close back in around me, but then Hunter said, "I think that's the first time you've called me Daddy outside of the bedroom."

My heart quickly dislodged itself from my throat.

"I've definitely called you Daddy in your living room, and probably the bathroom."

"In a non-sexual way," he corrected.

I swallowed audibly, tongue sticking to the roof of my mouth. He was probably right, and that…

"Is that okay?" I asked quietly. "We've never really talked about being this way outside of sex."

We hadn't talked about it, but I'd thought about it. I'd thought about it a lot, especially after talking to Keith and Verity. And especially after being around Silas and Marshall. Silas was always subservient to Marshall. Sometimes it was more obvious than others, but the dynamic was always crystal clear. At least it was to me.

"You can call me anything you want anytime you want," he assured me. "But if you want to start calling me Daddy and meaning it, things between us are going to change."

"I know, I—"

"I would want you to move in," he blurted, cutting off my protest. I pulled my arm away from my eyes, blinking my shitty popcorn ceiling into focus. "You what?"

"It's a responsibility, right?"

"Have you been talking to Marshall about this?" I asked.

"My brother is not the only resource for information about power exchange dynamics, Lincoln," he said, voice dry.

Of course he hadn't talked to Marshall about it. He didn't have anyone he could talk to about it without things getting weird, and I was over here sound-boarding our relationship off what felt like the entire LA kink scene. I was a shit, and I definitely didn't deserve him.

"I know you're not a submissive," Hunter said quickly. "That's not what I meant to imply."

"I know you didn't." I rolled onto my stomach and buried my face into the pillow, desperate to scream. "I just don't think this is a conversation to have over the phone."

"You're probably right." He exhaled a laugh.

"I was just calling to tell you how hard it makes me to see you come," I murmured.

"Obviously the feeling is mutual."

"I...I wanted to see if you had any requests. If I do film again today."

My second-round erection had definitely started to flag after the misdirection in our conversation, but if I ignored the words and thought about the end result, it was right back in full force between my legs. I secretly loved the idea of living with Hunter. I loved the possibility of him wanting to be more dominant with me. That didn't mean I was ready to let go of my own dominance, and I didn't think he'd ever ask that of me, but still...

"Are you hard?" Hunter asked.

I slid my hand down my stomach and circled my thumb and finger around the base of my half-mast dick. I hadn't bothered to get dressed after filming or editing, which had turned out to be great now considering the easy access to my dick.

"Yeah," I told him. Hunter was silent, and I swallowed hard before correcting myself and saying, "Yes, Sir."

I went from half-hard to rigid enough to facet diamonds in the blink of an eye.

"I don't want you to come," he said quietly.

I pictured him at work, sitting behind a desk in his expensive slacks and his crisp button-up. He had a purple tie on when he'd left in the morning, and I envisioned him smoothing one hand down the top of it like he hadn't just exploded my brain. If someone were to see him, they'd think he was discussing a deposition or whatever lawyers did. They definitely wouldn't think he was setting my entire nervous system on fire.

"I want you to get close, though," he said. "I want you to touch yourself until you're right there and then I want you to stop."

I groaned, rutting into the blankets and finally letting out the scream I'd wanted to loose earlier. On the other end of the call, Hunter laughed at me.

"Can you do that for me?"

"I'm sure I can."

"I'll make it worth your while," he promised me. "If you come over at the end of the night. I'll be done with dinner by nine."

It was barely one in the afternoon.

"That's an eternity from now," I whined.

"It's not so long," he said. "Prove to me you brought yourself right to the edge, and I'll make it worth your while after dinner. Deal?"

"I don't think these kind of relationships involve bartering," I grumbled.

"Don't they?"

I bit the inside of my cheek and wanted to curse wherever he was getting all of his extremely correct information about BDSM. It was almost unfair how naturally it all came to him. It was much easier for him than it was for me. Hunter had taken to dominance and submission like a fish to water, and I thought of Keith's partner Justin. And that wasn't to say dominance was work for me, but dominance was safety and it was protection, and I did actually like it. But submission offered me those things too. At least, it offered them to me with Hunter.

"Any other requests?" I asked.

"Would you wear a plug for me?"

Heat raced up my spine, and I wanted to throw a blanket over Feeny's tank for how embarrassing it was to burn as hot as I did at the very simple question. "Are you telling me to?"

"I'm asking if you want to."

It was almost unfair, I decided, for Hunter to be so accommodating. He had never tried to force submission out of me, and I was certain he never would.

"Will it make you hard?" I whispered.

"Knowing you're stretching your hole for me all day?" He laughed, rather sardonically. "Yeah, Lincoln. That will make me hard."

"Then yes."

"Film your video first," he said. "Get as close as you can without actually coming and then stop. Edit it however you want and send it to me. Then I want you to shower and prep yourself. And after you're clean for me, I want you to film yourself putting the plug in and send me that one too."

"Who are you?" I rasped, precum smearing across my sheets like a Vegas hotel fountain. "And what have you done with Hunter Covington?"

There was the briefest pause, and then he asked, "Was that too much?"

"No!" My voice was so fucking loud. How desperate. I cleared my throat and started again, "No. It was…it was perfect. I just didn't expect you to be so bold."

"You bring it out in me."

My eyes burned, and I rolled onto my back again, digging my fingers against the corners of my eyelids.

"Is there anything I can do for you in the meantime?" Hunter asked.

Only about a thousand things.

"Tell me you love me."

He exhaled a breath into the phone, straight into my ear. "Oh, sweetheart. I love you so much."

"I love you," I said back.

"I have a meeting, Lincoln. I've got to go. Do you remember everything I asked?"

"Wank, edit, shower, plug," I repeated.

"Perfect. I'll see you at nine."

It wasn't a question; it was a statement. It was a command.

The call disconnected, and it took all my strength to not throw my phone against the wall. I was so fucking hard and so fucking head over heels for this man. There was no saving me. My defenses? Gone. There wasn't a single wall I'd ever built that this man couldn't knock down with a word or a look. He knew all the ways to unman me, to weaken me, to hold me. To be so seen was fucking disconcerting, and I imagined this must have been how Silas felt in those early days with Marshall. Maybe it was a genetic trait possessed by all the Covington men.

"What are we going to do, Feeny?" I asked my fish, who swam around his tank oblivious to the mental struggle going on inside my skull.

Blindly, I fired off a text to Silas.

> Were you ever worried you were in over your head with Marshall?

He answered me quickly.

> Not in any ways that were real.

I understood the truth of that statement down to the marrow of my bones. This fear and this doubt that incessantly tried to tell me I wasn't good enough for Hunter or that things between us wouldn't last wasn't a real doubt. It wasn't a true fear. It was a defense and a response, and it had no place in my relationship with Hunter.

"Patron saint of being in too fucking deep and liking it," I muttered under my breath. Then I set up my phone, slicked my hand with lube, and did exactly what Hunter had told me to do.

CHAPTER 32
HUNTER

Lincoln's face when he stopped masturbating, the agonized pull of his mouth and the wide flare of his nostrils paired with a desperate little whimper…it was enough to make me combust. Thankfully—or not—I was saved from a miserable fate by the towering frame of my youngest brother outside of my car, rapping his knuckles against the passenger window. I fumbled my phone, trying to turn off the screen and shove it into my pocket before climbing out of the car and giving him what I hoped was a very innocent smile.

Smith eyed me warily, chewing at the inside of his lip. "You good?"

"Yeah," I said, "Yep."

He traced his tongue across the front of his teeth, a decidedly Marshall move before saying, "I know he does sex work. I've had sex with him."

"I know you have."

"It's not like…it's not like I haven't seen it before. Is all I meant."

It was a fair enough statement, though biting in its implication that there were no private moments between me and

Lincoln, that just because he posted videos online, there was nothing special just for us.

"That one was not for sale," I said, surprised at how protective I felt in that moment, not just of Lincoln's work but of our relationship itself.

I didn't want to fight with my brother. He was young, and the comment landed as I'd intended. Smith winced, dropping his head back and staring up at the sky for a breath before he looked back at me, earnest as ever. "You're right. That was… I'm sorry."

"It's okay," I told him. "I promise."

"I shouldn't have said that."

"Smith, it's…I get it." I slung an arm around my brother's shoulder and started us both toward the restaurant. "Lincoln's relationship with his friends is different than most people. His work is also…" I stopped myself from saying different than most, considering there was a time when he and I both had done different flavors of the same work. "Moral of the story, I know you didn't mean it poorly."

"I'm sorry, Hunter," he mumbled. "I've not been myself lately."

I imagined it was hard being Smith, on account of the fact he idolized Marshall very nearly to the point of detriment, and Marshall had just gently slid all of us, Smith included, out of being his first priority in life. It was like all of us seeing a different side of him for the first time, and while I was happy my brother was happy, I was not happy my other brother was not.

"There's been a lot of changes," I agreed.

We stepped up in front of Cunningham's, and I pulled the door open. Smith slipped inside first, waving a friendly hello to the hostess who looked at him like he hung the moon. I gave her a curt wave and jogged after my brother, snagging him before we got to the table.

"The hostess is pretty," I said to him.

Smith frowned, looked over his shoulder in the direction we'd come from. "What? Oh. Yeah, she's okay."

"Do you…I know you slept with Lincoln, Smith. Do you prefer men?"

My youngest brother rolled his eyes at me, looking like a petulant teenager all over again. "I don't prefer anybody."

"Is there a label for that?"

We came around the corner, and I saw Finn and Marshall already at our usual booth, both of them relaxed in some casual conversation. Drinks for all four of us were already on the table, Finn's mostly empty and Marshall's nearly full.

"No. I mean, maybe. But what I meant is I haven't thought about it at all."

I figured that was a lie, but I wasn't going to press the conversation in front of smartass Finn and doting father figure Marshall. Smith sank down into the booth beside Marshall, and I took my seat beside Finn. He glanced up at me, looking more himself than he had in weeks. Sometimes, I wished I knew more about these Neil and Annette people so I could track them down and ask them what the hell they were doing fucking around with my brother. Why had they hurt him so carelessly?

But I also knew, even if I did have a way to get in touch with them, I wasn't privy to my brother's sex life, just like none of them were aware of mine…though maybe things with me and Lincoln were a little more open book than if I had ended up with someone else. Silas knew what Lincoln did for work, and Finn knew what I'd dabbled in. Marshall most certainly knew about Lincoln, but I hoped Finn had held my confidence about my little experiments in sex work.

The night I'd come clean with him, I thought the floor was going to fall out from under me, but Finn had taken my secrecy mostly in stride. If anything, my confession had opened a new door for us to share more than we had before. Finn and I had always been close, but I felt closer to him now than I ever had. At least, I did when he wasn't turned upside down about the married couple he'd gotten involved with.

"Are you excited for tomorrow?" Marshall asked, drawing me out of my brain and back to the table.

Tomorrow.

Tomorrow.

Oh, right.

"Yeah, I am actually." Before leaving work, I'd chatted a little with Winters about the gathering Saturday. It was meant to be small and celebratory, no more than fifty people by most counts and a fair percent of the attendee group being my brothers.

"Is Andrew coming?" Finn asked.

"He is."

"Is he staying the night?"

I shrugged and took a sip of my vodka soda. "We haven't talked about it. I'm sure if he wanted to stay, he would get a hotel."

"Can he afford it?" Finn pressed.

"I don't know what his financial situation is, Finn," I said to my brother, somewhat annoyed at the line of questioning.

"Just ours then?"

Ah. It was the jealousy talking.

"You know more about my finances than I know about yours," I said. "Considering you help me with my taxes every year, but if you have enough money for that horrible pink paint we did your office in, I think you're doing just fine."

"Oh, my *God*!" Finn threw his hands up in the air, a sputtering laugh dying in his throat. "They use it in museums. It's supposed to be relaxing and introspective."

"Those are words you could use," Marshall teased, and

Finn gave both of us the finger before flagging down the waiter for another round and an appetizer.

I was definitely hungry, but I had big plans for the night with Lincoln, and there was no way I was going to eat a plate of lasagna before going home to him. The video he'd recorded for me earlier in the day was still burned onto my retinas, the desperate flush that spread across his chest with every stroke an addicting bleed I wanted to see up close and personal.

"Anyway," I said, clearing my throat and smiling at each of my brothers. "Seven tomorrow. They're having it at the office so you have the address."

"What time is Andrew coming up?" Marshall asked.

While I was annoyed they were still relying on me to be the middleman between them and our new brother, I was thankful at least for the interest. Their reception to the idea of a fifth brother had been chilly at best, sending Smith into a near spiral that eventually led him right into my boyfriend's bed, and I would like to avoid a repeat of that, if at all possible.

Instead of answering them, I pulled my phone out of my pocket and scrolled down to the group text none of them had used since I started it.

> Hey A. What time are you coming to town tomorrow?

Everyone's phones buzzed, and I set mine down on the table and shrugged at them. My screen hadn't even gone dark before another text came in, and I arched my brow at Finn, who swiped his screen on.

"Andrew says lunchtime," he repeated.

"Lincoln and I are going to meet up with him," I said.

"And you didn't invite us?" Smith frowned.

"I started a group text so you could make your own plans. So you could each have your own relationships with him," I told my youngest brother. "I'm sure if you want to join us for lunch, your presence will be more than welcome."

"I've got plans," Finn said, setting his phone facedown on the table.

"Of course you do," I said, shaking my head.

For as eager as I was to get home to Lincoln after dinner, I was equally invested in finding out what had crawled up Finn's ass and died. He was absolutely still reeling from whatever had transpired with the married couple, but it was very unlike him to carry any sort of attachment this long. I narrowed my eyes at him, and he matched my expression, waiting me out.

I was the first one to look away, breaking the tension. Beside me, Finn exhaled heavily.

"I need to piss," I said, climbing out of the booth and knowing without looking back that he would follow. He was so close behind me, I didn't even think he waited until my knees had cracked into place to start after me.

Locked in the confines of the bathroom, I poked my brother in the center of his chest. "What is going on with you?"

"I need a vacation," he answered. "And I need to repaint my office."

My tongue stuck to the roof of my mouth, and I swallowed down any sort of biting remark I wanted to land.

"Where do you want to go?"

"Someplace with a beach and endless daiquiris." Finn dropped his head against the wall, and I patted his cheek gently, not quite an embrace but a lingering touch just the same.

"Whatever is going on with you, Finn, you'll come out the other side of it," I promised him.

"I know," he murmured. "I'm just…I just miss what I had."

Then he nodded, rubbing the side of his finger against the underside of his nostril like he'd just made up his mind about something. He let out a loud sniffle, scrunching his nose and then straightening his shoulders, rallying and ready to go.

"You can have it again."

"Rather not," he said, grinning at me with the barest hint of mischief in his eye. "I learned the lesson the hard way."

"Finn."

Someone opened the door, and Finn cleared his throat, warning me, "Don't say a word about it to Marshall."

"Don't say a word about what to me?" Marshall asked.

Finn grimaced, banging his head against the wall. I shrugged my shoulders at him, not surprised in the least that Marshall had finally come after us. Ever the patriarch, always the fixer.

"I do hate the pink," Finn said, corner of his mouth pulling up into a smirk. "You were both right."

I shot a scathing look at my brother as the door to the bathroom opened again, and Smith crammed himself into the space with us.

"I can't believe you guys left me out there, and you're not even really pissing." He sounded actually hurt, and I leveled a look up at Marshall.

"I would love to, if everyone would shut up," I told Smith, edging my way out of the group and into one of the stalls.

"You're right," Marshall said next. "Come on."

It was under a minute before he'd herded Finn and Smith out of the bathroom, and not many seconds after that before my phone pinged with a text message.

MARSHALL

I'm worried about Finn.

He'll be fine.

Do you know what's wrong?

I have an idea.

> And it's nothing we can fix.

> You should be more concerned about Smith and his idolatry of you.

I know.

> Make time for him like you used to.

Marshall didn't have anything to say to that, which I took as a good sign.

Before joining the three of them back at the table, I turned down the volume on my phone and gave another watch to the video Lincoln had made for me earlier in the day. The things I was going to do to that man when I got home were unmatched, and if I made it through the weekend without convincing him to move in with me, I would be an absolute failure at life.

If he wanted to keep his apartment, that was fine, but I wanted him at mine. I'd bring the fish over myself if that was what I had to do. We could go over there first thing tomorrow or Sunday and transport Feeny to a new home on my dresser if that was what Lincoln wanted to do. Then we'd have lunch with Andrew, and at some point, I'd make time to fill Lincoln up with cum and shove a plug up his ass, just like I'd promised the night I invited him to the party. I was head over heels for Lincoln Summers, and I was ready for the whole world to know it.

CHAPTER 33
LINCOLN

At 8:45, I'd stripped out of my clothes and sank down onto my knees at the foot of Hunter's bed. He was due home sooner rather than later, but I needed the biting press of the floor against my bones to keep me from coming untouched. What a change in me, from being so certain of my dominance to leaning more into submission every day. I definitely appreciated the dichotomy of it, even if walking both sides of the line made things difficult for me mentally some days.

Reaching between my legs, I made a loose overhand fist and stroked gently down my shaft. The touch, even feather-light, was too much. I released my dick and grabbed my thighs, digging my fingernails into my skin until the sharp bursts of pain snapped me out of the haze. It was the plug in my ass that had done me in, the weight and press of it inside of me. Jostling with every step, every move.

Honestly, it had been the whole day, though.

Jerking off for him and not finishing, taking a shower and prepping myself for him before putting the plug in. It had turned the entire day into foreplay, and I had no fucking idea how Hunter had made it through work—in an office, no less—and dinner with his brothers without losing his mind.

I'd have my answer soon enough, because from the other end of the house, I heard the front door slam open, then closed. I scrambled off my place on the ground, hoping the redness on my knees didn't give away the position I'd been trying so hard to get comfortable in. Hunter came around the corner in a flash, shoes off, feet bare, one hand loosening his tie and the other fighting with his belt. When he saw me, his eyes went dark, the hunger apparent on his face. The sight of him was the same as drinking a whole bottle of wine. The hazy want and the unsteady legs. Trying to right myself, I swallowed hard and tweaked at one of my nipple piercings.

"Look at you," he rasped, finally winning the battle with his tie.

"I've been good for you all day, Daddy," I told him, voice shaking as badly as my thighs. "Now please get on your knees and let me come in your mouth."

Hunter's jaw quivered, his pants falling to the floor. He still had his shirt on, half unbuttoned. He stepped out of his pants and surged forward, grabbing me around the back of the head and crashing our mouths together. He kissed me hard and urgently, walking us both until we were at the edge of the bed. I expected him to push me onto my back and crawl between my legs, but what happened next was even better.

Hunter turned at the last minute, bending his knees and landing on the mattress with a soft puff of breath against my lips. He spread his bare thighs to make room for my naked body, the press of my dick against his stomach almost enough to get me off without any other stimulation.

"That's fine if that's really what you want," he whispered against the corner of my mouth. Hunter grabbed my cock and slid it over his balls and toward his own ass. "But I was hoping you could finish here instead."

Bracketing my hands on either side of his face, I put enough space between us that I could stare down at him to make sure he hadn't lost the plot entirely.

"Are you being for real right now?"

"Very."

My jaw went dry as a the desert, and I rocked back onto my heels so I could better appreciate the man beneath me. Hunter's cock was hard as mine, an angry pink and purple-looking thing with a slick crown and throbbing pulse of its own. His chest heaved with every breath, and I took my time undoing the remaining buttons on his shirt so I could spread it open and really see him.

Hunter Covington was a work of art, thick muscles and a sturdy build, with plush lips meant for kissing and dark eyes that had no place being out of the bedroom. And he was on his back beneath me, looking at me like I had hung him the fucking moon.

"I don't care if you come as soon as I touch your asshole," I said. "I want to take my time with you."

"You better," he murmured, grabbing my hips and pushing into me.

My dick pulsed against his hole, desperate to get inside. He was going to have to wait.

"Hunter…"

He shook his head.

"Daddy," I corrected myself, the honorific dragging a full-body shiver out of me. "Are you going to be my good boy now?"

"The best," he whispered.

Nodding, I groaned, pulling away enough to lean over the side of the bed. His clothes were scattered across the floor like breadcrumbs of eagerness. I snatched his tie up and ran the smooth silk through my fingers, pulling it tight and making a quick knot with two loops on either side.

"Can I?"

In response, he held his hands between us, wrists together in offering. If Hunter felt me shake while I tightened the binds around his wrists, he didn't call me out on it. Nor did he say anything when I leaned over the top of him, pinning his bound hands to the pillow. What he did do, though, was nip at my nipple, teeth catching on the barbell and making me wince.

I drew back quicky, grabbing his cheeks hard and pinching until his lips puckered out like a fish. The rush of control rolled through me like a heatwave, sweat immediately prickling against the back of my neck. It had been so long since I'd indulged this part of myself, and leaning into it now felt aligning myself with a place I was always meant to be.

"Bad boy, Daddy," I warned. "You said you were going to be good."

"I'm sorry, Sir," he murmured, nostrils flaring.

I must have died.

This had to be a dream, this perfect blending of dominance and submission wrapping around us and giving me everything I'd always wanted. Everything that had always been missing.

"If I let go of your hands, will you stay still?"

Hunter's chest heaved with every breath, but he managed a rough nod. For good measure, I pressed his wrists and his head down against the pillow before releasing him. My cock was so hard I could have beat him with it and left bruises that would last for a week, but I slid down his body, ignoring the way the plug in my ass weighed urgently against my prostate. I grabbed Hunter's thighs, spread him open, and buried my face between his cheeks.

The first thing I tasted was smears of my own precum, then Hunter's soap and his sweat. He arched off the bed with a desperate shout, but he did keep his wrists above his head where I'd left them. I would need to reward him for good behavior after all.

"I haven't—" he tried to stop me, but the words died when I licked a hot stripe from his hole to his taint.

"You taste like everything I've ever wanted," I promised him. "But I'll stop if you would rather I don't."

Hunter stared down his chest at me with frantic eyes. "Don't stop."

I licked him again, puckered my mouth against his rim, and speared my tongue into his asshole, rutting against the sheets the whole time, far too close to my own release for comfort.

"Do not come until my cock is in your ass," I warned, knowing that even though I wanted to…with Hunter like this, I could not take my time. He wasn't going to last and, honestly, neither was I.

I desperately needed lube, but the thought of peeling my face out of Hunter's ass for anything short of the apocalypse was a future I didn't think I could face. He looked too pretty with his hands bound over his head, though, so I reluctantly pulled myself away long enough to get the bottle from the nightstand. I made a mess of my cock and my fingers, an even bigger mess of him. I smeared lube up and down his crack alternating between teasing him with the tip of my aching cock and the press of my trembling fingers.

Hunter scrabbled his hands against the top of the pillow, the headboard, his cheeks so pink he looked like he had a fever. God, he was fucking perfect, and he was fucking mine.

It was a curious chain of events, I realized, that had brought me to this moment. From that fated and horrible night at Rapture where I'd thrown my best friend—accidentally— into harm's way, only for him to be rescued by the older brother of the man who'd flipped my life on its head. Hunter was everything I ever wanted and nothing I thought I needed, and sliding one finger into the tight heat of his asshole, I also knew he was going to be the death of me.

Hunter whimpered and bucked off the bed, clamping down so hard around my finger I had no idea how I was going to get my dick into him. Gently, I petted my free hand over the top of his hip, soothing him like he was a terrified animal, cornered and waiting to be branded.

"You're all right," I whispered, softly digging my fingers into his thigh until he startled and stilled. I had one finger up his ass, all the way to the knuckle, and enough lube between us he was probably going to need a new mattress. "Do you want me to stop?"

"No," he panted, shaking his head and screwing his eyes closed. "I want to be good for you."

My heart cracked in a new and unexpected kind of way, and I managed to get a second finger into Hunter, pressed tight alongside the first.

"You are the best," I promised him. "The best boy, the best Daddy, the best everything."

He swallowed hard, eyes still tightly closed. With every breath, Hunter's chest heaved. Staying still and calm was more than work for him, and I wished there was an easier way to get him ready for what he wanted that didn't feel so much like torture.

"You're so close, aren't you?" I asked, my free hand again petting calming lines down the angles of his hip and side.

He managed a nod.

"Open your eyes," I told him, and he did, the dark pools of his irises shining with barely restrained tears. "Is it too much?"

"No," he whimpered. "I just want…"

He didn't need to say anything more.

I wanted too.

I understood.

"I know I said I didn't want you to come until I was inside

of you, but I want you to come as soon as you need to." I eased my fingers out before pushing them both back in. Deep. His entire body shook with a tremor that reached all the way down to his toes.

"I can do it for you, Sir."

I bit down hard on the inside of my cheek, a violent taste of iron landing against my tongue.

"I can do it for you too," I said, moving my fingers into a scissor shape, slow as I could manage without setting him off. It meant something to him to follow this instruction, to not come until I was inside of him, but I couldn't hurt him in the process. I couldn't rush it, just like...just like he hadn't rushed me. Hunter had shown me nothing but patience and kindness, waiting for me to work out my own issues and come to my own conclusions about what I wanted and needed.

Now it was my eyes filled with tears, and I sucked in a sharp breath, finally pulling my fingers out of him and lining up my cock. In a perfect world, Hunter could have stood to take some more prep. Especially since he didn't bottom often— if ever—but it was equally cruel to drag this out when he was so desperate for it.

I was desperate for him.

Maybe there would come a day when I could eat his ass for hours, tease his prostate and milk the cum right out of him until he didn't have anything left to give me. Maybe it wouldn't hurt him to be stripped as bare before me as I often found myself with him. Today, though, today I needed to feel the heat of him surround me and nothing else.

"Are you sure about this?" I asked, hesitating.

"I'm not made of glass," he murmured, hands still above his head, the tail of the tie snaking through the dark waves of his hair. "But if you don't put your cock inside of me, I might crack open like I am."

"Okay," I croaked, notching myself against Hunter's tight opening. "Alright. Then…ask me nicely."

Hunter's legs gave a fierce shake, falling open wide on either side of the bed.

"Please fuck me, Si—"

He choked on the word as my cock pushed into him. His body was so hot, so fucking tight. Even with all the lube, getting into Hunter's body was a squeeze. I fought through it, giving him my whole length on one go, and then I cradled his shaft against my fingers.

"Come now," I demanded, and his cock spasmed in my hand, a thick rope of cum shooting across his stomach, followed by another and another, until it was nothing more than dribbles and pulses left. He held his legs open by sheer willpower alone, and it was my hands pressing him down into the bed while we both rode out the taut convulsions of his release.

His cock stayed hard in my palm, hot and heavy, and I gave him two more thrusts before the pleasure on Hunter's face pushed me over the edge right after him. My hips jerked, and I buried myself to the hilt, my entire body quaking from the force of my orgasm. I bent forward over his body and shook through it, sputtering and gasping, seeing stars.

"Perfect," Hunter moaned, raising his hands between us. I couldn't even see straight, but I understood the ask. It took forever to get the knot undone, but as soon as it was loose, Hunter had my cock out of his ass and my body pressed into the bed. He aligned himself behind me, sweaty chest against sweaty back, and he lifted my leg into the air with one hand and pulled the plug out of my ass with the other.

I shouted in shock and in arousal, and Hunter quickly replaced the silicone toy with the thick heat of his shaft. Sinking into me as thoroughly as I'd entered him, he went still with our bodies joined. He wrapped his arms around me and held me, both of us gasping for air. Something had…changed between us. Changed for the better, but all I could taste was the blood from when I bit myself earlier and the salt of tears I didn't realize I'd even been shedding. Pressing my head against his shoulder, I angled my face up for a kiss, which he gave me.

A gentle drag of his mouth against mine, a violent shudder as his cock pulsed inside of my ass, thickening to an impossible width that had me arching and crying out in Hunter's arms.

"I'm here," he whispered against the corner of my mouth. "I've got you."

One of his hands slid down my chest, and he stroked my cock until my body wasn't anything more than nerves and synapses, sparking and bursting beneath my skin. It was slow after that, slow and easy and too much and not enough all at the same time. After what felt like hours, Hunter rolled me onto my back and buried his face against the crook of my neck. He shuddered through another orgasm, pulling me along after him until his fingers and my thighs were sticky with cum.

"I'm your Daddy," he murmured into my sweaty and matted hair.

"Sir."

"Your good boy."

"Best boy," I croaked.

Hunter drew shapes in the swirls of cum I'd spilled onto my stomach, and he peppered kisses against my neck and my jaw.

"I want you to move in with me," he said.

And there was only one answer for me to give him. A tired nod not of concession but want.

"I'll move in, Daddy," I whispered. "I love you."

Hunter eased himself out of me, rolling us into as comfortable of a snuggle as our sweaty bodies would allow. He made no move for the shower, instead using his body to pin me against him, leaving a kiss against the top of my head.

"You've changed my life, Lincoln. And I love you too."

CHAPTER 34
HUNTER

Saturday morning came too soon, a wash of bright light through the window that cast a golden glow across the foot of the bed. Lincoln was asleep beside me on his stomach, both arms folded and hands pillowed beneath his face. The smooth planes of his back stretched down to the sheet tucked around his waist, and I tugged it lower over the globes of his ass with a low groan.

Being as quiet as I could, I searched around the bed for the lube. It was down past my feet, and I snicked the cap open and poured enough on my cock that pushing into him without prep wouldn't hurt more than he liked. Breathing heavily, I stroked myself until I was already close to coming, then I straddled Lincoln and dragged my cock through his crack. He was covered in flaking lube and dry cum. My tip dragged over his hole, and he moaned, bowing his back and pushing against me. I took it for the invitation it was, mounting Lincoln and sliding into him.

He was awake before I bottomed out, grinding down into the sheets to better take my weight on top of him. He groaned sleepily, and I braced my forearm against the top of his back and began to move. It was against my nature to not worry about Lincoln's pleasure in these interludes, but all I had to do was remind myself he *wanted* to be taken this way, and then it was easy to make way for my own arousal.

"Daddy," he whimpered, the word almost drowned out by the slap of our skin.

"Sssh, sweetheart." I dropped a kiss against the shell of his ear seconds before my hips stuttered and the first jet of cum spurted out of my cock. Letting all of my weight fall onto Lincoln, I rutted into him until my balls were empty before rolling off of him and flinging an arm over my eyes.

Lincoln made the happiest noises, wiggling his ass before turning his head so he could face me. His cheeks were flushed, his eyes closed, and his smile soft.

"That's my kind of good morning," he murmured. "Maybe next time get a toy in there too."

He was out of his mind if he thought I'd for one second forgotten his little double penetration fantasy. It was the opposite, in fact, permanently etched into my brain.

"I want you conscious and desperate for that," I said, reluctantly crawling out of bed and stretching my arms over my head.

"Is it time to get up?" he asked with a yawn.

"Not for you."

I pulled the sheets back up his legs, leaving his ass exposed to the air. He smiled into the pillow with a sigh.

"I'm going to make some coffee," I told him. "Check to see when Andrew will be up. I want you to stay in bed as long as you want, and then when you're up, I want to talk about last night."

While I spoke, I watched Lincoln carefully, monitoring his face for any signs of distress over my statement. None came. If anything, his smile turned to one of peaceful resignation, and it was hard to not feel like I'd won a war. With one last look at his almost-sleeping body, I forced myself to turn away. I was in desperate need of a shower, but coffee was more urgent so I pulled a pair of dirty underwear off the top of my hamper and stepped into them, hobbling out to the kitchen.

The apartment was dark, but the sky outside the window was light enough I didn't need anything artificial to see my way around. I allowed myself to dwell awhile on the fantasy of moving Lincoln in with me. Maybe it was too fast, but I would argue with any of my brothers over it if they tried to protest. Marshall had moved quickly with Silas, and I had judged him for it, but now with Lincoln asleep in my bed and his belongings in an apartment across town, I understood the urgency.

It made sense to integrate him, to make his things my things and mine his. There was no part of my life I didn't want him to have access to and nothing of his I wanted hidden from me. He might have other plans for the last part, but it wasn't anything I couldn't work through. Resting my hip against the counter in the kitchen, I set a pot of coffee to brew. I didn't have my phone, and when I shuffled back into the bedroom to get it, Lincoln was sound asleep in the position I'd left him.

Pulling my phone off the charger, I snapped a picture of him before heading back into the living room. I settled onto my couch and scrolled through the news and my social media. It was barely after seven. Andrew wouldn't be hitting the road for a handful of hours still, but I knew, of anyone, Finn would be awake.

He'd always been an early riser, so I fired him off a quick text.

You up?

His answer came quickly.

FINN

No

Are you lying?

Yes.

I stabbed my finger onto his name and turned on speaker phone, adjusting the volume low so the call didn't wake Lincoln.

"I am naked, though," Finn said in lieu of hello.

"I'm in yesterday's underwear," I countered.

"That's the most shocking thing about you," he said. "To what do I owe the early morning honor, brother?"

In the kitchen, the coffee pot beeped its completion. I went to get a cup before settling back in to talk to Finn.

"Had some time to myself," I said. "And I wanted to talk."

"This sounds like an intervention."

"Is there something happening that needs intervening?" I asked.

"Yeah." He snorted. "If you could help me stop going back to this couple…"

I hummed a thoughtful sound. "Why don't you tell me about that, actually. Now that you mention it."

"I don't know what there is to say." Finn groaned and the sheets rustled. He was definitely naked and probably still in bed himself. "Do you have coffee?"

"Of course."

"Can I come over?"

"You'd drive twenty minutes across town just because I have coffee made?" I cracked my neck, letting my stare settle on the large window on the far wall, the sky quickly getting bluer and bluer with every minute.

"Never mind."

"Of course you can come over," I told him. "Lincoln is here, and we're going to have lunch with Andrew at some point today, though."

"I can tolerate the first part but have no interest in the latter," he said. "If I come over, will you put on clean underwear?"

"Just for you."

"Thank God," Finn said, then the call disconnected.

With a weary breath, I took my first drink of coffee.

I was worried about Finn. Like, really worried about him. It had been years since his last serious relationship and he'd buttoned himself up tight after that had gone south. He'd absolutely had casual flings since then, but the level of distress he'd shown over this couple was quickly approaching relationship levels. I worried he hadn't been talking to anyone about what was going on, so of course he could come over. My brothers were always welcome in my apartment, even if Marshall was the brother who had the paternal instincts to accommodate us all.

Another drink of coffee and I headed for the bathroom, taking a quick shower and making sure there was no cum or lube left on my thighs by the time I finished. Cleaning the crack of my ass sent a shiver through me, a biting reminder of Lincoln's face pressed between my cheeks, his fingers digging into my thighs, his cock spearing into me…the way he pulsed and thickened when he came. The thought of it was enough to chub me up, but I ignored my dick for the first time in weeks.

When I got out of the shower, Lincoln was awake but still in bed, stretched out like a cat and tangled in the sheets. I crawled over toward him and left a gentle kiss against the corner of his mouth.

"There is coffee," I told him. "But my brother is on his way over."

He chased after another kiss. "Which one?"

"Finn."

"Do you want me to go?" he asked.

"I never want you to leave," I said. "We still need to talk about some of the things we said last night."

Lincoln twisted onto his back. "Is there time?"

I sat down and stroked a careful line from his shoulder to his elbow. "I meant everything I told you last night. I want you to move in here with me."

"I have a lease," he said.

"How long is left on it?"

"Four more months."

I wanted to spend the rest of my life with this man. I could manage four more months if I had to.

"Ask if you can break it," I said. "If there's a penalty, I'll pay it."

"You don't have to do that."

"Daddy wants to," I said, maybe a little sharper than I'd meant to. Lincoln's eyes went wide at the statement, and his brows knit together in confusion. "I meant that too. Didn't you?"

"Yes, but—"

"No." I shook my head, tutted my tongue against the roof of my mouth.

"Thank you," Lincoln whispered, blinking hard.

I brushed his hair back from his forehead, kissed his temple. I wanted to kiss every inch of his skin every day until the end of time.

"Do you need time alone with your brother?" he asked next.

I breathed deep, thinking about the truth of the answer. There wasn't anything I wanted to keep from Lincoln, but Finn might not feel the same way.

"What I need is for you to go to your apartment after you've had your coffee, and I need you to get your fish and bring him over here. I need you to get your sex toys and your clothes and the things that mean the most to you. I need those here before Andrew shows up for lunch."

Lincoln scoffed. "Trying to show off?"

"You are worth showing off," I told him, which earned me a flush on his cheeks. "But no, I just don't want you to talk yourself out of it."

He laughed at that, stretching his body out again with a sense of finality.

"We want the same things," he assured me. "I just don't trust it."

"Do you trust me?" I asked.

"Obviously."

Pride swelled in the center of my chest. "Then that will have to be enough. Now get dressed and come have some coffee. You need to be back here before noon."

Lincoln rolled his eyes at me, but followed the orders. We sat on the couch and drank coffee together, and he waited with me until Finn showed up in plaid pajama pants and an over-sized USC shirt that looked like it once belonged to me. They exchanged casual pleasantries, and Lincoln left with the promise to be back on schedule.

Finn observed it all from the kitchen, pouring himself a cup of coffee before collapsing on my couch with a very unhappy sound. I topped myself off and sat down beside him, angling our bodies together and bringing one leg up onto the cushion.

"This isn't like you," I told him simply.

He shrugged, pulling his lips between his teeth and glancing up at the ceiling. "I know. I just…"

"Whatever it is, it's safe here."

"They're getting a divorce," he blurted. "Neil and Annette."

"Oh."

I wasn't sure what else to say. I didn't think there was much else to say. I knew people where divorce was a good thing, but

Finn's demeanor proved this specific split could not have been worse.

"Do you want to—"

"Because of me," he said next. "They're getting divorced because of me."

My brother, the one Marshall and Smith jokingly referred to as my twin, the one I was the closest with, whose emotions I mirrored the most, took one more drink of his coffee, set his mug on the table, then curled himself into a ball on my lap and for the first time in two years, cried in front of me.

CHAPTER 35
LINCOLN

Packing up my apartment was easy because I didn't have much that mattered. I'd gone through such a massive purge after Silas moved in with Marshall, and I hadn't even bothered to take the collapsed boxes out to the dumpster yet. There were a lot of things that would need to wait, but I grabbed all of my clothes, my pictures and books, my sex toys. My life was contained in a series of boxes that fit on my bed, and while I could have carried them all down to my car one by one, I didn't really want to.

Sitting down in the middle of my life, I pulled out my phone and called Silas, who of course answered before it went to voicemail. He was very in love with his new life and his boyfriend, but he was still my best friend. I was the one who'd been pushing him away since he moved out, not the other way around.

"Hey," he said, happiness echoing through the phone so contagiously I couldn't help but smile.

"You busy?"

"Just having coffee while Marshall works a little. Why?"

"I could use a spare set of hands," I said.

"Yeah," Silas said without even knowing what for. I could

have had a body to bury. It would have made no difference to him. The blind dedication my best friend offered me had my heart expanding painfully against my sternum. "Where are you?"

"My apartment."

"Now?" he asked.

"Yeah, that would be good."

"Do you want me to bring coffee?" he asked next.

"I had some already, but it wouldn't hurt."

"Cool. See you soon, Linc."

Silas hung up and I tossed my phone onto the bed and waited. It took twenty minutes or so for Silas to get to my place, and when he walked in and saw the boxes stacked on the bed, he arched a brow at me in question.

"Going somewhere?" he asked.

"Hunter asked me to move in."

"That's quick."

I held up a hand to stop him, frowning. "Don't start with me."

"I just want you to be sure you're making the right decision."

"I didn't do this when you moved in with Marshall," I reminded him. Even though I'd wanted to, even though that had come from a place of jealousy.

Silas shoved his hands into his pockets and gave a quick scan to my apartment, the state of it, the state of me, and then the fight went out of his shoulders.

"You're right," he conceded, walking toward me until our chests knocked together. He dropped his forehead down low onto my shoulder, and it was second nature to slide my arms around his waist and keep him close. "That was dumb of me."

"You worry about me," I whispered against his ear. "I love that about you."

"He makes you happy?"

I nodded.

"Okay," Silas murmured, bringing his face up so we were almost eye to eye. "I just want the best for you."

"He is."

My best friend's mouth twitched up into a smile, and his eyes narrowed like there was a conspiracy between us.

"I never pegged Hunter as submissive."

The laugh that fell out of my mouth was violent enough to put physical space between us, and the look of confusion on Silas's face only made me laugh harder. I pulled him to the edge of the bed and tugged him down, holding his hand until I could breathe again through the tears.

"He's not," I said, shaking my head. "Not at all. Well…no. He's really not."

"But you…"

"It works for us," I shared, leaning in and pressing our foreheads together. "He's…"

The word lodged in my throat. It was one thing to use it with Hunter, another thing entirely to use it with someone else. Silas had always known me as a dominant, and not that it had any true bearing on the nature of our friendship, but would he look at me differently if he knew what I did behind closed doors? No. That was impossible. He was too good of a person for that, too kind and sincere in everything he did to think less of me for finding something different for myself.

"You don't have to tell me if you don't want."

"He's a Daddy," I admitted. "He's mine, but sometimes he calls me Sir and sometimes he gets on his knees for me, Silas, and it's fucking everything."

His face split into a huge grin, and he grabbed both of my hands, squeezing tight. "I love that for you."

Tears pricked the backs of my eyelids, and I swallowed hard, not wanting to cry in front of him.

"I love him," I rasped.

Silas tipped his chin and pressed our mouths together. He smiled against my lips, and I looped my arms around his shoulders before breaking the kiss and burying my face into the crook of his neck.

"I love him so much," I said.

"I know," he said. "I can tell. And he's lucky for it. He knows that, right?"

I nodded.

"If he hurts you, I'll kill him." Silas could barely get the threat out with a straight face, and his fake bravado had me laughing too.

"No, you won't."

"I would try," he said instead. "Marshall would."

"I doubt that."

"Hey." He grabbed my shoulders, gave me a little shake. "Marshall adores you. If you think he wouldn't come for Hunter if he hurt you, you're underestimating his affection."

I nodded my agreement.

"You got lucky with him, didn't you?" I murmured.

"Very. And so did you. With Hunter."

"Very," I agreed. "But I have to get these boxes and Feeny over to his apartment before lunch, and there's no way I can do it myself without an hour of whining."

"Good thing you've got me then," Silas teased, knocking his elbow into me.

It was all I could do to agree with him, even if the words were twisted into a knot in the back of my throat.

"I'm sorry I haven't been a good friend," I blurted, which earned me a very unhappy and confused look from Silas.

"How have you not been a good friend?"

"I just...I let you move and I know we see each other on Friday—"

"It's not enough."

I huffed a breath that puffed out of my cheeks, and I

shrugged at him. Because I wasn't necessarily sure that was the case.

"It's less than before," I said. "Different from before. But you want to be with Marshall, and I don't blame you for that. I want to be with Hunter as much as I can be too."

"Obviously." Silas grinned, gesturing at the boxes. "We will find something that works for us now. Something new."

"I don't want to be an imposition."

He stood up and scoffed. "You're my best friend."

"I know, but—"

"Maybe we can double date," he suggested, picking up a box without being told. I stood and grabbed one for myself, following Silas toward the door without being asked. "But I think if you call Hunter Daddy in front of Marshall, he might have an aneurysm."

My keys were on the counter, and I hooked my pinky finger through the loop. Silas managed the door open, and we shouldered our way into the hall together.

"It's not like that," I assured him. "That's…it's private for us."

"I love that for you," he said again, and there was no indication he didn't mean it. "But I do have to ask why *Daddy* Hunter isn't the one helping you move."

The way he said Daddy was laced with amusement, and I couldn't stop myself from smiling at how warm it made me feel inside. Even being a joke, I loved the idea of it, loved the feel of it when I thought of how Hunter treated me.

"Finn came over this morning," I said.

We'd made it downstairs to my car, and together we managed to get the trunk open. Silas dropped his box inside and I did the same, then straightened up and brushed myself off. He leveled a worried look at me, and all I could do was shrug. "Something's going on with him, but he's like a vault."

"All that attitude."

"Clearly a defense mechanism," I said, and Silas nodded his agreement.

"I really like Finn, but he's definitely the hardest of them to get a read on."

I closed the trunk, and we headed back upstairs to get more boxes.

"Have you met Andrew?" I asked.

Silas shook his head. "You?"

"Today will be the first time." I grimaced, walking back into the apartment and testing the weight of the boxes to see if I could get more than one on the next trip. "That's wild, though, isn't it? About their dad."

"About their moms," Silas whispered, like anyone was around to hear. "No wonder Finn plays his emotions close to the chest."

"Yeah."

I found two boxes of a tolerable weight and stacked them. Silas grabbed one, and we were back on our walk. It took three more trips to get everything, boxes stacked in the trunk and the back seat by the time we were finished. There were still plenty of things in my apartment, but none of them really mattered. I didn't need my bed when Hunter's was so soft, didn't need my TV or my nightstand when they were secondhand buys in the first place. But still, the thought of unloading them when they'd been mine for so many years had me feeling some kind of way. Like I'd told Hunter earlier in the morning, I had four months left on my lease and while I appreciated his offer to pay any early termination fees, that was a bridge I would cross when we got to it.

"What else?" Silas asked, following my stare around the apartment.

"Just Feeny," I said.

Silas frowned at the fish. "How are you going to get him there without the water sloshing everywhere?"

I frowned too. "I don't know."

"I'll hold him," Silas offered. "Then you can just bring me back here for my car."

"Are you sure?"

"Very," he assured me.

With the utmost care, Silas picked Feeny up from his home on my dresser, cooing down into the water like my fish was an actual, human baby. I rolled my eyes at them while I gathered up Feeny's food. I didn't bother giving my apartment one last look. It wasn't like I was leaving forever, and the things I was leaving behind weren't important. I locked the deadbolt and carefully trailed behind Silas, appreciating how slowly he walked so as to not splash any water over the edge of Feeny's bowl.

The whole way to the car, he whispered sweet nothings down to the fish, only handing him off to me to hold when he needed to get into the passenger seat. Once he was buckled, I passed Feeny back to him, smiling at the way Silas clutched the bowl securely in his lap.

"Do you and Marshall want to have kids?" I asked, sinking down in the driver's seat and turning the car on.

He looked at me with a horrified expression. "No."

"Okay," I chuckled.

"I don't have good role model in the parenting department, and neither does he," Silas reminded me.

"Isn't that a bonus, though? Like you know how *not* to act?"

That question landed a little differently, and Silas knitted his brows together in thought while I carefully pulled out of my parking spot and into the street.

"I don't think Marshall wants to have kids," he finally said.

"Do you?"

"I haven't thought much about it," he said, turning his attention back to Feeny and effectively ending the conversation.

I hadn't put much thought into the whole thing either, but

the way Silas had acted with my fish was so easily paternal, it was really simple to imagine him acting that way with an actual child. I couldn't quite imagine what it would be like to integrate kids into the lifestyle we chose to live, but it had certainly been done before. No matter, if Silas said no, it was a no.

He didn't say another word to me until we reached Hunter's apartment. "Is it okay if I come up?"

"Why wouldn't it be?"

"You said Finn was over. He was upset. I don't want to intrude."

I appreciated the sentiment, but if Hunter wanted his apartment to be my home, I was going to treat it like my home.

"It's fine," I promised, pulling out my phone. "But if it will make you feel better, I'll let him know you're coming up."

Silas's shoulders sagged in relief. "It would."

I helped Silas out of the car much the same way I'd helped him in. On the elevator ride up to the apartment, Hunter's… mine…I realized we were all in uncharted territory, but we were going to have to figure it out sooner or later, and there was apparently no time like the present.

CHAPTER 36
HUNTER

Finn cried on my lap for almost an hour, which was more than all the times I'd ever seen him cry in his entire life put together. He gathered his composure on his own, shaking free of the careful way I'd been carding my fingers through his hair and downing the cold coffee left in his mug.

"Better?" I asked.

He swiped the remaining tears off his lower lash line and nodded, standing up from the couch and walking into the kitchen.

"Just let me wash my face."

"There's washcloths in the bathroom."

But he was already bent over the sink, splashing cold water onto his cheeks. Finn returned with the coffee pot, topping both of our mugs off. Back to the kitchen to return the carafe to the warmer and he was on the couch beside me again, this time upright.

"Do you want to talk about it?"

"I'd prefer you tell me something interesting," he said, staring straight ahead. I opened my mouth, and he leveled a scathing look at me. "Not dinosaur related."

I made a show of snapping my mouth closed and scooting a little closer to him on the couch. He let me lean into him without much more than a grumbled protest. I wanted to tell him something good, something that mattered…something that would make a difference. In the end, the only thing I could offer him was hope.

"It won't be like this forever," I told him.

Finn sucked his tongue across the front of his teeth, eyebrows raised. "No," he agreed. "I imagine not."

He didn't say anything after that, but he did reach across me for the remote. I sipped my coffee while Finn flipped through the channels, finally settling on a show about aliens. I supposed there wasn't anything that needed to be said between us. Finn didn't want to talk, but he didn't want to be alone. There was a distinct difference between the two, and while I was happy to give him both, I couldn't force it on him. Just like Lincoln, Finn had to come around to his own wants organically. I was curious to know what appeal he found from being involved with a married couple, but that was something he would have to tell me on his own time.

The credits on the episode didn't even finish rolling before the programming segued into a fresh episode about different aliens, only punctuated by the sound of a key in the door and the rush of hallway air that always filtered in after the door was opened.

"I have Silas with me!" Lincoln called from the doorway.

Finn tensed but was quick to paste one of his usual, casual smiles on his face. He dropped his head against the back of the couch to better see the hallway, watching the two of them walk in together. Silas held a fishbowl protectively against his chest, and Lincoln had two boxes balanced in his arms.

"Where should I put my stuff?" he asked.

"Hi, Finn," Silas interjected, shrugging a shoulder in greeting. "Hunter."

"Gentlemen," Finn answered back, returning his attention to the TV. His smile faltered but held.

"Wherever you want," I answered, getting up and coming around to meet them at the end of the hallway. I took both of the boxes out of Lincoln's hands, relieved to find they weren't heavy. "The guest room maybe so you have time to go through it? Or my...our bedroom. Whichever."

The corner of his mouth twitched. Before he could say one way or the other, I took the boxes into our bedroom and set them down in front of the dresser. The two of them followed me in, and Silas looked around before setting the fish down on one of the nightstands.

"Do you like the light here?" he asked the fish.

"He doesn't care," Lincoln answered.

Silas shot a sharp glare at Lincoln before turning the bowl a quarter turn. That seemed to please him more, and he joined us on the other end of the bed.

"I don't know what I expected your apartment to look like, Hunter, but it's not this," he said.

I looked around at what I owned excited at the promise of how it would all look to see Lincoln's things interspersed with mine.

"Did you expect something more boring?" I asked.

"I don't know." He made a thoughtful sound in the back of his throat and looked at Lincoln. "Do you want to go get the rest of your boxes?"

"Yeah." Lincoln smiled up at me. "Do you want to help us? Less trips."

"Of course. I'll get Finn."

My brother was already shoving his feet into his sneakers in the entryway.

"I'm gonna go," he said when we all came back to the living room.

"You're gonna help," I corrected. "One trip and then you can go."

Finn grumbled a protest but went along with it. It took the four of us one trip down and back to get the rest of Lincoln's boxes, which was considerably quicker I think than Lincoln had expected it to take. He dusted his hands off on the front of his thighs.

"I just need to take Silas to my apartment to get his car," he said. "Then I'll be back."

"I can take him," Finn offered. "Unless you live in the valley."

"He lives here," I muttered.

"Hollywood," Lincoln advised.

"Better than not," Finn said. "Barely out of the way."

"Are you sure?" Silas asked, bracketing his hands on his hips. He'd met all of us, save for Andrew, but he hadn't really spent any time with us.

"Yeah," Finn assured him, wrapping me in a tighter than normal hug. I slid my arms around his waist and held him until he was ready to let go, giving one last squeeze before pulling away. "I'll see you tonight."

"Can't wait."

Lincoln and Silas said their goodbyes, then Finn and Silas were gone, leaving Lincoln and me in the apartment alone. It was oddly quiet, the TV show on mute since they'd arrived with Lincoln's things.

"How are you feeling?" I asked.

Lincoln toed off his shoes. "Good, I think. There's still a lot at the apartment, but I don't know if I want it."

"We can hire movers," I suggested.

"I don't know if I want it," he repeated.

"Well, when you decide."

Lincoln was next into my arms, a completely different sort of hug than the one my brother had given me. Lincoln curled his arms around my waist and pressed his face against my chest. I looped my arms around his neck and rested my chin on his shoulder, brushing a kiss against his ear.

"Do you want to shower?" I asked.

"Do I smell?"

"Like cum and sweat probably," I teased, breathing him in. "Like sex."

"Then no."

"God, have I told you today that I love you?"

Lincoln laughed and shook his way out of my hold. "I don't think you have."

He walked backward down the hallway and crooked his finger for me to follow. I made it two steps before he tutted his tongue against the roof of his mouth and shook his head disapprovingly. The warning sent a shock of pleasure up my spine, and when he pointed to the floor, there was no hesitation before I went to my knees.

"Crawl, Daddy," he whispered, and I did. One hand in front of the other through the apartment until we were in the primary bathroom. Lincoln stripped out of his clothes, kicking them to the side, and then he made a show of touching himself, sliding his hands all over his thighs and his stomach, tweaking his piercings and tugging on his cock. I rocked back onto my heels, feet together beneath my ass and my knees spread wide.

"Let me have you," I rasped.

Lincoln turned on the shower and tested the water before stepping in. Seeing the droplets rain down and slick his hair, chase each other down the swell of his shoulders and his hips…it was cruel and unusual punishment.

"Not yet," he whispered, shaking his head. "After lunch with your brother, when we're getting ready for your very fancy party."

The thought of Lincoln in *very fancy* clothes was almost

enough to make me come all over the floor. Just one touch of my fingers against my hole and I could easily see this through to the end right there. "Tell me more."

"You wanted me full of cum when I met your business partners," he reminded me, as if I could ever forget. "So, you'll have to make sure to make good on that."

"Oh, I will."

"I think if you come right now, you won't have enough later to make sure I'm *full*."

The way he drew out the syllable had me trembling so hard against the tile floor my knees ached. My cock throbbed aggressively in time with my heart, and I was helpless but to watch Lincoln drag soapy hands all over his body, cupping his balls and sliding through the crack of his ass.

"I'm sure I would."

He laughed at that, rinsed himself, and stepped out of the shower to get a towel. I watched as he dried himself halfway off, wrapping the towel low around his waist and knotting it below his navel.

"Your turn," he murmured, brushing past me and out of the bathroom.

Fuck, Lincoln was so hot when he wanted to be in control. The dichotomy of his moods and his needs would never get boring, and I was the luckiest man in the world to get to explore them both. The odds of us ending up together were stacked from the start, and if I had been any other man…his history with Smith might have been a dealbreaker, his casual affection with his friends, his work…*my* work. The stars had absolutely aligned for the two of us in the most unexpected ways.

"Shower, Sir!" he called out from the bedroom. "It's almost time for lunch."

The warning was a wakeup call, and I crawled the rest of the way to the shower, not quite sure my legs were going to carry me. I did manage to get washed and rinsed, dried and dressed without any further interruption. Lincoln had just settled himself on the counter in the kitchen with a reheated mug of coffee when there was a knock on the door indicating Andrew's arrival. I hesitated, rubbing my hands together before drying them off on my jeans.

"Are you nervous?" Lincoln asked, not leaving his perch.

"A bit," I admitted.

"Don't be. Do you want me to answer?"

"I can do it," I said, willing my legs to carry me to the door.

There was a flash of trepidation on Andrew's face when I opened the front door, but it was gone in a breath. It was the most Finn type of expression change, and I didn't think I'd ever stop being surprised at how much the five of us were alike.

"Hey," I greeted, stepping out of the way to let him in.

"Hey," he said nervously. "Hi."

"Hi," Lincoln blurted from behind me. He'd tucked himself under my arm and stretched his hand out for Andrew to shake. "I'm Lincoln."

"You're not another brother, are you?" Andrew asked, the question dry and biting.

"That would break several laws," he said with a smile. "I'm Hunter's boyfriend."

At the announcement, Andrew relaxed, if only slightly.

"Did you want to come in?" I asked, letting Lincoln drag me a little way out of the entry. It was a relief Lincoln had come home in a dominant mood because he took control of the situation like the absolute boss of a man I always imagined myself to be.

Fuck, this was hard.

My other brothers all assumed it was easy for me to be the contact person, that I enjoyed it, but that couldn't have been further from the truth. Andrew found me because of my work and my ties to some of the contracts our father had been working on recently. It was not my preference to be the unofficial Covington brother spokesperson, but I was the best suited for it.

Much to my dismay.

"You have a gorgeous home, Hunter," Andrew said once we were all inside. Finn's alien show still played silently on the TV, and Lincoln walked me to the couch and all but shoved me down into my seat.

"Did you have an easy drive?" Lincoln asked, sitting on the coffee table so Andrew could take the other spot on the couch.

"Yeah, I came up a few hours ago. Paid for early check-in at the hotel."

"That's good." Lincoln smiled, and as if on some magical cue, his stomach growled. "So, boys, what do we want to do for lunch?"

CHAPTER 37
LINCOLN

Hunter and Andrew were both content to let me steer everything for the afternoon, from picking the restaurant to deciding when we were going to call it a day. The two of them danced around each other like they were both waiting for the other to attack, but by the time we said our goodbyes, they were at least laughing together. Andrew was going to head back to the hotel for dinner and some relaxation before Hunter's party, and we were heading home for Hunter to make good on his promise of plugging me full of cum before meeting his colleagues.

He'd been off since I'd gotten back to the apartment with Silas, and it took all my willpower to convince myself it had to do with his brothers and not with me relocating almost everything I owned into his space. Once we were back in his room, he did stop to say hello to Feeny before stripping out of his clothes, and that had to be a good sign.

Right?

"Are you sure you want me to move in?" I asked, sitting down on the edge of the bed beside him.

"Very sure. Why?"

I shook my head because I didn't want to tell him he was

acting different. He had a lot going on with Andrew being in town and the promotion and me, and I absolutely did not want the me part of the equation to be an added stress for him since I knew the rest of it was.

"Just checking."

Hunter was quiet for a moment before turning to me, his eyes dark. "Which of these boxes has your toys?"

I chuckled, chewing the inside of my cheek. "Straight to it then?"

He swallowed hard, expression neutral. "Take off your clothes, Lincoln."

Hunter was already in his underwear, and it took me no time to find myself in even less. He hadn't moved from his perch on the bed, and I stood in front of him, my quickly hardening cock almost at his mouth.

"On your knees," he said next.

Sinking down to the floor was easier than it had been the first time I did it for him in the guest room, but still the same sense of nervous excitement coursed through my veins. I went all the way down so my ass rested on my heels, and much like he'd done before, Hunter left me there until I settled, until I quit fidgeting.

Tenderly, he slid his fingers into my hair and pulled me toward him with one hand, his other pulling his cock out from behind the waistband of his underwear. The intention was very clear and didn't need instruction, but he guided me down between his legs just the same and I swallowed him whole. Hunter was half hard, but he quickly thickened against the roof of my mouth. Precum pulsed against the back of my tongue, and I gagged around him a little, which earned me a low and rumbling groan.

"You're so good at this," he murmured, hips lifting off the bed so he could get deeper. Hunter's hand in my hair was steady, setting a much easier pace than I would have chosen if he didn't have my head under his control. The slow slide of my lips up and down his length was torture, but the sight of all the spit strings connecting us every time he pulled me up and off was enough to have my own dick leaking against my stomach.

"Can I touch myself?"

"No." The answer was firm and final, even as he reached to the drawer in the nightstand for a bottle of lube. "But you can prep yourself while I go find what plug I want to put inside of you."

I groaned, holding out my hand for him to drizzle some into my fingers. "Where's your toy box?"

"The one with the pink marker on it."

Hunter stood, rubbing his cock in my face before stepping around me to find the box in question. I didn't dare look after him. I already knew what he'd find. Instead, I paid attention to my own body, rocking back so I could get two slick fingers into my ass. Behind me, Hunter rifled through the box, thick silicone toys knocking against each other as he went. Every so often, he would make a surprised noise, which only had me spreading my fingers wider apart against my rim.

"You've given me ideas," he said after returning to the bed. He sat back down with his cock still out, a very average-sized plug in hand. "Are you ready?"

"Dying for it, I think."

Hunter smiled at me, swiping his thumb across my cheek.

"Come ride me then."

"Fuck." I scrambled off the floor and onto his lap. I replaced my fingers with his spit-soaked cock, sinking down around him with a breathy little whimper.

Hunter bracketed his hands around my hips, not guiding like he'd done before, only holding me steady so I could set my own pace this time. Rocking my body, I fucked Hunter until he couldn't hold my hips any longer. His hands freely roamed up my back and down my ribs, the reverent way he touched me enough to send me flying right toward my own release.

"Can I come?" I whispered, head thrown back. "Will you let me come?"

"I won't let you," he answered, curling his hand around my pulsing shaft. "I'll make you."

It was one stroke after that, and I came with a shout, spurting my load all over Hunter's strong fingers. I cried out, the only thing holding me up, his other hand splayed against the middle of my back. Hunter remained tense and focused, milking me dry, and only after I cried out from the overstimulation did he move. He grabbed me by the hips again, fucked up into me once, twice, a third time, then he went still. Heat poured into me, the girth of his cock pressing urgently against me as he came up my ass. He cursed under his breath and lifted us both off the bed, dropping me into my back and fucking into me once more for good measure. I trembled beneath him, hands against his chest and shoulders while he rode out the end of his release.

It was probably the most vanilla sex we'd ever had, but there was an unexpected intimacy between us that I hadn't anticipated. My own feelings only heightened when he eased out of me with a wince, then reached for the plug and made quick work of pushing it into me.

"God, Lincoln."

Hunter kissed the side of my throat, then my clavicle, and he worked himself down lower to each nipple, my navel, and further still until he was behind my balls leaving wet and open-mouth kisses against the place the plug breached me. "How am I going to make it through this party knowing my cum is sloshing around inside of you all night?"

"How are *you* going to make it?" I laughed weakly and covered my eyes with my forearm. "How am *I* going to make it?"

"You'll make it because I told you to," he whispered, smiling against the inside of my thigh.

I reached down and carded my fingers through his hair, messy and slightly damp at the roots.

"And you'll make it because I told you to, right?"

Hunter looked up at me without moving his face, just a slow shift of his attention from beneath the dark fan of his lashes, and he nodded, nose brushing against my still very sensitive balls.

"Anything for you, Sir," he whispered.

I managed another weak laugh before closing my eyes and sinking into the bed.

Hunter gave me five minutes of rest before dislodging himself from between my legs and urging me onto my feet. I grumbled every protest imaginable, only relenting once he walked us into the shower together and spent well over an hour lavishing more attention on me. By the time we were dry and dressed for his party, I was a live wire ready to spark into an inferno, and he didn't seem to be faring much better. Making a sex game out of his work party was probably not the best idea, but there was no going back from it now.

I didn't have fancy or expensive clothes like Hunter, but I settled on a pair of black slacks and a navy button-down shirt. He asked if I wanted a tie, and I asked if I needed one. In response, he looped one of his silk ties around my neck and knotted it at the base of my throat, and it felt like a collar to me, but if it felt the same to him, he didn't say.

"How does it look?" I asked.

Instead of answering, his mouth twitched into a smile that he hid with a kiss. And then we were off.

———

It was my first time to Hunter's office. My first time around all of his brothers at once, my first time feeling ashamed of myself for simply being who I was and not somebody different. The other partners at the firm were older and far more staunch than Hunter could ever be, but it was clear he'd spent years establishing respect and camaraderie. He wouldn't have made partner otherwise.

But to say I was feeling out of place would have been an understatement.

Patron saint of being in over my fucking head.

Hunter held tight to my hand, keeping me close to him as we made a quick round of everyone who'd already gathered. There was a makeshift bar set up against one of the windows that had my name on it, and I knocked my elbow into Hunter's arm to get his attention.

"Do you want a drink?" I asked.

"I would love one."

We'd been speaking with Smith and Finn while waiting for Andrew to arrive. Marshall and Silas were chatting with a man I'd never seen before, and for the most part, everyone seemed to be having a good time. If anyone was stressed, they were hiding it better than I was, but I hoped it wasn't anything a good drink wouldn't fix.

"Vodka soda?"

Hunter smiled, kissing my forehead. "You know me so well."

"Andrew is here," Finn said, and it felt like the perfect time to slip away to get us drinks. I gave Hunter's hand a squeeze and headed for the other end of the party.

I'd barely reached the bar when one of the other partners sidled up next to me. I didn't remember his name because Hunter had introduced me to four or five men all at the same time, and their names flew over my head as fast as he'd said them. I gave him a polite smile, turning my attention to the drink menu propped up beside the tip jar.

"Lincoln, you said?" he greeted, and I glanced up at him with a smile.

"Yeah. Hi." I nodded. "I'm sorry, I absolutely forgot your name."

"Shaw. Scott Shaw, but you might be more familiar with my username, Shaws-six-nine."

I scratched a sudden pressing itch along the underside of my jaw. "Why would I recognize a username?"

"Because yours is JayFxks, right?"

I had to physically look down, not convinced the floor hadn't fallen out from under me at his connection of my face to my job. This was my biggest fear, all my inadequacies coming to slap me hard across the face at the worst possible time and the worst possible moment.

"What can I get you?" the bartender asked, and I tore my stare away from Scott to face her, but the outline of her face was blurry around the edges, her dark hair blending into the sky outside the window.

"Vodka soda," I answered, thinking only of Hunter and not of myself. She mixed the drink, and I shoved some singles into the tip jaw before stepping to the side and praying I didn't drop the glass all over the floor.

Scott followed, staying close. "Does he know?"

"Of course he knows," I muttered.

"And he brought you here?"

I scanned the office for help, finding Hunter in a conversation with all four of his brothers, and they all looked so relaxed and happy. There was no way I would even entertain the idea of going over there and ruining things for him.

"How is it bad for me to make the videos but not for you to subscribe?" I dared a look at him. "How much have you paid me over the years?"

Scott's cheeks burned and he narrowed his eyes at me. "How I spend my money isn't your concern, but the strict guidelines in Covington's morality clause should be."

Hunter's drink squeaked against my palm, my grip bearing down around the glass. I hadn't imagined Scott would be able to make things worse, and yet here he was. I couldn't even keep looking at the party, couldn't risk Hunter turning around and seeing the terror written across my face. I turned on my heel and brought myself face to face with a window, momentarily wishing I could throw myself out of it. Suddenly, the plug in my ass felt like an anvil, the tie around my throat, a vise. I reached up and tugged at the knot.

Scott laughed, low and dangerous in my ear. "I could look the other way," he offered.

"If?"

"If you take a walk with me." His words were quiet, closer. My shoulders hurt for how tense I was, the glass seconds away from shattering in my hand. "I've been paying to see you come for a very long time, and I think I might be convinced to keep this between us if I could see it in person...whenever I wanted."

There was clearly no concern from Scott about *his* morality clause, but if I raised the issue, it would be my word against his, and who would they believe? Hunter would probably believe me, but why would the other partners? Why would anyone?

"You're asking me to cheat on him."

"I'm asking you to meet me in the bathroom," he elaborated, and I fought back the urge to be sick all over his shoes because I knew what was coming next. "And I'm not asking you for more than you already do, *Lincoln*."

The way he said my name sounded like a slur.

"Make yourself come and let me help," he said. "Whenever I want."

"No," I rasped, the weight of the word heavy on my tongue. This would be the end of my relationship because there was no way I would ever ask or want Hunter to give up his livelihood for me, and there was no chance in hell I'd ever let Scott see me naked in person, let alone see me getting off. I was going to delete his subscription as soon as I was in front of my computer, even though I'd probably need his money more than ever after Hunter broke up with me.

"No?"

"I don't accept your offer."

"What a piece of shit," an almost familiar voice said from behind me. Scott's entire body twisted, and he stumbled into me, losing his balance and sloshing Hunter's drink all over my pants. I managed to catch my balance, but Scott never stood a chance because Andrew's surprisingly strong right hook connected with his jaw and sent him straight down to the floor.

The whole room fell silent after that, all eyes turning toward the commotion. Andrew there shaking out his hand, me with wet pants, and one of the partners sprawled out on the floor of their office, barely conscious.

"Are you all right?" Andrew asked, taking a step toward me. "I heard the whole thing."

There was noise again and movement, Hunter navigating through the people who'd come closer to see what happened. His expression was a tangled mess of confusion and anger, barely any worry to be seen.

"I'm fine," I lied, stepping over the spilled vodka soda glass. "I've.. I've got to go."

And before Hunter could get to me, I did what I'd always done best.

I ran.

CHAPTER 38
HUNTER

My brother punched my boss in the face.

Well, Shaw wasn't technically a boss anymore since the party was meant to celebrate me becoming a partner like him, but Andrew definitely had still punched him in the face. Lincoln looked like he wanted to crawl under a table and evaporate into thin air, but instead he did the opposite. He bolted out of the party faster than I could even register what had happened.

"I'll go after him," Silas said, touching my arm.

I looked down at the point of contact, Silas's fingers soft and delicate around my arm. He didn't bite his nails the way Lincoln did, not a single hangnail in sight.

"I should go," I said.

"I'll tell him you said that." Silas squeezed, mouth twisted into a grimace. "I think you need to figure out what happened here first."

"He's right," Marshall agreed, and I looked up worriedly at my oldest brother. "We'll find him. He'll be in good hands."

"I know."

I wanted to be the one to go after him. I wanted to be the

one to find him and catch him, console him over whatever had transpired that had him fleeing the party with such a dramatic exit. He deserved it to be me, I thought to myself, but Silas and Marshall were already on their way to the elevator, and Andrew was heading for me, shaking out his hand. Lincoln called me Sir, called me Daddy. I should be the one to find him, to take care of him. But Andrew was in front of me, his knuckles an angry shade of red, his face flushed with just as much fury.

"What happened?" I managed to ask, frowning at my brother.

Shaw was still on the floor, but at least now he was seated on his ass with a welt across his cheek and blood pouring out of his nose. Winters was with him, the two of them speaking in hushed tones.

"That piece of shit was trying to blackmail Lincoln," he said.

"What?"

"I walked over in time to hear him proposition your boyfriend," Andrew explained.

I was a college-educated man, but I was in a bit of shock over the events that had just transpired, so I felt particularly daft when I stared blankly at my brother before muttering, "I don't understand."

"He said he'd been paying Lincoln for years, whatever that means, and he'd tell everyone if Lincoln didn't have sex with him. Were they involved?"

He'd been paying…

Oh.

"They weren't involved," I said.

Andrew swiped his finger across his nostrils, sniffing an inhale. "The rest makes sense, though?"

"Yeah. It makes sense."

Near the window, Winters helped Shaw to his feet,

gesturing with a jerk of his thumb toward the closest conference room.

"Sorry if I fucked everything up for you," Andrew apologized.

I shook my head before he even finished speaking, pulling him into a rough hug and clapping him on the back before he could think too long or hard about what happened.

"I would have done worse," I assured him. "Can you stay with Finn and Smith? I need to go talk to them."

Andrew followed my stare toward the backs of two of the partners at my firm before they disappeared into the conference room.

"Of course."

Smith looked so worried he was ready to crawl out of his skin, but his attention darted from Finn to Andrew and back again after I headed toward the conference room. This was definitely not how I'd imagined the night was going to go, but my brothers were with each other and Silas and Marshall were on their way to find Lincoln, and I would wrap this conversation up in record time before joining them.

I closed the conference room door behind me, crossing my arms in front of my chest and narrowing my eyes at Shaw. He sat on the edge of the conference table, still bleeding from his nose. No one had gotten him a towel, and I fought the instinct to be the one to do it for him. The collar of his shirt was stained red with blood already, and Winters looked sick from the sight of it.

"What happened?" Winters asked.

I shrugged and jerked my chin toward Shaw. "Ask him."

"Your brother hit me."

"Why?" I prompted.

"He didn't say."

"Was it because you were trying to blackmail my boyfriend?"

At the ask, Winters's brows shot up into his hairline, but Shaw didn't even have the decency to look offended.

"He's a cam boy."

"He's not yours," I hissed.

"You could be blackmailed or bribed because of him," Shaw went on. "Trying to keep his work a secret when the whole world has already seen him naked. What a violation of our morality clause."

"His work isn't a secret," I said. "And that's rich considering you were the one trying to blackmail him into sleeping with you."

"What?"

My comment was enough to shock Winters back into the conversation, his confused look landing on Shaw, whose nose had finally stopped pouring blood.

"You can tell him," I said.

Shaw, thankfully, didn't say anything.

"You tried to make my boyfriend sleep with you because you—incorrectly I might add—assumed I didn't know about his work, which is a preposterous observation. You, of all people, should know to never make assumptions about intent or impact in this line of work."

"Is this true?" Winters asked, and I didn't know which of us he was speaking to.

"Yes," I answered. "And if this is an issue, I'm happy to call all of this a wash and walk away from not just this offer of partner but the firm as a whole."

Winters held up both of his hands, one palm toward me and one toward Shaw.

"Not so fast," he said. "Let's not be rash."

"I'm not being rash, but I refuse to work with that man," I said, pointing a steady finger at Shaw. "So you can let me know later if I'm coming to work Monday or coming to pack my things, but I honestly have more important things to do right now."

"A complete lack of dedication," Shaw muttered under his breath.

I gave the man one last look and sighed heavily, glancing at Winters' unreadable expression before turning on my heel and leaving the both of them in the conference room. The party had absolutely thinned out, which was not a surprise, so the first people I saw after closing the door behind me were Andrew, Finn, and Smith. The three of them had fresh drinks in their hands and looked as comfortable together as they looked with me.

"Everything good?" Finn asked.

"I need to go find Lincoln," I told him.

"I'm sure he went home," Smith said.

"Yeah."

"Sorry your party was a bust," Finn added with a small grin. "But you can save the catalyst of that sucker punch for the next time I ask you to tell me something interesting."

I snorted, rolling my eyes at my closest brother before reaching into my pocket to dig out my phone. I don't know if I'd expected to have a message from Lincoln there, but I was beyond disappointed to find out I didn't. I texted Marshall, and he didn't answer, but Smith was probably right about Lincoln's final destination.

"Enjoy as much of the booze as they'll let you," I told my brothers. "I'll text you in a bit."

"Use the group chat," Finn said, reminding me of its existence.

I nodded and jogged to the elevator, already keying Lincoln's address into my nav. As soon as I pulled my car out of the garage and into the street, I called Marshall but he didn't answer. Lincoln didn't live terribly far, but it still took me half an hour of frustrating weekend traffic to get there. The lights in his apartment were off, and no matter how many times I banged on the door, there was no answer.

I called Lincoln next, that also going unanswered.

I texted him twice, pounding my fist against his door until one of his neighbors came out to yell at me over the noise. I apologized to her profusely, called Marshall and Lincoln again, then headed to my next destination, Marshall's house. I ended up running into the two of them in Marshall's driveway, Silas looking a little frenzied, phone held tight in his hand.

"Is he here?" I asked.

It made sense to me that Marshall's house would be a safe space for Lincoln to go when he was feeling off about things. It was, after all, not just Marshall's house now but also Silas's. It was also the place Lincoln had gone after our first scene together, back before we'd even known each other's names. It was the place everything had started for us, and I hoped it wouldn't be the place things ended.

"No," Marshall told me, his head tilted to the side in nervous concern. "We just checked his apartment, but he wasn't there either."

"That's where I came from too." I bracketed my hands against my hips and stared up at the night sky, not a star in sight. "There's no point in us chasing each other around the city all night."

"If he shows up here, I'll let you know," Marshall promised.

"I'm still trying to get a hold of him," Silas added, and I nodded at them both, dialing his number again for myself and finding nothing more than voicemail. "Okay."

I agreed because I didn't know what else to do.

"He can't be far," Silas told me, another gentle touch against my arm. "He's a creature of comfort. He'll want to be someplace safe."

"That's why I came he—" I snapped my mouth closed, cursing myself under my breath. "I know where he is."

I ignored both of their questions, hopping into my car and heading to my apartment. I'd been an idiot for thinking Lincoln would have gone to his apartment. That wasn't his home anymore. He'd literally moved his things—and his fish—into my place only hours before. If Lincoln had gone anywhere, he'd gone to my place.

He'd gone home.

My assumption proved right, as I found his car in a guest spot, the engine still warm. After the slowest elevator ride from the lobby to my floor, I all but sprinted down the hallway. The door was propped open, much like I'd done for him in the early days of our relationship, and something burned hot in the middle of my chest. He knew I'd come after him, and he'd wanted to make it easy.

"Lincoln!" I called out for him as soon as my feet hit the tile entryway, but I heard no reply. I did hear running water, though. The shower. And I found Lincoln with his back pressed against the wall and his eyes closed, steaming hot water splattering against his cheeks and his chest. His clothes were scattered across the floor, the plug I'd put in him hours before discarded alongside them.

"Lincoln," I said again, stepping into the shower without even bothering to take off my clothes. I wrapped my arms around him and yanked him into my arms, the tight scrabble of his fingers against my shoulder blades almost enough to crack me open on the spot.

"I'm sorry," he whimpered against my chest, and I curled my hand around the back of his head, pressing his body more fully against mine.

"Stop that," I warned. "You have nothing to apologize for."

"You deserve someone better than me," he argued, the words still muffled against my soaking wet shirt.

"There is no one better for me, Lincoln. I *want* you."

He said nothing.

"I need you," I whispered against the shell of his ear. "More than I've ever needed anything in my life."

Around me, Lincoln's arms relaxed, but so did his knees. It would be easy to hold him if we had more room, but once he'd landed in my arms, my adrenaline started to crash. I held him tight while we both slid down to the floor of the shower, and I opened my arms only wide enough for him to crawl onto my lap and curl into a ball.

"I've found you," I promised him. "Daddy's here, alright? Daddy is here. Sir is here. I've got you, sweetheart."

That promise, that vow, that was the thing that broke him, and Lincoln let out a breathy sob that rattled straight through my sternum. I held him tighter, like my arms could ever be enough to keep him together. Like I could be enough. An hour later, after the water ran cold, and I carried Lincoln to bed, it turned out I was

CHAPTER 39
LINCOLN

I woke up certain I'd been hit by a semi-truck, but as I blinked the bedroom into focus, I remembered the reality had been much, much worse. I was in bed with Hunter wrapped around me like a goddamn octopus, my head aching like I'd slammed it into a wall five hundred times, when in reality all I'd done was ruin Hunter's life, run to his house, and cry about it until I basically lost consciousness.

Call me the patron saint of…

I didn't even know.

"Are you awake?" he murmured into the back of my hair.

"Unfortunately."

"Can we talk?" he asked.

My tongue stuck to the roof of my mouth and I swallowed bile. "Can I have coffee first?"

"Yes. Of course." He made no move to get out of bed. "Here or the living room?"

"The bottom of the ocean," I offered as a counterproposal.

"The living room," Hunter said, giving me a squeeze before untangling his burning hot body from mine. I immediately mourned the absence of him, but it was my quest for closeness that pulled me out of bed and forced me to the couch. Hunter had put a pair of his pajamas on me at some point, and I appreciated that he'd dressed me in his clothes instead of my own. There was no real reason for it other than I liked it. I liked the way his pants were a little too big around my waist. That, even knotted, they hung a little too low.

Hiking them up so I didn't trip, I made my way to the couch and sat down. Hunter was there seconds later with a mug of coffee for each of us, his dark scruff looking soft and gorgeous. Just like the rest of him. Even with his hair wild from sleep and purple bags bruising beneath his eyes, Hunter Covington was a catch of a man. He deserved someone so much better than me, but he didn't seem to care.

"Are you breaking up with me?" I asked, burning the words out of my mouth with a swallow of still too hot coffee.

"What?" His brows raised, and bless him, he looked genuinely shocked.

"Are you breaking up with me?" I asked again, the words hurting marginally less the second time. I wondered how often I'd need to utter them before the sting lessened to something manageable.

"Why would I break up with you?"

"Because of what happened last night."

"How was any of that your fault?" he asked.

I didn't appreciate the obtuse conversation, and I had half a mind to pour my scalding coffee all over his head.

"It was because of my job," I reminded him. "Or did you not get the whole story from your brother or your business partner?"

"My brother told me my *former* business partner was trying to blackmail you," he said, setting his coffee down on the table and grabbing my knees. "That's not your fault."

"It...what do you mean former?"

"Former," he repeated. "I told them last night before I left I wouldn't work with someone like that. He can leave or I will; it makes no difference to me."

"How can you say that?" I leaned over and set my coffee next to his, frowning down at the way his fingers wrapped around my kneecaps like they'd been molded to fit there.

"How could I not?" he asked, moving his hands from my legs to my face, the same thoughtful grip against my cheeks, fingers sculpted to hold me in all the right ways, and I blinked hard, fighting back an embarrassing wave of tears. "I love you. I'm in love with you, Lincoln."

I clenched my jaw, fighting the way my chin quivered at his confession, at his truth. It was far from the first time he'd told me he loved me, but maybe…it was the first time I believed it.

"I'm sorry," I whimpered, hating the water in my words, the tremble as I fought through every syllable.

"I'm not." He brought our faces together, mouths so fucking close. "I'm the opposite of sorry."

"Did you lose your job over me?"

"If I lose my job, it's because of Scott Shaw, not because of you." Hunter exhaled against my lips. "But I hope the right decision is made, and if not, that's better for me in the long run anyway. I don't want to be tied to a firm that rewards that kind of behavior."

I wanted to believe him.

He sounded so earnest and true, but it was hard. It was so fucking hard.

"I was so scared when I couldn't find you last night," he said next. "I went to your apartment first, then I went to Marshall's, and then I realized what a fool I was. I knew exactly where you'd be."

"I came home," I murmured, blinking hard.

Hunter's fingers swiped stray tears off my cheeks, and I went slack in his arms, letting him hold me up. He pulled me in, curled his arms around my shoulders and held me like he had the night before in the shower. The level of coddling should have been embarrassing, but I'd never felt more protected than I did when Hunter held me, and I needed that to be okay.

My relationship with Hunter had taught me so much about myself, and not just in the dominant and submissive way. He'd given me a safe and non-judgmental space to explore parts of myself that I'd tried very hard to keep in the dark, and in shining a light on them he'd shined a light on me. I was whole because of Hunter, but more than that, I was loved.

"I know you did." He kissed the top of my head, and I relaxed against him.

Hunter didn't complain, didn't groan, didn't even move. He held me there on his couch for as long as he'd held me on the floor of his shower. Maybe even longer. When I pulled away from him to drink some coffee, he watched me quietly like I was a deer about to bolt in front of a car in the middle of the night. It felt a little like that, I realized, swallowing the room-temperature coffee before sliding off the couch and onto my knees.

"What are—" he protested, trying to hook his hand under my armpit and pull me back up. "What are you doing?"

"Daddy," I whispered, placing my hands on my thighs palms up, something I'd seem Silas do more times than I could count. Fuck, it was powerful. Heat surged through me, up from my stomach and into my throat, making me sit straighter, chin tipped up even as my lashes fluttered.

"What do you need?" he asked, pushing my hair back from my face. "What do you want?"

"Just this," I said softly. "Just you."

"You have me," Hunter promised, climbing to his feet and standing in front of me. His dick was soft, but he pulled his pants down anyway and dragged his flaccid tip against my mouth. I opened for him because it felt like the right thing to do, and he fed the entire soft length of his shaft onto my tongue. He was in me fully, my nose buried in the trimmed hairs at the bottom of his happy trail, and I huffed a breath out of my nose that had Hunter shivering against me.

"You're perfect," he said softly, fingers sliding through my hair as his cock thickened against my tongue. "You're everything I've ever wanted. More important than any job or any other man could ever be."

I knew he meant his brothers, and I blinked hard.

"My priority is always you," he said next, another promise. "Whatever you need, it's yours."

Precum pulsed out of his cock, painting the very back of my tongue. It was impossible to breathe without getting erect myself, his cock very nearly fully hard, pressing against the roof of my mouth and my throat. I swallowed around him, smiling to myself at the way he groaned and thrust his hips against my face.

"Is that what you need?" he asked, tightening his grip in my thoroughly finger-combed hair. "You need this cock in your throat?"

I groaned and nodded, reaching between my legs when Hunter started to pump into my mouth in earnest. Precum smeared around my mouth, and I was desperate for the taste of him, the stretch of him. I wanted Hunter deeper inside of me, and not in my mouth, but I trusted him to know what I needed and give it to me. He always had, and I was certain there on the floor of his living room—of our living room—he always would.

I nodded around him, groaning low when the first burst of cum shot against my tongue. He was so deep in my mouth I barely tasted him, but he spilled his load into my throat, entire body going tense until his orgasm settled into something soft around the edges. Hunter tugged my hair until I looked up at him, and the admiration in his eyes was almost enough to send me over the edge myself.

"I don't want you to come yet," he said, pulling my mouth away from his cock with an obscenely wet pop. Strings of saliva connected his cock to my mouth, and the way his chest heaved with every breath was hotter than it had any right to be.

"I'm close," I warned, rubbing my palms over the tops of my thighs.

"Well..." Hunter licked his lips and stroked his half-hard cock inches away from my face. "Don't make that my problem."

A shiver tore through me, and I managed a jerky nod.

"Yes, Sir."

He licked his lips again and, on instinct, I licked mine, chasing the sweaty and musky taste of his dick down my throat.

"I like that. But I think you forget who I am sometimes, don't you?"

Another hot rush of tears filled my eyes, and I offered him another nod, this one weaker.

"Yes, Sir."

"Is that my fault?"

"No," I rasped.

He disagreed, "I think it is."

"Daddy—"

"I'll make it right, though," he interrupted me, tucking his dick back into his pants and taking a half-step away from me. "I'll make sure you never forget who I am to you...who you are to me."

I'd never felt so weak and so strong at the same time. I wanted to crumble and build myself up with the same breaths, the same actions.

"Go back to bed," Hunter said slowly. "Get some lube and one of your toys."

Of all the things he could have said, that might have been the last thing I ever expected. My first instinct was to question it, but the look on his face stopped me in my tracks. Hunter was in full Dom mode, something he rarely let himself slide into on account of the fine line he and I walked in that regard, but he looked so at home in his skin and I felt so good on my knees, I didn't want to ruin it for either of us.

"Yes, Sir," I whispered, climbing to my feet and scrambling into the bedroom.

He didn't immediately follow, instead giving me more than enough time to dig through my box of sex toys and find the dildo that most closely resembled Hunter's cock. It was longer than his by an inch or so, but the girth was almost spot on, and while I didn't know if it was for me or him, it would be fun either way. I tossed the dick and the lube onto the bed and sat down on the edge, nervous but ready.

Ten minutes later, Hunter finally appeared in the doorway. He had his coffee in one hand and both of our cellphones in the other. He tossed his onto the dresser, then turned mine around a few times in his hand before setting it down next to his. There was an unspoken question there about filming whatever was about to happen next, but I didn't want to press him on asking it. The same way Hunter always waited for me to be ready, only pushing when he knew I was ready for it, I needed to wait for him. His expression shifted, chest expanding with a long breath.

"Daddy," I whispered, a low moan dying in the back of my throat every time I called him the honorific. "Did you want to record it? Did you want to save it so you can watch us later?"

Hunter sucked his tongue across the front of his teeth and set his coffee down beside our phones.

"I want to fuck you with whatever toy you picked out of that box," he told me simply. "And then I want to fuck you with my cock alongside it."

It was my biggest fantasy come to life. I was going to die a miserably undeserving but happy man.

"I..." he trailed off, rubbing his palm over the bulge between his legs.

"Film it," I told him. "Prop the phone up against your mug, the angle's fine."

"Are you—" he stopped, nodding. "Yes, Sir."

The versatility of our scenes was going to be the actual death of me, the easy way Hunter moved between dominant and submissive, modeling for me what it meant to be so fully devoted to another person you could be everything they needed in every single moment you were together. He was that for me, and the dark want in his eyes promised that no matter what my traitorous brain told me, I was the same for him. Hunter set the phone up against his mug and pressed record, then he turned his sights on me and closed the bedroom door.

My heart jumped into my throat.

I fumbled blindly for the dildo and the lube, slicking the shaft and my hand in the process. Hunter crossed the room, sinking down to his knees between my spread thighs. He stared at me, eyes hooded, and stroked his hand up and down the plastic cock until his fingers were slick with lube. Without looking away, Hunter eased me back onto the bed and pushed his fingers into me.

I was a little sore from the plug the night before, even more from the loss of what the night should have been, but Hunter's fingers inside of me were quick to massage away that loss. He found my prostate with ease, teasing me with a precision that had my dick leaking against my stomach. I don't know if he was already too primed to wait or if he only took pity on me, but he lowered the dildo between us and replaced his fingers with the plastic cock.

The stretch of the toy was shocking, more unforgiving than the warm stretch of his actual dick, and my hands scrabbled against the sheets, back arching as he buried the toy inside of me. Hunter used his body to move the toy, fucking me with it just like how he'd move if it was his actual dick. I spread my legs, and he growled at the sight.

"Grab your ankles," he said, voice low. "Hold yourself open."

I did as I was told, pulling my legs apart so Hunter could see the place he penetrated me. He cursed under his breath, slicking more lube down the shaft of the toy before pushing one of his fingers in alongside the shaft. One and then another, and a third, the fourth pressing against my rim with every thrust of the toy.

"Please," I whimpered, giving him my throat, my vision blurring around the edges as he stretched me open to take his cock and the toy at the same time.

His hand went still, fingers still hooked into me.

"I wish you could see yourself," he murmured, the leaking and swollen head of his cock pushing against my hole. "You were meant for this. For me."

One finger out, another, a third, and then the biggest, sharpest stretch I'd ever felt in my life as Hunter pushed his cock in on top of the dildo. I should have picked a smaller one, should have had more manageable aspirations because with two cocks inside of me, there was no way Hunter wasn't about to fuck to me to death.

A sob tore out of me, and Hunter went still. He was half-folded over me, one hand between our bodies and the other smoothing hair away from my sweaty and tear-stained face.

"Do you want me to stop?" he asked. "Slow down?"

"I want you to ruin me," I told him. "Remind me there is no one for me but you, nothing for me but this."

He growled, thrusting hard against me with a sharp snap of his hips. I tightened my hold around my ankles and relaxed as much as my body would allow. The tension rolled off of him in waves, the arousal and the restraint enough to leave my own cock pulsing. The pressure inside of me with every push of Hunter's hips almost enough to render me unconscious.

"Tell me you deserve this," he grunted, teeth bared against my ear. "Tell me you deserve this, or I won't let you come."

"Daddy."

The word caught in my throat, wrapped around my desperation.

"Tell me you deserve it, or I won't come inside of you," he said next.

I dug my fingernails into my ankles and slammed my head against the bed with a frustrated whimper. The words were right there, but they would cost me everything. I wasn't certain I believed them, and I didn't want to lie to Hunter, not here and not like this.

He shifted his hand between us and pushed the dildo deeper, pressing the base of it against his stomach so every thrust he made into me drove the toy cock deeper inside of me, deeper than his dick, deeper than I deser…

"Lincoln," he warned.

The taut pull of his muscles and the skittish pace of his body gave away that I could make a liar out of him if I wanted. Hunter was seconds away from coming whether I confessed what he wanted to be the truth or not. But even if I didn't deserve him, he didn't deserve that.

"I love you," I told him, locking my ankles around the small of his back and grabbing his face with both of my hands. The change in my legs squeezed him tighter and Hunter closed the space between us, sinking his teeth into my lower lip with a muffled shout.

"I deserve your cum," I whispered next, groaning as his entire body shuddered and stilled. "I deserve to come too."

He made a tight fist around my dick and stroked me right

over the edge, both of us convulsing as he spilled into my ass, and I shot across his knuckles.

"I deserve to be happy," I whispered next.

Hunter smiled against my mouth, licked the place he'd bit me, and I knew, for the first time in our relationship, we both believed it.

CHAPTER 40
HUNTER

Winters had begged me not to leave, but I'd made myself clear. They could have Shaw or they could have me. That had been two weeks ago, and the promised management committee meeting was wrapping up while I packed up my bag to leave for the day. I was heading straight to Cunningham's to meet my brothers for dinner, then home to Lincoln. He'd sent me a particularly cruel video over my lunch break that involved the dildo I'd used to DP him and a vibrator, and to say I was eager to return home to him was an understatement. I'd been sporting a chub since 12:30 and running into a sullen-faced Scott Shaw on his way out of the conference room was the only thing that could sour my mood.

He shot me a scathing look, which confirmed everything I needed to know. The committee had invoked the termination clause in his contract and most likely bought out his equity share in the firm. Them choosing me over him was a bold statement to my skill and dedication to the firm, and it was also a vote of confidence that was not lost on me. Winters left the conference room next, the other partners in tow. He greeted me with a definitive nod of his head, which I returned before slipping out of the office and heading for the elevator.

Downstairs in my car, I texted Lincoln to let him know the happy news, and I sent him an extra message for good measure letting him know just what I planned to do to him once I got home from dinner. He replied to me with a grinning devil and a picture of his asshole, black plug splitting his cheeks and all. That man was going to be the death of me, and I would welcome each and every one of my final breaths.

When I made it to Cunningham's, Marshall and Finn were already there. It was unusual for Smith to be absent, but I chalked it up to traffic on a Friday. Sliding into my usual seat beside Finn, I jabbed my elbow into his ribs.

"Scott Shaw separated from the firm today," I said.

Finn let out a whoop, raising his glass and waiting for me and Marshall to cheers him. They'd already ordered for me and Smith, which was one of the things I appreciated the most about them.

"It does feel wrong to celebrate someone's demise," Marshall said after taking a swallow of his wine.

"He brought it on himself," Finn reminded, and I nodded my agreement.

The party had been two weeks ago, and it had simultaneously been the longest and shortest fourteen days of my life. We'd expeditiously finished moving Lincoln into the house, which had ended with a Silas and Lincoln slumber party in the guest room. Marshall had assured me I'd get used to it, and I believed it. Lincoln was so safe with me, he didn't feel the need to hide his affection for his best friend—or my youngest brother—and I was beyond grateful we'd found each other and I was able to give him that. He deserved so much more than anything I'd ever be able to provide, but I was happy to continue trying to prove myself the kind of man he told his friends I was.

Smith bustled into the restaurant, sinking down into the empty space at Marshall's left. He had on an oversized hoodie, which was out of character for him, and I arched a brow in question, but Finn was the one to ask him, "Whose hoodie?"

Smith plucked at the well-worn material and shrugged. "I've had it since college. I don't know where I got it."

I narrowed my eyes, but the flush on Smith's cheeks was enough to let me know it was a conversation he didn't want to have. If I respected Finn enough to not press about Neil and Annette, I had to respect Smith enough to not ask where he'd stumbled across a three-sizes-too-large hoodie for a college none of us went to.

"How was work?" I asked instead.

Smith swirled his wine and took a drink. "It was work."

"Do you still hate it?" Marshall asked.

He scratched the side of his neck and gave us all another weak shrug. "I don't know. Depends on the day."

"That feels normal," Finn said, earning a smile, so he kept talking. "That piece of crap from Hunter's firm got shit-canned today."

My brother's brows lifted toward his hairline.

"The trash takes itself out or something," I said.

My phone buzzed against my thigh, and I pulled it out to find a text message from Lincoln, another picture. This time he had on short black shorts and a black leather harness with a mesh top that didn't even reach his navel piercing. It looked like he might have on eyeliner, but the lighting was dark and the picture was taken in a mirror.

He was in the bathroom at Rapture, Silas beside him with his arm slung over Lincoln's shoulders.

Marshall checked his phone next, undoubtedly getting the same photo. We both set out phones down on the table, and Smith frowned at mine.

"What?" I asked.

"Is that Lincoln?"

"He's out with Silas. They spend Fridays together since Marshall and I are here."

"Where are they?" Smith asked.

Marshall made a choked sound in the back of his throat, and I was quickly reminded of the awkward conversations I'd been forced to have at the start of my and Lincoln's relationship about our proclivities and how they aligned with his best friend and my oldest brother. But Lincoln and Smith were friends, they'd been intimate, and there were probably little to no secrets between them.

"Rapture," I answered.

Marshall looked like he wanted to crawl under the table and die, but that must have been a side effect that came from being an elder millennial with younger siblings.

"Oh," Smith said, another shrug.

Finn leaned forward, propping his elbows on the table and his chin in his hands. He smiled sweetly at our baby brother. "Have you been?"

"Have *you* been?" Marshall asked.

"Don't assume you're the only person in town who likes kinky sex, Marshall," Finn answered, which had Smith mirroring the choking sound Marshall had just made himself.

"I've been," Finn said conversationally, like we were talking about going to the park on the weekend. "I'm sure Hunter has been. Marshall, obviously. I don't know if this is genetic or not, but—"

"I've been!" Smith blurted, maybe louder than he'd intended.

"I don't want to know," Marshall muttered.

Smith threw him a sidelong glance and turned his attention back to his wine.

"Do they want to make you an equity partner now that Shaw is out?" Finn asked, and I was grateful for the change in conversation.

"I'm happy with the current terms," I answered.

And I was.

Two weeks, and everything in my life had settled into everything I'd never dreamed could be mine. Watching Marshall fall in love with Silas had been agony, not because he didn't deserve it, but because it had drawn into such a startling clarity how much I *did*. After a life spent pretending I didn't care about that kind of partnership, Lincoln had come into my life like a hurricane and proved me wrong in a thousand different ways.

I was glad he was mine. Glad I would get to go home to him at the end of the night.

The rest of dinner passed as it had before, with friendly conversation about work and life. We were supposed to see Andrew again in a couple of weeks. He'd endeared himself permanently with our three other brothers after he'd laid Shaw out in front of everyone at the party, and the group chat hadn't quieted down ever since.

At the end of the night, I said my goodbyes to Marshall and Finn, the latter looking like he'd finally recovered from the heartache over Neil and Annette. I wished he would tell Marshall because he'd always been better about matters of the heart than me, hence why he'd been the sounding board for all of us, Lincoln included. But I respected it wasn't something he wanted to share. Maybe someday it would matter enough to him, but I knew once Finn fell in love again, it would be for the last time. He was witty and whip smart, but his heart was the biggest of the five of us, and it could only bear the weight of so much repair before it collapsed entirely.

When it was time to say goodbye to Smith, he hesitated, weight shifting from one foot to the other.

"What's up?" I asked, knowing he needed the prompting.

"Can I come over?"

I thought about the laundry list of vile and depraved things

I'd planned to do with Lincoln upon his return from Rapture, then mentally folded it in half and slid it into my pocket.

"Always, but what's up?"

"I just…"

"Of course," I assured him. "No explanation needed."

I wanted more than anything to ask why Smith had attached himself to me not Marshall, but I suspected Marshall might be part of the problem. Not that he'd done anything wrong, but I had the distinct impression Smith was desperate to break out of the shadow he'd stepped into, and separating himself from Marshall was a huge part of that.

I told Smith I'd meet him at home, then fired off a text to Lincoln to let him know not to burst into the door naked and ready to fuck. My boyfriend didn't seen fazed at all that another Covington was going to be in the house upon his return, and I thought about that the whole drive home. Again, the comfort, the welcome, the safety that Lincoln had brought out in me, that I'd been able to share with not just him but also my brothers.

At the apartment, I fed Feeny and dug out some pajamas for Smith. He changed in the guest room and came back out, hoodie still on—which was suspicious.

"Did you want me to turn the heater on?" I asked.

He shook his head, and I wondered if his neck was covered in hickeys or something else that he wanted to keep hidden. Not that it mattered, so I poured us both a drink and together we settled in on the couch. I gave him the remote and let him put on a show. It took an entire episode, but Smith finally relaxed.

Three hours later, Lincoln made it home. He gave me a kiss on the lips, then kissed Smith on the corner of his mouth, and promptly dragged me off to the bedroom, laughing the whole way. Smith took it in stride, assuring me he'd turn off the lights and lock up when he was ready to call it a night.

Lincoln kicked the door to my bedroom closed behind us and made quick work of stripping out of his clothes. His shorts were around his ankles, harness still strapped across his upper body when he bent over the bed and spread his ass cheeks apart, giving me an up close and personal view of the plug he'd sent a picture of earlier.

"I need you, Daddy," he whimpered.

My cock immediately hardened, and I pulled it out of my pajamas on my way toward him. Smoothing my hands over the warm globes of his ass, I gave him two gentle pats against the backs of his thighs. Lincoln groaned and pushed back against me with a playful wiggle.

The limits of our scenes were a constantly shifting thing, but not in a way that felt impossible to manage. Lincoln was still learning how to lean into submission without losing himself, and pain was sometimes now a part of that for us. Dragging my hand to the inside of his leg, I pinched his thigh, and Lincoln whimpered again, burying his face in the sheets.

"You have to be so quiet," I chided, flipping open the lube and smearing some down my shaft. "Can you do that, or do you need help?"

Another whimper.

"Help," he croaked.

"Okay," I told him, twisting and tugging the plug until it slid out of his ass with a plop. The resulting gape had precum pulsing out of my dick, and I wasted no time plunging all the way into him. "Daddy's got you."

Fully buried in Lincoln's ass, I grabbed his harness with one hand and hauled him up so his back arched in the sexiest angle I'd ever seen, and I slid my other hand over his mouth, ready to stifle whatever noises he was about to make. His mouth was wet against my palm, and I set a pace intended to drive him right to the edge and over it. Lincoln had been teasing me with his body all day long, and it was time for him to pay the price.

The sound of our skin slapping together drowned out the grunts and groans he loosed against my hand, and I held tight to him until a familiar heat started to burn low and hot at the base of my spine. Taking my hand away from his mouth, I grabbed Lincoln around his waist and started to fuck into him in earnest, harder thrusts designed to make me come.

"That's it, Daddy. That's so good. You're so good," he stammered, trying to be quiet. "You're the best boy, oh fuck. Nobody fucks me the way you do."

"Touch yourself," I demanded.

He grabbed his cock and stroked himself twice, not even trying to stifle the cry that tumbled out of his mouth when he came. I shoved his face down into the sheets and drove into him once more, the pressure of my own release finally exploding. I came inside of him with a rolling growl, fingers gouging into his hips to hold him steady.

Another thing I'd learned was how to be rough with Lincoln in the ways that made him feel loved. He truly enjoyed being manhandled, and I trusted him enough to take him at his word. We still talked all the time about what we wanted to try and what we liked or didn't, but there was a lot of *knowing* that existed between us, and I truly believed that was what kept us going so strong.

Beneath me, Lincoln collapsed on the bed, his hand pinned between his stomach and the comforter. Gently, I eased out of him, a feral sound building in the back of my throat at the sight of his gaping and cum-slick asshole. I gave him a harder smack against the side of his thigh, and Lincoln crawled onto the bed, then flopped onto his back.

"I think I want you to spank me," he said, eyes bright and clear, not hazy like they sometimes were after he came.

"I can spank you."

The corner of his mouth twitched. "I know you can."

I gave one last overhand stroke to my half-hard dick and pulled my pajamas back up. My throat was parched, and I was in desperate need of a drink.

"I was thinking, I'd like to bottom again for you soon," I admitted, biting the tip of my tongue between my teeth.

Lincoln was a phenomenal top, but on account of the fact I came within seconds, it was something we'd still only done that one time. At my ask, though, he lifted his hips off the bed and stroked his cock, pointing it at me.

"I'll make it so good for you," he promised.

"I know. I'm going to go get some water. Do you want anything?"

"Well, now, just to fuck you." Lincoln laughed and kicked free of his leather shorts.

"Did you and Silas have dinner?"

"We had snacks," he said.

"I'll make us a sandwich to share." I bent over the bed and brushed a kiss against his temple, then headed out to the kitchen.

I didn't think we'd been fucking that long, but the house was already dark and buttoned up, save for the light spilling down the hallway from the guest room. As quietly as I could manage, I pulled all the ingredients out of the fridge and set to making a turkey sandwich that would hold me and Lincoln over until the morning.

Gathering the plate and a glass of water, I made my way back toward the hallway. The light in the guest room flipped off, but the hall light turned on just as quickly. Smith was there in front of me, clearly on his way to the bathroom, but he'd finally taken off that damn hoodie. His brow knit together over the bridge of his nose, and he had his phone in hand, frowning down at the screen. He didn't even see me.

"You good?" I asked.

Smith jumped, almost dropping his phone but managing to save it against his chest. He blinked up at me like a raccoon caught in headlights, not quite fast enough to make it out of danger.

"You startled me," he said obviously. "I was just going to brush my teeth."

He gestured toward the bathroom to my right, and that was when I saw it. The dark shadows, the elegant script, and designs that stretched from my brother's wrist to his forearm.

"Smith," I said slowly, not wanting to grab him but also not wanting him to move. "When the fuck did you get a tattoo?"

ALSO BY KATE HAWTHORNE

Club Rapture: Risk Aware

Love by Design

Burden of Proof

Club Rapture: Giving Consent

Worth the Risk

Worth the Wait

Worth the Fight

Worth the Chance

Trophy Doms Social Club

Humbled

Edged

Praised

Bound

Shared

Trophy Doms New York

All In

Tied Down

Cried Out

Roughed Up

All in Good Time

Necessary Space

Necessary Time

Duality

Dual Destruction

Dual Surrender

Dual Defiance

Two Truths and a Lie

A Real Good Lie

A Cold Hard Truth

A Matter of Fact

Room for Love

Reckless

Heartless

Faultless

Fearless

Limitless

A Very Messy Motel Brothers Wedding

Relentless

Secrets in Edgewood

A Taste of Sin

The Cost of Desire

A Love Made Whole

Secrets in Edgewood: The Complete Series

The Lonely Hearts Stories

His Kind of Love

The Colors Between Us

Love Comes After

Until You Say Otherwise

<u>STANDALONES</u>

Rebound

One for the Road

Daybreak - Vino & Veritas

Unfettered

Dreams

A Thousand Lifetimes

<u>COLLABORATIONS</u>

With E.M. Denning

Irreplaceable

Future Fake Husband

Future Gay Boyfriend

Future Ex Enemy

With J.R. Gray

May the Best Man Win

ABOUT KATE HAWTHORNE

Kate Hawthorne is an author of character-driven LGBT romance, known for crafting emotionally intense stories with high heat and a kinky twist. Creating worlds where passion and angst collide, Kate's books bring you complex protagonists in fearless pursuit of self-exploration and happy—if not sometimes unconventional—endings for everyone.

Visit her website
http://www.katehawthornebooks.com

Sign up for Kate's newsletter
http://www.katehawthornebooks.com/extra

patreon.com/katehawthorne

instagram.com/kate.hawthorne

threads.com/@kate.hawthorne

facebook.com/authorkatehawthorne

www.ingramcontent.com/pod-product-compliance
Lightning Source LLC
Chambersburg PA
CBHW010734310726
48971CB00010B/2834